> I am about to pull the curtains when,
> at the margin of my vision,
> a woman falls out of the sky.

I do not see how it began. All I see is that she falls, feet first but tipping forward, arms stretched out as if to break her fall, her clothes as chaotically twisted and tossed as the rain, and the weight of her body carrying her down through the currents of air straight to the earth like an anchor. For a moment my brain cannot register what my eyes clearly see, what my ears hear: a scream that tangles with the whine of the wind so that they become one miserable chord. The moment she hits the ground the sound becomes thin again, just the wind on its own once more.

ACCLAIM FOR *FALLING OFF AIR*

"FALLING OFF AIR is a first-rate thriller that is also a parable for the modern age, a compelling exploration of love, ambition, and misguided ideals wrapped in exquisite prose. I devoured this book whole."
—Amy Gutman, author of *The Anniversary* and *Equivocal Death*

"Harrowing."

—Oklahoman

"Definitely a talent to look out for."
—Murder and Mayhem Book Club

Please turn to the back of the book for a preview of Catherine Sampson's new novel, *Out of Mind.*

more . . .

"The novel possesses a unique flavor, with moments of humor and an enjoyable suspense element that will appeal to mystery fans. Recommended."

—*Library Journal*

"The mystery and its solution are satisfyingly convoluted. Fans of British mystery will enjoy this one."

—Romance ReadersConnection.com

"This engaging amateur sleuth tale is kept fresh by the beleaguered heroine who finds her own community is ready to devour her as a wounded piranha."

—*Midwest Book Review*

FALLING OFF AIR

CATHERINE SAMPSON

NEW YORK   BOSTON

Mysterious Press
Warner Books

Time Warner Book Group
1271 Avenue of the Americas, New York, NY 10020
Visit our Web site at www.twbookmark.com.

The Mysterious Press name and logo are registered trademarks of Warner Books.

Printed in the United States of America

Originally published in hardcover by Mysterious Press
First Trade printing: August 2005
10 9 8 7 6 5 4 3 2 1

The Library of Congress has cataloged the hardcover edition as follows:
Sampson, Catherine.
    Falling off air / Catherine Sampson.
        p. cm.
    ISBN 0-89296-813-3
    1. Political activists—Crimes against—Fiction. 2. Motion picture producers and directors—Crimes against—Fiction. 3. Women detectives—Fiction. 4. Single mothers—Fiction. 5. Twins—Fiction. I. Title.
    PS3619.A459F35 2004
    813'.6—dc22   2004001964

ISBN: 0-446-69523-8 (pbk.)

Cover design by Diane Luger
Cover photo by Marc Yankus

For James
and
For Martha

Acknowledgments

I am very grateful to several people for their help with the writing of this book. Elizabeth Aylett advised me on chronic fatigue syndrome. Jennifer Schwerin and Nancy Fraser gave me technical guidance on filmmaking. Martha Huang read drafts tirelessly and ruthlessly. James Miles, my husband, gave me his constant support. My parents, John and Joan Sampson, gave me and our three children shelter from SARS at a critical stage of preparing the manuscript. I am deeply indebted to Amanda Preston, my agent, and to Sarah Turner and Amy Einhorn, my editors.

Chapter 1

THE shouting starts at around seven in the evening. A hot day, an oppressive dusk, and my neighbors the length of the street fling their windows wide open in the vain hope of admitting a breeze. The air smells singed. At first the voices are no more than a whisper. I have gone to the front of the house to put out the rubbish and, this being prime soap time, I assume the noise is scripted and broadcast. One of the voices is male, one female, but this early in the argument restraint still keeps them low if urgent, and I cannot tell one word from another even if I wanted to.

Within half an hour, shrieks of indignation and hoots of ridicule are bouncing off our terraced, slate-clad walls, then back onto the curlicued red-brick mansions opposite. The voices seem to be amplified in the still air, and accusation and counteraccusation flow in through the open windows undistorted and devastating. By this point I am kneeling on the floor wrestling the twins into their pajamas but I am soon distracted by the yelling. I sit back on my heels to listen, letting go of Hannah, who crawls off cheerfully, believing herself for once victorious in the nightly struggle to go to bed naked. I am tempted to go to the window to get a better sense of where the voices are coming from, but they have enough problems without me sticking my nose in.

"Of course you don't understand, you selfish bastard," a woman screams, "you won't let me . . ." Here her voice continues, something about spending money, but a man's voice is overlaid, calling the woman a bitch repeatedly until she falls silent. Unchallenged now by her, he gains in volume. "You're a lying, blood-sucking whore," he yells, his voice breaking with emotion, muttering something that I cannot hear, then roaring, "What the fuck's been going on in my house?"

"Your house? Your . . ." She—whoever she is—comes back at him enraged, but then a third voice intervenes, the light, anxious tones of a child, and there is no more screaming.

I grimace, my mind's eye in someone else's sitting room, windows open, a frightened girl or boy summoning the courage to say something, anything, to shut his parents up. The argument is ugly even at a distance. The red cloud of rage lifts, of course, apologies can be made, accusations retracted. In this case, however, it is difficult to see how life can continue as normal, unless calling your wife a lying whore is normal.

My neighbors, both sides of the street, are a modest lot. They don't yell in public, they don't venture into the street naked, and God forbid they'd smile a hello to a stranger, but weather like this strips everyone down. We have been promised rain, but instead it just gets hotter and hotter, the air heavier and heavier for three days in a row. When the rain comes, it will empty the heavens.

––––––––––

I was depositing William in his crib as the first clap of thunder broke above us and the rain descended like a waterfall, drumming suddenly against the window like someone trying to get in. I wondered whether our house was waterproof. It seemed unlikely that such a flimsy structure could be anything more than splashproof. It is perhaps overstating it even to call it a house. The real estate agent talked about "council house chic." God knows how long it took him to dream that one up. It's like a little flat turned vertical, standing upright on its own patch of earth, its walls barely solid enough to hold it up. There are two feet of paved ground in front with a low concrete wall that has no function except to serve as our boundary, and a tiny garden at the back fenced with flimsy wood and chicken wire. Inside, mostly by virtue of its size, the house is cozy. I've had no time to do much to it, so it remains much as it was when I bought it, complete with garish paintwork and stained carpets. The best and warmest thing about it is an open fireplace. The agency advertised it as a "period feature," and it is indeed a Victorian fireplace. Of course when the house was built forty years ago that particular Victoria was long gone.

This is not the house I would have chosen. It is the house I could afford. A single income, double child-care bills, and zero windfall on the horizon all added up to the smallest mortgage I could find. Our house and its little string of neighbors are a gray British version of shanty-town shacks compared to the red-brick Victoriana that graces the opposite pavement. They have intruder alarms and leaded windows like jewels in their heavy wooden doors. I have a doorbell that plays "Greensleeves" off-key and a cracked window at the back where next door's eleven-year-old hit it with a tennis ball.

By eight o'clock I'd fed, bathed, and wrestled Hannah and William into their cribs, and plugged bottles of milk into their rosebud mouths. I felt as though I'd run a marathon. I wiped the sticky remains of the twins' teatime from my sleeves, poured myself a glass of merlot, and twitched the sitting-room curtain open, perching on the arm of the chair to watch the storm. My back was aching and I rolled my shoulders, feeling the crunch at the base of my neck, trying to ease the stress. The combined weight of the twins was now much the same as that of a baby elephant. Outside the ominously oppressive day had given way to an angry night. The trees and shrubs in the gardens opposite shuddered, and rain fell in great swathes through the orange darkness, tossed and twisted by the wind.

The family who lived opposite hadn't pulled their curtains shut yet, and I could see the cool blue of their high walls, the brass picture lights above framed prints. I frowned. Was it my imagination or could I hear voices again, straining over the storm. Surely everyone would have shut their windows. Unless, I thought, one was too distraught to notice a gale howling outside. A fork of lightning lit up the sky and then, just a moment later, a clap of thunder burst and shook my frail little house. Still, unlikely as it was, my ears caught at fractions of words, at shrieks and wails that seemed too human to belong to the storm. I gazed up the street, then down it, but the rain had driven everyone inside.

I am about to pull the curtains and shut out the weather when, at the margin of my vision, a woman falls out of the sky. I do not see how it began. All I see is that she falls, feet first but tipping forward, arms stretched out as if to break her fall, her clothes as chaotically twisted and tossed as the rain, and the weight of her body carrying her down through the currents of air straight to the earth like an anchor. For a moment my brain cannot register what my eyes quite clearly see, what my ears hear: a scream that tangles with the whine of the wind so that they become one miserable chord. The moment she hits the ground the sound becomes thin again, just the wind on its own once more. The weather and everything else of no consequence is fixed in my mind for good now because of that moment of violence; scar tissue forming around the memory.

I stood up in agitation, my heart pounding, eyes wide, staring at the heap in the pathway of the house on the other side of the road. What should I do? What could I do? Energy flooded to my muscles and I ran, flinging open my front door, damp air filling my lungs. I reached her, squatted down, had to force myself to look closely. Until that point some part of me believed that the wind and the rain must have played a trick on my ears and on my eyes, but it was as I feared. The broken heap was, or had been, a woman. She was wearing something flowing and loose that was now caught around limbs that had broken on impact, and long hair covered her head, her face turned into the ground. The rain was driving against the top of my own head, pouring down into my eyes and I had to peer, eyes half shut, down at her. It seemed to me that another, darker, liquid was seeping from under her head, but I couldn't be sure. I couldn't tell if she was breathing so I laid my fingertips lightly on her back to see whether I could sense a rise and fall. I could detect nothing.

I stretched my neck back, straining my eyes against the darkness and the elements. Where had she come from? On the third story a tiny wrought-iron balcony extended from the brickwork. I got to my feet, my hair hanging in wet ropes across my face. I could do nothing for her. If she was still alive she would drown if she stayed here. I was wasting time. She needed an ambulance. I took four paces to the front door and rapped on it, then kept my finger pressed on the doorbell. There was just one anonymous doorbell, which meant the house was not divided into flats, that it was occupied by one family or one person, perhaps the one person who lay shattered on the ground behind me. Yet even as the thought occurred to me I knew it was not the case, knew I'd seen other people letting themselves in at this door. A big well-dressed man, grungy teenagers, these were the images that came to mind. No one, however, came to the door.

The noise of the rain, like waves slamming against a shoreline, meant I could not hear whether there was movement inside the house. I took a step back. There was only one light on as far as I could see, and that was in the third-floor room with the balcony. I stepped back farther, and I could see now that there were French windows opening out and that drapes of some light fabric had been lifted by the wind and were blowing into the night. I banged on the door again, shouted, then gave up. I turned back toward my house, making for the nearest telephone, then stopped dead in my tracks. My front door had blown shut. Hannah and William were inside. My hands went to my head, clutching great handfuls of sopping hair.

"Shit, shit, shit," I heard myself shout.

I had left them safe in bed, of course, but at that moment, in the face of sudden death, neither fire nor earthquake seemed impossible or even unlikely. I vaulted the brick wall between the house with the pale blue walls and its neighbor. I hammered on the door with one hand while I pressed the bell with the other. For a moment I thought I heard footsteps, but then nothing. No one. I could have sworn someone was on the other side of the door.

"Please open the door," I shouted. "I need your help."

Still nothing.

"It's an emergency," I yelled.

I gave up, climbed over the fence into the next pathway, pounded on that door with the same results, gave up, clambered over a low hedge, tried again. There were three bells here, three flats. I pressed all three with my palm, kept pressing and thumping at the door, my fist numb. All of a sudden the door opened and a young man peered out, outraged at my invasion. We had passed each other in the street many times but never so much as nodded hello. Tall and athletic, with cropped hair, he was dressed in a short raincoat, carrying an umbrella, dry as a bone, getting ready to venture out and get soaked.

"For Christ's sake, what—?" He took in my bedraggled state, my crazed eyes, and I saw him want to close the door in my face. But he didn't. Anyway I wasn't going to let him. I was half inside already.

"Your phone," I gasped, dripping all over his threshold. "I have to phone for an ambulance."

He let me shove past him and stood awkwardly, hands pushed angrily into his pockets, while I grabbed the phone on the hall table and dialed 999. All the time I spoke to emergency services, telling them about the woman who had fallen, and about my house locked with my children inside, I was looking at him, needing him to understand too and to help me. He had the sense to keep quiet, anyway, while I spoke. The anger lifted from his face as he listened, and the expression was replaced by one of shock. By the time I'd given my address, he was heading out into the rain, leaving me alone in his hallway.

I hung up, then looked around. How long would it take them to get here? I couldn't wait. There was nothing but the hall table, a spindly antique affair about a foot square, no room for anything but the telephone, which I tipped onto the floor. I lifted the table, liking the look of its long legs, and I ran back across the road with my loot. The man had stopped by the woman, bending over her. I didn't stop to see what he was doing. I stepped over my front wall and swung the table at the window, holding it by its legs, leaving the wooden edge of the tabletop to do its demolition work and turning my face away as the glass shattered. I bashed around a bit more to get rid of the shards of glass, then dropped what was left of the table. It was more delicate than I'd thought, and it hadn't fared well. I pulled off my sweater and wrapped it around my hands for protection, then pulled myself carefully over the sill and into my sitting room. I pounded up the stairs and into the tiny room that was the twins' bedroom. Inside all was quiet, two cotton-suited bottoms stuck in the air, faces half-hidden in the mattress, lips working, dreaming of sucking.

I stood there for a minute just looking down at them, catching my breath. So peaceful. I had an overwhelming desire to stay here and stand guard over them. Outside I heard sirens approaching. I turned and left the room. I ran back down the stairs, grabbed my keys from the kitchen table and, just to make double sure, wedged open my front door with a copy of the *Guardian*.

The street was full of flashing blue lights. Not only that: This street, abandoned as a ghost town when I had needed help, when I had shouted and yelled for help, was now as populated as a rush-hour station. Faces peered from windows and from behind half-open front doors. The more adventurous had grabbed some sort of protective clothing and made their way into the street, where they stood in ones and twos, not really knowing how to talk to each other, not wanting to be involved, curious nevertheless and therefore conversing. How to form a community, I thought. Kill one of them.

Suddenly the door of the house from which the woman had fallen burst open. A slight figure raced from it and before anyone could move, hurled itself on the woman's body. An animal cry rose into the night sky and my blood ran cold. The small figure, scarcely more than a child, was hugging the limp flesh, burying his face in her wet hair, for all the world as though he was trying to breathe life back into her. Then the police and paramedics closed in, forcing the boy away, protecting what could no longer be protected. He tried to fight them off, pint-sized fists pummeling the living bodies that dragged him tenderly from the dead. The rain hissed down, drowning his shrieks and drenching us all.

———

Later that night, when the body and the boy had both gone, a young woman, Detective Constable Mann, took my statement. She had stamina, and I fed her stamina on cups of tea. She tried every way she knew to stir my memory, to search it for the thing I did not even know I knew, for the elusive glimpse of the unusual, the out of place, the clue. I was pleased by her doggedness because I needed to have what I had seen examined and reexamined. I needed to repeat it aloud, and to someone other than myself. I needed to have it recorded.

From my work I know that what is remembered as the truth may be only a version of the truth, so I knew I would return to this record that D.C. Mann produced to check and retune my memory in the days to come. By the early hours of the morning my statement was a marvel of description on everything from the state of the weather to the exact angle at which the woman had fallen, the altitude at which I had first spotted the body falling, the degree of lifelessness with which the woman's body had lain broken on the saturated ground.

I recited to D.C. Mann what I could remember of the screamed argument earlier in the evening. It was strange to sit there in my kitchen in the midnight silence and calmly recite the words "whore" and "bitch." I told her I had no idea which house the argument came from, no idea whether it had anything at all to do with the woman's death that came later. I was telling her about the argument only because she wanted to know the story of the whole evening, from beginning to end. Then I hesitated. When she pressed me to say what was on my mind, I told her that I thought I had heard voices again just before the woman had fallen, but that—and this I stressed—could have been sheer fancy. This time there were no words to give her, no splinters of sentences, just my impression that I had heard voices mixed with the noise of the storm. She did not want to use words like "impression" in the statement, wanted me to firm it up, but I could not. I ended up wishing I hadn't even mentioned it.

The woman, she said, had not yet been formally identified, but I learnt the name of the family who lived at the house from which she had fallen. She said the house belonged to the Carmichaels. I told her the name meant nothing to me. I read my statement and reread it. My words had been transformed into police language. I would not myself have chosen to describe the woman who died as "Caucasian female, middle-aged, wearing light-colored night-dress." Just as I would not, in my first breath of description, have described D.C. Mann as black, although she was. The statement simply did not sound like me, yet nothing that Mann had written was inaccurate. I signed every page, scratching lines through the empty space at the bottom of the last page so that nothing could be added. Every detail was there, but nothing I had witnessed was the slightest clue to the heart of the matter: why this woman had fallen and how.

Chapter 2

THE electronic mangling of "Greensleeves" roused me from sleep. It took a moment for the memory of the night before to hit me, but when it did it fell like a sledgehammer. I hauled myself from my bed, my eyes barely open, and pulled on the same jeans, T-shirt, and sweater that I'd peeled off three hours before. I could smell sweat on them, and fear. I peered at the clock. It was six A.M. Even standing upright I could still feel sleep, like the pull of gravity, dragging me back toward my bed. I resisted it and padded barefoot to the front door.

A large man stood there, the man I'd seen entering what I now knew to be the Carmichael house. His broad face was working in distress, his eyes red and heavy. He wore a creased business suit that I guessed he had put on yesterday morning and had not yet had a chance to change.

"They said you saw her fall," he said, and I was surprised to hear an American accent. He stepped inside without further introduction.

I closed the door behind him and led him the two steps that constituted my hallway. Upstairs I could hear the twitter of the twins' voices, awoken by the doorbell. I ignored them. I knew I had a few minutes' grace while they chatted before calling for me. I opened the door to the sitting room, wondering absentmindedly why I'd closed it, then remembered as a blast of damp air hit us both. He followed me in and stood staring at the broken window. D.C. Mann had been due to go off duty when she'd finished taking my statement, but instead of going home she'd helped me sweep up the glass and then vacuum, to make sure we got it all up before the children started crawling around on it.

"Next time take a key," she'd suggested drily.

She'd tried ringing a couple of twenty-four-hour glass repair shops too, but the earliest anyone could come was nine. So we'd found a grimy plastic sheet in a cupboard and taped it across the window.

Between us we'd done a pretty good job, but overnight the wind had dislodged some of the tape with the result that we might as well have been standing in the street outside. Carmichael gestured interrogatively at the window.

"My wife . . . ?" he asked, confused. How, after all, could she have fallen out of his house and into mine?

"No, no, something else," I reassured him. I invited him to sit down. I doubt he even heard me, he was so agitated, and because he did not sit down neither did I. I stood hugging my sweater around me and watching him pace like a caged animal in my tiny room. He seemed to fill the space and reach the ceiling. I had the feeling that he was used to assuming control of situations and places and that, unable to control this situation, he was doing his best to master at least the ground under his feet. He paused by the fireplace and examined the framed photographs I'd put there, picking each up and replacing it, forming a line much straighter than the original display. I don't have many strangers visiting the house, and his attention unsettled me until I realized it was only this attempt to impose order that was stopping him falling apart.

"I'm so sorry," I told him. "How is your son?"

"Kyle. He's not . . . He's sleeping, the doctor gave him something. Look, I don't understand," he turned toward me, making a visible effort to articulate his confusion, "what happened."

"I didn't see . . . I saw her falling, that's all. I was looking out of that window." I gestured toward it, and he walked to the place where I had stood and looked out through the drizzling rain toward his own house as if he expected to see her falling still. "I saw her falling, and then, when . . . she was on the ground I went to her, but there was nothing I could do, so I called the ambulance."

"You didn't see how it happened?"

Surely he must already know this from the police, unless they had decided for some reason to leave him in ignorance. I shook my head. The uncontrolled dive had haunted my night. What could make a woman loosen her hold on safety and step out into the void, surrender herself to plummet unchecked, inevitably to shatter on the earth below?

"Did she say anything to you?" His eyes fixed on mine, and I was struck by their blue intensity. "They said there was some time between her falling and you calling the ambulance."

I tried to ignore the implicit criticism, shook my head.

"I'm almost certain she was already dead when I reached her. There was a man from a few doors down who was with her for a few minutes after me, but I really think she was dead by then."

He nodded, glaring through watery eyes, then touched his fingers to his lips like a child. Upstairs there was a bang, then a wail. He jumped, his nerves giving him away.

"I'm sorry," I gestured upward, "I have to go and get them . . ."

He frowned as though I had added a whole new level of complexity to an already impossible situation.

"I have children upstairs," I explained, making for the door.

When I came back downstairs a few moments later he was back by the photographs. He turned as soon as I entered the room and resumed his interrogation without apparently registering the fact that I had a pungent child wriggling under each arm.

"Did you see anyone?"

"See anyone?" I repeated stupidly. Did he mean inside the house? Outside? Then I realized it made no difference. I bent down, put the children on the floor so they could move around and play—I hoped we'd got all the glass out of the carpet the night before—but they were hungry and uncomfortable and they just sat there and bawled.

"No one," I told him.

"But they said there was shouting, arguing."

"That was earlier," I corrected him, then remembered the wisps of argument I fancied I'd heard through the storm just before his wife fell. "I've no idea whether that was connected or not."

"Of course not. That is for the police to say. What I am trying to determine is whether you had any reason to believe my wife was with anyone before she died."

"As I said, I saw nothing and no one until your wife fell," I said, a little abruptly. I had made myself clear the first time.

He seemed to recover himself slightly, looking down at the children as though seeing them for the first time. Hannah's nappy was about to burst.

"I was out at a dinner, my wife didn't want to come," he explained to me. I had to strain to hear his voice over the children. "My elder son was at a friend's house for a sleepover. He doesn't know yet." He glanced at his watch. "I have to go. I have to go get him." His mouth worked again, and I thought I saw his chin tremble. He took a deep shuddering breath, and must have remembered that he had not introduced himself. "I'm Richard, Richard Carmichael," he said, holding out his hand and making an attempt at the social niceties. "We've been neighbors for a while now, six months almost."

"I'm Robin Ballantyne." I took his hand and we shook. I could feel the misery seeping from the flesh of his palm. Then, made unthinking by the children's demands for attention, I asked, "Did you know that your wife might do this?"

He didn't like the question, withdrew his hand immediately.

"How could I expect this from Paula?" he snapped.

Well, if I didn't like him so much as glancing at my photographs he was allowed to be a little prickly when I asked him if his newly dead wife had been suicidal. After that he made for the door, muttering that he would see himself out. I made a move to go after him. I might even have apologized for my insensitivity, but Hannah grabbed my leg and wouldn't let go. I heard the door slam.

I gazed down at the children, overwhelmed by my lack of sleep. They were shouting as though they'd been abandoned in a snowstorm at the top of a mountain without food or drink. At moments like these I never knew where to start. Milk or nappies? Hannah or William? Milk, nappies, milk, nappies, Hannah, William, Hannah, William—it was like a crazed chant. My hands started to do the right things, gathering wipes, clean nappies, placing bottles of milk in the microwave, and all the time this other part of my head was working on something else entirely. He'd called his wife Paula. Paula Carmichael.

The only Paula Carmichael I'd heard of was a prominent social activist. She was a Labour member of parliament who sat on the back benches and irritated the party leadership. But that was almost marginal to who she was: so flamboyant and inspiring in her public speaking that during the past year or two she had begun to make a social conscience fashionable again. She had hundreds and thousands of people volunteering to do good works on their Saturday mornings. Even the home counties had become a hotbed of Carmichaelites. Some of them had added a zero or two to their regular charitable giving. Others had actually got off their gin-logged backsides to try and find someone, anyone, in their affluent communities to help. More a poet than a politician, she used the power of her rhetoric to shame men on both sides of the house. "All over this country volunteers are picking up your pieces," she'd famously harangued the prime minister on one occasion, "sticking together lives that should never have been broken, attempting to cure with compassion and a collection box what should have been prevented by good government."

I had not seen the face of the woman who fell, or enough of the rest of her to identify her, and yet there was something even in the manner she had fallen, even in the voice that had called out through the night that was not unfamiliar. I would never have chosen to watch anyone die like that, but Paula Carmichael was a woman I knew something of, a woman I liked and respected. I felt ice form in my veins, and I shivered.

On autopilot I cleaned and changed the babies in turn, lifted them one by one into their high chairs, then toasted bread and cut up apples and bananas. I poured milk into two cups and twisted lids onto them. With food and drink in front of them they stopped complaining. I turned on the radio, but before I got to hear so much as a headline the doorbell rang. I sighed, abandoned the children again and went to open the door. It was Jane. I had hardly seen her since she realized that I had a problem making child-free lunches—in fact I had a problem with child-free anything—and she had a problem with children. I let her in, along with another squall of rain. The whole house felt damp, as though the rain were leaking into its joints.

Jane shook herself like a dog, spraying a mist of water all over me, then took off her raincoat, handed it to me, and raised her eyebrows.

"What a thing to happen, eh?" she said.

Jane is of Chinese descent, with a high forehead, sharp cheek-bones, and black hair that hangs almost to her hips. She looks positively imperial. It's all undermined though when she arches an eyebrow, opens her mouth, and a strong Perth accent emerges. Her parents settled in Scotland in the late fifties, fleeing Mao and getting farther than most. Her mother and father, both physicists who spoke no English, opened what must have been one of the first Chinese restaurants north of the border. They retired after a couple of decades, but Jane's sister now ran the business, which had diversified into fish and chips years ago and was about to go up market and launch a Thai menu. Her parents, fearing her Scottish accent would hold her back, sent her to elocution lessons, but Jane refused to cooperate. Instead, defiantly, she became more Scottish than ever.

Jane looked tired, the early morning light illuminating the dusting of feathery lines around her eyes and across her forehead.

"You're up early," I said.

She gestured over her shoulder toward the Carmichael house.

"I was working into the wee hours. I put two and two together. It was you who found her, was it not?"

I nodded.

"The address was on the agency copy," she explained, heading into the sitting room. "I—" She stopped dead, staring at the window.

"Come into the kitchen," I turned to lead the way, "and I'll get you a towel for your hair."

I boiled the kettle while Jane arranged herself on an upright chair, rubbing the towel I gave her over her head and watching Hannah and William, not touching, not talking to them, clearly at a loss as to what to say. Well it's hard to coo over a baby when you've suggested to its mother that she have it aborted. Without someone to share the load they would ruin my life, she'd told me, and of course they had, in the nicest possible way.

"Well," she said at last with rare diplomacy, "they're thriving." Then, with less diplomacy, "Hannah's the spitting image of Adam."

I scowled.

"What? Do you not think so?" Jane protested.

"I prefer to think they were an early experiment in cloning."

"William's got his mouth as well, so no one will believe you."

There was silence as I poured boiling water into the coffeepot, and I became very aware of my baggy sweater with a hole at one elbow and the remains of Hannah's regurgitated apple on the other. Under Jane's cool and elegant scrutiny I could feel the bags under my eyes swell to balloonlike proportions. I felt resentment prickle at my neck. I had not invited her here to observe me.

I turned to face her, leaning my hips back against the counter, allowing the coffee to steep.

"Why are you here?" I asked, although I had already as good as guessed.

Jane held my gaze.

"The police aren't ruling out foul play." It was her work voice, confident, persuasive. "Did you see what happened? Was there anyone there but her?"

Only the few of us who knew Jane very well could hear the slight increase in pace, the increased intensity of the accent, the breathless undertone when she was on an adrenaline high. I could hear it now, and it confirmed my identification of the woman who had died. No garden variety Paula Carmichael would have excited Jane like this.

"Why are you assuming she didn't kill herself?" I asked.

"I'm not. But why should she?"

I glared at her. I had a sick feeling in the pit of my stomach and my head was beginning to throb. There was a time, when I was working with Jane, when she held no terrors for me, I gave as good as I got or else I ignored her, but I knew I was about to be bullied and I was out of practice.

"You'll do an interview for me, won't you? I haven't spoken to Jez yet, but I'm just going to hand him a fait accompli. We'll be doing a special tonight, and we'll get friends and family on board of course, but if you could do that 'I saw her plunge out of the sky,' moment, that would be a really moving counterpoint. Frankly, if you could talk to us, and not to anyone else, I'd really owe you."

We gazed at each other, and she must have misinterpreted my reluctance, because she plowed on.

"When I say . . . I mean I don't see how we could actually pay you—"

"Jane," my hackles had risen, "talk to me like that and you can leave right now."

Silence, a couple of heartbeats long.

"I'm sorry, I wasn't implying . . ."

"Of course not."

"I only said it because I know Adam gives you nothing, and while he's busy swanning around on the telly here you are living in a slum bringing up his . . . For God's sake, it should be you editing *Controversies* tonight, not me . . . I cannot bear to see you—"

I slammed a cup of coffee down in front of her so that a tidal wave of liquid slopped onto the table. It stopped her in midflow.

"This isn't a slum," I said through gritted teeth, "and they're not his children. Not anymore."

I eyed the twins who eyed me back. I could say these things now and they wouldn't question, wouldn't complain. How many years would that last? Jane was staring at me, eyebrows raised.

"Adam gives me nothing because I want nothing from him," I

said, miserable because this was so obvious to me and because other people seemed to have such problems with it.

"Of course, of course." Jane was struggling, which isn't something you see every day. "I'm sorry. I wasn't thinking . . ."

"Forget it."

It took Jane exactly five seconds to recover herself and forget it. Then she was back on the scent like a terrier.

"So did you know her?"

"I don't think so." I knew it sounded ridiculous. Surely either you know someone or you don't. Only minutes before I had dismissed the thought that Paula Carmichael lived opposite me as fanciful, but now my mind was, of its own accord, presenting me with shreds of memory dug up from months back. Pushing the twins in their stroller one day in the summer, I'd passed a woman walking under the pigeon-infested bridge by the underground station, and I had nodded at her in recognition, only moments later realizing why I knew her face; that I had seen her on television and that she was Paula Carmichael. She had been hurrying, a briefcase in her hand, papers sticking out of it as though she had stuffed them in, and it had not occurred to me then that she was going home, or indeed that home was anywhere close at hand. This little person—she couldn't have been more than five foot two— seemed too small and insignificant to be the huge persona that Paula Carmichael had become. Even her hair, dark and untamed on television, seemed a graying brown in real life. I remember that I had looked around after her when I realized who she was, and that I had caught her doing the same thing, twisting to look back at me. Catching each other's eye, we had turned back quickly, embarrassed at ourselves. I knew why I had wanted a second look, but why in the name of God had she turned to look at me? I had been having a bad hair year, but did I really look so outlandish?

A second memory, but out of kilter, a week or so before the first.

In Sainsbury's, both children attempting to hurl themselves out of the stroller so they could roll in the aisles, me at my wits' end trying to juggle stroller and shopping basket. A woman wearing dark glasses, long graying hair pinned back from her face, clothes elegant but fraying, two large pepperoni pizzas in her basket. I thought at first that she was angry that we were blocking the aisle, but when I managed to haul the stroller out of the way for her she gave me a big sympathetic grin. "Been there, done that," she said cheerfully, and I gazed after her, pleased and surprised by the camaraderie. I had not recognized her then, and I had not made the connection even when I later saw Paula Carmichael under the bridge, but now my subconscious made the leap.

"I think I ran into her a couple of times," I amended. As I spoke, William started to grunt and groan and fight the straps that held him in his chair. "But I hadn't realized she lived so close by."

William threw a bowl of cereal on the floor and Hannah burst into noisy tears for no good reason. They had been tolerant, but their goodwill had run out. My time was up and Jane knew it. She glowered at them.

"Look, Jane, I'll think about the interview and give you a call," I said.

"Okay." She didn't look happy, but there wasn't much she could do about it. She got up. The twins upped the volume another notch, and Jane had to shout, "There's one thing you should know, because you're not to bite my head off later. I'm getting Adam in to talk about her too."

"What the hell . . . ?" But the twins and Jane all drowned me out.

"He knew her quite well," Jane spoke rapidly. Perhaps she thought that if she spoke fast enough I wouldn't hear what she was saying. "They worked on a program together a while ago. He'll be great about her, you know he will. If I ever die, I'll want Adam to do my eulogy, and he doesn't even like me. Anyway, I just wanted to let you know. It makes no difference to you. I'll keep a good distance between you."

I found myself shaking my head and caught sight of my reflection in the window, mouth pulled down at the corners, eyes narrowed. I sat down hard on a kitchen chair, looking blankly at Hannah, who was screeching in my face. Her big dark eyes, Adam's eyes, were round and angry.

"I swear, Robin," I could hear Jane saying, "you won't have to see him. I'm assuming you don't want to . . ."

"Damned right," I said. I felt as though another body had just slammed to earth at my feet.

Chapter 3

Wἱᴛʜ Jane gone I picked the children up and peered out into the street through the plastic sheeting that was my window. The wind had dropped and the rain was no more than a mist, but everything looked as though it was in shock after the onslaught of the night before. Shrubs drooped under the weight of rain that had fallen on them, blossoms had been dashed from plants and trees by the wind, and the assorted fast-food wrappers that usually blew around on the pavement lay waterlogged in the gutters. A yellow and black ribbon defined the place where Paula Carmichael had fallen and what therefore might or might not be a crime scene. A single police car was parked outside the Carmichaels'. The house looked peaceful. There were a couple of lights on but no conspicuous movement inside. I wondered whether Richard Carmichael and his elder son were back home yet. How much digging would the police do inside the house before they satisfied themselves that Paula Carmichael's death was suicide?

Photographers and reporters were already gathering. I counted around a dozen men and a couple of young women standing chatting in small groups. Jane was quick off the mark, but with a story like this every news organization would deploy its forces quickly and efficiently. I would become a prisoner in my own house if I stayed put. For a year I had hidden myself away in here, bonding so tightly with my children that we were almost an indivisible organism, breathing, sleeping, waking, emptying our bladders and our bowels in total synchrony. For a year I had been too tired to feel an adrenaline surge. Too tired to feel an anything surge in fact.

But when a woman falls out of the sky in front of you it gives you a jolt. I felt electrified by the shock, as though part of my brain that was dead had been charged and regenerated. Disaster euphoria. It's an ugly concept, but, for all my disapproval, Jane's excitement was contagious. I had put my working life aside, I had put all my passions behind me, and I was so far exiled from the working world that I scarcely missed it, but this morning, Jane had paraded my previous existence in front of me, and I wanted it so badly I could scarcely breathe. I present it as a logical argument, and of course it all makes sense, cause and effect, but the truth is that that morning I just felt in my guts something that had been building up for months and was bursting out of me like a need for some narcotic. I had to get out of the house, and I had to get back to work.

Standing there at the window, with the twins in my arms, my head was buzzing. I was chasing ten trains of thought in ten different directions. I tried to focus. I needed help. I needed a babysitter.

I called my mother, who is a babysitter only in extremis. I called her mobile, because I never know whether she'll be at her house, or at my older sister's. Lorna has had chronic fatigue syndrome, or CFS, for almost two years now, and my mother spends two or three evenings a week with her, as well as running her own law practice in Streatham. Which is to say that my mother has enough on her plate. But she came because it was an emergency. Or that was how it felt.

An hour later I closed my ears to the petulant squawks issuing from Hannah and gently disengaged myself from William, who had fastened his arms around my neck and his feet around my hips. I pecked my mother on her cheek and guiltily murmured my thanks. Then I walked out of the front door and pulled it shut behind me. There. It sounds so easy.

Light as air, with no stroller to push, no babe in arms, I walked over to the black gloss door of number twelve, the only door that had been opened to me the night before. I wasn't sure which of the three doorbells was the one I wanted, so I rang all three just as I had the night before. At the top of the house, a window screeched open and a woman leaned out in a dressing gown, hair unbrushed, face white with exhaustion. It was like looking in the mirror.

"What is it?" She frowned down at me. "Do I know you?"

"I'm looking for the man who opened the door to me last night, I—"

"I don't know who you're talking about. I've got a sick child in here. He's been up all night," she said in desperation. "Just go away."

The window was slammed shut. A child? I hadn't noticed a child going in and out all the time I'd lived here. I had learned more about my neighbors in the last twelve hours than I'd learned in the last year, but perhaps now wasn't the time to suggest a get-together.

I didn't dare ring again. I looked at my watch. It was nine on a Wednesday morning and my man had probably left for work by seven. I dug a paper and pen from my bag, sat on the step and scribbled a note.

> To Whosoever Opened the Door Last Night,
> Thank you for helping. I'm sorry about the table. It seemed like a good idea at the time. I'll reimburse you for the damage. Just let me know how much I owe you.
> Robin Ballantyne, number 19

I slipped it through the letter slot, glancing guiltily back at my house, where the small pile of wood in the front yard was all that was left of the table. Whatever sentimental value it held had been comprehensively bashed out of it. I just hoped it wasn't a priceless antique.

———

I sweet-talked my way past Gayle and into Maeve's office, and Maeve was as surprised to see me as I was to be there. She looked up from her papers and her face broke into a smile.

"Well, hello stranger. My God, Robin, what's brought you back to the land of the living? I hardly recognized you."

Which was a polite way of saying I looked a wreck. What had I been thinking of to make my office debut in yesterday's jeans? I hadn't washed my hair for three days now. Four perhaps. I tried to think back. Had I brushed my teeth before I left the house? Maeve had half-risen from her chair as if to come and kiss me, but I wasn't sure it was safe for her to come that close. I retreated and sank into the low leather chair in the corner, and she sat back down. She could scarcely see me across the top of her desk.

"I e-mailed you a month ago to ask whether we could discuss my return to work," I reminded her. Maeve is head of the Current Affairs department's Documentaries for Television division. Which makes her HCA(DTV), just one of an army of managers who run the Corporation's vast broadcasting empire. Day to day she has no hands-on program-making responsibilities, which is just as well since she has never made a television documentary in her life. Her responsibilities are primarily to oversee the commissioning process and to mastermind personnel. She is a bureaucrat born and bred, and seems to have an army of minibureaucrats working under her.

"You did," she agreed, her smile slipping. "You did indeed." Her eyes ran over me, and I saw her take in the scuffed boots, the mysterious white stains on my jeans, the baggy sweater, the hair that hung limply around my makeup-free face. I wasn't what you'd call dirty, but I didn't exactly sparkle.

"Do you feel ready to come back?" she asked, working to keep the doubt from her voice. "I'd hate to snatch a mother away from her little ones." She made it sound like a cat snatching a mouse away from her litter.

"Absolutely," I was trying to sound professional. I was supposed to be a journalist, however, not part of the news, so something kept me from mentioning Paula Carmichael. "I'm sorry I'm a bit of a mess this morning. I was involved in an incident yesterday, and I spent most of the night giving a statement to the police."

"Oh dear." If anything she looked more concerned now, as though perhaps she thought I was hallucinating from lack of sleep.

Maeve is used to vanquishing government spin doctors and hysterical program editors with a flick of her whiplike tongue, but I was problematic. I could sense it in the way her manicured forefinger was rubbing at her lower lip.

"Well we're all dying to have you back on board," she said, her eyes not quite meeting mine. "Terry never stops talking about you."

Good old Terry—my biggest fan, also my immediate boss, which helps, but a mere handservant to Maeve.

"How do you see yourself fitting back in?" she persevered. I could tell that the question was just a way of killing time while she worked out a way to get me off her back.

"I just want to make programs again," I said. "I'll find a way to make things fit."

Maeve stuck out her jaw and nodded slowly. She'd been hoping for a longer answer.

"Of course, of course, it's what you're best at. It's what you win awards for." She gave a little smile, then heaved a sigh and looked me in the eye for the first time. "Well we'll see what we can do, Robin, but I have to be honest, we're implementing some stringent streamlining measures here."

"You're cutting editorial jobs?"

"We're," she hesitated, "losing people. Mostly through natural wastage. You've been away, you probably haven't heard . . ."

"I'm guaranteed a job on return from maternity leave." I gritted my teeth.

She nodded again, and this time she didn't even try to cover her discomfiture with the words. Then her face brightened.

"Have you thought of a move sideways?"

"Sideways?"

"Well sideways and upwards actually. I mean into a more managerial role?"

I would have laughed if a heavy hand hadn't grabbed at my heart.

"The reason I ask," she pressed on, "is that we've just advertised for an EGIE."

"For a what?"

"An ethical guidelines implementation editor," she spelled out for me, as though I were a particularly thick child. "It's a new post."

I still didn't know what she meant.

"Someone who checks that programs are being made ethically," she explained wearily. "You know, Robin, that we're doing all the things we should be doing, and not doing the things we shouldn't. That we—and the independents we commission—are all sticking to the Corporation guidelines, broadcasting with integrity. You'd be perfect for it."

I put my head on one side.

"Why the sudden concern?" I asked.

"Robin, where have you been? Read the papers. The world

moves on. The media are constantly under fire for infringing some journalistic principle or other, and we've got to be seen to respond."

The accusation that I was out of touch was unfair. I spent my days with the radio for company, and my evenings with the newspapers. Radio and print reported on the goings-on in television as if it were an unruly younger sister: a scene staged here, an actor hired for reality TV there. Radio and newspaper journalism aren't immune, of course. One person and his mouth are enough to give birth to a lie. You don't need technology, but somehow with more technology and the multiplication of media, there's simply more to play with, and while playing is not usually good journalism, it often makes for a good story. The Corporation had so far escaped scandal, but its own managers were paranoid that they, or someone they employed, would be caught out. Journalism operates on trust. The reader trusts the journalist, and the employer trusts the journalist. However, managers aren't naturally disposed to trust. Which of us is? They know every contract gets broken. Sometimes they even encourage it.

"Cover our back, you mean."

Maeve pinched her lips together and refused to rise to the bait.

"You've heard about Paula Carmichael's death, I suppose?" she said, making a leap I couldn't follow. "Or has that managed to pass you by too in your domestic idyll? Look, I've got a meeting and I'm already late. Go away and enlighten yourself, so that at the very least you know what I'm talking about. Then come back to me next week and let me know if you want it, and I'll see if I can swing it for you."

Maeve stood up and whisked a briefcase from beside her desk, dropped a floppy disk into it, snapped it shut, and made for the door. I got to my feet, wondering how I'd ended up in this particular mess.

"But for God's sake, Robin, get a haircut. There's a limit to what

I can swing." She paused again, remembered what she was supposed to say, then added sweetly, "Did you bring any photos of the little ones?"

I shook my head. I'd never been this far from them before, never needed to consult a photograph.

———————

I headed straight for the bathroom and spent long minutes looking in the mirror. There were days I didn't look in the mirror from the time I got up in the morning to when I dropped into bed at night. I mean of course I washed when I had the time, but the finer points of grooming had sunk to the bottom of my list of priorities and it showed. I had never plastered myself in makeup but even I had to agree that I needed something to counteract the deathlike pallor of my skin, something to disguise the bags under my green eyes, something to give my lips a little life. And then there was the hair. It made my scalp prickle just to look at it. I combed some water in with my fingers and tried to push it into shape, any shape. I splashed cold water on my face and rubbed it dry with a paper hand towel in an effort to produce some color. I stared hard in the mirror again, but all I could see was a thin shabby woman with lank red hair and a blotchy face.

"What a loser," I said aloud to my reflection.

Behind me a toilet flushed and a door banged open. A woman emerged from the stalls and came to wash her hands at the basin. She was wearing black, well-cut trousers and a tailored jacket over a clingy purple T-shirt with a gold chain at her neck. Her hair was highlighted blond, cut close to her head. She ignored me, gave herself a brief, approving glance in the mirror while she dried her hands, then strode out, her heels clattering in a businesslike fashion on the tiled floor.

I went to find Jane, skulking through the hushed corridors in case I ran into old colleagues. When I found her, I saw it in her eyes too. It was beginning to piss me off.

"I know, I know," I told her. "I should have smartened myself up a bit."

She didn't actually say yes, you're right, but she looked it. I had to admire her. She'd been working half the night, then out to see me in the early hours, and here she was back at her desk, not caring about sleep when there was a story to cover. She still looked tired, but she'd done something to her hair, twisting it up on top of her head and skewering it with what looked like a hatpin. Jane is aware that she works in an open-plan office. It's one of the secrets of her success. She is always on show.

I filched a chair from the desk behind Jane's and rolled it over to sit next to her. A television monitor hung from a bracket on the ceiling, showing Corporation news output. Jane's underlings wouldn't be in until later that day, and the desks in front of her were empty, but people working on earlier programs were occupying desks around the edges of the room. I felt more at home here, where at least fifty percent of the workforce was wearing jeans. I couldn't vouch for it, but some of them may even have borne traces of their children's breakfast.

"What are you doing here?"

"I came to apologize for shouting at you about Adam."

"Accepted. So what are you really doing here?"

"I went to see Maeve. She offered me a job."

Jane raised her eyebrows.

"EGIE. Ethical guidelines implementation editor." I was keeping my voice low. For all I knew people high and low were fighting for the job.

"A poisoned chalice," Jane murmered back. "In fact a great big vat of arsenic."

"Quite."

"What are you going to do?"

"What do you think? Turn it down."

Jane pulled a face and leaned close to me. "No one's job is safe," she said, "not even Maeve's. You may not be able to pick and choose."

I started to ask her more but she shook her head, indicating with her eyes that this was not the time or place.

"Later," she insisted. "But to get back to my original question, what are you doing here?"

"Paula Carmichael," I changed the subject. "What are they saying?"

"Too early to draw any conclusions. That's the police. Shocked and saddened by the loss of a true friend, that's the prime minister thinking she's probably more use to him dead than alive. Meanwhile everyone else is speculating wildly."

Jane was tapping at her keyboard, summoning up the agency copy on Paula Carmichael. I read over her shoulder and learnt quite a bit: That Paula Carmichael was forty-nine when she died. That Richard Carmichael, aged fifty-six, was the stepfather of the boys, that Paula Carmichael's first marriage had ended in divorce. That Richard Carmichael had also been married before, and that his American wife had alleged he had beaten her, and that she was an alcoholic. That Paula and Richard had met at a government-sponsored seminar on the social responsibilities of business enterprises. That Paula's social activism frequently took her far away from home. That one of the sons, George, had been arrested for being drunk and disorderly at a football match. That their Lambeth house was worth at least a million pounds, but that Richard had lost close to that gambling on the stock market. That Paula Carmichael's former husband was now living in Aix-en-Provence and running a café with a new wife. All this, I guessed, must have been collated from library clippings. Editors had just summoned up the Paula Carmichael file and reworked the news stories that had come up in the past two or three years since she became well known. There hadn't been sufficient time for anyone to do any proper digging.

"But nothing that tells us why she jumped . . ." I murmured.

"So she did jump?" Jane seized on my terminology.

I shook my head, irritated. "I don't know. I've told you, I didn't see."

"Looks to me like they've got the husband lined up as the killer."

Jane looked at the television set and tapped my arm to make me look too. It took me a second, because Gladstone Road looked fresh and new, and not like where I lived at all. Then I realized they were showing the front of the Carmichael house, and that there were photographers blocking the road outside. Whoever was filming must be standing right outside my front door. Even inside it perhaps.

"Shit," I muttered. I wondered how my mother was coping.

As we watched, the door to the Carmichael house opened, and Richard appeared. A man emerged and stood behind his right shoulder, a police officer I guessed. He wore a nondescript gray suit and his dark hair could have done with a brush, but even on television you could see his eyes were busy, watching constantly, moving from the faces in the crowd to the faces of his uniformed officers, who in turn kept glancing at him. Next to the gray-suited police officer, Carmichael was physically vast but he seemed to have shrunk into himself, and when he spoke there was hurt and anger in his voice.

"I have a statement here asking for help with the police inquiries into the death of my wife, Paula." He flourished a piece of paper and cameras flashed. He cleared his throat. "But I'm going to tear it up and tell it how it is." At this point the gray-suited man beside him briefly closed his eyes, and I could have sworn he was praying.

"I know you British all think I should shut up and grieve. Let sleeping dogs lie and all that bull, but I'm a loudmouth American, and I say it how it is. My wife was the best thing I ever saw about this country. By a long way. And you're all a bunch of ungrateful bastards. You won't let anyone rise above you. You just have to knock them down." Carmichael raged on, and the journalists loved it, pressing in close with microphones, photographers jostling each other. I spotted at least three uniformed officers looking expectantly at the gray-suited man, waiting for him to put a stop to it. But he just gazed into the middle distance, apparently letting the unorthodox press statement wash over him, which wasn't perhaps as stupid as it looked. I doubt anything could have stopped Carmichael in midflow, and it would have been an unsightly scene to have the police physically restraining the widower. Carmichael ranted on.

"Some months ago my wife was making a documentary commissioned by the Corporation about her work, and all they wanted to do was dig the dirt. They had no respect. They just wanted to humiliate her, and she began to doubt herself and everything she had done. Ever since, she started to talk about retiring from public life, about stopping her work. Now this. She's gone now, so are you happy?"

He stopped short then, as though he was going to say more, but changed his mind. Within a moment he had turned and vanished again inside the house. The journalists surged forward. One, a young woman, tried to slide into the house through the open door, only to find her way blocked by the gray-suited man. He nodded politely at her, stepped smartly into the house himself, and shut the door in her face. I heard a guffaw of laughter from somewhere in the crowd of hacks. For a moment the television screen went black, and then the coverage switched back to the studio.

I felt dizzy and the picture on the screen blurred in front of my tired eyes. I had a sense that something was deeply wrong, that I found myself at the heart of something in which I had no part.

"Now there's a wee gem for the EGIE," Jane snorted.

"Then it's someone else's problem," I replied.

"What's someone else's problem?" The voice came from behind my shoulder, and I turned to find Suzette there, eyes bright, her head cocked interrogatively.

"Everything." I grinned at her. We hugged and her delicate frame felt tiny against me. I fancied I could even feel her heart beating, like a bird's. "Everything is someone else's problem. I thought you didn't work here anymore."

"I won't have anything to do with her," Jane muttered, teasing, still gazing at the TV monitor. "She's a traitor. I don't know how you can hug the wee thing."

"I had a meeting," Suzette explained, "so I thought I'd drop by, see if Jane was here to say hello. Don't ask me why, I suppose I just felt the need to be abused. You're the last person I expected to see."

We left Jane there, grumbling that it was all very well for those who had no work to do, and we headed out of the building and walked until we found a coffee shop.

"It's twelve," Suzette pointed out. "That's lunchtime."

For someone so tiny, she eats like a horse. So we ordered coffee, and then we ordered baguettes. Suzette slipped out of her coat, a lithe body with a dancer's poise. Her blond hair was scraped back from her porcelain features and she was dressed in black as she almost always was, a tight sweater over a full skirt, ready to step like a swan into any corps de ballet. She bent to brush some crumbs from her chair and managed to make it look like an elegant thing to do. When she speaks she uses her delicate hands for emphasis. It makes whatever she says sound like music. She has the personality of a diva too. She is capable of relaxing, but only when there is no alternative.

"You look great," she said, sitting down, pulling her chair close.

"You're kidding," I laughed.

"You look great considering, put it like that then," she said, smiling. Suzette was busy, just as Jane was, but she had found time to drop by many times over the past year. She had helped with the children once in a while and never came empty-handed: nothing over the top, just a bottle of wine here and there, perfume for my birthday, fancy soap, little things that helped me to feel human.

"And how have you been?" Sometimes I felt guilty. My own life was so full that I tended to forget Suzette had her own challenges.

Jane, Suzette, and me. We had worked our way up through the Corporation ranks together. Somehow the three of us had bonded like iron and what had started off with shared lunches in the canteen became once-monthly dinners that lasted for hours and had us all talking about our lives and our work in a way I believe none of us did with anyone else. If we'd been more alike it probably wouldn't have worked, but Jane's arrogance was somehow balanced out by Suzette's self-doubt, and when Suzette's cool logic was too much for us, then Jane would start giggling, and that would be an end of that. Whenever we were together the conversation bounced around and went to interesting places. Strangely, we did better as a threesome than in any combination of two.

"Well, I'm busy," she said, stirring sugar into her coffee, "but I'm getting by."

She was the only one of the three of us who'd been gutsy enough to break away from the Corporation. Jane had stayed inside the organization and had become the editor of *Controversies*, while Suzette and I had both added camera skills to our production training. With the new generation of 3-chip cameras that produce broadcast-quality footage from machines that weigh in at just over three pounds, a lot of our work was done without the traditional camera crew. I'd stayed inside the Corporation too, but Suzette had always been less tolerant of bureaucracy, and had never known how to fight her battles. She had always needed to be her own boss, and her own production company seemed to have given her the freedom she needed. "But tell me about last night."

"Oh." I hung my head, reluctant to bring it all back. For a moment there I had been enjoying the pleasure of meeting Suzette. "There's nothing really to tell. It was just awful."

"Well, I mean, you saw her fall, right, so what did you see?"

I gazed at her. Suzette, Jane, myself—we all spend our lives with images. It's how we think.

"I saw her falling through the air, fast, and landing and crumpling." I shrugged. "It was over in an instant."

"Was there anyone else there?" Suzette's eyes were fixed on my face, mesmerized.

Always the same questions, I thought. Why was it that no one else in the world seemed to consider that Paula Carmichael might have committed suicide.

"I didn't see anyone."

Suzette nodded, thinking.

"But you heard arguments in the street."

"That's getting so blown out of proportion," I objected. "There was some row going on in the early evening. Everyone heard it, they must have. Then I may have heard voices again around the time she died, and then again I may not have. There was a storm, it was noisy, it was probably my imagination."

Suzette caught my tone of exasperation.

"Sorry, I didn't mean to interrogate you." She backed off. "It's just that I knew her slightly, so it's . . . well, it's just all rather strange . . ."

"I didn't realize you knew her."

"Only slightly," she repeated, and sniffed. In Suzette's vocabulary that small, controlled sniff meant that she did not intend to expand on this.

"You sound as though you didn't like her." I was surprised. "I thought everyone loved her."

"Including Paula," Suzette said drily. She stopped for a moment, then changed the subject. "Look, I'm going to have to run because I have an appointment, but I was going to ring you anyway. I heard you're thinking of going back to work, and I wondered whether you'd be interested in joining me at Paradigm."

I stared, and she grinned at me, delighted at my surprise.

"We've had some teething problems, mostly financial, but I really believe they're over now, and I can't think of anyone I'd rather work with."

"It's certainly worth thinking about." I struggled for words.

"So think about it. Let me see, how about more food, let's say a working lunch on Monday?"

"Okay," I said slowly.

"And look," Suzette said, "I know things are tough. If you need anything, just let me know. Babysitting, whatever."

"Right," I said, smiling at the earnest look on Suzette's face. "Thanks."

Chapter 4

AFTER Suzette left, I went and bought myself some makeup and a potion that promised me shiny hair. I retired to the washroom to try to make myself presentable. Then I did Jane's interview for her. I kept it as low-key as possible, no dramatics. After I came out of the studio Jane forced a smile and told me it was "Great, perfect, just what we needed," but I can smell Corporation bullshit a mile off and I knew she was disappointed. With any luck, I thought, I would end up on the cutting-room floor. Still, I spent the rest of the day feeling sick at myself, as if I'd been filming pornography, not an interview for a news analysis program. I should have just taken what I had seen the night before and wrapped it up and locked it away in my head. What good did recycled death ever do anyone?

By the time I'd got home from the Corporation there was a thin but steady stream of people coming by to take a look at where Paula Carmichael had fallen. There were journalists staking out the Carmichael house too, and police cars coming and going. I was glad to get to my front door unaccosted.

My mother opened the door to me before I had a chance to get my keys out.

"We've been looking out the window watching for you," she explained. "The children think all the activity is great fun."

Sure enough, the twins were having the time of their lives. Ma had set up their high chairs so they had a good view of the street. She'd provided them with drinks and biscuits, a baby version of dinner theater. While the babies were busy rubbernecking, she'd been tidying and vacuuming. My father abandoned Ma, my two sisters, and me when I was little. Somehow she brought the three of us up on nothing but debts—because that was what my father left us with—and completed a law degree in the bargain. My mother could write the book on multitasking.

"They're all ghouls," I said, as another car double-parked outside and a couple of middle-aged women got out.

"Not at all," Ma said. "Look what they're doing."

As she spoke, one of the women reached back inside and emerged with a bouquet of white roses. The two of them pushed their way through to the Carmichael house, and as the way cleared for them I saw that the pavement was now scattered with flowers and cards. The street was rapidly becoming a shrine.

"My God," I murmured, "just like Princess Diana."

"People liked Paula Carmichael," Ma said sadly. "They respected her and she respected them. She was never smug. Now everyone's heartbroken. Look at the policeman, even he's sad. Why would she do that?"

Fresh from the newsroom it was a new perspective for me to look at how sad the policeman looked, but my mother was right.

"It's so depressing," my mother said in a low voice. "If she couldn't bear to live, how can any of us?"

I watched for a few more moments, turned away, then turned back again. This house was so small, I couldn't retreat to a tower and pretend that nothing was happening outside. For a good while yet the pavement outside the Carmichael house would be the arena and my house would be the grandstand.

"I've got to get out of here," I muttered.

"I'm at Lorna's this evening," she said wearily, "but come and have dinner with us."

And so it came to pass that my mother cooked us dinner. Which consisted of pouring drinks all around and ordering Indian take-out. The twins shared a plain naan, mashed chicken korma, and some spinach. Once they were asleep on the guest-room bed breathing garlicky little snores we reheated the rest. Ma spooned out three portions, one for me, one for her, one for Lorna.

"Lorna's tired," she said, handing me Lorna's plate. "I think she'll stay in her room."

Lorna's room is the most peaceful place I know. That night she had chamber music playing softly and the lights were dimmed. She glanced over as I entered, but she said nothing. She was lying on her bed. By this point in the day she is usually exhausted, but even when she sleeps the quality of her rest is poor.

"You don't feel like joining us?" I asked gently. She smiled and shook her head of red-gold curls, gesturing that I should leave her plate on the table by her bed.

"Busy day," she said softly. Her voice was a contralto, surprisingly vibrant coming from her weary body.

Often, we would eat together. Once the most sociable of people, Lorna's instinct was still to seek out human contact even if it drained her of the last ounce of energy, which it always did. A year earlier, when the CFS was at its worst, I sometimes had to carry her to bed, and when I did I always remembered my mother scolding a seven-year-old Lorna for picking me up, three years younger, three years smaller, and swinging me around and then dropping me hard on the floor.

There was a time when I was jealous of Lorna. She was a bossy older sister, overzealous at school but still the most popular girl in the class, excelling at hockey and tennis. When she was seventeen I was fourteen, bookish and arty and hopeless at sports. I looked on bewildered as my girlfriends fought for the favor of a smile from Lorna and the boys followed her around like puppies. From there she disappeared to Cambridge, and the stories of her achievements both academic and otherwise came to me secondhand. There was no way I could even hope to step into her shoes at school, but at least I could get on with my life outside the shadow cast by her sun.

Now Lorna has chronic fatigue syndrome. Even medical experts refer to it as an illness "of ambiguous status and uncertain cause." They fight a fierce clan war over its name. It's also known as myalgic encephalomyelitis, chronic Epstein-Barr, and atypical poliomyelitis, even yuppie flu—which, if it wasn't so derogatory, sort of fitted Lorna. Cambridge led to a fast-track career in merchant banking, and now she had the money to move on from hockey to more exotic activities. It was on a cycling holiday in Nepal that the trouble started. A day into the expedition she was struck down by a fever, some mysterious virus never identified, but quite probably something she had picked up in Britain before she left. She spent two days on her camp bed in a tent, forcing the fever down with Panadol, then tried to plow on. It wasn't like her to admit defeat, although it is true that until then most things in her life had come with relative ease. Anyway, this time she found herself unable to continue. She returned home and was adamant that this was just a temporary setback.

The exhaustion that she insisted would not last long went on for months. A year later, one day after she resigned from her job, she was diagnosed with CFS.

No one could tell us why it had happened. Lorna's case did not fit any one of the medical models perfectly. It is possible that CFS involves a link between physical and psychological factors, but the nature of that link, if it exists at all, is still a matter for speculation. CFS affects all socioeconomic and ethnic groups, we were told, is more common in women than men, with a typical onset between the ages of twenty and forty. All of which meant little to Lorna, who at the worst of it was tortured by sleeplessness, an excruciating sensitivity to noise, and was racked by muscle pain. She would try to get out of bed and get only as far as the door before collapsing.

There is no cure, and we don't know if or when it will go. Experts have difficulty with any sort of prognosis because there have been few long-term studies. However, Lorna is better than she was, her progress marked in small steps back toward independence. She has a tendency to rush at things, so when she does feel better she pushes herself to the limit, and then profound exhaustion overwhelms her again. Still, her progress, even if she takes one step backward for every two forward, gives us hope that one day this strange affliction will leave her altogether.

I put the tray down and bent to kiss Lorna's forehead. Her huge green eyes looked up at me. They smiled that sad dark smile that had been hers since the dazzle left her. Those eyes haunted me.

I busied myself drawing the curtains. When she was tired like this, she had no energy to do anything for herself. It was already dark outside and God knows it would depress even the happiest soul to stare out into the night for hours on end. She hauled herself into a sitting position, and I fixed the table over her so that she could eat comfortably. She began to pick at her food and I sat down in the armchair next to her bed.

I tried to make a couple of visits a week. It tended to be in the evening, by which time she was usually exhausted. I would sit with her for a while, not saying much—chatter tires her at the end of the day—but it would be companionable all the same. Since the birth of the twins I had often come frazzled into this room, near the end of my tether. Despite the awfulness of Lorna's condition the enforced tranquillity had given me a few moments of respite. Once I had dozed off in that armchair and my mother had come to find me an hour later, only to discover me fast asleep and Lorna lying in bed watching over me.

Tonight, though, I couldn't get ahold of the tranquillity. I was frustrated. I wanted the old talkative Lorna back, not this silence. I wanted the Lorna who would regale me with her victories, and who would listen to my troubles with at least an attempt at sympathy, then make me laugh, felling me with some hilarious observation that was always spot on. Today there were things I'd have liked to get off my chest, like how it feels to watch someone plunge to their death, and how grotty I felt about doing Jane's television interview, but depression hovers over Lorna. It has lifted somewhat with the improvement in her symptoms, but nevertheless suicide didn't seem to be a good late-night topic of conversation. What I had to say was not calculated to soothe, so I kept quiet. Nevertheless, Lorna seemed to have sensed that something was wrong. She had stopped eating and was looking at me.

It nearly burst out of me then. The words were there waiting, a mouthful of poison ready to be spewed. For God's sake, snap out of it, Lorna. Pull yourself together!

I bit it back.

"I'll see you later, my food's getting cold," I muttered, standing and leaning over to kiss her again. Then I made for the door. I felt the full force of Lorna's eyes on my back. Lorna's my big sister and I've always been scared of her.

My mother was in Lorna's lilac and walnut sitting room with a tray on her lap. Her face was long and strained and I assumed she was worrying about Lorna.

"How's she doing?" I asked.

Ma heaved a breath, as if I'd dragged her away from some other train of thought. She pulled a face.

"Oh, not bad at all," she said, "but she wipes herself out. She did a little exercise this morning, and she spent all afternoon on the Internet."

"She must know more about this disease than her doctor."

"On the contrary," Ma gave a strained smile, "she's educated him very well, and I'm sure most of her time on the Net is spent educating other people."

"Strange how she manages to be as bossy as ever," I commented drily.

It was Lorna who had insisted that she would continue to live in her own home, a flat in an Edwardian terrace that she had had expensively renovated in the months before she became ill. The flat is ideal because it is close to me, and to Ma, and to our baby sister, Tanya, but not so ideal because it is a first-floor flat with a steep staircase down to the front door. For a long time she simply didn't go out. More recently she's ventured down on Ma's arm and into the street. One day they went for a drive to Richmond Park, another day to a coffee shop. Lorna does her supermarket shopping on the Internet. She has part-time home help. Lorna wants, I know, to think she is still being independent, but Ma spends at least three evenings a week there so that Lorna doesn't feel isolated. Tanya moves heaven and earth to leave her three children with her husband, Patrick, and sit with Lorna twice a week. I was pretty useless because Lorna couldn't take the noise of the twins for more than a few minutes at a time and I had no one to dump them on. Except, of course, for my mother or Tanya. Which brought us back to square one.

"She's got an acupuncturist coming tomorrow to take a look at her," Ma said.

I caught her eye and we both broke into broad grins. Ma was full of scorn for alternative medicine. She waved an arm expansively.

"Next week it's a cauldron and some frogs, what the hell. If she wants to try it, that's fine by me." She laughed, shaking her head, blinking back tears. Anything Lorna wanted had always been fine by Ma. She was Ma's golden daughter, her delight, the success plucked from the disaster of her broken marriage. Lorna had not always returned the devotion. As a teenager she found Ma's intensity irritating. She'd rejected her advice whenever it was offered, and never asked for help. I often wondered how she felt now, with Ma ministering to her every need.

I tucked into my food. I was ravenous. My mother and I are regulars at the Haweli around the corner from Lorna. We know the menu back to front. It's my version of a social life, to have takeout, put the children to bed and sit in front of *ER* with my mother, like an old married couple. Sometimes it unnerves me when I think of the two of us, both single independent women yet dependent on each other for company, my face an echo of my mother's thirty years ago. It's like looking into my own future and seeing the loneliness stretching forever.

"Prefer the masala," I commented between mouthfuls.

"Hmm." Ma still didn't seem to have her mind on the food, and she spoke very quietly. "I can't . . . Have you spoken to Tanya?"

I shook my head. "She left a message last night, but I haven't got back to her."

"I know. I saw her last night after she'd tried calling you." Ma paused to sigh again. I'd stopped eating now and was watching her. She looked suddenly older, her face creased along lines of worry that I had not seen, even with Lorna's illness, for years.

"She was quite upset. Apparently your father turned up on her doorstep and invited himself in."

We stared at each other.

"My father?" I echoed. Ma shrugged her shoulders at me, as if to say she couldn't help it, it was nothing to do with her. "I thought he was dead," I said. Which wasn't strictly true, but he had vanished so comprehensively from my life when I was four that he might as well have been.

"Evidently not." Her voice was stretched thin, barely under control. "Tanya sent him packing, but she thinks he'll be back, and she wanted to warn you in case he tries to contact you. He asked her for money."

I snorted.

"Talk about being out of touch . . . Can she be sure it's him? I mean, where's he been all this time? And how did he find Ta—"

Ma stood up abruptly, her face sagging.

"I don't know and I don't want to know," she snapped. "I'm telling you in order to warn you, nothing more. As far as I'm concerned he has been dead for thirty-odd years. All three of you know that your father is not to be trusted. He's a crook and a con man and my greatest regret is that I ever had anything to do with him."

I sat there, gazing after her, stunned as much by my mother's outburst as by my father rising from the dead. My mother disliked anger, feared its unpredictability. In us, she had always counseled repression. "Just put it aside," she'd advised in every crisis, and we all knew she told herself the same thing.

I looked down at my plate. The curry was cold, fat congealing around the edges of my plate. I felt sick with apprehension and excitement. My father had been purged from our lives, all talk of him was taboo. I had dredged through my memories time and again to find a face in my memory, a voice, anything. I had found almost nothing. Now I would meet him.

Chapter 5

THE damp weather had cleared and the heat of the sun was direct. The carpet of flowers outside the Carmichael house was still soggy from the rain, and condolence cards had been mashed into the pavement. Now the whole sodden mess would be cooked. There was a police officer stationed outside the house looking uneasily at the grunge at his feet. He kicked a couple of rotting bouquets into the gutter and then, after a moment, he bent to pick up a fresher bunch of lilies and place them in the relative shelter of the doorway. I found a note shoved into my letter box.

> Robin,
> Don't worry about the table. It belongs to the landlord. I'll stick something else there and with any luck he won't notice it's gone. If it was worth a fortune I'll fake a robbery and he can claim it on the insurance. You might want to chuck away the remains.
> Pretty foul introduction the other night. Hope to meet again in better circumstances.
>
> Dan

I smiled, turned the scrap of paper over. It was a dry cleaning receipt. Two suits, six shirts. The name at the top was Dan Stein. I put the note in my pocket. I liked the idea of a neighbor with a sense of humor.

————

When D.C. Mann rang to ask me to come to the station, I couldn't bring myself to ask her whether she doubled as a babysitter. Nor could I ask my mother again, so I dropped the children off with Tanya. My sister and Patrick are both nurses, and they work shifts at the hospital. Tanya was still in her nightgown when she opened the door to me, and her hair was standing on end.

"Shouldn't you be asleep?" I said guiltily.

"I just got the girls off to school. I'm going back to bed for a couple of hours," she said, holding out her arms for the twins, "but Patrick will look after them until I get up. Then he has to get going."

Patrick appeared behind her, pulling on a sweatshirt over jeans.

"Hand them over," he said. "I'll knock them into shape." Tanya handed William to her husband and Patrick started to tickle him.

"You look like you should be in bed too," I said over William's squeals of delight.

"Nah, I've had my six hours, it's Tan's turn. I'm fine."

With three girls and a perpetually empty bank account Tanya's life was a complicated one. Whatever arrangements she and Patrick made usually worked simply because there was no space for them not to work. How the two of them ever got to see each other with their head-to-toe schedules I couldn't work out, but perhaps that was the secret of their success. I was two years older than Tanya and in the past I'd maintained a somewhat superior attitude to her. She wasn't as ambitious as I had been. She had allowed herself to get distracted by hearth and home. Now I just felt humbled by her. She was so much better at the whole thing than I was.

"I heard about your visitor," I told her as Patrick retreated into the house with William.

"Nerve of the man," she muttered. "I'll tell you all about it later. Off you go. Tell the nice policeman you didn't do it."

———————

Which I thought was a joke, until I met Finney, the police officer who had stood by and let Richard Carmichael rave: the same gray suit, the dark hair still unbrushed, the same cool, watchful eyes, and, most powerfully, what the television had not begun to convey, the sense of restless energy and intelligence that washed over the room the moment he walked in.

He walked with a slight professorial stoop. There were gray strands in his hair, his trousers were perhaps an inch too short. A badly knotted tie veered violently off course exposing a missing button on his shirt that in turn revealed a patch of white skin and dark hair. If you had asked me right then whether I was intimidated, I'd have said I tended to be intimidated only by people who were capable of dressing themselves in the morning. He must have been about the same age as me, and I wasn't about to defer to him.

"Good morning, sir," D.C. Mann said, standing. She didn't seem frightened of him, but she did seem alert, as though she was waiting for something.

Finney flashed her a smile that transformed his face and nearly floored D.C. Mann. The smile jolted me too, just on rebound. That, I thought, was what she had been waiting for. By the time he turned his attention to me the smile might never have been. Grave-faced, he introduced himself, pulled out a chair on the other side of the desk, flopped into it, and then said in a voice that was almost a drawl, "I saw you on the telly last night."

I felt I should defend myself, but I had done nothing wrong. I nodded.

"The word 'confidentiality' mean anything to you?" Finney asked mildly. I saw D.C. Mann wince.

"I said on television exactly the same as I said to D.C. Mann. How can that influence your inquiry?"

"I hate television," Finney growled. I remembered the door to the Carmichael house that Finney had slammed in the face of the journalist. Our eyes locked. Challenge and counter-challenge passed silently between us like an electric charge. Television was my life, or had been. This was a declaration of war, and I savored it.

"You can never tell what's true and what's lies," Finney complained, dragging his eyes from mine. "Don't you think, D.C. Mann?"

Mann agreed, lowering her head, her eyes on him.

"Television is man-made." Automatically I parroted what I said to others in my life who were critical of what I do. "It can lie, it can tell the truth, just like the people who make it. Often it falls somewhere between the two, but in many cases it may reveal a different truth."

Finney gazed at me. I wished I'd kept my mouth shut.

"Well, here we have a bit of a problem with a different truth." His voice dwelled with contempt on those last two words. Then he glanced at his notes. "On television you made no mention of the voices you heard shouting yesterday evening, but you told D.C. Mann that you heard an argument just before you saw Paula Carmichael fall. Can you explain that?"

"I wasn't asked about the arguments in the television interview," I said. "You know as well as I do how these things work; it's just intended to be a sixty-second snapshot, not an exhaustive investigation."

"Really," Finney said sarcastically. "Useful to know how these media techniques work, but I'm more interested in the voices you heard."

"I told D.C. Mann very clearly last night that I was not sure whether or not I heard voices before I saw Paula Carmichael fall. I wasn't sure then, and I'm still not sure."

Finney raised his eyebrows, looked interrogatively at Mann.

"That's right," she said, looking uncertainly first at him then at me, as though she was unsettled by our skirmish and not sure which side she should be taking. "I tried to make that clear in the statement. There were two different incidents. Loud voices earlier in the evening that everyone heard, and then Miss Ballantyne looking out of the window and thinking she may have heard someone shouting around the time Paula Carmichael fell."

Finney bent his head over my statement again.

"That's not as clear as it might be," he grumbled.

"Sorry, sir," Mann muttered.

" 'May have heard,' " Finney repeated the phrase with disgust. "What the hell does that mean?"

Neither I nor D.C. Mann answered, and after a second he asked, "Do you often hear voices?"

"Only when I'm not taking my medication." I gave him a hard look.

"Your medic . . . ?" He trailed off, uncertain how to continue, then saw that I was winding him up.

"No, I do not hear voices," I said firmly. "There was a lot of noise from the storm. I thought I heard something that sounded like a voice, but I may have been mistaken. I wish I'd never mentioned it. I was just trying to be helpful." Finney pursed his lips, then turned again to Mann.

"Have you asked anyone else in the street whether they heard voices around the time Carmichael fell?"

"There's some confusion." Mann was relieved to be able to offer him something by way of reply. "We've had a couple of people saying they heard shouting in the street around that time, but of course Miss Ballantyne was the only one who saw her fall, so she's the only one who even knows exactly what time we're talking about. And immediately after she'd fallen, Miss Ballantyne started shouting in the street herself, and I think that's what our witnesses heard. The storm may have distorted Miss Ballantyne's voice, because nobody seems to have been able to tell us what she was shouting."

"I don't think that's true," I interrupted. "I think they heard, I think they just don't want to admit that they heard me yelling for help but didn't open their doors."

Finney was silent for a minute, reading over the statement again.

"Try and clarify that," he said shortly.

Mann grimaced.

"Now, moving on, last night you told D.C. Mann that you didn't know the woman who died."

"I didn't recognize her," I clarified. "It was dark and I scarcely saw her face."

"In fact," he had the transcript of my TV interview in front of him, "you'd met her twice."

"I said I thought I'd bumped into her," I said, frowning. "Paula—I think it was her—said a total of four words to me."

"You implied you were friends on TV."

"I said I thought I'd bumped into her," I repeated.

Finney blew softly, not hurrying.

"So what were these four words?"

"Been there, done that."

" 'Been there, done that,' " he repeated it slowly, wonderingly.

I explained the context then, that I'd been struggling with small children in the supermarket, but Finney still looked bemused.

"I think Carmichael was being sympathetic," D.C. Mann interjected, "saying she'd been through that too."

"Been through what?" Finney scowled and I saw D.C. Mann cringe.

"Dealing with small children," D.C. Mann spelled out, remembering at the last minute to add, "sir."

Finney went a little paler, as though one of us had mentioned menstruation. He breathed deeply, then fired a series of questions at me. I say fired, but he had this slow, deep delivery that meant you only felt the kick afterward.

"Did you ever visit the Carmichaels?"

"I told you, I don't know them."

"Were you ever inside their house?"

"No."

"Did you speak on the phone?"

"No, what is this? I told you, I—"

"Did you have mutual friends?"

"No."

That last question and answer started to bother me, but I was too distracted to think why.

Finney's eyebrows rose.

"Well, you'll have to help me out here, Miss Ballantyne," he said. "We've been spending a lot of time looking through Mrs. Carmichael's things, as you can imagine."

Looking for a suicide note, I speculated, but I wasn't about to open my mouth.

"Mrs. Carmichael left a lot of papers," Finney went on, "and I mean *a lot*. It's still early days, so we're still paddling in the shallows, so to speak, but we've come across a bit of a mystery, and I'm hoping you can put me straight."

Here I was gripped by a sense of foreboding so strong that I felt deprived of oxygen. Finney looked up questioningly at me and I managed to jerk my head to indicate that he should go on.

"Could we open a window in here?" I asked.

Mann got up and went over to the window, fiddled with the catch for a moment, then turned and shrugged at me apologetically. Finney did not seem to have noticed her failed efforts.

"Mrs. Carmichael kept diaries," he was saying. "She kept work diaries, she kept family diaries, she kept a personal diary. We're drowning in diaries. How she found time to do anything but write in her diaries I do not know. It's her personal diary that we've been having a little look at, and in it she mentions you."

My eyes fixed on Finney's. There was unhappiness there, there was impatience there, but I could see no shadow of a lie in them.

"It mentions me," I echoed.

"Yes. Can you tell me why that might be?"

"I can't imagine."

Silence, and I knew he wanted me to talk into it.

"How do you know it's me?"

"Robin, two children, same names, right ages, living opposite. Same physical descriptions. Slim, red hair, green eyes . . ." He paused to clear his throat. "Couldn't be anyone else."

I forced myself to carry on breathing, tried to make my brain turn.

"There is no explanation that I can think of," I said, as calmly as I could, "but maybe if I could see the context . . ."

He produced a photocopied sheet and pushed it across the table at me. His fingers brushed mine, and we each pulled our hands away as if burnt. I stared across at him, then down at the sheet, trying to focus. Most of the page was blacked out. Only one paragraph remained for me to read. I pulled the sheet closer to me and forced myself to concentrate.

Robin goes back and forth to the supermarket like a mother bird with worms for her young. So much of her life is full of grim determination. How lonely she must be at the end of the day when Hannah and William are asleep. She never seems to go out. But yesterday I was walking across the Common to the underground. It was a real summer's day, everyone going about with no clothes on and radios blaring, and there she was, there they all were, lying sleeping in the sun. She'd rigged up an awning for them so they were shaded, and she'd got hold of each of them even in her sleep, and you just knew that the slightest stirring would waken her. They were all three in shorts and T-shirts. Oh, and the babies' little fat legs, and plump white arms, all hither and thither. What abandon, what sheer joy to sleep in the sun. It's the first time I've seen them truly at ease. How I envied them their innocence. I wanted to lie down on the grass beside them. Oh, how I wanted to sleep in the sun without guilt.

I picked the sheet up and read it through again, cool and forensic. I was beyond feeling uneasy, beyond feeling that this was all terribly strange. This, these words on the page, were beyond coincidence. This woman had watched me. She knew my name and the names of my children. Instinctively my body and my brain reacted as if under threat, tensing, adrenaline racing to prime me for fight or flight. I tried to calm myself, willed my heart to slow its pounding. She was dead, I told myself, there was no one to fight or to flee. I examined the date on the diary entry. Early September, just weeks before. It was mid-October now, and the extreme heat of the past few days was a strange climactic blip in the middle of an autumn that was fast advancing toward winter. I remembered the day Paula described, remembered how refreshed I'd felt after that sleep: sleep without guilt, without dreams, sleep without interruption. I'd had to wake the twins as the sun disappeared, so we could wend our happy way home. I read the passage over and over again until I realized that Finney was impatient.

"Obviously she knew me," I said slowly, exactly, needing to convey this distinction, "but I did not know her."

Both D.C. Mann and Finney gazed at me in disbelief.

"Are you accusing Paula Carmichael of being a stalker?" Finney asked, almost amused. "Because I don't think that's going to go down very well."

———

After the interview with Finney I went for a walk on the Common. I knew the children were at Tanya's, knew I should pick them up before Patrick's shift. Tanya had made it clear to me more than once that, while happy to help when they could, their lives were already fraught with the demands of work and children. They needed a holiday, and they couldn't afford one, and here was I taking advantage.

My head was full of questions, but they kept getting pushed to one side by Finney's smile, which lingered there far longer than was decent. The man annoyed and intrigued me in equal measure. His attitude had been antagonistic, but the prospect of tangling with him was not entirely unpleasant. Adrenaline was rushing through my bloodstream. Adrenaline and something else, something seductive, was making my head light and threatening to dull my sense of danger. Paula Carmichael's death was unremittingly awful. Yet here I was, just hours later, excited and intrigued by a man for the first time since Adam left. I was appalled at myself. How could my emotional life be so distorted that a woman's death would have the effect of reawakening me to the joys of sexual attraction? I was in a state of temporary insanity. I despaired.

I didn't just want to walk, I needed to walk. I needed to walk on my own. I walked as though my life depended on it, arms swinging at my side. With every step I felt calmer.

I was scarcely aware of where I was walking, but I know the

Common like the back of my hand. I know the large open lawn where mothers push strollers and where for much of the year the wind howls across the flat expanse; I know the run-down playground, where the slide is forever surrounded by metal barricades that entice the children in. I know the duck pond, the graffiti-covered snack bar, the toilets with no paper and no running water, the sheltered wooded area where men cruise for sex of one kind or another and prostitutes loiter just in view of the passing motorists.

I sat down on a bench and gazed at the spot where, in the summer, I had lain asleep on the ground and Paula Carmichael had watched me. Had she sat down on this seat, I wondered, or hurried on by, briefcase under her arm, just as I had seen her that day under the bridge. The grass where we had lain was now a muddy patch. Despite the sun, no one was lazing on the ground today; it was still too damp from the storm. I sat there in solitude, but it was as though Paula sat with me, beside me on the bench, silently challenging me to work out our connection. How did Paula know me? How did she know my children, my circumstances, even my loneliness? Certainly she had lived as good as opposite me, but that in itself was not a sufficient explanation. None of my neighbors could have put my name to my face let alone named my children.

"She doesn't know me from Adam," I whispered to myself. It's a hazard of living alone.

Then the words I had said started to fade and reform in my head, and synapses sparked. What had Jane said? That Adam had worked together with Paula Carmichael on a documentary. Of course that didn't mean they were so much as friends. It was probably nothing. As far as I knew, Adam had remained pretty secretive about what had happened between us. Leaving children fatherless was hardly something you boasted about at the dinner table. So the leap from knowing Paula to sharing his secrets with her, to her living opposite me was all too much. I was clutching at straws, but there was only this one straw to clutch.

———————

I was back at home with the children when Terry phoned. I was trying to get us all a late lunch. We were suffering from low blood sugar and I was just managing to hold it down until the food was ready, but Hannah and William were falling apart. The last thing I wanted was a work call.

"Terry, how are you doing?" Terry, my favorite manager. No doubt Maeve had told him to ring.

"Good, and you? Getting any sleep?"

"Here and there," I said lightly. I felt about a hundred and three.

"Still, worth it all in the end."

"Absolutely," I said, thinking: Speed it up here, Terry.

"Well, I was just ringing to touch base," he said, "and find out whether you've given Maeve's offer any thought."

"Um, I need more time," I said. I still intended to turn the job down, but I was afraid if I said that right now Terry was programmed to try to persuade me and I'd be there all day. I just wanted him off the line.

"Well, you've got a day or two to play with," he said, "but after that Maeve says she's going to have to open it up."

"Okay. I'll let you know before then." Couldn't he hear the impatience in my voice? He could certainly hear the children fussing.

"Meanwhile, do you fancy a night out?" His voice became playful, a fairy godfather offering Cinderella a trip to the ball. "I've been left with an extra ticket to the awards ceremony at the Grosvenor House Hotel on Saturday, and everyone will be there. It would get you back in the swing of things, remind people who you are. What do you think?"

I couldn't see the harm.

"The children will love it," I said, waiting for Terry's sharp intake of breath before adding, "Just kidding. Of course I'd love to come."

Chapter 6

THE awards ceremony required some lifestyle changes. I hired a babysitter—I mean a babysitter who charged an hourly rate that was the GDP of a small nation, an agency nanny called Erica from Sweden—because I couldn't stretch my mother's goodwill any further, and Tanya and Patrick had for once screwed up their shifts, so that they were both working at the same time. They were wondering what to do with their own kids, let alone mine. Erica's main qualifications consisted of a black belt in judo, which seemed a little irrelevant, and a stellar career at a Swedish nannying academy. I got a haircut, short and sleek. I got a new subscription to Sky digital television. I'd been economizing for the past few months, but if you're going to work in television you've got to have access to all the news that's out there and this way I could watch everything from CNN to China Central Television. I dusted off my mobile phone and charged it up. If I was going to leave my children in the care of a total stranger—albeit a stranger with impeccable references—at least she could contact me when they choked or knocked themselves out, as they inevitably would. I even bought myself a new lipstick.

Terry came miles out of his way from Putney to pick me up and tooted his horn outside my door at six-thirty. Terry is nearly sixty and gay, but he loves to play Prince Charming and take a woman out on a date once in a while. He has the car for it, a macho four-

61

wheel drive, high off the ground. There aren't many white Range Rovers around. They tend to show the mud, but Terry's is always spotless.

"Robin, you look wonderful," he said with surprise as I climbed into the passenger seat. "Maeve said—" He stopped short.

"She said I looked like shit," I guessed.

"Maeve would never use language like that."

"Maeve should try getting up a dozen times in the night."

"She should try getting up to all sorts of things in the night," Terry said. "She's certainly missing out on something."

We drove through the streets of south London toward the city center in companionable silence, warm air billowing through the open windows. I love driving, and four years ago, back in the days when I still indulged myself, I bought a 1990 BMW. It accelerates like a sports car and does a hundred smooth as cream. I love its understated lean lines, but bits of it keep dropping off or going wrong and, weight for weight, spares are probably more expensive than solid gold. It had got to the point where I was afraid to drive it for fear of something else going wrong. I used it to pootle to and from Lorna's and Tanya's, and recently to and from the police station, even though it was developing some alarming rattles. It was due for its inspection and I knew it was barely roadworthy and I was dreading the expense, so when Terry had offered a lift, I had grabbed it.

Usually I love to be driven as much as to drive, to be free with my thoughts, gazing out the window as the world passes by. Tonight I could not completely relax. I was flailing in a pool of unease. I took some comfort from Terry's presence at my side. It was easy to make fun of him, he did it himself all the time, but it was people like Terry, talented, creative, collegial, who still gave the Corporation a gilding of style. Old school and Oxbridge educated, with a passion for hand-embroidered silk waistcoats and a halo of curly gray hair around an otherwise bald head, Terry had made his way easily up the Corporate ladder. Then he'd hit a ceiling because he didn't have the raw ambition to make it right to the top like Maeve. In the Corporation he was comfortable, relatively safe. His creativity had become stifled by a career in management, but out in the raw competition of the independent producers someone like Terry would have been ripped limb from limb. I had always assumed he would sit out his career at Maeve's knees, perfectly content. Then I remembered what Jane had said and wondered how long Maeve would have knees for Terry to sit at. It was strange, I thought, that Terry should be happy to sit just this far up the ladder, making no apparent effort to climb. Meanwhile Jane, Suzette, and Maeve were driven by red-hot ambition to go that extra step. And me? What was I driven by? There had been ambition, as strong as Jane's. I had banished it for the past year, but I could feel it lurking, and I feared that if it had lost none of its heat, its return would condemn me to a life of frustration. Could I tame my ambition so that I would not be constantly torn between my children and my work?

"Penny for them," Terry said.

I shook my head.

"It's weird being out and about without the children. Nice but weird."

"You'll go mad if you don't work, Robin." He said it softly.

I sighed.

"I have to work or we'll starve. I just don't like the children being with anyone but me."

"You'll have to get over it."

"I am aware of that, thank you, Terry." Silence fell. I felt guilty for snapping at him, but really there was no need for him to be so damned patronizing.

"You should take the job," he said eventually.

"It's not me," I grumbled. "You know it's not. I don't want to be some sort of policeman, going around slapping wrists when people step out of line."

"Someone's got to do it, and better you than some twenty-year-old with a nose ring through her brain."

"Can't do it anyway," I told him. "Paula Carmichael's death will be top of the EGIE agenda, and the police seem to think I'm a prime suspect."

He laughed at that, thinking I was joking. I wished Finney could have seen him.

"Anyway," he said, when he'd sobered up, "Paula Carmichael's death is right off the agenda. Her husband's retracted his statement, at least the stuff about the Corporation."

"What?"

"The lawyers were onto his statement the moment he made it. Then the director paid him a visit to express his condolences: flowers, gifts for the boys, everything. While he was there he pointed out a few of the finer legal points, reminded Carmichael how expensive it would be to fight a libel charge and, hey presto, he backed off. He made a statement this afternoon saying he was very upset when he spoke to the press yesterday, and he'd been mistaken to say Paula had been upset by the documentary. Indeed, she'd been flattered by their interest. The lawyers are double-checking it as we speak. It'll be all over the bulletins."

I puffed out my cheeks and exhaled slowly.

"Great," I said, "first the Corporation humiliates his wife, then him."

"Rubbish," Terry protested. "The documentary about Paula Carmichael was never aired, no one ever saw it."

I frowned.

"That's the documentary she made with Adam?"

"Strictly speaking, it wasn't even a Corporation project," Terry explained. "It was a Paradigm production, you know, the company Suzette Milner set up, but it was commissioned by the Corporation, and Suzette hired Adam to do the presenting."

"Really?"

Terry nodded without comment. They weren't the best of friends, Terry and Suzette, so I didn't say what I was thinking, which was that Suzette had played that particular card close to her chest when I had seen her on the morning after Paula's death.

"So was Paula Carmichael depressed or wasn't she?" I tried to clarify. "What's her husband saying?"

"The man's a mess," Terry said. "He probably doesn't know what he's saying himself."

He leaned forward and turned on the car radio to see whether there was any mention of Carmichael's retraction on the news. There was none. "Still being digested by the lawyers, then," Terry commented. The weather forecast predicted a sharp drop in temperature the next day and hazarded to speculate that autumn would now continue its more normal path downward into colder temperatures. We made the rest of the journey in silence. For the past year I had hardly set foot outside south London, and now, as dusk settled, I gazed out on the grandeur of the Thames and at the fairy-lit bridges. It didn't look like the city I lived in.

We pulled up outside the Grosvenor House Hotel.

"Nice frock," Terry commented as I clambered out.

I humphed. It felt all wrong, as though there'd been some horrible mix-up and I'd got someone else's clothes on. I couldn't believe I'd ever felt comfortable in anything but boots and jeans and layers of T-shirts and sweaters. I hadn't worn a dress since the third month of my pregnancy. The one I'd dug out of my wardrobe for this evening was navy silk, cut just above the knee, high at the throat, very simple. It hung looser on me than it had before, I guess I'd lost more weight than I'd realized. I'd wrapped a light woolen shawl around my shoulders. I waited as Terry handed the car keys to the valet, and saw Maeve arriving. She was clearly worried about that drop in temperature, because she carried a fur stole over one arm, like a lapdog.

Inside, people had gathered in the bar and I saw that Maeve was in her element, networking like a fiend. She caught sight of me, saw with obvious relief that I was out of my jeans, and beckoned me over, introducing me to a rickety old man in a cummerbund.

"I'm grooming Robin for the new ethics post," she told him, patting at my silk-clad shoulder like a cat. "So you see, we are responding to your concerns."

The old man had sharp eyes, and they gave me an appraising glance before returning to Maeve.

"We put the mink on your back, my dear," he said in a shaky voice, "so you'd better be, don't you think?"

Maeve laughed, a tinkling, nervy sound, and when he moved away, she patted the offending skin as though scolding it and whispered in my ear, "He meant they pay my wages, nothing more."

"Maeve, what do you mean you're grooming me?"

"Well, I should have said you're grooming yourself," she said, with another tense giggle. "Great haircut."

I took a deep breath. It crossed my mind that the redoubtable Maeve might be dabbling in illicit substances.

"Maeve, I can't take this job, it's just not me. I just want to make programs."

She looked at me pityingly, then.

"Maeve," I tried again, sotto voce, unwilling to make a scene but suddenly overwhelmed by the urgency of the situation. "I'm guaranteed a job on return from maternity leave . . ."

"And a rather long maternity leave it's been, hasn't it?" she threw back at me, waving her hand and flashing a smile at someone I recognized but couldn't place. "Besides, we've offered you a job. Now it's time to decide what your priorities are. Just don't embarrass me, Robin. I can't afford to have that happen."

Frustrated and angry, I stood and watched as she moved off through the crowd, air kissing anyone and everyone who crossed her path. At one point she lunged for a young man in a tailcoat only to realize at the last moment that he was a waiter. A media crowd is almost pathologically sociable. I could see a couple of uniformed hotel staff trying to usher people into the ballroom, but my colleagues were like a bunch of children in the playground, unwilling to go and sit down in the classroom where they'd have to stop chatting with their mates.

I'd lost Terry, but then I saw him deep in conversation with one of his old cronies, heads together, backs fending off casual socializers. I spotted Suzette on one of the high chairs by the long black bar. Her back was to me, but I could see her face in a mirror. She was wearing a little black dress and pearls, with her long blond hair scraped back in a severe chignon and her face pale and clean of makeup. I waved at her, and she spotted me in the mirror and turned to mouth "Monday" at me, and I gave her a thumbs-up. Perhaps Suzette was the way out. A partnership in Paradigm productions would give me the creative freedom I craved, and I liked her; she was bright and serious and very thorough. She had a great visual sense and huge reserves of enthusiasm. We had worked together a couple of years ago on a series about schools, and we'd got on just fine. We could do it again.

I saw Jane, then, on the arm of the Corporation's political editor Quentin Browne and caught her eye. She was a picture of Chinese chic, wearing a tailored red cheongsam split to the thigh. Jane is tall and not at all willowy, so it was not what you would call a subtle outfit, especially when almost everyone else was in shades of black. She winked at me and wiggled her substantial hips against Quentin, who turned to her and kissed her full on the lips. I must have looked astounded, because when she emerged from his embrace and saw my face, she laughed out loud. I could hear her raucous bellow from where I stood, and her date put his hands over his ears and said something to her which made her laugh more. It appeared there were many things I'd missed in my seclusion.

Jane was working her way through the crush toward me when there was a tap on my shoulder. I turned, expecting Maeve again, my heart sinking. Then I stood stock still while my heart did something else entirely, and my jaw dropped.

It was Adam. Why hadn't I anticipated exactly this? I cannot say. Except, perhaps, that I had erected such substantial barriers in my head against him that I had assumed they had actual physical existence. Somewhere deep in my psyche I must have thought he could not actually get close to me, not to my head, not to my body.

"Hi," he said. "Are you talking to me?"

He smiled and it was a smile from the bedroom and the breakfast table. My heart twisted. That smile would warm my lonely hours. The kids would love that smile. He would seduce me. All over again. He would let me down. All over again. This time he would let us all down.

"In principle," I said slowly, "but actually I have nothing to say to you."

For an instant his smile faded, and I could see that behind it he was nervous. That was fine by me. Let him suffer. He cleared his throat.

"How are Hannah and William?"

I raised my eyebrows in mock surprise.

"You know their names."

He had the grace to look sheepish.

"Suzette told me."

I nodded. I couldn't help noticing that heads were turning, that people were watching. Too many people knew our history for this to be between the two of us. Suddenly I needed it to end. I turned to walk away, but he grabbed my arm and didn't let go. Out of the corner of my eye I saw Jane step toward us, but I shook my head.

"I've been thinking," he said, moving closer, lowering his voice. "I was a jerk . . ."

He still had my arm, and he held up his other hand to fend off my interruption. I could smell his soap. I could smell booze too, and guessed he'd been drinking for a couple of hours already. He looked thicker around his chin, almost jowly, and right at that moment he was displaying none of his old devil-may-care charm.

"I'm not saying we can go back," he hurried on. "I'm just saying could I see them sometime, could I help out, maybe financially? I feel bad . . ."

"Too late," I hissed back at him, my face burning. I twisted my arm out of his grip.

"Oh for God's sake, Robin, they're my children as much as yours." He was getting angry now, moving his weight from foot to foot, his face too near to mine, and with a broadcaster's voice any whisper is a stage whisper. Everyone was getting this loud and clear. "You can't keep them all to yourself forever. I just didn't want the whole domestic deal."

I wanted to hit him then, or shout at him—something about domestic deals and love, and how one didn't work without the other—but I didn't, because even in the white hot fury of the moment I was too ashamed of my own bitterness to share it with the world. That was for his ears only. That was for later. Right now I just needed to shut him up.

"Adam," my voice was barely under control, but I leaned in close so that the material of his suit brushed against my skin. I put my hand on his shoulder and spoke in his ear. "I want to talk to you too. I want to talk to you about Paula Carmichael and why my name and the names of my children are in her little book, and then perhaps you can explain it all to the police."

He stepped back from me as though I'd slapped him, his face white, eyes wide. Then he turned on his heel and was gone.

Chapter 7

"Y OU'RE going to hate this," Jane warned me on the phone the next morning. "I'm only telling you because someone's got to, and you'd rather it was me."

It was Sunday lunchtime, and Jane was calling from Quentin Browne's flat, where she was reading the newspapers over eggs and bacon. She didn't volunteer that they'd only just got up, but I could tell from her tone of voice. Quentin had picked up an award for some news story or other, and there's nothing like a prize to tickle a man's fancy.

"Okay."

"Are you sitting down?" I was standing by the breakfast table. The children had just finished eating and we were having a competition to see whether I could clean up the floor before they ate all the bits off it.

"Just get on with it." I knew I was being short with her, but we weren't all languishing in a postcoital haze.

"Okay. I'm reading the diary section of the *Chronicle*. Here goes. 'At a glittering awards ceremony at the Grosvenor House Hotel last night, broadcaster Adam Wills picked up the Nice Try award for romantic melodrama. The great and good of broadcasting were treated to the spectacle of Wills chasing after his old flame, award-winning producer Robin Ballantyne, and practically throwing himself at her feet. Ballantyne, who had two children by Wills and

71

is said to be deeply bitter about Wills's failings as a provider, gave him the brush-off and left him looking distinctly silly. After hounding him for money for the past year, it seems she is now the one playing hard to get.' That's it."

For an instant I was speechless, and then it burst out of me, "Playing hard to get?" I was furious. "Hounding him for money? Where did this come from?"

"It didn't come from anywhere." Jane sounded taken aback. She tried to calm me. "They've just invented it. You know how these things work."

"I've never asked him for a penny," I ranted on. "I don't want a . . . a provider. I . . ." but I couldn't carry on.

"Robin, this is just silly. I didn't mean to upset you. You should be laughing . . ."

"Why, Jane, are you laughing?" I snarled and hung up.

I rang the *Chronicle* then and demanded to speak to the editor and told him that I'd sue him for libel unless he printed a retraction. I should have known better. It's a new newspaper and it sells itself as the prime purveyor of political and media gossip in the capital. It is written in tabloid style but it gets most things at least broadly right, so that what starts out as gossip in the *Chronicle* is often picked up by the heavyweight papers. Its circulation has boomed because it appeals across the board, and because no one can afford to dismiss it.

"A retraction of what?" he challenged me. "He chased after you, you gave him the brush-off. Dozens of people were watching."

"I've never asked him for a penny."

"We only have your word for that."

"So whose word do you have for what you wrote?"

He almost laughed in my face then, and told me I couldn't expect him to say who his "news sources" were, but that if I wanted to put my own side of the story in his newspaper, he'd be happy to print it.

I wanted to scream at him, but I'd already made things bad enough, so I hung up instead.

————

The day passed in a blue cloud of depression and the children caught wind of it and whined. Nothing would please them, and to tell the truth I was only partly with them. I made sure they were fed and clean and clothed, I even tried to entertain them, but my thoughts were in another place, with Adam. I thought I'd got rid of him for good and now he was insinuating himself back into my life, even into my dreams.

After our public row at the Grosvenor House Hotel I had left, waving away Terry's offer of a lift, just climbing into a taxi and going. I needed to be on my own, and for once I didn't care about the fare. I paid Erica and sent her home, very pissed off. She'd just been settling into a video and was looking at another three good earning hours ahead of her. While she was putting her coat on and phoning for a taxi I bent and kissed the twins, almost hoping one of them would wake up and I'd have to cuddle them back to sleep. When Erica was gone I went back downstairs and switched on the television. I watched mind-numbing shows until midnight, then forced myself to turn it off and go to bed. I read myself to sleep with the light on. I did all I could, all in all, to stop myself thinking about Adam while I was conscious. Then, the moment sleep hit, I dreamed about him.

You can't repeat a dream and have it make sense, but this one had woken me at four with the deepest feeling both of sadness and of foreboding, as though my subconscious was not only chewing over the past but preparing me for something monstrous to come. In my dream Adam and I lay together, naked, and I could feel his skin, his arms around me, his long legs tangled around mine, his warm breath on my neck. I had come home, I was at peace and yet, somehow, I was outside my dream. I say this because I was capable of identifying this sense of peace, and because I felt a deep sense of loss and betrayal because I knew that this sense of peace was a false one. In the dream, I moved in the bed and bumped into another body, a lifeless dried-up thing, naked too, and sexless. I screamed, and Adam reached toward me, but instead of drawing me to him he shoved me away and off the bed. Then I was standing, looking down, and Adam reached out to the naked sexless thing and caressed it, and it seemed to come alive at his touch, its wizened hand stretched out to Adam. Its eyes opened and it laughed at me, mouth wide and toothless, blood seeping from its gums. I awoke then, feeling physically sick. I sat on the edge of the bed for several minutes, my head hanging down, then I switched on the light, went to the bathroom, and doused my face in cold water. I looked in the mirror, and for an instant I saw the creature looking back at me. I shook my head, and stared into the mirror again, gazing into my own eyes, dissolving into myself.

"Get a grip," I muttered and turned away.

———

I went for a walk on Wimbledon Common with my mother. It was cold, as promised, and it seemed colder still in contrast to the heat of the past few days. The children were wrapped up like Michelin men, two sets of eyes peeping out from between scarves and hats. Ma was horrified that I had so much as caught sight of Adam. The fact that we'd exchanged words positively distressed her. When she heard what I was thinking, she looked as though she were about to explode.

"But you're doing so well without him, Robin," she protested. "You don't really think you need him, do you?"

"I don't need him and I don't want him, but I can't just think of myself. The children are going to need some sort of father figure . . ."

"For what? What could he possibly provide that you can't?"

"William will need a role model," I said vaguely. "Hannah . . ." In truth, I wasn't quite sure what it was that they would miss, since I'd had no father myself after the age of four, but Tanya's Patrick seemed to do a good job of it, in between working night and day to stave off bankruptcy. I tried again. "Look. I need to go back to work. My savings are gone, we have to live, and if I'm going to work I need other people to help me out. I'm going to need nurseries, babysitters, and that's all going to cost money too. Maybe I have to say okay, I give in, you can help me out."

"Adam Wills babysitting?" My mother's voice was filled with scorn.

"Ma, I cannot do it all." I was getting angry. My mother's face was set and pained.

"I did," she said.

"That's just not true." I didn't pause to think, just leapt right in. "We had aunts and uncles coming out of our ears."

She was pushing the double stroller uphill, her shoulders hunched over with the effort and also, it seemed to me, with hurt.

"Ma, I'm not criticizing you, and I'm not belittling what you did, but it's different now."

Uncle William, my cousin Hannah, these were the names that came to me when the nurse bent over me and placed a baby on each arm, asking me what I was going to call them. There were half a dozen names—Katherine, Donald, Meredith—that would have done just as well. My mother's older siblings and their offspring had been my extended family. A couple of my cousins had found work in Croydon. The better-heeled were now in Surrey and Sussex. There was no one left in Streatham except my mother. We all kept in touch, but the bond that was so strong and proud when we were young was now stretched and weakened by distance and time. It was only at Christmas that we managed to get together.

We paced on in silence, keeping to open patches of ground, aware that the light was fading fast.

"I thought I'd brought you up to be self-sufficient," my mother said eventually, her tone at once disappointed and disapproving. I bit back a reply and continued to walk in silence, but my mother couldn't let it be.

"Adam Wills is not an avuncular presence," she hissed, hurrying ahead and turning to face me so that I had to stop or run the stroller into her. "If you let him back into your life, he'll take over. He's a dominator. You'll never escape from him."

I steered the stroller around her, kept on pushing.

"Okay, end of conversation," I told her over my shoulder. "This is pointless."

We walked in silence back to our cars, put the children into their car seats, and went our separate ways.

———

That night he rang as I had known he would. His voice was full of apprehension as though he half expected me to hang up, but I was too drained to fight anymore, and too unsure of my own position.

"I thought I'd leave you twenty-four hours to cool down," he said.

I had been lying on the sofa, but now I sat up straight, swinging my feet to the floor, the better to concentrate. If I was lying down he would walk all over me.

"I didn't look good in the *Chronicle*, did I?" His voice was light but I could hear the strain under the surface.

"It did me no favors either. Who fed them that crap?"

"I have no idea. I'm sorry. Look, I want to apologize about last night. I was stupid, insensitive. I'd had a drink or two. I was, you know," he tried for a jokey tone, "tired and emotional."

"Forget it."

I had lit the fire and now I gazed into the flames, trying to pretend that this phone conversation could go on at the margins of my consciousness, that I did not have to get involved, did not have to get hurt. I stared at the flames, and they leapt and they played and they soothed, but when Adam spoke it still seared right through me.

"Look, I meant what I said, I mean about wanting to help with the children, but I'm not going to interfere. I promise. It's your life, they're your children. I mean mostly yours. I'd just like to have a little bit of them. Whatever you think I deserve, which probably isn't much."

A tear found its way down my cheek, and then another. I fumbled for a tissue but had to make do with my sleeve.

"You can't expect . . ." I tried to control my voice, but I could hear it waver, and I had to start again. "If you meet them, even once, you have to stick with it."

I sounded like a sergeant major, as if I could order undying loyalty.

"I know, I know, I understand all that."

It was too glib for my liking.

"I mean you can't be their father and then not be their father. That would be worse."

"Well, like you said, I hardly qualify anyway."

I rubbed my hand over my forehead. I was too upset by all this to be able to read him. I couldn't tell what he wanted. I couldn't tell how much he wanted it.

"Look," he said, "this is impossible over the phone. How about we meet? I mean, we can do it on neutral territory, and we can talk about things, you can tell me what the ground rules are, we'll go from there."

I heaved a breath. He was handing me the initiative, but it's not something you can give away. You have to seize it and I thought he had probably already done that.

"No," I said slowly, "you come here."

Let him see, my brain was telling me, let him see how life is. If he can't take it, you'll know then. And only when I saw him together with the children would I know whether I could bear it.

"All right, if you're sure." He sounded taken aback. "Um, when should I come?"

"How about Tuesday." It would give me a couple of days to psyche myself up. "At six-thirty," I said. Bedtime. Life in the raw.

We said our good-byes and hung up. I sat and stared at the flames some more. They leapt and they played and they soothed. Then I picked up the telephone and hurled it at the wall.

Chapter 8

A DAM," I told Jane, "wants to talk." Jane had rung to apologize. Her judgment, she said, had been warped by too much sex. She had emerged from Quentin Browne's flat, presumably sated, and returned home only in the past hour or so. Then she picked the five minutes after Adam phoned me to call me herself. She was lucky to find my telephone in working order.

"Tell him to go fuck himself," Jane proposed.

I sighed. I couldn't find the words to argue it with her.

"You're not really going to talk to the wee shite?"

"Shouldn't you be a bit more mellow after a day in bed?"

"I'm bursting with love for all mankind, except for Adam. And don't change the subject."

"He's coming here on Tuesday, at six-thirty. He's going to meet the children."

There was silence on the other end of the line.

"And anyway, how much of a shit is he?" I was thinking aloud, trying to persuade myself. "Maybe I've been unreasonable. He was honest with me, he told me he didn't love me, so I told him to go. No one can change the way they feel, after all. I as good as threw him out."

"Robin, don't do this. Don't rewrite history. We all heard him the other night. The whole domestic deal, that was his problem. It was nothing to do with loving you or not loving you." She paused, but I didn't say anything, and she realized she had to say more to convince me and plowed right on, pressing home her advantage. "When did he tell you he didn't love you? Was it before or after you told him you were pregnant?"

"Weeks after I told him I was pregnant. Roughly ten minutes after I said it was twins," I admitted.

"Robin." Jane sounded appalled. "The man's a bloody great shite."

Jane's outrage echoed in my ears. It wasn't the greatest recipe for a peaceful night and indeed I scarcely slept. No sleep, no nightmares—there's always a silver lining.

———

The next day Erica was back on duty for my lunch with Suzette. I was learning to schedule the child-care handover twenty minutes before I left the house so I had time to wash and change my clothes. This time I even went to the remarkable lengths of brushing my teeth before I went and asked for a job. Then I gathered up an armful of bills that had come through the mail slot. I had no time to deal with them, and I shoved them in my bag to open on the tube.

Suzette and I were to meet in Covent Garden at one, and I miscalculated the tube time and arrived fifteen minutes early. I got off at Charing Cross and walked through the underpass, buying a copy of the *Big Issue* from a man with a nice smile, a dog, and a low-key sales drive. He nodded his thanks and took a sip from a paper cup of cappuccino as I stepped out into the sunlight and headed up the Strand. It was one of those bright autumn days when the chill in the air seems festive and the blue sky promises spring instead of winter. Covent Garden was bustling. There were crowds of eager easy-to-please tourists around the street clowns and strains of *Carmen* coming from the open-air café under the arches. I strolled around, too unused to shopping and too aware of my empty bank account to buy anything, but lapping up the buzz of commerce.

Suzette and I found each other and we headed up Long Acre to a Japanese restaurant where she said they did a good affordable sushi lunch. I was happy to eat anything that wasn't Indian or baby food, but I tried to greet the suggestion with only mild enthusiasm, as though I ate Japanese at chichi restaurants at least once a week. I was trying hard to act like a professional all over again, but I kept having out-of-body experiences looking down on myself striding around in central London in work clothes and makeup and wondering who the hell I was.

The restaurant was all stripped pine benches and rice paper blinds. We found an unoccupied booth and slid in, and ordered set lunches with mineral water. Suzette was looking pale and tired. Her fine skin seemed stretched tight over her bones and there was a rim of red around her huge eyes. She was wearing a dark gray sweater that just about showed her ribs, and made her skin look even paler.

"I got about three hours' sleep last night," she said, pulling chopsticks out of their paper sleeve and fiddling with her place setting. "Everything was spinning around in my head . . . I shouldn't say that, I'm supposed to be persuading you to come and work with me."

We smiled at each other.

"I don't mind hard work," I told her. "I like the idea of freedom if that's what's on offer."

"That's exactly what you'd have," she said, "and no bureaucrats who know nothing about program-making dictating how many shots you take of what and quoting guidelines at you day in, day out."

"But you have to sell the programs, and they still give you a budget," I pointed out.

Suzette nodded, sitting back as a Japanese waitress brought a tray and placed it in front of her. It was followed by a tray for me. I plunged a tempura prawn into the sauce and then into my mouth. I was starving, and I nearly groaned with pleasure as I bit through the crispy batter and into the tender meat.

"It's not perfect," Suzette said, taking a little wasabi on the end of a chopstick and mixing it into the soy sauce, "but I feel freer here and now than I did when I was with the Corporation."

We talked for a while about Suzette's plans. She was full of ideas, as I'd known she would be. She read voraciously and a line in a book or a magazine article, even a picture caption, could be all the catalyst she needed to set her off. A television producer has one aim, and that is to get pictures that will shock or amuse or delight the audience. No pictures, no story. Suzette was scathing about bad television, damning about the lackadaisical approach of others, insulted by images that weakened the story. To her, the picture was the mission, and her almost obsessional approach gave Paradigm the energy that I knew many others lacked. Paradigm, in her eyes, would become a great name in documentary making if it could get through the early and financially sticky years of obscurity. She'd done a lot of thinking about how I would fit in and what I could bring to the company, where our skills would complement each other and where I would be able to take the lead. It sounded exciting and attractive and I found myself wanting to do it. The more I heard about the financial side of it, however, the more I became uneasy. She didn't say it outright, but it was pretty clear that she was living hand-to-mouth, and I tried to pin her down on how much I could expect to earn. I needed to know at least to within the nearest five thousand pounds, but she didn't want to commit herself even to that.

"It's really difficult to talk in those terms," she said, with an apologetic grimace. "A couple of years from now, if we can make our name and be the obvious choice for commissioning editors, we'll be on much surer ground, but right now we're competing hard on price. What you or I take home depends on what we make week to week and month to month."

We concentrated on the food for a while. The sashimi was good, fresh and firm. I warmed my hands on the cup of miso soup.

"I'm not sure whether I can take the financial risk," I said eventually, unwilling to introduce my domestic situation but wanting to be honest with Suzette.

The comment seemed to annoy her, or perhaps she was just disappointed that I was having doubts.

"I know you have responsibilities, we all have responsibilities of one kind or another. I wasn't suggesting you should work for charity, but you have to take risks if you want rewards. You stay in the Corporation and you'll suffocate."

Maybe she was right, maybe in my role as mother hen I had just become risk averse. My alternatives, after all, were bleak.

"Did you know Maeve wants me to do the ethics job?" I said.

Suzette gave me a sickly smile and said, "You're not going to turn me down to be ethics czar?"

I shrugged.

"Terry tells me I couldn't do better."

Suzette just pulled an unimpressed face and shrugged, so I changed the subject. "I hadn't realized the documentary Richard Carmichael was complaining about was a Paradigm production."

"In the end it wasn't an anything production, it was a total non-event," she said, and shrugged again. "There was nothing to say. I wasn't keeping anything from you."

"I'm not suggesting you were, but what went wrong?"

She heaved a deep breath and put her head on one side, looking at me with some amusement.

"Why all the interest?"

"For God's sake, Suzette, the woman killed herself in front of me."

"Or was killed," she reminded me quietly. She thought for a moment, fiddling with the table setting again, then looked up at me.

"This isn't for general release," she said, "because it all got extremely messy. Basically, we did a lot of filming and then Paula pulled out. She wanted a puff piece, no negative stuff, just two hours of how wonderful Paula Carmichael is . . . or was, I should say. When I pointed out that we weren't in the business of hagiographies she refused to cooperate."

I frowned. The waitress arrived at our table and refilled our teacups with green tea.

"Couldn't you have gone ahead with what you had? It must have been financially crippling to dump the whole thing."

"It cut Paradigm's projected revenue by more than thirty percent last year." Suzette sounded grim. "Anyway, it's over. I really don't feel like going through it all over again. Carmichael's retracted, so there's no more to be said."

"But why would he have made it up? It makes no sense."

Suzette speared a slice of apple with a cocktail stick.

"Paula Carmichael had a big ego," she said, keeping her voice low, her eyes flitting around us to see if anyone was listening in. I would have thought her paranoid if it were not for the fact I myself had recognized two former colleagues at another table. Paula Carmichael was, after all, still news. "If Paula got depressed it was because she thought she was going to get great publicity and then she realized we were going to show her warts and all, and she didn't like that. But no one wants to think their wife is as self-obsessed as that. Maybe her husband just saw it differently."

She popped the apple into her mouth. I considered what she had said.

"So what were her warts?"

Suzette chewed and swallowed. She thought for a moment.

"She was a megalomaniac. She thought we should treat her like Mother Theresa. I'm not going to go into all the stuff that happened, because it would take forever, but she seemed to have left reality behind some time ago, and that's the nice way of putting it."

"Everyone's eulogizing her now."

"Yes," Suzette gave a wry smile, "well, that's the power of the media, for you. For the most part, she handled it like a pro. We just took our brief very seriously. Too seriously for her."

I sat back on the bench and looked at Suzette. Maybe Paula had always been too good to be true. I felt a little sad. Since her death I'd kept that exchange in the supermarket with me, that grin, the sympathetic, "Been there, done that." I didn't want to hear that she'd been a cynical media manipulator.

"Still, you don't jump out of a window because someone didn't show you due respect."

"Maybe," she said harshly, "if you're Paula Carmichael you think it will immortalize you."

I shook my head. It wasn't worth arguing.

"Adam and Paula got on well, didn't they?" I was guessing, but if it was Adam who had told Paula about me, as I suspected it was, that surely pointed to friendship.

Suzette watched me carefully. "What do you mean?"

"I heard they got on really well."

"Really?"

"You didn't see any evidence of it?"

"They seemed to get on fine, I mean Adam is always professional, but I didn't see much of them together. I really have no idea what they got up to, I wasn't with them every minute of the day . . ."

Suzette appeared to have misunderstood my question, and to resent it.

"I'm not suggesting an affair or anything like that," I said.

"Oh." Suzette was quiet for a moment. "Well, I don't know then. I suppose I would say that Adam kept out of the arguments about the content of the documentary," she said eventually. "He was working on other projects at the same time, it probably didn't mean that much to him when the whole thing fell through."

———

I managed to get a seat on the Northern Line, and gazed at the ads above the heads opposite. There was a poem about urban greenery that kept me occupied for the length of time it took me to read its four lines. Teenage girls in uniform were standing by the doors, their arms draped around each other's shoulders, whispering and then once in a while bursting into giggles. Next to me a middle-aged man with a huge paunch and purple veins on his cheeks smelled of urine. I'd done all the thinking I could about Paula Carmichael. I needed some other distraction. I looked in my bag to see whether I had left a book or a magazine in there. I hadn't, but I came across the letters I had shoved in on my way out. I thumbed through and pulled one out of the pile, a fresh white WH Smith envelope. I frowned. It had been addressed in a hand I did not recognize, to Adam's flat, my old address, then redirected in what looked like Adam's hand. It surprised me, for a minute, that he knew my new address. Then I realized when we had spoken on the telephone he had not asked where he should come to see me. This thought delayed me for a moment, but somewhere around Waterloo I opened the envelope, unfolded two sheets of handwritten paper, and started to read.

My dear Robin,

I hesitate to approach you in person since an unfortunate misunderstanding with your sister earlier today.

My heart began to pound and I glanced back at the top of the page. No address, but it was dated the day on which Paula Carmichael had fallen. The wrong address and redirection had taken nearly a week. I continued to read.

I am afraid that because of her bad feelings towards me Tanya misinterpreted my visit. Please let me assure you that I have only the best of intentions. I just wish to make contact with the daughters I have never forgotten while I still can.

If you would consider meeting me, I will be in the lobby of the Victoria and Albert Museum on Monday at 4. Perhaps we could have tea.

I raised my head, but if you asked me what I was staring at I couldn't have said. We were pulling into Stockwell. The doors opened, people got out, people got in. Just as the doors were closing I pushed my way out and onto the platform, and stood there, reading to the end of the letter. When I had read it through once, right down to the signature, which read, "Your father, Gilbert," I started at the top and read it again. I read and reread. At least three trains came and went. I was elbowed and kicked by the hordes rushing on and off. Then I stopped reading. I looked at my watch. It was three minutes past four.

Chapter 9

I tried all the same. And failed. By the time I walked into the great entrance hall of the V and A there was no man of any age or any description anywhere to be seen. Still, I hung around for half an hour, reluctant to admit defeat, clinging to the fantasy that he would appear, that I would know him, and that this part of my life, which had not been all right, would be in some way transformed.

Afterward, when I gave up on him, I didn't want to talk to anyone about anything. My father's letter and my subsequent failure to meet him had revived a lifetime of regret in me. All that evening I stayed at home with my children and left the telephone switched to the answering machine. A couple of times someone tried ringing but hung up when they got the machine. My mother left a message—Lorna had raved about the acupuncture. Patrick left a message—I'd left a baby bottle at their house, did I need it urgently? Suzette left a message—could I call her please?

I tried not to dwell on my father, and instead took pleasure in the domestic chores that so often frustrated me. I washed my children and I hugged them tight and they laughed and prodded me, sticking little fingers up my nose, pulling my hair. We rolled and played and laughed, and I wondered then why I could not live like this for every minute of every day.

Hannah had learned a whole new trick. She would push her little chair around, then abandon it for an instant, arms in the air, and do a little knee-bend and a kick before reaching for her support again. William, who rarely got up off his bottom, was a highly appreciative audience, applauding her and giggling wildly. It was the kind of moment that would have been good to share with someone.

But not with D.C.I. Finney, who rang the doorbell in the middle of it. I still felt annoyed at him for making me feel ridiculous. My face must have fallen when I opened the door and found him waiting.

"I rang you, but you didn't answer," he said.

"And it didn't occur to you that I might be out," I replied. Or that I might not want to see anyone.

"I've just been at the Carmichael house, your lights were on, and I could hear voices. Laughter actually. Either you were in or something very strange was going on."

"Elementary," I conceded and let him in. "I'm afraid it's bathtime. Can we talk while I do that?"

He didn't look happy about it and eyed Hannah and William with barely concealed distaste, but I stood my ground.

"You can't just turn up on my doorstep at the children's bedtime and expect to conduct a formal interview." It had been a long day, and my voice was irritated, ready for a fight.

He grinned. It came out of nowhere, the same blast of sunlight that had dazed D.C. Mann. The smile created deep creases at the side of his mouth. He must have been smiling like that since he was a kid. Then, as before, the grin vanished as quickly as it had come, leaving just the shadow of good humor in his eyes. I stood stock still, transfixed. I had to tell myself to break the spell.

"I'll just run the water," I turned on my heel, "if you could keep an eye on them for a moment."

I hurried up the stairs two steps at a time to the bathroom, turned on the taps, squirted in a dash of bubble bath and allowed myself a couple of seconds with the mirror. The new haircut was holding up well to my neglect. I pushed the hair back behind one ear, examined my profile, and set off downstairs again.

I'd been gone a little more than one minute, but the twins had left the sitting room and got to the bottom of the stairs, where they were both wailing an insistent "Mama, Mama, Mama," and hurling themselves at Finney's legs. He was standing at the bottom of the staircase like a goalkeeper, trying to block their way up without actually bending to touch them, and looking down at them with near panic in his eyes.

"Thank God," he murmured as I reappeared.

"There is a gate you could have closed," I pointed out.

I whisked the children away from his legs, one wriggling body under each arm. Finney followed me up to the bathroom, and stood well back while I stripped the children, removed nappies, wiped bottoms, and dunked them into the water.

"Your choice of paint?" Finney asked. I glanced at the walls. Orange gloss, red trim. It had been like that when we moved in. I scarcely noticed it anymore.

"Good warm colors," I replied noncommittally.

The children had calmed down now they were in the water. Hannah was using a flannel to clean the sides of the bath and William was sinking a plastic boat.

"Have you given any more thought to why you were in Paula Carmichael's diaries?" Finney asked.

"I think," I said, "that we may have had a mutual friend. It's the only explanation I can come up with."

"Who would that be?"

"That would be someone I'm going to speak to in the next couple of days." I was watching Hannah and William, but I could see

Finney's face in the mirror, gray against the orange wall. "I'll find out whether that's the link or not. Then I'll let you know."

Finney was quiet for a moment. He must have known that I was warning him off.

"The diary's a problem for me," he told me. "Anything I can't explain I have to dig into, that's my job, and so far I can't explain the diary, which means it's a problem for you too."

I mulled over what he had said in silence. It could have been an apology, and it could equally well have been a threat. Or perhaps some kind of one-man good-cop-bad-cop routine. He was watching the children, but distractedly, as though his mind were somewhere else. Belatedly I realized William had got hold of a bottle of shampoo and had already squirted liberal amounts into the water.

"I need to ask you a few questions," he said, "but they mustn't go anywhere else. I mean it."

I turned toward him.

"You mean don't broadcast them."

"Right. This is all secondhand, and . . ." He sighed. "Well, Richard Carmichael says that Kyle, the son who was home, saw a visitor—someone who'd called before, and who she'd argued with—on the evening of her death."

I frowned.

"You mean Kyle saw someone inside the house with his mother?"

Finney grimaced. I stared at him.

"Well did he or didn't he?"

"Carmichael won't let us speak to the boy at the moment. Says he's too upset. So, like I said, so far it's all secondhand."

We exchanged a look that was, for the first time, the look of colleagues. Journalists and detectives both know what secondhand information is worth.

"I know you've already told us that you saw no one on the night of Paula Carmichael's death," Finney returned to his halfhearted attempt at interrogation, "and I'm assuming that's still the case."

"Yes, I still saw no one."

"Right. But you obviously spend a lot of time at home, and you look out of the window regularly, and you live opposite, and I'm asking whether you saw anyone visit the house in the few days before her death."

"I do not spend my life looking out of the window," I laughed in disbelief.

"I wasn't implying . . ."

"No, I saw no one." I was still smiling at Finney treating me like a little old lady. "But there could have been whole armies visiting her house, for all I know."

"Okay, okay," Finney held up his hand in defeat, "I get the message."

We stood, not speaking, for a moment.

"Those voices you thought you heard, around the time Paula fell," he ventured. I knew what was coming.

"I can't help you. I'm sorry. I have no idea what I heard or what I didn't. Has anyone else mentioned hearing anything?"

Finney pulled a face.

"Nothing conclusive. One or two people say they may have heard something just before she fell, but it could just be the power of suggestion. Everyone had heard the shouting earlier in the evening, they may've been expecting to hear a second installment."

"What about the devoted couple who were yelling at each other earlier? If you found them, you could ask them whether they resumed their argument later."

"Number twenty-nine," he said. "By their account, by the time Paula fell they were tucked up in bed."

"Really? In the same bed?"

Finney pulled a face.

"Whatever turns them on," he said, "but I wouldn't put money on their golden wedding anniversary."

We fell silent for a moment.

"How are Richard Carmichael's finances?" I asked.

"Why?" Finney sounded defensive, but then perhaps he was regretting talking so openly with me about the progress of the investigation.

"I don't look out of the window much, but I do read the papers."

"I believe the newspapers have reported that his wife's death might get him out of some financial trouble," he said, "but that the insurance policy doesn't cover suicide."

I looked questioningly at him, and he nodded.

"But when he spoke the day after her death he was clearly implying that she'd been hounded to suicide," I continued.

"He won't be the last person who's ever done a U-turn when it suited him."

"That was just because the Corporation threatened to sue him. Do you mean he's really saying it wasn't suicide?"

Finney raised an eyebrow and pulled a face.

"A man's allowed to change his mind," he said.

"So he is." I thought for a minute. "But has he found anyone else to blame?"

"I believe he asked you whether you'd seen anyone at the scene."

I nodded. "And I told him the same as I told everyone else."

"Well now he's somehow got hold of your suggestion that you might have heard voices, and he's very enthusiastic about that." Finney sounded resigned. I had the distinct impression he would rather I had kept my imaginings to myself. "Especially combined with this mysterious visitor the son's come up with."

"Of course." I could hardly change my story just because it wasn't convenient for Finney.

"Well," Finney had been leaning in the doorway, but now he glanced at his watch and straightened up, "I'd better be off. I'll see myself out."

"Okay," I said. "I'm sorry I can't be more help."

He shrugged.

"Don't forget I need to know how you got into that diary." He turned toward the stairs. I watched as his shoulders receded. As he reached for the front door, the bell rang. Finney opened it. I couldn't see who it was, but I heard a male voice.

"There's a Dan Stein here," Finney called up to me.

I leaned out into the hallway, peered down the stairs, and Dan Stein poked his head around the door.

"Hello?" He looked flustered, but then he probably hadn't expected Finney.

"Hi." I hoped he wasn't having second thoughts about the antique table. My visitor glanced around him in confusion, trying to trace my voice, and Finney pointed up the stairs toward me.

"Ah!" Dan Stein looked relieved. "Um, I was wondering whether you wanted to go out for a drink," he said awkwardly. Finney was still standing there, holding the door open for Stein and listening to the exchange.

"I'm afraid I'm a bit tied up," I said apologetically, feeling like an idiot, my cheeks burning. "The children are in the bath."

"Ah, well . . ."

He carried on standing there, apparently with no intention of leaving.

"Um, would you like a coffee?" I offered reluctantly. "I can be down in a moment if you don't mind . . . you could just wait for me in the sitting room."

I expected a retreat at that point but instead he just said, "Okay, take your time," and strolled past Finney. Dan vanished into the sitting room. Finney looked up at me. I couldn't read his face.

"I guess the rest of us had better stand in line," he said. Then he was gone. I went back to the bathroom and stared down at the children, seeing nothing.

"What is wrong with you?" I hissed at myself.

I ran the conversation with Finney through my mind, angry that I had let my defenses down. The whole situation, him standing there in the bathroom while I bathed the children, the two of us chatting almost like friends, everything had been too easy. Which could only mean that Finney knew he had disarmed me and was making use of it. I groaned in embarrassment. Then I remembered that Dan was downstairs waiting for me, and I groaned again.

I had no energy for small talk but Dan seemed instinctively to know that. In fact, when I appeared with two naked babies, two nappies held under my arm, and two sleepsuits slung over my shoulder to dress them, he seemed to take the whole situation on board in an instant and to know what I needed. He asked nothing of me. I just sat back and smiled, my feet curled under me, as he bounced and swung Hannah and William in turn until they were two little balls of writhing flesh, giggling hysterically.

"Sorry," he said ruefully, as Hannah shrieked in pleasure, "the only thing I know how to do with babies is chuck them around. I suppose you wanted them calming down for bed."

I shook my head.

"It's fine. They'll be worn out."

He didn't really know what to do with nappies, but he took a good stab at it and had the children—and me—laughing along the way.

When they started to cry from sheer exhaustion I took them up to bed while Dan sat back with a newspaper.

"I'm sorry," I said when I reappeared, "I never got you that coffee."

Dan put the newspaper down and smiled at me.

"You know," he said, "if you've got a beer I'd as soon take that."

We both had a beer, and as we sat and chatted it occurred to me that this was something I hadn't done for ages. Because of time and circumstance, my friends had been whittled down to my closest circle and I didn't go to pubs or clubs to meet new men. This was really very pleasant. It was aesthetically pleasing to have Dan sitting there in my front room, although his office suit and tie jarred a little. We were unencumbered by the past, and it was comforting not to be alone. He examined all my photographs as well as all the books on my shelves. He asked about my friends and my life, and I told him about the strange path I'd traveled in the couple of years that I now thought of as the run-up to Paula Carmichael's death.

"Did you know her?" I asked him.

"Only to say hi to," he said. "We used to get each other's mail sometimes, so I'd drop it round. I never got to know her."

He told me that he was a personnel manager for a major financial institution, and I knew immediately that he was good at it, that he would listen and sympathize and advise.

Eventually he stood and stretched and said he had better get going.

"Do you mind if I drop by again sometime?" he asked.

"I'd like that," I told him.

He left at nine forty-five, and I decided to ring Suzette back— if I was going to work with her, I didn't want her to think I was difficult to pin down. I thought maybe she had managed to come up with a ballpark figure for my salary. God knows I wouldn't make a fortune at the Corporation. What I needed was a regular income, not a huge one—but money, it emerged, was precisely the problem.

"Robbie, I'm sorry, I've screwed up." Suzette sounded anxious and miserable. "I came back here this afternoon to look at the books again, but I keep coming back to the same thing. I don't want to mess you around. I mean I know your situation, so I'm going to be straight with you. You cannot afford to work here, because I cannot afford to pay you."

"You can't afford to pay me," I echoed.

"I mean I can't afford to pay you enough. It's all right for me, I'm on my own, but I can't do that to you. I feel bad enough . . . I want to do things properly, I don't want to hurt anyone. I don't want you to hate me, and . . ." She drew a shuddering breath and seemed to have trouble controlling herself. "Believe me, you would grow to hate me."

"Suze, I'd never—" but she cut me off.

"I don't know what I was thinking. I just wanted so much to have you with me—but this is what grown-up people do, isn't it? They make the right decision in the first place, they don't dig themselves into a hole they can't get out of . . ."

"Look, Suze, I'd rather know now. Don't beat yourself up over it."

"I just wish I could have you working with me." Suzette was disarmingly sweet about it. Indeed I was surprised how upset she seemed, on the edge of tears. "You keep me sane, Robbie."

It was a sad phone call, but it seemed to confirm our friendship in some strange way, and when it was over I felt resigned. One door closed, another was creaking ominously open. It was already ten, but if I didn't do it now I would chicken out. I called Maeve. I tried home, but she wasn't there, so I tried her mobile. It turned out she was still in the office. I told her I'd take her job.

"That's really great news, Robin," she told me. "You're not going to regret it."

I knew I would.

We settled on Wednesday as a first day at work, which gave me exactly a day to sort out child care. Maybe in time I could wangle a place in the Corporation nursery, but for the moment it would have to be the redoubtable—not to mention expensive—Erica.

"There's just one thing," Maeve was still talking. "This thing with Adam Wills, it's not going to happen again is it? I mean frankly it's already an embarrassment."

"No, Maeve," I said, my heart heavy, "it's not going to happen again."

Chapter 10

"SO how did he ask you for money?" The next day I still couldn't get my father out of my head, and I was questioning Tanya closely.

She looked at me over the rim of her coffee cup. At her elbow was a home improvement magazine and it was open at a double-page picture of a model kitchen, everything about it glossy and bright, a pot of tulips on the polished marble, a puppy capering in the sunlight on the Italian-tiled floor. I knew Tanya fantasized about a kitchen like that, and I knew she couldn't afford it.

I sipped my coffee. It was the first time I'd had instant coffee at Tanya's house. This was serious belt-tightening. Today the children had been offered generic economy digestives in a plain white wrapper.

"You think I made it up?" she asked.

The three girls were at school. Patrick was doing the washing up and making sure that my two were happy while I talked to Tanya. He had given them saucepans to bash with wooden spoons and a bowl of water with soapsuds to whisk, and they were making a noisy and delighted mess on the linoleum floor.

"Well, did he look hard up?"

"Appearances are deceptive, my dear," she said wryly, holding out her polished nails for my inspection. "I had a manicure, but it doesn't mean I paid for it. It just means Patrick's pretty handy with the nail file."

At which Patrick turned and took a bow.

Tanya rolled her eyes and I smiled thinly at him. I knew he could feel the tension between Tanya and myself as we discussed our father, and I knew he was trying to break it.

"He looked clean and tidy, if that's what you mean," Tanya said. "He was wearing a raincoat."

"Did you recognize him?"

"I did once he'd said who he was. He looked like that photo, the one in the drawer, you know the one I mean? He was older and grayer, but it was him I'm sure. Same face."

The photograph. The only surviving photograph of my father. God knows what my mother had done with the rest—burned them probably. This one had been of our father lolling on the beach and grinning into the camera, with the three of us clambering all over him. He looked tall and gawky, with a clear bright smile and oiled hair. It had been kept in a drawer in my mother's bedroom, and was only brought out when my mother deemed it necessary. "Necessary" usually meant that a school friend had been teasing one or other of us about not having a father. The photograph would be produced as proof to quash the friend's scurrilous allegations. Sometimes I invented a playground feud just so I could see it.

Tanya was two years old when our father left, hardly more than a baby. You might have thought they would have done some bonding by that point, but there wasn't a trace of it left now. Over the years we'd had variations on this argument a million times. Was the mysterious Gilbert Ballantyne really a crook, or was that just an invention of our mother? Was he dead? If not where was he? And, most important, what would we do if he came looking for us?

Tanya was the most fiercely protective of Ma. She had also had the toughest time at school and had hated not having a father. Her position never wavered. She would have nothing to do with him.

I had always been more ambivalent. Lorna, I realized now, had consistently been uncharacteristically silent on the matter.

"The thing about money . . ." Tanya was thinking hard. "It wasn't the first thing he said. He said . . . I mean I said I didn't . . . then . . . Sorry. You need the context . . . I open the door, this man is there. He doesn't look like a tramp. Still, I'm on my guard, you know, he shows up unannounced, I haven't a clue who he is, he could have been anyone. People are always getting robbed in broad daylight in this street. He says, 'Hello, you don't remember me but I'm Gilbert, your father.' I say, 'Why are you here?' He says, 'I just want to see you, I've never forgotten you, I want to make contact.' I say, 'Well you've made contact, you've seen me, good-bye for another thirty years.' He says he doesn't want to go. But by this point he thinks I'm about to close the door in his face, and he starts to talk in a panicky sort of a way about how we're family, we should stick together, and I suppose when he gets panicky, I panic too. I don't want him to come inside, I don't want him to see the children, and I end up almost shouting at him, asking what he wants, anything to make him go away, and at last he says something like, 'I want help.' And I say, 'You want money from me?' I mean I'm amazed at the effrontery, and he just stands there silently for a minute and then he has this strange look in his eyes, really hard, and he says, 'Will you give me money? To make me go away?' And I slam the door in his face," she made a gesture with her hands, "and that was it. I looked out the window a few minutes later, and he was gone."

It was pretty unambiguous. I rubbed my hands over my face, then reached down to William who was crying and clinging at my knee, and hauled him onto my lap. He was still clutching the wooden spoon, and he bashed me on the chin with it. I removed it from his grasp, and he yelled and wriggled to get off my lap and onto the floor again. I set him down and he grabbed another weapon and set about my ankles.

"The whole thing's left me with a horrible taste in my mouth," Tanya said. "I'd have felt more kindly disposed to him if I'd never seen him again. It would be better if he'd died."

"Tanya," Patrick scolded. Tanya had worked hard to find a man like Patrick. He was solid, he was kind, and he would never leave her. Sometimes I found his goodwill to all mankind hard to take, but mostly I was just glad for Tanya that she had him.

"Well it would," she insisted.

I didn't join in the argument. I didn't want to believe in this down-and-out father.

"Tanya, could he possibly have said 'I want *to* help,'" I put the stress on the third word, "not 'I want help'?"

She looked at me as though I were mad.

"How could he possibly help me?"

"That's not the point. What I mean is could he have meant that? Could you have misheard?"

"No." Tanya screwed up her face, convincing herself. "And anyway, he asked for money. You think I misheard that too?"

I threw up my hands.

"I don't know what to think," I said to Tanya. I got up to pour myself more coffee.

I hadn't intended telling Tanya and Patrick that Adam was coming to see me that night. I had assumed that Tanya would disapprove of any contact with Adam, just as she disapproved of contact with our father, and I didn't think I could face another prefight analysis. But too many secrets can be a burden and so I changed my mind and told them. It came as a relief to me that Tanya was not immediately horrified. Indeed she hardly seemed surprised.

"We all need all the help we can get." She shrugged. "And Adam's a good man in some ways. He's funny, he's sweet, he's got a good job. He screwed up as a lover, but you've both had time to cool off."

"He'll fall in love with the kids," Patrick said. "Although I keep asking Tanya why on earth we had three of the blighters. Just don't have another."

"There's no danger of that," I said.

Talking to them had been a comfort, as though I'd heard the voices of reason. I felt as though this was a day of touching base, drawing nourishment from my roots, building up my strength for the confrontation to come. I was under no illusion that my meeting with Adam would be easy, because there were no obvious solutions to our situation, no clear objectives. My parting with Adam had been raw with emotion and as rapid as it could be. Jane had asked me a few months afterward whether I felt we'd achieved closure, and I hadn't even been able to grasp what she meant, let alone say yes. How could there be any sort of closure with the twins a giggling, squirming memorial to what had been? Every time I looked at the children I saw Adam. But if there was to be no closure, then I was left with the same old problem, which was how to coexist with him.

When I left Tanya's house I dropped the car off for its inspection at her local garage, then unloaded the children, put them in the double stroller, and walked from the garage to my mother's house. A watery sun was in the sky and the exercise helped to keep my anxiety about the evening ahead at bay. What's more the movement lulled both the children to sleep, so that when I arrived I had the rare luxury of parking them in the hallway and settling down to a cup of tea and the newspapers at the kitchen table. As long as I can remember, which means since the departure of my father, my mother has never felt the need for her house to be a show home. Her idea of interior design is sheer self-indulgence. Food sits in cupboards and in the fridge until it is capable of speech and can ask to be put out of its misery. Mounds of books and magazines cover every surface. If she sees something she likes, whether it is an essay on international relations or a cartoon or a photograph, she sticks it in a clip frame and puts it on the wall. Her house is like a giant scrapbook.

"Did you see this?" My mother had folded the diary section of the *Guardian* and marked a small item with a cross. I read:

> After a series of scandals about editorial standards in day-time talk shows and months of spirited resistance, the Corporation has finally given in to government pressure and appointed its first Ethics Czar, former award-winning television producer, Robin Ballantyne. Industry insiders say the appointment is tantamount to an admission by the Corporation that it has a problem. But Maeve Tandy, head of television, last night told this diarist that it was "a simple restatement of our commitment to high-quality programming. I would be very surprised if Robin Ballantyne finds that we are not fulfilling our editorial standards." Robin Ballantyne has kept a low profile for the past year, and is believed to be taking up her high-visibility position at a time of personal strain.

My heart sank. I hadn't expected Maeve to be so quick off the mark, but I imagined she wanted to get the newspapers off her back. I knew it was only propaganda, but still, the tiny article sounded like a death knell for my career.

"A girl's got to do what a girl's got to do," I told my mother, handing the article back to her, and turning to the other papers to see what was happening in the Carmichael case.

I'd noticed that the mourners making a pilgrimage to the house had thinned to almost nothing, and the newspapers, like Finney, seemed to have few new leads to go on. Jane's suggestion that Richard Carmichael must be a suspect had come to nothing. The initial debate about what would become of the Carmichaelite charities had been largely settled by Paula Carmichael's deputy, a woman called Rachel Colby, who had made a public statement saying that their work would continue and expand. Already, she said, sadness over Paula's death had galvanized more people to become involved in the work she had pioneered. However, the news coverage had discovered a new lease on life because Carmichael's funeral was taking place that afternoon.

"Why didn't anyone tell me?" I looked up from the newspaper in alarm.

"What do you mean?" said my mother from the stove, where she was boiling tortellini for lunch and heating a ready-made carbonara sauce.

"This woman watched me out of her window, she wrote about me in her diaries, and then I watched her die. I can't not go to her funeral," I said with a wail. "Why didn't Finney tell me?"

"Isn't it in Birmingham?" my mother said. "That's where she was from."

"Well, Birmingham's hardly the end of the earth," I grumbled. "I could have got on a train."

I went back to reading. There were endless column inches filled with who would attend and who would not. In particular there was the question of whether the prime minister would be there. The commentators suggested that he could make political capital out of going. Soon I realized that my mother was wrong. The funeral was to take place in London. Paula Carmichael had been Roman Catholic, at least in name, and her funeral was to take place at a local church right there in south London.

"Ma?" I took a deep breath. "Would you mind taking the children for a couple of hours?"

Chapter 11

I arrived with fifteen minutes to spare, but the overflow from the church was spilling onto the street, and there was a move under way to set up speakers outside so that the funeral service could be heard there. I dug out my Corporation pass and convinced the man at the door that I belonged to a television crew.

"All right, love, but don't make a racket," he whispered, as he pushed open the heavy door for me. Inside, the organ was playing Bach, and there was the softest rustle of low conversation from the congregation. The pews were full, and extra benches and chairs had been brought in at the back of the church. I spied a small empty space in a pew near the front and walked quietly along the side aisle until I reached it, glad that I had taken time before I rushed out of my mother's house to borrow a black skirt and jacket. Luckily we were about the same size, my mother and I, but she wasn't as tall, and I was uncomfortably aware that the skirt was shorter than was ideal for a funeral.

In the side chapels hundreds of candles had been lit under representations of the Madonna in paint and stone. I reached the pew and only then did I see that the space I had identified was smaller than I had expected and it was next to Detective Chief Inspector Finney in a black suit and tie. I hesitated and he glanced up at me, his eyebrows raised in recognition. I gestured weakly at the space and he and his neighbor moved along a few inches to make more

room. It was still a tight squeeze, my hips pressed against the end
of the pew on one side and against Finney on the other. I could
feel the warmth of him through the layers of fabric that were between us. My skirt rode up over my thighs. I tugged it down, but
to little effect.

Beside me I felt Finney tense and I looked up. Richard Carmichael
had arrived, and was walking down the central aisle with his step-
sons trailing behind. All wore black, even the youngest was in a
black polo neck sweater and blazer over black jeans. Carmichael
himself looked grim, his mouth tight, jaw muscle working. He was
holding hands with the elder son, who nevertheless did not walk
at his father's side but a step behind. Carmichael nodded in ac-
knowledgment at the murmurs of condolence that followed his
progress.

I did not see his elder son's face, but the younger one had clearly
been crying. His eyes were red, his face puffy, and his hands were
clenched into fists at his side as though he was holding on for dear
life. His ear was multiply pierced and the row of silver rings caught
the light that trickled down from the small circular windows in the
dome above us. The Carmichaels were ushered into a reserved pew
at the front of the church next to an elderly woman who I assumed
was Paula Carmichael's mother. I saw that the prime minister had
made a low-profile entrance and was being guided in from a side
door to take his place just behind the family.

I spotted other familiar faces and realized that Finney had posi-
tioned himself carefully, not for a view of the pulpit, which was
partly obscured, but for a view of the congregation. I saw Suzette
and Adam a row apart on the other side of the church. I had expected Adam to be there and felt at peace with his presence. We
would go to battle later. We exchanged smiles. Many of the pews
were filled not with politicians or media, or even with family, but
with the Carmichaelites themselves. They were mostly women, but

that was the only generalization one could make about the gathering. In other ways—race, status, wealth—my impression was that all the world was there. Two pews had been removed to make space for a row of wheelchairs. Without exception everyone looked grim, as though they would never smile again.

The organ ceased and the silence took on the quality of expectation. Paula Carmichael's coffin seemed very distant, on a trestle to the left of the altar, and piled high with wreaths. I thought of her body, all broken, her hair soaked around her head.

The priest, Father Joe Riberra, was a young American with spectacles and a goatee, who spoke as though he was at the dinner table, quietly and conversationally. He talked as though he had known Paula Carmichael well, and at points his voice was so low that I could only just make out what he was saying. The congregation was silent, straining to hear every word.

He told us that the only possible response to Paula Carmichael's death was grief, but that we were also there to celebrate the life of a woman who had given birth to a great movement for social regeneration. He described Paula's life. She was not, he said, born to a privileged family. Her father was a trade unionist, her mother a teacher. It was from them that she had learned of the importance of principle and social activism. He had visited Paula's home and seen that her bookshelves were full of the biographies of those who had tried to change the world.

"Paula wasn't terribly good at modesty. I'd have said she wanted her own biography up there next to the great men of history, and I'd say she may yet get it, that she probably should. But towards the end, she wasn't happy. Things changed, none of us really knows why. She told me she didn't want to be remembered. Well, I hate to contradict her even in death, but we're here because she made an impact on our lives.

"I should tell you I had an argument with Paula. It was about the terrible things life throws at us, the things that make us feel like hell, and that we simply cannot comprehend. Those of us who are Christians still find ourselves asking how God can allow these things to happen. War, famine, sickness, and decay. Violent death, suicide. What in God's name is their purpose?

"I told Paula that all I can think is that we're never going to understand and we're always going to struggle against these things, but that God is always there. At all times, in all situations, with us and beside us and right smack in the middle of the awfulness. She disagreed with me and many of you will know that having Paula Carmichael disagree with you was pretty scary. Those are the times and the situations, she said, when we realize there is no God, and it is in those minutes of most profound loneliness that men and women turn to other men and women for their salvation. Sometimes other people come through for them, and sometimes they don't. Now I'm not going to try and kid you that the difference in our positions is only semantic. It's not. But nor are they mutually exclusive.

"The second thing I want you to go away with," Father Riberra continued, "is the Carmichael challenge: 'So what are you going to do about it?' If anyone had asked her what she wanted on her tombstone, that would have been it. Don't whine, don't pass the buck. Put yourself there, smack in the middle of the awfulness. Alongside God, I'd say. Alongside humanity, she'd say. Don't walk away. Get your hands dirty."

The priest dropped his head, as though the homily had simply run out, and there was silence.

Then all of a sudden there was a clatter from my right and I turned my head. Adam was out of his seat and pushing past mourners to the central aisle, apparently not caring about the disruption he was causing. He glanced up, his face suffused in panic, and for an instant he caught my eye and paused, as if he were about to address me. Then he shook his head in confusion and turned away. The entire congregation must have watched his stumbling exit. Only the priest kept his head bowed.

Finney, observing Adam's departure, had caught the moment's connection between Adam and myself and turned to me now, his eyebrows raised again, this time in interrogation.

I shook my head wordlessly. All that I had seen in Adam's eyes was pain.

————

"You know him, the man who walked out?" Finney pursued me out of the church at the end of the funeral mass. The sky had darkened and heavy drops of rain had begun to fall. Some of the crowd was hurrying off, but for the most part people seemed to be rooted to the spot, as though the funeral hadn't ended, as though there was still something to wait for.

"I used to work with him."

"At the Corporation," he clarified. "I've seen him on television."

I nodded.

"Why's he at the funeral?"

"I think he worked with Paula Carmichael at one point."

Finney gazed off over my shoulder and seemed to focus on someone else in the crowd. Then he came back to me.

"Is he the mutual friend you mentioned who might be the link with Paula's diaries?"

Interesting, I thought, that he's using her first name as if they've grown to be friends, as though she had reached out beyond the grave to him to smile and say, "Been there, done that."

"It's possible. I'm going to ask him."

"Don't let me put you out," Finney scowled. "I'll talk to him myself."

"No." The thought of Adam and Finney having a heart-to-heart was, for some reason, not good. "I'm going to see him this evening, it's all been arranged."

He nodded, his eyes distracted by Richard Carmichael's emergence from the church and the forward thrust of the media. I had no idea whether Finney had really heard what I said. He turned away and snapped at one of his officers to clear a broader path for the mourners. The crowd and the outside broadcast TV vans had all but blocked traffic, and horns were blaring. D.C. Mann materialized at Finney's side and acknowledged me with a dip of the head.

"I'll speak to you tomorrow," Finney told me. "We have to clear this up." He moved away.

I was jostled from side to side by the crowd, then I felt a hand on my elbow, and turned. I had assumed Suzette was there out of duty—she had hardly been full of praise for Paula—but she looked shaken all the same. She wore a charcoal gray dress, and a gray pillbox hat with black feather was perched on her gathered blond hair. We hugged and kissed on the cheek, the nature of the occasion making us more demonstrative than we would otherwise have been. The misunderstanding over money still sat uncomfortably with me, but we were friends and we started to walk side by side. The bottleneck had eased and the current of mourners swept us along.

"Do you know what that was all about?" I asked her.

"Adam?" She pulled a face. "I suppose he wasn't feeling well."

"You think so?" I said it uncertainly, although of course it was the only sensible explanation. It just hadn't looked that way to me.

"I spoke to him before the funeral and he said he had a headache," she said.

I had misinterpreted the pain I saw in his eyes, then. Adam had a history of occasional but severe migraines that made light and noise unbearable and made him vomit. When they struck he needed medication immediately, but because the headaches were rare he often forgot to carry his pills with him.

We paused and watched as Richard Carmichael, still hand in hand with his older boy, the younger standing a yard away, stood and chatted with journalists for a moment.

"It's hardly the time, you'd have thought," Suzette murmured.

"He seems to think he can use the media," I said, "but they'll be just as eager to destroy him if things turn that way."

"He's still trying to peddle this line that someone was seen visiting Paula Carmichael before she died," Suzette said thoughtfully. "Although there seems to be only the son's word for it."

"You don't believe him?" I said. We were talking in low voices, aware that Carmichael friends and family were all around us.

"Carmichael needs the money," she said softly. "That means Paula can't have committed suicide, and he can't have killed her. That's a bit of a tightrope." She paused and sighed. "Was that man you were talking to with the police?"

"Finney." I nodded.

"Does he think it's suicide?"

"I don't think he knows what to believe."

Suzette gave a tight little smile.

"Welcome to the club," she said.

———

I headed to my mother's first to pick up the children, because I knew she had to go out.

She was waiting for me, dressed in a suit, her bag on her shoulder, and clearly annoyed.

"I'm supposed to be there already."

"I thought you said you were leaving at four-fifteen," I said, my heart sinking, stretching out my arms for the twins.

"I had to be there by four-fifteen, I'm sure I said."

I put Hannah and William in the stroller, apologizing profusely. Then I walked back to the garage where I'd left the car and wrote a check for three hundred pounds of work on it, which did nothing to lift my mood. I loaded the children and headed home, wishing I'd never agreed to see Adam.

Chapter 12

I get home at five-fifteen and busy myself with the children's tea. Once they are eating I look in the mirror. I have already thrown the black jacket over the back of a chair. The short black skirt has to go too or I will look like a French waitress in a farce. My hair could do with a wash. I drag some jeans and a striped T-shirt out of the basket of clean laundry and iron them. I pull the blind closed and strip down to my underwear. Then, still in the kitchen, I wash my hair in the sink. The children watch this, fascinated, and all the time they keep stuffing food in their mouths. This is great. I should do it every mealtime. I comb my hair through, leaving it to dry, and pull on the clean clothes. At six I examine myself critically in the mirror. I could do with some lipstick and mascara, but this is not a date. All I want is for Adam to see that I am strong, that I have not fallen apart, that I do not need him, that we do not need him, that we are all fed and clothed and happy and clean. I clear up the tea things, wipe hands and faces with a flannel, check their nappies, change them into cuter clothes.

I glance around the flat and look for the first time as through Adam's eyes. He will think it poky, which it is. He will be surprised I've put up with the bizarre color schemes, but I have. The best I have done is to jolly it up in places—I've made mobiles out of magazine pictures, framed lots of photographs, filled vases with my childhood collection of peacock feathers, painted mirrors and lampshades. These tasks have filled lonely evenings when the children are in bed. I have no money to spend on anything but food and clothes, but I want them to feel their home is a warm and happy place. As I look at it through Adam's eyes my efforts look amateurish and cheap. I could clear my pathetic handicrafts away, but I will not. At least it is clean and tidy. Adam always said he didn't care about tidiness, but he would have cared if he'd had the mess of children around him. I pull more laundry from the drier. I will fold it and take it upstairs before he comes.

At six twenty-five the phone rings. It is probably Adam, I think, my heart pounding, Adam saying he's been delayed. It is Terry.

"You're going to take the job, that's brilliant." He hears my silence, tries to jolly me along. "I know it's not exactly what you want, but there are people losing their jobs left, right, and center. It's a promotion, for heaven's sake."

I sigh, my heartbeat still failing to slow. I look at my watch. Six-thirty. I hear a car pull up in the road outside.

"I'm sorry, Terry, I really can't talk right now."

"I just feel we should have a chat before you start at work, and you're starting tomorrow."

"Fine. Good, we'll talk, but not now," I plead. "I'm in the middle of something. I'll explain later. Really. I'll ring you."

He doesn't like it of course, but he says good-bye.

I hurry into the sitting room and look out of the window, but if a car had pulled up it has moved on again. There are no free parking spaces outside the house. By this time of day the road is always lined with returning commuters, and a green Toyota is sitting outside the house, parked badly in a space that could have taken two cars.

By six-forty I am a wreck. My hackles rise like a dog's with every passing vehicle. When a nice man knocks on the door at six forty-five to ask for a charitable donation I nearly bite his head off. At six-fifty I try calling Adam. Perhaps he has forgotten. But I just get his answering machine and I decide that it is a good sign and he must be on his way.

Just before seven there is a knock on the door and I open it ready to punch the man who stands there. It is Dan Stein. His face falls.

"I've come at a bad time again," he says, looking at my expression.

"No, no." I try to smile, but it doesn't really work, and I realize I have to explain, "I've had some bad news, a family thing, but I'm fine."

"Okay." He doesn't know how to go on. He's embarrassed by this talk of family because we are not yet familiar. I am not being exactly welcoming. I haven't invited him in this time, and I cannot. Not tonight.

"Could we go out for a drink on Saturday," I offer, managing a smile of sorts. "I'm sorry, I'll be in better shape by then."

"You're in great shape right now," he says, and grins to tell me the remark is intended in the best of taste, just meant to comfort me.

I manage to smile back.

"Why don't you come over at around eight?" I suggest. "And we can go to the George."

"Or for a meal," he suggests. "If it's going to take this long to arrange one date, it might as well be a good one."

"Okay, but not Indian," I say, trying to make conversation but not wanting to.

"Are you sure you're okay?" he asks softly.

I nod, my jaw set. He lifts his hand, and for an instant I think he is going to touch my face. I draw back and his hand goes to his pocket for a pen to write down his telephone number. We agree that we will see each other on Saturday, and I close the door on him. Tonight was not the right time to entertain a suitor. Nevertheless, he is persistent and I like that. He has met the twins and he is still persistent. I like that even more. He has sympathetic eyes, but he looks so young and pristine, especially this evening, dressed in chinos and a leather jacket. Surely I am too old for him, too old and bashed around.

I bathe the children. I dress them in their nightclothes. At seven-thirty I try calling Adam's mobile, but it rings and rings and no one answers. At eight I give up on him. I mean I give up properly, forever. He has not managed this one simple thing. He has been delayed by some trivia, diverted by some irrelevance, one way or another there's something he would rather do than meet his own children. He has as good as turned his back on them. I contain myself until the children are in bed and then I pace the floor fuming and fulminating, cursing myself for ever having listened to him, hating myself for wanting him to come, despising myself for ever having believed in him.

By ten I have calmed down. The first trickle of relief has found its way through the hurt. I am not going to have to deal with Adam. There will be no agonized discussions about his involvement in our lives, the children will be all mine again. I am under no obligation to him. For the first time since Adam and I parted I go and kneel by the cupboard where my papers are stored and I pull out a box of photographs that I have avoided like the plague. I stare down at the picture on the top of the pile, Adam and I, arms around each other's shoulders on holiday in Morocco, both tanned, happy grins on our faces. I put the photographs down and go and pour myself a whiskey in the kitchen, then I return to the photographs with the bottle and sit cross-legged on the floor and work my way through the images of our time together. It is a grand farewell. Laughing, hands clasped, arms entwined, even one of us kissing, his hands on my face, pulling me to him. I close my eyes, lean back against the sofa, and run our time together like a movie in my head.

I was working for financial news and documentaries and I'd got a whiff of scandal before the country knew it as a scandal. I'd had word that Paper Money, a young but outstandingly successful investment company, was concealing huge losses from the public with the help of some creative accounting. It was nothing more than a whisper, and small investors couldn't resist, continuing to throw their money into the void. For six months I pushed and probed and combed the company accounts. I wined, I dined, I flattered. I even flirted, which is something I only do under duress.

It was at this point that I met Adam. He egged me on, even as Paper Money got wind of my interest and tried to intimidate me with talk of lawsuits. Eventually my breakthrough came in the form of a Deep Throat from the Serious Fraud Office. Then Adam presented the forty-minute documentary that caused Paper Money's demise and won me a prestigious award. It wasn't the award that gave me a kick so much as the fact that I'd single-handedly brought Paper Money down. I was drunk on my own power and I was hungry for the next challenge. I don't know what that challenge might have been because I fell in love with Adam and, after a few months, became pregnant with twins, and then he left.

Adam was my best friend as well as my lover, but all of it was tied up with work. Work was who we were, both of us. We talked endlessly about it, laughed about it, we made love after it and before it. When I started to change, when the double helping of life inside my belly started to move my head and my heart in new directions, Adam stayed where he was. And when he found himself alone in that place he looked around for a new companion.

I didn't know the details, the who or the where or the how many times, but that there was someone else I am certain. I suspected it in the week before his declaration of non-love for me. Then, when

I challenged him, he didn't deny it. It made all the difference to me. If there had been no one else, if Adam was just afraid of how parenthood was going to change his life, I would have dragged him kicking and screaming into domesticity, but when I knew there was already someone else, then I knew he'd made a choice and that choice was not to be with me and with our children.

"To closure," I murmur and raise my whiskey glass in a farewell toast. I sip. Time for bed.

But "Greensleeves" shatters the silence and I haul myself to my feet. I find Finney and D.C. Mann on my doorstep.

"Miss Ballantyne," Finney says, "do you own a red 1990 BMW?"

"Yes, what's—?"

"Can you tell me the license number?"

I recite it and Finney nods, and looks sadder than I have seen him. Which makes no sense.

"We need to come in," he says, and I stand back, mystified.

We go, all three of us, in the sitting room. The glass in the window has been replaced, but during my evening of fury I have not once paused to pull the curtains closed. I can see the Carmichael house, all lit up, on the other side of the street. Finney runs his eyes over the room. I see him take note of my tumbler of Laphroaig, the stack of photographs scattered where my foot caught them carelessly when I went to answer the door.

"I need your car keys, Robin," Mann says.

I stare at her. Go automatically to my bag. I search for the keys, first calmly, then upending everything on the table. My house keys tumble to the floor and I seize them up, then realize that the car key isn't on the key ring as it usually is.

"I don't . . ." My brain has gone blank. Then I realize what must have happened. "I had the car inspected this afternoon," I explain, "so I gave the key to the mechanic, and I suppose I didn't put it back on my key ring when I picked up the car . . . I had my hands full . . ."

"So where is it?" D.C. Mann is not interested in my story of domestic life.

"If it's not here . . ." I shake my head at the contents of my bag. "Sometimes I leave the key in the ignition when my arms are full. Usually I realize when I get to the front door, and I have to go back, but this evening I had my house keys, so I might not have noticed . . . Has my car been stolen?"

"Where were you this evening, Robin?" Mann asks. She and I had struck up a fledgling friendship the night Paula Carmichael died. She is wearing brown trousers that cling to her thighs, and a volcanic orange sweater that drapes over a figure honed in the gym, but I can feel the hard professionalism under the informality. The earth underneath us has shifted and I cannot find my footing.

"I was here," I say, "all evening. Hannah and William are asleep upstairs."

Mann glances at Finney and he gives her a small nod. She turns and leaves the room and I stare at him as I hear her run lightly up the stairs, pause outside the children's room, push open the door, step inside.

"What the fuck is going on?" I demand, approaching Finney. Our eyes meet, and I learn from what I see there that something awful has happened. I wait in shocked silence, and in a moment Mann reappears and nods at Finney. She is relieved. He is reassured.

"What was that all about?" I ask again, but she ignores my question and waves me to sit down. I continue to stand and she perches on the arm of the sofa to continue her interrogation.

"You didn't go out even briefly?" she insists, glancing at Finney. "You didn't nip out to the corner shop or anything?"

"I told you," I say, my voice rising, "I've been here with the children. They've been asleep since eight o'clock. I couldn't have gone out even if I'd wanted to."

"Well what did you do all evening?" she asks, her voice taking on a chatty tone.

"Nothing," I say.

I know at once that "nothing" is not enough. I waited, was what I should have said, I waited for Adam. I should have come clean then, but it is none of their business, and I cling to the mistaken belief that if I am stubborn they will just back off.

"Did you watch television, Robin?" Mann persists.

Finney squats down at my feet and picks up the pile of photographs. He looks up at me and our eyes meet.

"Do you mind?" he asks softly.

"Do I have a choice?" I snap back.

He stands then and walks over to the light, his back to me.

"No," I say, my eyes glued to Finney, knowing that if I lie I will be caught out, "I didn't watch television."

He takes a photograph from the top of the pile, replaces it at the bottom, works his way through the pictures, pausing now and again, head bowed.

"Did you eat dinner, Robin? You must have eaten something." Mann is losing patience. "You can't have just sat here all evening doing nothing."

I shake my head. There is a tight feeling in my chest, and what has been an amorphous sense of unease is turning into downright panic.

"What's this all about?"

Finney sighs, hands Mann the pile of photographs.

"Where did you park your car?" he asks wearily.

I shake my head.

"It's up the road," I say. "I couldn't get a parking space."

"When did you last drive it?"

"This afternoon, I told you. Look, I refuse," I say as calmly as I am able, "to answer any more questions until you tell me what this is about."

Finney regards me with disdain, and this frightens me as much as anything else. He and I were as good as playing footsy twenty-four hours ago. What has happened?

"There's been an accident," he says, his voice low and relentless, his eyes like a hawk. No, I want to correct him, that was days ago. Paula Carmichael fell out the window days ago, what's taken you so long? But his voice is already taking me beyond that, his words like a wrecking ball, demolishing my life.

"Adam Wills has been killed by a speeding car, just up the road," he says. "The car was a red 1990 BMW, registered to you."

I stare at him, past caring what he sees in my eyes. Then my knees give way and I slump onto the sofa. My stomach seems to fold over itself.

"What am I supposed to think?" he defends himself, as though I have challenged him. "You own a car, it killed a man. I've seen his body. The deceased is the man you told me you were going to see this evening. And what the fuck am I supposed to make of these?" He snatches the photographs from Mann and brandishes them at me. Several fall to the floor.

D.C. Mann reels. "Sir?" she says uncertainly.

I am overwhelmed by nausea. A deep chill has seized me by the shoulders and is shaking me with huge racking tremors. My stomach is a fiery ball, leeching heat from my body. What energy I can harness I use to shake my head over and over again. Mann comes over to kneel next to me in concern. She puts her hand on my arm.

"The children are his," I say to her. How can they think I would kill my children's father?

"What?" Finney has not heard.

Mann stays where she is, her hand clutching my arm, but she turns her head toward him.

"She says the children are his."

It comes as no surprise to him, not after the photographs. He nods grimly.

"Hey presto, a motive," he mutters, sarcastic as ever.

I look up at him and our eyes lock. I cannot begin to fathom the disappointment I see there. Here is a man who makes me distrust myself, who weakens me. But I cannot afford to be weak, not with my children upstairs.

"I want a lawyer," I say.

————

When my lawyer comes, her skin is still soft from bed, her hair hangs loose around her shoulders and her eyes are wide with anxiety and love. She, my mother, encloses me in her arms where I still sit on the sofa, but I am numb. The blood is departing from my limbs in order to keep my vital functions going. I am cold, shivering. As if at a great distance I see my mother's face fall as Finney talks to her. She seems to be arguing with him, but he shakes his head and talks in a low voice to her. They both turn to me and I hear words that inform me that the house is to be searched. Ma tells me that she has given my permission for the search and has told Finney that a warrant is not necessary. Her eyes seek mine out and I understand that she wants to confirm that she is doing the right thing by volunteering cooperation, but I am not capable of involvement in their negotiations. I force myself upright and to the door. I climb the stairs, their eyes on me. I open the door to the room where, I now understand, Mann went to check that I had not murdered my children in their beds. There is no space for a chair in there, so I seat myself cross-legged at the foot of their cribs and wait for the men to come and tear our home apart around us.

Chapter 13

THE search of my house the night before did not, as far as I was aware, uncover anything more sinister than dust and grime, great clumps of which emerged from hiding behind the sofa and underneath the fridge. The police did not trash the place, but things were not as they were. I found the cutlery upended into the kitchen sink, clothes off hangers and papers sorted and resorted until they were in no order at all. My peacock feathers were trampled into the dirt and one of the mirrors I'd painted had sweaty fingerprints all over it. I tossed the feathers and the mirror into the bin and for good measure followed them with the mobiles I had made. Everything felt grubby to me now.

All that they had taken away were the photographs of Adam and me, and some letters and documents belonging to Adam that had got mixed up with my things, and that I had retained only because I had not been aware that I had them. I signed a receipt for these items and thought nothing of it. They couldn't be incriminating because I had committed no crime. I was in no hurry to get them back.

I half expected to be arrested on suspicion of murder, but after Finney had talked again to my mother, they let me stay in my own house. As I pulled the curtains I saw a patrol car sitting in the road outside. I doubt it was for my protection.

When Finney had gone, I went to bed. I closed my eyes and in my head I opened the car door and looked inside. There were the keys, in the ignition. There, with a foot on the accelerator, sat an ill-defined shape, a figure not male not female, silent, anonymous, a figment of my imagination were it not for the fact that Adam was dead.

I hardly slept and then somewhere around five in the morning I fell into a sleep as deep as death. I awoke at dawn to a cry from William. My son's father was dead. The knowledge paralyzed me. I could not get out of bed to go and get William. I could scarcely breathe and my chest seemed bound in iron. I lay there, every muscle clenched. I heard my mother go and fetch the children from their cribs, shushing them in case they disturbed me. I gazed at the ceiling, moved my eyes slowly to the curtained windows and then to the pile of clothes on the chair by my bed. Even the familiar room seemed strange to me, as though I had stepped through some portal into another world. All this time I had thought Adam was not with me, but he'd been part of everything all along. The children wouldn't even know he'd gone. They would grow up with their father not just absent but dead, nowhere to be found. Tears welled, then worked their way down my cheeks and down, soaking the pillow. I curled into a fetal position. I closed my eyes. I slept again. This time, when I awoke, I was ready for the wave of loss that washed over me. I sat on the edge of the bed, jaw set. I weathered it. I got up.

———

The night before, Finney had looked like a wreck. This morning, at the station, he was clean shaven and he'd put on a new white shirt, but the bags under his eyes matched mine for volume. He nodded a hello and gestured at Mann to switch on the tape recorder. He glanced at me, then glanced again.

"You look upset," he said. It was a professional judgment, nothing more.

I had soaked my eyes in icy water, but they were still red-rimmed and swollen from crying and from sleeplessness.

"I *am* upset," I agreed. I sat down opposite him.

He looked away, avoiding my eyes, and Mann asked a question.

"Is there any other way you would describe the way you feel this morning?" Her voice was kind, sympathetic, and it pierced holes in my defenses.

I gazed at her.

"I am . . ." I felt tears rise and then words burst out of me, "so sorry . . ."

Finney's head snapped up. I struggled to regain control and felt the tension in their silence.

"I'm so sorry he's not here, I mean that he's not anywhere," I tried to explain, my voice still shaking. "And I'm so sorry my children will never meet him."

Finney's mouth twisted. Was he disappointed not to have a confession? He reached into his jacket pocket and pulled out a piece of newsprint, folded. I knew what it was before he had spread it out on the table and pushed it across to me. He took care that his fingers did not touch mine.

"I'd like to ask you again about your relations with Mr. Wills," Finney said. "I'm assuming you know what's written here."

I pushed the *Chronicle* clip back toward him.

"Don't believe everything you read."

Mann intervened.

"Robin, do you want your lawyer present?"

I shook my head. My mother was outside, last seen with her head bent over a newspaper. I had told her I did not want her to sit in on the interview. I wanted to make no admission of weakness and I wanted to rely on no one but myself. I was volunteering all the help I could. I'd given my fingerprints, I'd given blood. If only Finney would stop riling me, I would give him my cooperation too.

"You were seen arguing in public last week," Finney carried straight on, his voice distant. "Mr. Wills was begging you to let him see the children."

I made a couple of false starts, then settled on a way of explaining that I thought clarified matters.

"It was the first time he'd ever asked to see them, I wasn't keeping him from them, he just left long before they were born. I can't see," I added for good measure, "what gives him the right to see them."

Finney's eyebrows twitched upward again and for an instant that look of arrogance returned. It annoyed me.

"Adam was pretty unconcerned about what became of his sperm," I added wearily, "until he decided it would improve his reputation if he was a devoted father."

Something flashed through Finney's eyes and his jaw tightened. He leaned back in his chair, tipping it on its back legs, waiting for me to go on. Police and journalists, we all do it. Shut up and wait for someone to talk themselves into a trap.

"Look," I said, leaning toward him. My lips were quivering with exhaustion. "He rang me on Sunday night and we talked. We didn't have a row. I agreed that he would come around last night and we would talk things through. I didn't want him to see the children, but we would have come to some sort of an arrangement. I was sitting there all evening waiting for him to come . . ."

There are times when your head goes AWOL, and at this point my brain decided without any encouragement from me to take a few moments out to consider where Adam had been while I was waiting. Until this point my mind's eye had refused to envisage an impact of metal on flesh, bones grating under pressure, blood leaking through mashed muscle and shredded skin. Now all this and more flashed before me, as immediate as if it was taking place in front of my eyes, but it was stylized, in slow motion. Adam's mouth gaping open with the shock, arms flung wide, body hitting the ground, bouncing upwards, settling. I cleared my throat. Adam's broken body lingered stubbornly in my head. His body lay crumpled like Paula Carmichael's, she fallen on pavement, he flung on the tarmac, both of them just yards from my home. Was this an end or a beginning to the symmetry?

Finney was looking at me expectantly. I let the silence stretch. I was incapable of speech. The muscles around my jaw shuddered under the strain.

"You left us in midsentence, Miss Ballantyne." Finney's tone was razor sharp.

There must have been sirens of course, but there were always sirens. It wasn't that I had not heard them. I must have heard them and ignored them.

"I'm not angry at him anymore," I said, realizing this to be the case as I said it.

"I'm delighted to hear it," Finney said, his voice heavy with sarcasm and bringing his chair back to earth. I looked at him, frowning. I expected better of him than this. We had liked each other, I thought, at least in a combative sort of way. Now he seemed to hate me. Finney dropped his gaze and reached for the newspaper clip, putting it back in his pocket. He changed the subject.

"You saw Mr. Wills leave Paula Carmichael's funeral yesterday," he said.

I nodded.

"I'm going to ask you again whether you know why he walked out."

I shook my head and then added as an afterthought, "Suzette said he had a headache."

"You think he made a scene at a funeral because he had a headache?" Finney repeated the words with scorn.

"He gets migraines." It sounded weak and even as I was saying it I realized that, in all the time I'd been waiting for Adam the night before, it had not once crossed my mind that he was not well.

Finney let another silence stretch, but I ignored it and eventually he spoke again, this time in a more persuasive voice.

"Miss Ballantyne, I want to take you back over the past few months." He leaned toward me, his elbows on the desk between us. "I understand what you've told me about your relationship with Mr. Wills. No one would deny that you've been through a hard time. There's been ill feeling and you think Mr. Wills has neglected his duties."

I caught my breath and I gave Finney a look I thought was guaranteed to shut him up, but he looked at me blankly and plowed right on.

"So please be assured that if you answer these next questions honestly, people are going to understand. Miss Ballantyne, have you made phone calls to Adam Wills in the last two months?"

I frowned, remembering a series of questions like this about Paula Carmichael, and again the two deaths merged in my mind and I found that part of my brain was coolly working on the problem and had already decided that the two must be linked. That they knew each other was indisputable, that I was known to both of them and involved even indirectly in the death of each was also clear. That they should meet violent deaths within days of each other was surely too much of a coincidence.

"I didn't phone Adam," I was speaking slowly, trying to be accurate. "Not apart from the call I told you about on Sunday, and then it was he who rang me."

"Maybe you've sometimes just dialed his number, then hung up when he answered?" he suggested.

"Why would I do that?"

Finney glanced down, and I saw that he had placed a small notebook on his desk at his elbow.

"Did you ever go and wait outside his flat, perhaps hoping to bump into him?"

"No." I was beginning to get angry.

"Or send anyone with a message on your behalf?"

"What is this, you think I'm a stalker?"

I looked at Finney's face, then at Mann's. They had averted their eyes, and that told me everything I needed to know. My brain started to creak back into action.

"Adam had a stalker?" I asked, incredulous.

Finney closed his eyes for a moment and Mann stepped into the breach.

"Miss Ballantyne, I think it would be helpful if you didn't try to second-guess us. Helpful to you, as well as to us."

I ignored her. I was already working on this new information.

"Did he report it? He must have reported it."

Finney let Mann do the cool denial, but I was sure I was on to something, and I warmed to the interview.

"Okay. What do you want to know?" I challenged, sitting back in my chair for the first time. Perhaps I could learn more.

Finney gazed at me and puffed out his cheeks, Mann put her head on one side and regarded me like a naughty child. We sat without speaking for a minute, the battle lines redrawn. Outside the interview room, men were talking in loud voices in the corridor. One of the men swore, then he was hushed, and a herd of footsteps receded. I knew, now, why the police had not simply thrown me in a cell the night before. There was another suspect, a stalker, and while they might like to believe the stalker was me, it was looking more likely to them that we were two people. The information filled me not only with profound relief but with the zeal of the wrongly accused. With information like this I could fight an offensive game, not hang around waiting for Finney to take a potshot. Finney had read my mind, and I could see him trying to decide on a strategy. He didn't want to give me information, but every question he could ask would tell me something.

So far the police had told me nothing of the circumstances of Adam's death, except that he had been hit by my car. What little I had learnt, I had heard on the radio. Adam, who hated driving, had caught the Northern Line to Tooting Bec station and had walked up from the tube toward my house. When he crossed the road to turn into my street, a car—my car—had hit him before proceeding in the direction of the city. The radio suggested that there had been witnesses, but gave no detail of what had been seen. My car had been found abandoned near the Oval.

"If you're out of questions I have a few."

Mann rolled her eyes but Finney ignored her.

"How did you know where to find the car?"

Neither of them answered me.

"Why look at the Oval of all places? And why go looking for my car at all? I hadn't reported it missing, and I doubt any of your witnesses could tell you more than the color and make. You do have witnesses, do you?"

"You'll choose a better hiding place next time than the Oval, will you?" Mann parried, fighting a rearguard action. I didn't bother to answer her. I thought for a moment, and something occurred to me.

"Did you get a tip-off, was that it?"

"Or did you give us a tip-off, was that it?" Mann came back, but too quickly. She'd let the information slip. Someone somewhere had told the police about the car. I put the information aside to be analyzed later and moved on rapidly, while I still had the upper hand.

"Don't you think Adam's death might have something to do with Paula Carmichael's?" I said.

"You mean to say," Finney said slowly and carefully, "you want us to consider Paula Carmichael's death, where you were the first at the scene, also a murder?"

"You've been investigating it as though it could be a murder," I pointed out.

Finney shook his head. "That investigation's over." He paused, searching I thought for a decision about how much to say, then decided on total disclosure. "We're satisfied that Paula Carmichael's death was suicide. We have records now from her psychiatrist. The woman was clinically depressed. She'd been prescribed Prozac, but she hadn't taken it for several days before she jumped. She even wrote about committing suicide."

I frowned at him. His sympathy for Paula Carmichael seemed to have evaporated. I had never heard him refer to her as "the woman" before. Did he feel that by committing suicide she was wasting police time?

"What was she depressed about?" I wanted to know, but Finney had had enough, and he held up a hand to stop me in midflow.

"Would you object very much," he asked, "if we had a go now?"

Chapter 14

THERE must have been a dozen of them. Not all men, but in general the job still attracts more men than women. I won't dwell on the symbolism of the zoom lens and the victim laid bare, but that morning it felt like rape.

They were huddled around my front door, and I told the minicab driver to stop fifty yards away, so I could decide what to do next. I paid him and got out, then stood on the pavement for a good thirty seconds without a single bright idea in my head. They are paid to be observant, but they were chatting and laughing, their eyes reaching no farther than the end of their cigarettes, knowing that as long as they sat outside my front door they would eventually get what they were waiting for, my fellow journalists, some of them no better than vultures, and with nastier habits.

I wanted to run—or to punch them, and it was that urge which set me walking toward them. I had put on sunglasses to save my swollen eyes from the early morning glare, but now I took them off and put them in my pocket. If I was going to face the cameras—and sad to say that was more likely than that I could fell them all with one left hook—then I must engage the cameras. To cover my eyes would be to cut myself off. To let the camera gaze into my eyes might be to garner some sympathy. When you've been in the media too long, such cold-blooded analysis of the business of communication becomes second nature. It was in my favor, for instance, that I had put on no makeup. I would look shell-shocked, as though this thing had hit me from nowhere, not as though I had planned a murder. Was I calculating? Absolutely. But then I really hadn't planned a murder.

"Excuse me, gentlemen," I said as the human wall loomed in front of me. There was pandemonium for a second. I might just as well have said, "Mob me, gentlemen, please." Then the cameras exploded in a flurry of clicking and I found a microphone thrust in my face.

"Did you kill Adam Wills?" someone shouted at the back of the crowd, and there was some amused cackling from a man I knew slightly, and whom I had thought better of. Other questions were shouted, but the theme was similar, and my brain was speeding along its own path. I turned slightly, so that the television cameras had my full face, and I tried to look into the eyes around me as I spoke, so that I didn't look shifty or as if I had anything to hide. My legs were shaking under me, not from nerves but from exhaustion and misery. I could smell the stale cigarette smoke on the breath of the nearest hack and I wanted to vomit. It would have made for great television, and it would have been the end of me. Set the agenda, I murmured to myself, set the agenda. Don't let *them* set it.

"As you probably know, Adam Wills was the father of my twins," I said, counting down the words to a thirty-second sound-bite. That's long for a soundbite, but this was a big story and I was a big suspect. If I was editing this story I would give me thirty seconds. I tried, moreover, to structure my statement in such a way that if they chopped it up, it would not misrepresent me wherever they cut. There was no point in saying "I wanted to kill Adam Wills but I didn't," because those first six words would make the perfect headline and the last three would end up on the floor of the editing suite. What I said instead was, "Whatever happened between us, I could never have wished Adam any harm. I know the police have to eliminate me from their inquiries, and I support whatever they have to do. I hope they'll be able to find the stalker too, if only to eliminate him. They have to find Adam's killer because one day my children have to know what happened to their father, and I have to know too. I'm sorry, I have to go . . ." I elbowed my way through the shouted questions to my front door.

Already I was regretting what I'd said. It would sound too cocky, too polished. The strange thing was, as much as I'd calculated what I had to say and how to say it, I had still had a hard time not breaking down. I meant every word of it. As I emerged from the shock of the night before, my need to know was growing like a gnawing hunger in my gut. It was almost incidental that I had to clear my name. I was shaking too much to find my keys, and it set my teeth on edge that they managed to get a few shots of me like that, scrabbling around in my bag, head down, incompetent. I swear one man tried to follow me right inside my house, and my foot reached behind me and made sharp contact with his ankle. As I shut the door I heard his voice behind me, complaining, "The bitch kicked me." I locked the door and sat down hard at the foot of the stairs.

Erica emerged from the sitting room, her face as pale as her Swedish hair. I had not enlightened her, when she arrived, about Adam's death or my car's involvement in it, but now I could hear the television and Sky News updating us live. The children scuttled around her legs and came to me. I scooped them up. Erica didn't come too close. I was a suspected murderer, after all. Who knew what evil I was capable of? A baby on each arm, I could still kick.

"I have telephoned to my agency," she said, crossing her arms in front of her, a buffer in case I tried to headbutt her to death. "They know about my situation. I have informed them I am leaving when you return."

I stared at her. Leave! I wanted to shout. Get out of my house! Instead I begged.

"Just stay for today," I said. "Please. This is all a horrible mistake and I need some time to get things sorted out."

"There is no mistake," she said. "Their father is dead."

Her hips, her shoulders, everything about her down to her slightly freckled jaw was set. I looked at my watch. It was nearly two already. I'd been at the police station since eight-thirty. Five hours of questioning and I knew it wasn't over yet. Outside the sky was clear and blue, the temperature the fresh, sharp cool of autumn. The children were already stir-crazy, wriggling in my arms and begging to be put down, then crying to be picked up again. We would all be carried out in straitjackets if we were imprisoned in here all day. There was a good chance, however, that the press pack might be sufficiently stupid that they had not realized there was an alternative way out. It did not look like it from the front, but a small lane ran along the end of the back garden. I had no gate onto it, but after the storm part of the fence had collapsed, creating an adequate escape route.

"Help me out 'til five," I pleaded, "and I'll pay you double."

Now she shifted to look at me.

"Cash," I said. Her arms unlocked and fell to her side.

She shrugged and nodded. She was not willing, but she was mine. I had three hours to salvage my life.

———

Maeve's face fell when I walked into her office.

"Robin, I thought you weren't coming in until all this blows over. You look terrible."

"I've done nothing wrong, Maeve," I looked her steadily in the eye, "and this *is* supposed to be my first day back at work. I thought you'd be glad I've made the effort." She gave me a twisted half-smile and glanced away, pulling a file of papers toward her then pushing it away, just for something to do. She gestured me toward one of the low armless chairs that put all her visitors at a disadvantage. She was wearing black, no sleeves, her arms tanned and taut. There were no love handles on Maeve, no cuddly cellulite. She was all bone and rippling muscle, honed in the gym morning, noon, and night.

"You look great." I tried to bring us back to some sort of normality. "Is the black for Adam?" I nodded at the dress.

"It is." She brushed a speck of dust from her modest breast. "I notice you, however, are not in mourning. Is there anything we should infer from that?"

"How dare you." My voice was low.

"I'm sorry," she said after a moment. "That was unfair. I know that the two of you . . . were very close at one time."

It was true that I had given no thought that morning to what might be appropriate, simply pulling on jeans and a leather jacket against the chill in the air, but I was in mourning as surely as Maeve was in black.

"Maeve," I said softly. "We've known each other a long time. Either you think I'm a murderer, in which case you shouldn't even be talking to me. Or you're just pissed at me because my private life is messing up your professional life. If you think I killed Adam, just ask me to leave now. If you don't, then could you please cut the crap?"

The silence stretched. Maeve examined her fingernails for what seemed like several minutes, and then she leaned back in her chair.

"I'm not going to ask you to leave, Robin," she said, "but don't underestimate the shit we find ourselves in."

I realized I had been holding my breath. Now I breathed out, grateful for the "we," and for the "ourselves." My relief was short-lived.

"You look like death, Robin," Maeve continued, leaning forward again. "It's only hours since Adam was killed. You're giving yourself no time to recover. I do appreciate you coming in, in the middle of all this, of course I do, but take some time off."

"What are you saying?"

"What do you mean, 'what am I saying?' I'm saying take some time off."

"I don't want time off."

"Well, as your manager," Maeve attempted a mischievous smile here, then gave up on it, "I'm telling you that you need time off."

"You're suspending me."

Maeve held up her hand and waved it to and fro.

"Not at all," she said. "Don't be so melodramatic. We just want to let the dust settle. Let's call it compassionate leave."

"I don't want leave, I don't want compassion."

Maeve passed her hand over her forehead.

"Robin, you can't walk in here and expect . . . Look, you'll be on full pay, and of course we'll be very excited to have you back the moment this is all over. It's just very difficult for us right now. We've lost Adam, which is a personal blow to many of us who knew him. And how, for God's sake, can we cover his death when he was run over by one of our own . . . I know, I know, not *you*, just your car. I didn't mean to imply . . . but you must see it's very difficult for us. Very, very difficult all round. For us as well as you. I know that if there's anyone who is sensitive to the needs of the Corporation, it's you, so I'm sure you'll understand . . ."

"Understand? Understand?" I could scarcely fit words together, and I stood there repeating it like an angry parrot. "Understand? You're screwing me, that's all there is to understand."

I walked out then in a red haze of anger and marched through the corridors that linked offices and studios and canteens like a blood supply to vital organs. For all its backstabbing, its petty fights, and its many inadequacies I had still loved this place. Adam had loved this place. I saw no one I recognized and in my head they were all cowering under their desks, too frightened to say hello. A black hole was opening up inside me: The Corporation was no longer my home. I was in exile.

Chapter 15

W HAT on earth possessed you, at a time like this, to go and talk to that woman?"

I was at my mother's, where I'd sent Erica and the kids when we escaped out of the back door. Erica had managed to take the kids onto Streatham Common for a walk without getting mobbed, and she informed me that they had tottered and tumbled around without a care in the world. We could sleep at my mother's to stay away from the press for as long as we wanted. Now my mother was helping me bathe Hannah and William. Which is to say that I was sitting on the toilet seat, a glass of merlot in hand, and my mother was perched on the edge of the bath with her customary glass of sherry. Between us we had about a quarter of an eye on the children. Their discarded clothes lay wrinkled and muddy like shed skins all over the floor, but in the past twenty-four hours domestic concerns like laundry had rapidly descended the list of life's priorities.

Why indeed had I spent my only three hours on a visit to Maeve? It certainly wasn't loyalty to the new job I'd never wanted. Nor was it some misguided attempt to pretend everything was normal, which it clearly was not. Of course I had been canvassing support, knowing that if my employer (and Adam's employer) showed faith in me, then that nebulous thing known as my reputation would receive a boost. But I was not so stupid as to think the Corporation could save me.

"The Corporation was Adam's life," I said to my mother, as though that explained it.

"You still haven't told me why you had to go there," she pointed out softly. She'd been very gentle with me ever since Adam's death. She was my mother and she saw the pain in me where everyone else assumed there was none. Still, I sensed that deep down she was alarmed by what was happening.

"Well, if I want to find out why he was killed and who killed him, some of the answers have to be there." I thought it was obvious and I gave her a look that must have said she was a fool. My mother gave me a similar look in return but I carried on, caught up in the urgency of my mission. "There are people I need to talk to, and all of them are there . . . What the hell can I find out at home? I was just trying to keep my foot in the door. Damn Maeve."

I almost spat the last words and my mother heaved a sigh.

"I don't want to interfere," she ventured. "You must do whatever you decide of course, but—"

"I know, I know," I interrupted, snapping at her. "I should just put it aside, right? Like everything, always, pretend it's not happening, put it aside."

She was stunned into silence. In an instant I knew I shouldn't have said it. My sisters and I had frequently laughed at my mother's maxim behind her back, but none of us, as far as I knew, had ever taunted her with it before.

"I'm sorry," I muttered. "I'm really sorry. I shouldn't have said that. But someone did this and tried to frame me, and frankly, if you don't want to see me in jail, I have no choice."

She bit her lip and gazed back at me, then shook her head sadly.

"Let's get the children out," she said, subject not closed but put aside.

We got them out of the bath and into their nightclothes. I dimmed the bedroom light, laid the children down, and leaned over to kiss them and murmur in their ears. Their first day fatherless and they were oblivious. When they were older they would ask me about it. Would they half remember, half imagine a chill in the air, a cloud in their mother's eyes, the echo of sirens, the stern presence of the police? I prayed that there would be no more mystery about it by then. I needed to be able to say this is what happened and why, this is who did it and why. I needed to be able to say it was awful, but it is over. I stroked Hannah's hair. She was as good as asleep already, gazing up at me dreamily through heavy-lidded eyes, her mouth pulling on her pacifier. I resolved that their father's death would have no impact on their days. They would not be the tragic offspring of a murdered parent. Not if I had anything to do with it. Not if I could stay out of jail. Which did not seem then, as I stood over my children, as much of a challenge as it would seem an hour later.

I went to bed just minutes after the children. I had no appetite for food. I was so drained that I could barely lift one foot in front of the other, and even if my mother and I had anything to say to each other, I would not have been able to articulate the words. I fell into a deep sleep and then half woke to voices downstairs. Despite my exhaustion, my brain was in such a state of excitement that I could not simply ignore them. I sat up and listened, but the words were muffled, so I crept to the door and opened it softly.

Mann's voice, "We understand absolutely, Mrs. Ballantyne, but this is a murder investigation. It's only eight-thirty, it's not as though it's midnight."

"Let her sleep, for heaven's sake. Why can't you leave it 'til to-morrow? This is nothing more than harassment." There was a brief silence after my mother's speech, and her claim of harassment might well have swung things in her direction, but I could not sleep knowing that there was some news. Good or bad—and my instinct was that it was the latter—I had to know. I pulled on my jeans and T-shirt and padded down the stairs in my bare feet. Finney was there too, which for some reason came as a surprise. They were all looking at me by the time I reached the foot of the stairs, and I wished I had taken a moment to splash some water on my face and put a comb through my hair. In particular I wished I'd pulled some underwear on. I felt vulnerable, exposed.

"What is it?" I asked.

Finney's eyes went in one easy move from my sleep-creased face to my bare feet.

"We're sorry to disturb you," Mann said, "but we need to ask you a few more questions."

"You could have rung first," my mother complained.

"We tried. We got the answering machine," Mann said. I exchanged a glance with my mother and she nodded. The calls were piling up both here and at my own house: Terry, Jane, Tanya, Suzette, a dozen others. I'd rung none of them back. Not yet, not until I'd sorted things out.

"Okay," I said, and led them into the sitting room. My mother told me that the press were outside too. My escape had been short-lived.

Mann sat on the sofa next to me, and looked around at my mother's collection of kitsch while Finney pulled up a wooden dining chair from the table. My mother hovered behind me, and I wished at this moment that she would be one thing or the other, that she would leave the room and leave me to it, or remain and be professional. Her anxious, sympathetic presence was irritating me and that in turn was distracting. I could practically feel her breath on my neck.

"We need to ask you some questions about your house," Mann started. "How long have you lived there?"

Behind me my mother gave a little snort, as if the question were clearly irrelevant, and therefore justified her claim that I should not have been woken up to answer it. My own reaction was more cautious. Why the house? What did they know that I did not?

"Just over a year. Why?"

"You moved there from Mr. Wills's Upton Park flat?"

"I was here at my mother's house briefly, while I bought mine. Why? What's this about?"

"Why did you choose that particular house?" It was Finney this time, but I was getting increasingly annoyed at their assumption that I was not to be told anything. To me it was an assumption that I was guilty.

"I liked the paintwork," I snapped at him. He looked at me levelly.

"You did not like the paintwork," he said.

"Well, why do you think?" I said. "I had no money. It was cheap."

"You have a job," Mann interjected. "You probably have savings."

"Child care is going to cost me nearly all that I earn," I spelled out to her, incredulous that another woman should be so obtuse.

"And your savings?"

"I put down a large deposit on the house so I could afford the mortgage payments," I explained wearily, hating to discuss what were essentially private matters. Even my mother didn't know all this. "I also took an extended maternity leave, most of which was unpaid. As of now I have no savings, no prospect of saving in the next eighteen years, and two children to feed, clothe, and send on school skiing trips."

"So that little council house is your future," Finney said. "Two teenagers in bunk beds, taking turns at the kitchen table to do their homework, and no space to swing a cat."

"Thank you, yes, but we'll have to pass on the cat."

In the moments that followed, when no one spoke, I wished I had not let that note of bitterness into my voice. I wasn't even sure where it had come from. Then Finney spoke again, dropping words like depth charges into the sea.

"Well, you'll be all right now," he said, "won't you?"

I frowned. I turned around to face him.

"What do you mean by that?"

Finney's eyes had a tired, world-sick look to them, and his next words were impatient. "You know perfectly well what I mean."

"I don't," I said distinctly, "know what you mean."

I could feel my mother, very still, behind me.

"Who inherits Adam's flat?" he asked softly.

I gazed at him, lost for words, alarm bells beginning to ring, then clamoring, deafening me.

"I have no idea," I said eventually, but I could scarcely hear my own words for the noise of danger in my head.

"You know perfectly well everything comes to you," he said, not even attempting to keep the contempt from his voice.

"This is outrageous." My mother saved me from having to speak. She had stepped out from behind the sofa and forward, as if to shield me from Finney. "You come here, you wake up my daughter, and while she's still half asleep you produce some half-baked accusation to try and provoke her to an ill-considered response."

It was a performance worthy of any defense attorney, but this time Finney brushed her away like a fly.

"It's all in black and white," he told her, "and it's been in your daughter's possession for more than a year."

He drew a long buff envelope from the inside breast pocket of his jacket and handed it to me. For a moment I just held it on my knee. My hands were shaking too much to open it, and besides, I knew what it was. After a moment I handed it to my mother.

She took it from me, wide-eyed, and opened the envelope. It was not sealed. It had never been sealed. She stared down at it, her eyes moving over the text.

"The last will and testament of Adam Wills," she whispered, and handed the paper back to me as though it had scalded her fingers.

Chapter 16

I was all alone in my mother's house. Alone, that is, with the children. My mother had gone to work.

"I can't not go, I've got appointments all day long," she said defensively. "I've been putting people off for the last few days, but there are clients waiting for me. I can't just palm them off on someone else."

My mother specializes in refugee and immigration work. She listed for me the clients who were waiting for her attention: a refugee woman who'd been in Britain since her childhood, now fighting deportation; a young man injured in a police cell who was accusing the officer of racism; a middle-aged man completing the paperwork to bring his recently widowed mother from Bangladesh to Britain. They all sounded a great deal more worthy than me.

She bustled around the house, gathering up papers and files, losing and then finding her car keys.

"Life must go on," was my mother's parting shot as she slammed the door shut, but mine was going nowhere. My mother seemed to be distancing herself from me, as though she were preparing to lose me. She had not challenged me about the will. After Finney's departure the night before, we had gone to our beds with only the minimum of conversation. I'd slept badly for the second night in a row and I'd woken when the children did, at a quarter to six, with my head pounding.

My mother's silence over the breakfast table had been frightening, and the thought that she might be doubting my innocence just intensified the pain in my head. I would have challenged her, forced her to talk to me, but I was capable of little more than holding my head in my hands. I could not face food or caffeine, and preparing the children's porridge made me feel sick. When the door slammed shut behind my mother and I heard her rev the car and drive off, I felt abandoned. I glanced from the window and saw the press gathering already, several of them sipping from cardboard cups, the steam from their drinks rising into the chilly air.

Hannah and William didn't know what was going on, but their mood had become brittle and dissatisfied in reaction to the tensions around them. My nerves were stretched taut and every whine sounded to me like fingernails on a blackboard. There was no way the children could know that any minute Finney might decide he had enough evidence to arrest me for murdering their father, but they clung to me like drowning kittens to a raft. And I could not bear their touch. As gently as possible I disengaged myself time and again from their clutches, but they welded themselves to me with increasing desperation.

These things I had done automatically for months: kneeling to wipe up the mess after breakfast even as more mess fell to the floor around me; wrestling clothes onto cobra-like limbs; shielding myself from kicking feet while I changed nappies, shit leaking all over their clothes, little heels pounding in the excrement, then pounding me. For months I had let these things wash over me, shit and all. On that morning, the second day after Adam's death, with the pain in my head threatening to burst my skull open, these same things drove me to tearful distraction.

When my mother had been gone about half an hour several things happened in quick succession.

Hannah was screaming because I had taken away from her an

open carton of milk that she was pouring on the floor. I gave her a bottle to calm her, but she rejected it, stamping her feet and pointing at my glass of juice. Too weak with anxiety, exhaustion, and pain to argue, I handed it to her. She took one gulp, two, then carefully placed the glass on a stool, before swiping it to the floor with a purposeful right hook. The glass broke, showering William's legs in glass and apple juice.

I yanked him up, but not before he put his hand down on a shard, which forced its way into his palm. Blood oozed from the cut, he screamed, and I saw Hannah about to pick up a dagger of glass that would have severed an artery the moment she touched it. I yelled at her and lunged, with William still in my arms, pushing Hannah away from her trophy, but toppling her at the same time so that she fell and hit her head on the table leg.

At this moment the doorbell rang. I ignored it. I couldn't have done anything else. William was still howling, holding his hand away from him, the blood dripping all over us both. Hannah was in floods of tears, face down on the floor in the middle of the minefield, and when I tried to help her up she thrust me away. At that point something in me snapped. I couldn't help myself. I stood over Hannah and shouted down at her. I shouted in fear that turned into anger against the world. I don't remember what I shouted and I don't particularly want to. At the same time I grabbed her arm and hauled her out of danger. It must have hurt, but she yelled as though I was amputating it.

I twisted around to deposit Hannah on a safe bit of floor, and as I turned I became aware that there was another person in the room. Adam's mother, Norma, was standing behind me, her face white, jaw slack with horror at the tableau we presented. Hannah was dangling by one arm but refusing to be put down, her legs locked around my leg. I was in danger of losing my balance.

"The door was open." Norma was always a stickler for courtesy.

"Help me," I said, but she didn't move. Instead she seemed to swell with righteous indignation.

"What on earth is going on?"

"Just help," I insisted. "William's hurt his hand. Take him from me."

She stared and went, if possible, whiter, but after a moment she came nearer and held out reluctant arms. I passed William to her, realizing as I did so that my bathrobe was gaping open, but Norma would not have noticed if I was naked. She was too busy inspecting the bloody and screaming little boy in her arms. His face had gone red and blotchy with distress and Norma looked at him as though he were a martian.

With two hands free I gently lifted Hannah under her arms and loosened her legs from mine. She was sobbing as though her heart had broken, which I suspect it had. I had never shouted at her before. Even when I had her in my arms she refused to look at me, and even when the tears dried up, her bottom lip still pouted and quivered. I gave her a quick once over, but could find no cuts. Then I carried her to the bathroom and with one hand grabbed cotton wool and antiseptic spray for William. By the time I returned to the sitting room, Norma was on my mother's sofa and William had calmed enough for her to be able to dab at his hand.

"Why are you here?" I was still standing, on the defensive, Hannah in my arms.

"These are my grandchildren," she said in the precise tone that had always driven me mad. She did not look at me as she spoke. Cleaning William's hand gave her an excuse not to. She didn't raise her voice, but she was almost spitting.

"You have kept them from me for quite long enough. I had to learn about their existence from a newspaper."

"I am sorry about Adam," I said. It had to be said and I wanted to distract her from her grievances against me. It was Adam, not I, who had kept them from her, but this was not the time to split hairs. The woman looked shattered, a good century older than she had when I last saw her nearly two years before. She wore all the right things: the Country Casuals coat over the Jaeger skirt and the Bally boots. I'm guessing of course, but she's a woman who sticks to her brands. What was unusual was that it was all thrown together, nothing matched, and her white hair, usually so neatly coiffed, was flying in wisps around her head. Her mouth was working desperately as though she were chewing on something, and there was a tic at the corner of her eye. Here she was, holding her dead son's son in her arms, and all my animosity was washed away in a flood of pity. What I only understood afterward was that she was crazy with grief.

"You kill my son, and then you have the effrontery to say you are sorry." She took a deep breath, and her shoulders rose in out-rage. She stood with William still in her arms. He had stopped cry-ing and was watching his grandmother's face closely. It was a new face and it was doing interesting things.

"I didn't kill your son," I said softly.

"Look at you, you slut," she hissed. "Not even dressed, broken glass on the floor, yelling at your children. You are not capable of looking after them and you have forfeited whatever rights you ever had to be their parent."

She turned and started walking toward the door with William still in her arms. For a moment I stood paralyzed. I could not be-lieve what was happening, that this woman should walk in off the street and seriously attempt to kidnap my child. A red tidal wave of fury rose inside me.

"What are you doing?" I caught up with her by the door and stood in front of her, blocking her exit. She lunged to the left and I obstructed her, but the coat stand toppled to the floor missing us by an inch.

"He's in danger, you'll kill *him* next." She was shaking with anger.

"Give him to me," I ordered her, but she ignored this and tried to step around me. I managed to block her again, but I was hampered by Hannah who was clinging to me, whimpering at the anger in our voices.

"Sorry," I whispered to Hannah, and tried to put her down beside me on the ground, but she would not let go and Norma seized the opportunity to push past me to open the door. I grabbed her arm, put out a foot to jam the door, and suddenly we were wrestling, Hannah still clinging to my ankle, William shrieking in distress, holding out his arms for me, his hands clawing at my bathrobe, pulling it away from my body.

Norma hauled the door open, and we fell, a jumble of flailing limbs. Then, all at once there were people over us, hands lifting William from my neck, where he had attached himself like a limpet. There was something wet in my eyes, I rubbed it away and saw blood. A hand seized mine. I pushed myself to my knees and stood, only to be faced by a surprised cameraman who never expected that the story would fall at his feet.

"Get inside," Finney muttered and shoved me back through the door as cameras clicked behind us. I looked around in panic for the children and gathered up one under each arm. Mann, never far behind Finney, was with Norma, who was sitting at the bottom of the stairs, her head in her hands, shoulders heaving. I carried the children, sobbing and clinging, into the sitting room. Finney followed me, agitated.

"What the hell happened?" His eyes took it all in, the broken glass on the floor in a pool of juice, the wad of bloody cotton wool.

I shook my head, robotically patting and stroking, comforting my children. I was shaking with anger and humiliation, and I could not trust myself to talk.

"She's an unfit mother." I heard Norma's voice from the staircase, still precise even in the midst of hysteria. "I won't let her kill my grandchildren just as she killed my son. I won't allow it. The court will take my side. They will live with me. I'll take good care of them . . ." And here her voice trailed into sobs.

Finney blew out his cheeks.

"Here," he said. He handed me the packet of cotton wool. "Clean up that cut. D.C. Mann will take her home. We had some more questions for you but they'll wait."

When they had gone I cleaned up the glass, then myself, and I sat the children, who were calmer now, in front of the television to soothe them. I rang my mother and told her what had happened.

"There's no way she could claim custody is there?"

"I doubt it," she said, but I knew her tone of voice too well. She was worried and she could not give me the cast-iron guarantee I needed.

Chapter 17

WHAT was I thinking? That Richard Carmichael would open the door to me and say, "Ah, the girl who drove her car over her lover, come on in, what can I do for you?" I suppose I was still operating in an alternative universe where I was innocent until proven guilty. It's amazing how one can get so old and still be so naive.

In fact it went more like this. Under cover of early darkness, as press thin out, murder suspect leaves house by back door and walks around block to approach door of neighbor with whom she has recently had relatively civilized conversation after death of said neighbor's wife. Murder suspect lifts brass ring, knocks on door. Neighbor takes a while but eventually opens it and stares at her in disbelief, frown lines between eyes. Murder suspect, already on defensive, starts to speak. Starts to gabble really.

She wonders whether her neighbor might spare her a few minutes, she's trying to throw some light on the deaths of her former lover and the neighbor's wife. Neighbor, more lionlike than ever, eyes narrowed, jaw dropping, draws his head back as if to launch a bite at this irritating creature.

"I don't like to be rude but you have to be kidding," he says. "If you'll excuse me."

And neighbor shuts the door on neighbor.

───────

I have read what Paula Carmichael wrote about suicide. It's not a note. It is an entry in her diary, dated for the day of her death. Now it has been transferred from that diary to the newspaper. Intensely private, it sits uncomfortably next to an ad for exercise equipment. Underneath it, in a desperate attempt to justify publication, is an article by the newspaper's resident doctor, advising of the symptoms of depression and suggesting a visit to the doctor if the reader recognizes them in him or herself. There is, the doctor suggests cheerfully, a solution to everything. But Prozac was surely an inadequate response to Paula Carmichael's anguish.

If only there was solace in sleep I could carry on, but I wake in the middle of the night brooding before I am even conscious of being conscious. My joints ache with guilt, my brain scrabbles around looking for meaning. Finding none it becomes crazed. It starts to hurl itself against the bars. Logical thought, perspective, all these things are now foreign to me. I am stripped and ugly, I am bloated, heavy with the weight of all that I have not done, all that I should have done. I have no one to show this ugliness to, no one to lift it from me. Mortality and black shadows approach, I cannot lift a hand to stop them.

I read it every which way for meaning. That Paula Carmichael was not happy is clear, but to be overwhelmed by the approach of mortality, to be so weakened as to be unable to fight it off is surely not the same as embracing death. To jump off a balcony is to mobilize your muscles to push off, to launch yourself into space and rush toward your own death. I remain unconvinced that this diary entry is a suicide note.

———

After Norma's attempt to kidnap William my mother has abandoned her aloofness. She is back beside me, fighting shoulder to shoulder. She tries to get Finney to make a public statement to the effect that there is no evidence that I am responsible for the death of Adam, but we all know he can't prove a negative. I know she will not win this battle and I suspect that any such statement might backfire on him and me. Finney shakes his head. He can't, he won't do it. I am not surprised. What does surprise me is that there is an apology in his eyes. He would have liked to help me out. All this is utterly intangible, my perception of a feeling glimpsed fleetingly in someone else's eyes, but it cheers me nevertheless. I must gather around me the people who believe in me, the people I can approach for help, or at least trust not to stab me in the back. I write a list of the people I love. It is short on quantity but long on quality.

———

My list did not include Erica. She would have been on another list altogether, but later on the Thursday of Norma's visit, when I was at my lowest, she called. She had spent the previous evening in the pub, she said, "And my friends told me I was perhaps insensitive, and they asked what are you like, and will you kill someone, and I said I do not know you well, but I do not think so." Then, moving right along from that smidgeon of doubt, she asked whether I had made alternative child-care arrangements. I had not, and it was driving me wild with frustration. As I saw it I had a choice. I could sit back and look after my children and leave Finney to sort things out—most likely he would get it right eventually—or I could go out there and try and sort it out for myself, in which case I had to be able to come and go at a moment's notice. I had to follow wherever this sorry mess led me, and I had above all to know the kids were safe. Norma's attempted abduction of William might have been halfhearted, but I had no way of knowing what was going through her grief-sickened mind. I had moved back to my own house. Now the press had my mother's staked out as well, there was no advantage in being house guests any longer.

I hadn't had the heart to ask my overworked mother to be my babysitter as well as my lawyer. Tanya and Patrick had kids and troubles of their own, and Lorna was hardly up to playing at bodyguard. I had called a nanny agency, but once the woman on the other end of the phone had asked my name and inquired about my requirements it hadn't taken long for her to put two and two together. When I had mentioned that the nanny might possibly also be required to foil a kidnapping she had cut me off and said stiffly that theirs was not the agency for me. All of which seemed to leave me with only one option and that was to leave Finney to get on with it. I just couldn't do that.

"Because you know," Erica was saying, "I like your children very much, they are so sweet, and if you like I will come back."

I leapt at it. It would cost me a fortune, but I was back on the Corporation payroll, even if I was on enforced leave. I couldn't stand Erica, but the children seemed to tolerate her and I knew she would take good care of them. Perhaps more important, right now, was that mention on her CV of her martial arts training. A high kick to the shoulder and Norma would cease to be a problem. I only wished I could be the one to administer it. All in all Erica was the answer to my prayers. Even when she asked smoothly for time and a half, "because, you know, I am afraid of the stress," I didn't blink an eye. I welcomed her back with open arms. She would start that evening, so that I could go and meet Jane.

"You look like hell," Jane greeted me. She had the sense to speak in a low voice. This was a public place, and the last thing I wanted was to draw attention to myself. Even when I'd left the house, just after dark, there had still been one dogged cameraman outside. Soon they would get wise to my back-door escape route. I'd rung a local firm to hire a car. With mine in the care of the police, I didn't want to have to expose myself to the gaze of strangers on the tube or on buses.

Jane unwrapped a long striped scarf and took off her coat, draping them both over the back of her chair. She frowned at the speaker that hung over our table dispensing a particularly frenetic school of jazz.

"Isn't there anywhere quieter?"

I shook my head. The music system had been playing Handel when I got there. It had seemed like a quiet little bistro, perfectly empty, but there's probably no such thing on Aldwych. In the twenty minutes I'd been waiting for Jane the place had filled up with people fresh and noisy from work. I'd turned up the collar of my jacket and buried my head in the menu, but already I was feeling the eyes of other people on me.

We each ordered a glass of white wine, but when it arrived I couldn't bear the sour taste in my dry mouth. I asked for a jug of water, but the waiter pretended not to understand. I ordered an Evian, but that didn't come either. After a few moments I looked around for the waiter but he was flitting from table to table at the other side of the room, looking increasingly fraught.

"They're busy," Jane commented.

"I can see that," I snapped, then apologized. "I'm sorry, I just really don't want to be here."

"Then let's not be," Jane said. She got some money from her bag and laid it on the table to pay for the wine. We pulled coats and scarves back on and stepped out into fresh air and what seemed like silence. We didn't talk for a long time, just walked, following our noses down Surrey Street and toward the river. We passed a late-night deli, and Jane stopped.

"I'm ravenous," she said. I followed her in. I didn't want to eat anything but she ordered me a toasted BLT and a chamomile tea anyway.

"You have to eat, girl, or you'll be no good to anyone," she said. I took the brown paper bag reluctantly and we continued toward the Thames. It was much too cold to be out in the evening, but we found ourselves a bench under a streetlight and sipped at our hot tea. A man on a neighboring bench eyed us dolefully. He was wrapped in cardboard and newspaper against the night air and our conversation seemed to be disturbing him, so we dropped our voices.

"You do know I didn't do it, don't you?" Jane was at the top of my People I Trust list, and I needed her to stay there.

Her hesitation was minuscule but it was there, and when she spoke it was not what I wanted to hear.

"I need to know about the will," she said. "That's what looks the worst. How on earth could you forget something like that?"

For a few moments I couldn't speak and she didn't hurry me. I think she knew what was going through my head. I'd needed unqualified loyalty and she couldn't give it.

"Every instinct I have tells me you didn't do this," she said, looking out over the dark water. "I'd trust you with my own life, but I have a brain that's asking me these wee questions, and I can't just shut it up. All I'm asking for is an explanation."

"I shouldn't need to explain myself when I've done nothing wrong." My voice was gruff with anger. The silence stretched between us, and after a few moments I calmed down a bit and made myself imagine that it was the other way around, that she was a murder suspect and I was her friend. I supposed that I would have questions too.

"You remember," I said, "when Adam made that program *Front Line?*"

"Afghanistan."

"Afghanistan. About humanitarian workers who risk their lives in war zones."

"That was when you found out you were pregnant."

I shook my head. "That was when I told you I was pregnant. I found out a week before he went, and for that week he was the happiest man in the world. Except that he was off to Afghanistan, and it really spooked him. He kept saying what would we do without him if he was killed, should he call it off, and I said don't be silly you're going to be fine. Anyway, he told me he'd contacted his solicitor and he was making a will, and I just laughed at him. I don't know why I was so blasé, plenty of journalists did get killed, it must have been something to do with my hormones. And his insistence that he had to support us, that he was going to be the breadwinner, that just annoyed me. Then, the day before he left, he told me if anything happened to him I'd find a copy of his will in the desk. I didn't even take him seriously, I was just rolling my eyes and saying 'Yeah, yeah, you'll be fine.' I never gave it another thought. I never saw it in the desk. It must have been pretty well tucked away."

"But the police found it in your papers."

I shrugged. "When I left I just grabbed all the papers from the desk—it was mainly my stuff in there, he didn't really use it—and threw it all in a box. I didn't look at it then, and I've had no reason to touch it since, not 'til Finney took it all. Anyway, they'd have got it sooner or later. His solicitor must have it."

"You've told all this to the police."

"Several times."

"And they don't believe you? It sounds entirely plausible to me."

"You're a sympathetic audience. Finney's not. To him it just sounds like a plausible lie."

We were silent for a few moments, watching the patterns on the water, the constant hum of traffic like white noise.

"How do you feel now that he's gone?"

I shook my head. "I can't understand it. I feel bereft. He left a year ago, I've been fine without him, and suddenly wham, he's dead and it hits me between the eyes as though he'd never gone."

"Most of the world is assuming you're glad he's dead."

"And here I am with a broken heart."

Jane put her arm around me and I lowered my head to her shoulder and let it rest there for a moment, then forced a laugh and rubbed my eyes.

"I'm freezing my butt off here," I said. "Let's find a pub."

"What you're feeling," she said as we strode toward the Lion's Crown, "maybe it's because you never had a chance to grieve when he left. You were too busy with the children."

"Maybe," I said.

The fresh-from-the-office crowd had largely departed for the commute to bed, and we found a place next to the fire. I went to the bar and got Jane a glass of red wine and myself a whiskey. I wanted something clean and strong and straightforward. Something that burnt a little as it went down.

"I'm going to need your help," I told her when I returned with the drinks. She'd taken off her coat now and I did the same.

She was looking at me as though I were mad.

"Who's this then? Robin Ballantyne, ace detective?"

I refused to smile. "I'm in trouble, Jane."

"I know. But—"

"I get in any deeper and they're going to start talking about taking the children away."

Jane shook her head and wouldn't look at me, but she didn't say anything. She didn't want to believe it. I didn't want to believe it myself, but Jane hadn't been there the night of Adam's murder when Mann went upstairs to check I hadn't killed my own children. Most murders are family affairs and some murderers, once they start, can't stop.

"I'll help if you think I can do anything," she said eventually. It was reluctant, but it was good enough.

"Okay. I think Adam's death is somehow linked with Paula Carmichael's," I told her. She started to interrupt, but I stopped her. "Just hear me out. It's too much of a coincidence. They knew each other, they'd worked together. If Finney's telling me the truth, the police aren't even looking at Carmichael's death anymore. If I can do anything the police can't, it's here. It's where Carmichael and Adam intersect, and that means the link is something professional."

I stopped and waited for Jane's objections, but she was just looking at me, her head slightly on one side.

"Suzette doesn't know anything about a friendship between them," I went on, "so maybe whatever happened between them only happened after the documentary was canned."

"Maybe they hated each other's guts," Jane suggested. "Maybe Adam killed Paula. Did you think of that?"

I stared at her.

"I'm not sure I can think of that," I said slowly.

"Some investigator you are," Jane grumbled. "But if you insist, for argument's sake, let's say they loved each other."

Silently we considered the implications of this.

"I'll talk to Ray," she said.

"I keep leaving messages for him, but he never calls me back."

Raymond McLean was covering Adam's murder for the Corporation. He had good contacts in the police and we used to be friends, but it seemed that counted for nothing now.

"I'm going to tackle Maeve and Terry and try to do some digging into the background of the documentary," I told her. She nodded, sipping her drink, and I nodded back. We had a plan of action. Of sorts. It was progress.

Chapter 18

I threw myself on Maeve's mercy. I was counting on the fact that she had none, and I was not disappointed.

"No can do," she said lifting her perfectly manicured hands up in an elegant gesture of refusal. "Of course if it was up to me you'd have your job back right away . . . but it's not."

"Maeve, I had to fight through a mob of cameramen to get here this morning, including someone from the Corporation. How do you think that makes me feel? You saw the op-ed piece this morning calling for my arrest." I quoted it from memory, " 'Ballantyne's suspension from the Corporation is a clear withdrawal of their support for her. What do they know that the police do not?' Is that what you want, Maeve? You want the Corporation to give me the thumbs-down?"

Maeve shook her head and her helmet of dark hair scarcely moved. I sensed that her position had become more entrenched since the last time I spoke to her. I knew, although I did not want to acknowledge it, that as the evidence mounted against me those who had sat on the fence previously were now settling on one side or the other, and Maeve was on the other. I guessed most of the Corporation management were with her. I was too hot to handle, I'd let the side down, I was no longer Corporation material. All these things I could hear echoing around a conference room, but whether this meant Maeve believed I had killed Adam was strangely hard to say. She had greeted me civilly, but with no warmth. It could have been punishment for being a murderess or simply for causing Maeve a bureaucratic headache. There was no fear in her eyes, but nor was there any friendship, even the paper-thin friendship she so specialized in.

"If you were making the tea, or filing, we might manage it," she said, "but what we need from an EGIE is a stainless reputation for moral integrity. And," she soldiered on over my objections, "you'd be dealing with highly sensitive information, and you'd be under great stress. The answer is a simple no, you cannot return to work."

I sighed a great breath of frustration that was no act. I'd expected it, but the injustice of my situation still burned like acid.

"Okay then. Look, I can't sit at home all day. I'll do anything, I'll do what you said, I'll make the tea. At least it would show you trusted me not to poison you all."

Maeve told me that no, I could not make the tea either. So I settled into my chair and suggested a couple of other menial jobs that I knew she'd say no to. All I wanted was to wear her down, and sure enough, after a few minutes of discussion about potential openings for lavatory attendants, she tried to throw me out.

"Look, Robin," she said, glancing at her watch, "I've got another meeting in a few minutes and this is really getting you nowhere."

"Is Terry going to be there?" I asked.

She nodded warily, although I was pretty sure she was making the meeting up.

"Well, I'll tag along if that's all right. I need to speak to him."

She lowered her forehead into her palm and rubbed. "Robin—"

I interrupted her.

"Maeve, you've put me back on the payroll, but you never issued me with a new pass to the building," I complained. "I have to sign in like a guest. It looks like you've fired me, as if you're frightened to let me in. At least let me come and sit in the library and do some research, let me tell the press I'm working on a proposal, show them I'm planning on a future here and not in some women's prison. Then I'll stay out of your hair. I promise."

Maeve gazed at me for a moment, then she heaved a sigh.

She swiveled her chair and tapped something out on her keyboard, then printed it out, read it through, signed it, and handed it to me. In my hand I held a signed instruction to the personnel department to issue me a Corporation pass.

"Thank you," I said, without a smile. This was all I had wanted.

"It's the least I can do," Maeve said drily. Which was true.

———

I went to find Terry. He'd been reduced, in the last redesign, to a large Perspex cubicle, like a fish tank in the middle of the newsroom. It was supposed to be a model of soundproofed transparency, but most staff had simply brushed up their lip-reading skills. It was an evolutionary thing, like growing longer thumbs to play video games. Terry's eyes were constantly flitting beyond me, watching passers-by watching him.

"You're missing a meeting with Maeve," I told him.

"I am?" he said. He pulled a Palm from his pocket and poked at it for a minute before hissing at it, throwing it down, and thumbing anxiously through a desk diary. "I don't think . . . no . . . no, not 'til Monday."

He slumped back in his chair, his potbelly sticking out. I hadn't seen Terry since the night of the award ceremony. He was sweating slightly. Despite the cold outside, the building was hot and his little greenhouse was hotter.

"Robin, Robin, Robin, what are we going to do with you? This is a fine mess you've got yourself into."

The nervous banter irritated me, and the underlying accusation irritated me more.

"Someone else got me into this," I said bluntly, sitting myself down opposite him. He pushed his chair backward as if to retreat from me. "Someone stole my car to run Adam over then rang the police to tip them off. Someone's framing me."

Terry's eyebrows rose a little, but his eyes avoided mine.

"Whatever you say, my dear. I wouldn't like to be the one to upset you."

I stared at him, but his face was still turned away from me. He seemed to be looking at his left shoe, a rather fancy wingtip. If I wasn't mistaken he was sufficiently unnerved by Adam's death, and my alleged part in it, that he could no longer look me in the eye. Terry was high on my list of people to be trusted, but it looked distinctly as though he'd have to be struck off.

"Has Finney been to see you?" I asked.

"Finney?" He shook his head in genuine confusion.

"The police."

"Ah. Yes. A young black girl took a statement from me, about my phone call, you know."

"Of course." I had known that they would check telephone records to my house—they had my full permission to do so, among a thousand other invasions of my privacy—but still it made my skin crawl. "What did you say?"

"Well," Terry puffed, "that you had cut me off saying you were in the middle of some crisis. That you were clearly distraught." Terry glanced upward and caught sight of my face. "What am I supposed to say? That's what happened. I'm not about to perjure myself."

I had come here to ask him for information about the *Carmichaelite Mission* documentary, but I had lost my appetite for it.

"Well, I just dropped in to say hi." I stood up.

Terry looked sheepish. "Where are you off to now then? We could get a coffee."

In the light of our conversation the suggestion seemed ludicrous. "I don't think so." I pushed open the door so that his staff could hear my farewell. "I'm really glad I can count on your support," I said loudly, and forced myself to kiss him on his unwilling cheek. Then I turned and left him staring after me.

I found Suzette in the canteen. A wintry sun was shining through the high windows and casting great patches of bright light over the tables and chairs, most of which were empty. A group of kitchen staff chatted and laughed near the buffet. A panorama of London spread beyond the glass. Suzette had chosen a table as far away from the sun and from other people as possible. She was sitting alone, facing the wall and contemplating a plate of something green.

"Suze," I said, and she jumped at her name, twisting to see who had spoken and spilling liquid from the white teacup in her hand.

"Sorry." I grabbed a paper napkin and dabbed at the mess. "I didn't mean to give you a shock. What's the matter?" I caught sight of her ashen face, eyes swollen, and pulled up a chair opposite her. "Suze, you look worse than I do."

She gazed at me, then shook her head wordlessly. She hadn't touched her open sandwich. The lettuce was beginning to wilt and the ham was taking on a nasty sheen, and I wondered how long it and Suzette had been sitting there. I could see her struggling to pull herself together, and eventually she spoke.

"I rang you but you didn't ring back."

"I'm sorry, it's been a really bad time."

"I came in for a meeting with a commissioning editor, but . . ."

She shook her head, on the verge of breaking down. "Adam and I used to have lunch here sometimes. Christ, what a thing . . ." She attempted a watery smile.

I sat and stared at her. Something in her expression was like a lightning bolt in my head, suddenly illuminating the landscape of the past. I had introduced Suzette and Adam, and I knew they had worked together more than once. I knew they had liked each other. Now Suzette's face was telling me something more, almost as though she were willing me to know. Still, for a moment, I could not bring myself to say anything, and she too sat there silently, staring at the table. There was a sense, I think, that for either of us to take a step forward from that point would be to enter a mine-field, but eventually I could not resist asking the question.

"Were you and Adam seeing each other?"

She stared at me with huge sad eyes, but she took her time over answering, just sitting there, her hands in her lap clutching a screwed-up tissue.

"No one was supposed to know," she said at last. "I'm so sorry."

I felt as though she had slapped me—and as though Adam had risen from the dead to slap me too. We sat there for a moment, but there were more questions that had to be asked.

"When did it start?"

"When you split up," her voice was a whisper.

"So you mean, all the time you were dropping by to give me moral support," I couldn't help dwelling on those two words sarcastically, "you were with him?"

She nodded, tears overflowing onto her cheeks.

"I'm sorry," I had to lean in close to hear what she was saying, "he didn't really want me." She passed the tip of her tongue over dry lips. "He wanted news about you and about the children . . ."

I stared at Suzette and she started to sob softly, dabbing at her nose and her eyes with a paper napkin. "I felt so bad for you." Her voice kept breaking up. "I wanted Adam, but I could see what you were going through, and I wanted to be your friend too. I'm sorry."

I shook my head.

"Have you told the police about your relationship?" My voice was accusatory and Suzette jumped again.

"They haven't asked me."

"What did you do, communicate in code? They must realize he was seeing someone."

She shook her head for a long time before she could stop crying enough to speak. "We split up months ago, there's nothing the police need to know. It just, you know," she looked at me sideways, "fizzled."

I gazed at her waxen face. Fizzled wasn't a concept I associated with Adam. After a moment Suzette shrugged.

"We just got bored," she said.

I gazed some more and she shrugged again.

"There always was someone else with Adam, wasn't there?" Then she said, "I really want to know who did this."

I wanted to get this straight. "It was over. So when you invited me to work with you at Paradigm, you weren't going to work alongside me and then go home to Adam at night?"

Suzette wouldn't look at me, but she shook her head.

I sat and stared at her. I felt drained. Drained and hugely disappointed, and as though, if I had to lose another friend, I would disintegrate. At the same time something inside me was hardening. The earth beneath my feet was crumbling, but in some strange way I was finding my footing. This was not the time for forgiving and forgetting. Indeed that time might never come—I saw no particular reason why it should—but, whatever became of our friendship in the long run, in the short term I needed Suzette.

"I'm not going to tell you what I think of you right now," I said to her. Her eyes lifted, and I saw relief flit across her face. "But if you want to know who killed him, you have to help me. I think Adam's death has something to do with Paula Carmichael's."

That put a stop to the sniveling at least.

"Why do you say that?" She wiped her eyes.

I told her what I'd told Jane and managed to overcome her initial skepticism as I had with Jane too. By the time I'd related all the coincidences, she was listening carefully.

"Adam and I were together when we were working on the documentary," she said thoughtfully. "We spent our spare time together. I've already told you, as far as I'm aware he had nothing but a passing professional relationship with Paula."

I scowled. There had to be something.

"Is there any film from the documentary knocking around anywhere?"

"I don't really see how that could . . . I'd have to take a look, I don't know off the top of my head," she said eventually. "I don't understand what you're looking for."

"Anything that tells me anything. I'm clutching at straws here."

"Well," she said, "I can have a look . . ." Her voice trailed off and we sat in silence for a moment, Suzette scrutinizing my face.

"So this is some sort of investigation then," she said uncertainly.

I held up my hands, defending myself.

"I'm just trying to dig myself out of a hole," I said.

Suzette nodded.

"I can see why you would want to do that," she said.

The silence stretched between us. Suzette seemed much calmer now, but she was lost in her own thoughts, her eyelids heavy. The canteen was getting noisier as teatime neared and I didn't want to have to face my former colleagues. With Erica on a stopwatch I couldn't afford to hang around with Suzette, even if I'd wanted to, and frankly I didn't want to. Her morose state of mind depressed me, and her betrayal had left me angry and hurt. Right then I could not foresee any time that I would seek her out as a friend. Just as I was about to get to my feet and make my excuses my mobile started to ring in my pocket. It was my mother. She was with Lorna, in an ambulance, on her way to accident and emergency at St. Celia's. She would explain when I got there.

Chapter 19

ST. Celia's accident and emergency was a prefab shack next to the car park. Two nurses sat behind what might or might not have been—but probably should have been—bulletproof glass. They listened wearily to my pleas to be given access to my sister and assured me that they would try to find out where she was, if only I would just take a seat.

It took a while, during which a procession of mildly injured and sick-looking people arrived and joined the forlorn queue. Now and again someone would be ushered through a scuffed navy door into the inner sanctum of the hospital itself and a shudder of excitement would run through the room. I tried to track my mother down by calling her mobile, but she had switched it off.

Eventually I was summoned to the desk and informed that Lorna had been admitted. Was she all right, I wanted to know, but they couldn't tell me how she was, just where she was. I should exit the waiting room, turn left through the car park, left again at the main entrance, then follow the signs. I was almost crying with frustration by the time I was led through a ward to a curtained-off corner, and it was nothing less than a miracle when the blue drape was drawn back to reveal my mother and my sister.

"What happened?" I hugged my mother, then leaned over Lorna. Her red curls fanned out over the stark white of the pillow. There was a dressing on her forehead, her eyes were closed, and I could scarcely make out the rise and fall of her chest. I turned back in alarm to my mother, but she shook her head.

"She's sleeping," she said. "She'll be fine, they're keeping her in for observation because she lost consciousness."

"What happened?"

My mother looked haggard. "She fell down the stairs."

I frowned my incomprehension.

"Your father came to Lorna's flat," my mother said in a voice that shook with emotion. "I opened the door and saw him there, and I don't remember what I said, but Lorna must have heard and thought I was in trouble. She came to the top of the stairs and she tripped and fell."

I winced.

"She's broken two ribs and her right wrist," my mother recited, "and she hit her head on the edge of the radiator by the door. She's had stitches just above her eye. There was so much blood, I thought she was dead."

I stared down at Lorna's still face. Her normal state looked animated by comparison.

"What did he want?" I murmured, not expecting an answer. I turned away from Lorna and looked at my mother. "Did you shout at him or something? How did Lorna know anything was going on?"

"I don't know . . . I don't think I shouted." My mother sighed miserably.

"I'm not blaming you," I reassured her. "I'm just trying to understand how it happened."

She nodded. "I know. I suppose I must have raised my voice. I told him to go away. I think he was trying to tell me that he wanted to see Lorna. I suppose he raised his voice too. I told him Lorna didn't want to see him."

"What did he say to that?"

"Oh . . . 'You're wrong,' something like that."

"Could Lorna have seen who was at the door?"

"I doubt it. I was trying to push the door closed."

"But she'd have heard the sound of his voice."

"Well, it wouldn't have meant anything to her," my mother said. "She hasn't heard his voice for thirty years. She hasn't seen him either, come to that."

I gazed at my sister. Lids lowered, lips pressed shut, she was the ultimate in inscrutability, but then she had been pretty inscrutable for years. Even before CFS hit there were always areas of her life that she refused to share, despite her enormous enjoyment of conversation and friendship. Maybe my stressed-out head was imagining things, but it seemed to me that Lorna's panicked reaction to the man at the door and his confrontation with Ma indicated that she knew exactly who was there.

"What did he do when she fell?"

"We were both . . . distraught because Lorna wouldn't come round. He asked me where the telephone was, and he called for an ambulance. Then I told him to go, and not to come back."

We both sat and contemplated Lorna, my mother in the regulation visitor's chair, one hand resting on her injured daughter's hand. I had propped myself uncomfortably against the edge of the bed. Through the window I could see the power station. I was too wired to sit playing guardian angel for long.

"I'll get you a cup of coffee," I told my mother, and slipped out between the curtains.

A nurse pointed me past the reception desk into a bleak corridor, then I followed a sign toward a cafeteria. Better that, I thought, than prefabricated coffee from a machine. The cafeteria was closed, but I spied a vending machine a few yards beyond in the lobby. A gray-haired man in a raincoat was standing there feeding coins into the machine, and instinct made me stop well back and watch. There was something about his face. Was my mind playing tricks? He glanced toward me, then past me. So he did not know me. Or did not think he knew me. I hung back. He turned and went to the information desk. I heard him ask to use the phone for an internal call and I saw the clerk jerk his thumb at it, and then get up and wander off. At which point I walked quickly to stand behind the man. He dialed the operator, and asked to be put through to the ward where my sister was. Then he spoke to a nurse.

"Could you let me know how Lorna Ballantyne is doing?" he asked. There was a pause while he listened. "My name is Gilbert Ballantyne, I'm her father." He replied to a question I could not hear.

I stepped smartly backward, repelled. All my distrust of this man was revived by what had happened to Lorna.

"I see, that's good, thank you," he said. "Would you kindly pass on my best wishes for her recovery?" His voice was a revelation. Even as I moved away from him, shreds of memory resurfaced, splinters of the past, dimmed voices, arguments, my mother in tears. They threatened to disable me. He replaced the handset and moved away, toward the exit. I stared after him for a moment and then, not conscious of having made a decision, I began to follow him.

I'd had no practice, of course. All I could do was follow as far behind as I dared and hope he didn't look around. The worst bit was through the echoing corridors of the hospital, then a residential street of terraces where we were the only two pedestrians. He must have been preoccupied. Preoccupied or deaf. Anyone else would have picked up on my footsteps, would have looked around anxiously, convinced they were not alone. For some reason my father did not.

He turned left along High Street toward the underground, and

I followed, relieved to be among the crowds of shoppers. I had been here before, pre-children, pre-Adam even, on a hot summer day. I remembered pausing to admire a cool white sari on a headless mannequin in a shop window, buying a mango from a fruit stall and sitting on the Common to eat it, its sticky pungent flesh making me thirstier still. Today, I kept my eyes fixed on that raincoat.

Once I thought I had lost him. I came to a halt and gazed around until I spotted him in a newsagent's. I waited for him to emerge. The shop was busy, there was a queue at the cash desk. I watched my father approach the newsstand, watched him bend, reach out, pick up a copy of the *Financial Times,* watched him slip the pink broadsheet inside his raincoat, turn unhurriedly, and head for the door. For an instant, after he stepped back onto the street, I stood rooted to the spot. I had just watched my father steal a newspaper, and at the very least I expected someone to shout after him, but he proceeded down the street unchallenged.

I followed him past the tube station, off to the right past Marks & Spencer's, then to the left, past a church and a betting shop. This was an area like mine, where the houses were surging in value as middle-aged blue-collar workers sold their homes for a quarter of a million pounds and moved farther out of town. Meanwhile, moneyed young things moved in and set about a flurry of home improvement, ripping out walls, sanding floorboards, and fitting power showers.

My father turned into number sixty-two, a crumbling terrace, its peeling woodwork surely an embarrassment to its freshly painted neighbors. He had a key, and vanished inside. I came to a halt outside the house. Coffee-colored lace curtains hung unevenly at the windows, obscuring any view I might have had of him. I hesitated for no more than a second. I had followed him this far, but why hadn't I simply gone up to him and confronted him? Because that, surely, was what I wanted.

I ran up the steps to the front door and pressed the doorbell, but I couldn't hear it ring. Instead I knocked, and after a few seconds the door was opened on a security chain. I could see a section of face, elderly and female.

"Who are you, what do you want?" she challenged me.

"I've come to visit Mr. Ballantyne."

"Who?" Her face creased even more, the skin hanging loose from deep wrinkles.

"Mr. Ballantyne. I saw him come in here a minute ago. Are you his wife?"

She hooted with laughter at that and, to my surprise, opened the door wider to reveal a bony, lopsided frame clad in shiny polyester pajamas. A smell of boiled cabbage and stale urine wafted out onto the air.

"There's no one here by the name of Ballantyne," she said, "and no husband either."

With the door open I could see that this was a boardinghouse. A yellowing sheet of instructions titled "Rules of the House," was stuck with tape to the nearest wall. The instructions—the last one was "Pull the Frigging Flush"—were handwritten in big, rounded letters and the paper was curling at the edges.

"The man who just came in here, wearing a raincoat, who is he?"

"None of your business, is it? My guests like their privacy, so if you'll excuse me . . ." She shut the door firmly in my face.

I knocked again, and tried the bell, but I couldn't be sure anyone heard. I walked up the street, then down, full of indecision. I glanced at my watch. I could lay siege to the house, I could wait for the man I thought was my father to come out, but my children were waiting for me at home and Erica was watching the clock. I started to walk back toward the hospital, where my mother and Lorna were waiting for me too. I couldn't even be sure that the man I'd followed was my father. I could have sworn I had seen him on the hospital telephone, and that I had heard him give his name. Perhaps I had lost him in the crowds and started to follow the wrong man. I tried to think back over our route, to identify how and when things might have gone wrong. I began to feel foolish and my pace quickened, away from the boardinghouse. It was possible, I realized, that I had followed a total stranger.

Chapter 20

ON Saturday, news from St. Celia's was encouraging. Lorna was feeling much better and was to be discharged. Tanya would pick her up when she went off duty. My mother had appointments to catch up on that afternoon, and groaned on the telephone to me that she hadn't prepared properly, and that she had indigestion.

"Why oh why," she wailed, "is hospital food so totally vile?"

It was such a commonplace complaint that it made me feel better, as though perhaps that day would be more commonplace than the ones that had preceded it.

I was more tired than ever. Hannah had reacted to my long absence the day before by staying awake all night to be with me, which was flattering but devastating. She had cried every time I put her down in her crib, and eventually fallen asleep with her warm tummy pressed against mine, pinning me to the bed. Now, the only thing keeping me going was my own hunch that Paula Carmichael's death and Adam's were somehow linked. But with exhaustion came self-doubt.

Jane rang.

"I interviewed the Colby woman this morning, you know, Paula Carmichael's deputy, and when we'd finished I told her what you think about Paula's death. She'd like to speak to you if you want to see her."

"I'm willing to speak to anyone who's willing to speak to me."

"She's read all about you. Says you intrigue her."

"Why, for God's sake?"

"Something to do with being a single mother of twins?"

"I always said it would come in useful one day. Lucky I didn't abort them, eh?"

There was silence from Jane, then her voice, embarrassed.

"Look, do you want my help or don't you?"

I apologized and thanked her, and she told me where to meet Colby, which was at a women's shelter in the north of the city, just off the Caledonian Road near King's Cross.

For the first time, there were no photographers outside my door. I thought their editors were probably disappointed that I had not yet been arrested. Or maybe something had happened to distract them. Leaving the house once Erica had arrived was easy, except that Hannah was upset, and that upset me. I found my way, through the traffic, to a four-story Georgian terrace in a crescent. There was no visible sign that this was a hostel. No nameplate, just a bell, which I rang. Only then did I notice the small closed-circuit camera above the doorway. I raised my face toward it and an instant later was buzzed in. Inside the doorway was a small antechamber and a second security gate, which was opened by a young woman with a blond crew cut who extended her hand and said, "Hi, Robin isn't it? Come on in."

If I had been listening to my usual complement of radio news, I would have known that Rachel Colby was Australian, but as it was I hadn't and I didn't. Rachel led me through a sitting room decorated in minimalist style with what I guessed were donated secondhand armchairs and a television set. One woman lolled, watching Oprah Winfrey, and another sat at a small table, writing what looked like a letter. They glanced up as we walked by, and I followed Rachel into a small office opposite a kitchen. She waved me to a chair while she stood and poured mugs of coffee from a pot. Somewhere Radio One was playing.

"I used to work here all the time. This was my baby, my project," she told me. "I set the whole thing up. I love it. Miss it like hell now I'm a bloody bureaucrat. I'm only here today because there's a dispute with the neighbors, and the women here are a little bit nervous. So if anything blows up today, if we get any media interest or anything, I'm the troubleshooter."

"The neighbors don't want you here?" I asked as I took the coffee from her.

"Well, they sort of do and then they don't," she answered with a grin. "They're all good tolerant liberals, and they're all very sympathetic to the Carmichaelite name, particularly at the moment, but we had a domestic two nights ago. An angry husband put a brick through the window. Wouldn't much matter if it was ours, it's happened before, it'll happen again, but he got the wrong house. He put it through a neighbor's window, into a room where the kid was sleeping. She wasn't hurt, but that's not the point, and then he followed it up with some colorful abuse and the threat of arson. Well, I wouldn't be too happy about that myself if I had kiddies upstairs in bed. It's a tricky one, and the ridiculous thing is that we may end up having to identify ourselves more clearly, so that if men do follow their women here, they at least attack the right house. You know, paint a nice big bull's-eye on the window or something."

She grinned, and I knew at once not only that she would solve this particularly knotty problem without a bull's-eye, but that she'd solve many more. She was young, and energy and confidence and competence breezed out of her.

"Jane said you have twins," I said.

"No way," she laughed. "Is that what she said? Ha! Me with twins, that'll be the day."

"Then why . . . ?"

"Why did I want to see you, when no one else will talk to you? Paula was obsessed with you, she told me all about you. You were this mythical figure in her eyes. She used to call you the reluctant earth mother. How could I not want to meet you?"

I smiled politely. The reluctant earth mother. How very charming.

"Doesn't the fact that I killed Adam Wills put you off?"

"You didn't kill him," she assured me. "It just doesn't fit and believe me, I know about these things. I'm an expert on murderous spouses."

She didn't seem inclined to elaborate and I didn't push her. I already knew I hadn't killed Adam. Besides, if she was going to detail her theory I'd rather she did it to Finney, not to me.

"You know Paula and I were never introduced," I said.

Rachel Colby grinned. "That was part of the charm. Paula always said it was like watching a lab experiment."

"Well, it is great, obviously, that she spied on me," I said, trying not to show my irritation, "and that I gave hours of pleasure. But why me?"

"She'd heard about you before she ever saw you," Rachel explained. "Adam poured out his soul to her one day, and she was immediately hooked and wanted to know what had become of you. Then she and Richard had to move, and the real estate agent took them to see this house, and she told Adam about it, and he said that was your street, and she told him the number and he said it was right opposite. Richard doesn't know it, but you're why they bought the house."

"She bought a house because of me?"

I was incredulous, and Rachel smiled at my expression, then her face became serious.

"I know it sounds spooky," she said, "but that's not how it was, it wasn't anything threatening. Richard wanted to buy it anyway, and he knew nothing about you. When I say she was obsessed by you, she never peered through your windows or anything like that. She just liked to keep a kind of motherly eye on how you were doing. It may have been a bit wacky . . ."

"Was it something to do with Adam?" I was having trouble finding Paula's fascination with me endearing. "Were they having an affair, was that why she wanted to watch me?"

"No," Rachel said, then reconsidered. "Well, I don't think they were. This whole thing with you, that wasn't about Adam. It was about Paula. There she was, hugely successful, achieving all the things she'd dreamed of, and helping lots of people into the bargain, just like she'd always wanted—but she hardly had a moment for her own kids. All the time she was traveling, or she was in Parliament, or she was giving speeches. And in those speeches she was telling other people to take better care not only of their own children, but of all the children in society, because they are our future, they are the world of tomorrow . . . but at the same time she was all chewed up with guilt over Kyle and George. I used to tell her: Look, they're teenagers, they don't want their mum hanging round their necks anyway. But she tortured herself—every time any little thing went wrong she said it was because she wasn't spending quality time with them. Watching you took her back to when Kyle and George were babies too, before she had to be everything to everyone, when she was just a young mother looking after her kids. Babies never have problems with drugs, or fall behind in class, or mix with the wrong kids. As far as I could make out, it was nostalgia that drew her to you. Nostalgia and regret. Great combination. Paradise lost." She paused and thought for a moment. "Nostalgia, regret, and Adam Wills would be an even more potent combination, I have to admit."

"You say they weren't having an affair, but they were close."

"They were really close." Rachel was as far from inscrutable as you could get. Everything she said was accompanied by an expression as readable as a book, open and direct.

"But they weren't lovers?"

"You have to understand, Paula was very depressed before she died, and Richard was no good at dealing with it. She was getting no support from him, and she was lurching around, trying every damned thing to get some satisfaction. As far as I know, she and Adam were never lovers, but they were very intense. Even I don't know what went on between them."

"Was Paula always depressed?"

"Well," Rachel paused to think. "She was always up and down, very volatile. Her ups were great, except that none of the rest of us could keep up with her, and her downs were miserable. But this last time was different. It came on quite suddenly, and it was . . ." She shook her head. "It was really distressing to watch for anyone who loved her. She just couldn't shift it. Suddenly she was disillusioned by the whole Carmichaelite thing. She even wanted to close everything down. I never really got a good reason from her . . ."

Rachel's voice trailed off. When she started to speak again her words were slower, more considered. "We did have a problem . . . This goes no further, is that agreed?" I nodded. "I mean you swear on Paula's grave?" I nodded again. "Because this has never reached the press. We had a problem with fraud. Thousands went missing. We never did find what happened to it. It seemed to be the thing that triggered the depression. I tried to tell her it was just a tiny bit of the picture, but she seemed to think it made the whole thing rotten and corrupt. It changed her whole attitude to everything we've achieved. I mean—and this also, on Paula's grave—by the time she died I'd been carrying the organization for months."

She heaved a sigh and sat back in her chair, giving me time to digest all this. I gazed at her, and she was the sort of person who didn't mind. She didn't avert her eyes, just sat there content to be inspected.

"Do you have any idea who took the money?"

Rachel shook her head.

"There was no obvious suspect. It was done by manipulating the accounts, which were all on computer, and a lot of people had access. Paula refused to involve the police. It was something we disagreed on, quite badly in fact. I said we had to make it public if we were going to maintain our integrity as an organization. She said the police would trample all over the private lives of our volunteers, and that we'd end up convicting some poor chap who just needed to pay his rent, and that we'd lose the goodwill of donors too. She said we'd conduct our own investigation, but she was busy with that documentary that never got shown and really there never was any investigation."

"Charity accounts have to be audited," I pointed out. "You can't just have thousands disappearing and cover it up."

"You can if Paula pays the cash back out of her own pocket," Rachel corrected me.

"Which is what happened?"

"Which is what happened, but you never heard it from me. Look, Paula would have gone to the end of the earth for all of this. Never mind good sense. She was all about instinct and inspiration and devotion and loyalty. She expected a lot from people, she expected them to do the right thing time after time after time. It really hurt her if they didn't. I mean it was like a physical pain. Don't get me wrong, I'm devastated that she's dead, but this Carmichaelite thing . . . well, ultimately Paula couldn't have kept it up. She was exhausted by it, drained. It's a wonderful thing, there's a real energy there, but it's not a fairy tale. There are thousands of people involved now, each with their own agenda, and just because it's charity doesn't mean people are nice together. Now

Paula was a great leader, but she was no good with factional fighting, and cliques, and egos that belong to people other than herself.
She could have motivated a sloth, and she wanted people to take
the initiative, that's what it was all about, but she just got irritated
when people started arguing, and let me tell you that six months
from now that's what every Carmichaelite in town will be doing.
The movement is just too big, too unfocused. You can't keep up a
feel-good factor like we've had."

"If you feel like that . . ."

"Oh, I'll defend it to the death . . . but realistically, if we're
going to keep any impetus going, we'll have to narrow the focus of
the movement, pull out of some projects, concentrate on others.
People are going to get hurt. It'll be very messy."

"You've given this a lot of thought," I said. "I mean what happens, post-Paula."

"I was thinking about it long before she died. We'd have got to
this point whether she was alive or not."

"But you've been telling the press that the movement is going
full speed ahead."

She shrugged.

"It's not a good time to announce a major restructuring," she
said. "And there's this huge surge of interest that Paula's death has
inspired. I'm not going to knock that on the head."

There was a tap at the door, and Rachel left the room. Her assessment of Paula's legacy was a sobering one, but I was not sure
that it got me very far. When she returned and told me she was
running out of time, I asked her about the Corporation documentary.

"Paula really didn't say much about it afterwards. She got very
tight-lipped any time I brought it up. I think she talked to Adam
a lot more. They didn't meet until they were working on the documentary, and it was only afterwards that they became bosom

buddies. Anyway, I got the impression she and the producer had a personality clash." Rachel pulled a face, and added, "These things happen."

"But not between you and Paula," I said.

Rachel smiled, and there were tears in her eyes.

"No, not between me and Paula."

"What about Richard? Do you see a lot of him?"

"Paula had compartments for things. It was how she got such a lot done. Anyway, Richard was one compartment, I was another. I knew what was going on with him, but only from her. He was watching her like a hawk at the end. He knew something was wrong and it scared him. He just didn't get that it would have been better to talk to her than to yell at her and listen in on her phone conversations."

"He did that?"

"Uh-huh." Rachel nodded. "Well, he wouldn't be the first husband to do it, but it didn't help when Paula was saying she felt claustrophobic, hemmed in, as though everyone was watching her, waiting for her to fail."

The doorbell rang, like an alarm in the tranquillity of the hostel. Rachel glanced at the CCTV monitor next to the desk and grimaced at me.

"Here comes our petition," she said. "It's showtime."

Chapter 21

MY route home was dogged by traffic jams. By the time I got there, and Erica delivered the children into my arms ready fed, bathed, and dressed for bed, I hated myself for things which were actually totally beyond my control.

"Was everything okay?" I asked

"Okay," Erica parroted. "Nobody came here, but there was a phone call. From someone who wishes you well."

"What was the name?"

Erica stared at me.

"Somebody who wishes you—" she started.

I interrupted her. I guess I was a little brusque, but all I wanted was to kiss my babies and cuddle them before they fell asleep. "Yes, I got that," I snapped, "but that's not a name."

Erica gave me a look that said I was being unreasonable.

"No name," she said, "but someone who knows you, someone who has visited here because they know where you live."

What was this? Twenty questions? I rolled my eyes at the ceiling. I know I shouldn't have done that. She'd been taking care of my children, freeing me to do what I needed to do. I couldn't have done it without her, but why couldn't she just take a message?

"They say you are doing too much." She said it as if she was scolding me.

I shrugged. Kind, but I wished people would keep their noses out of my business.

Just then the doorbell rang. I would have ignored it but Erica was standing right there, pulling her coat on, and she just went ahead and opened it—without looking through the spyhole first, I noticed. Perhaps a day without the press camped outside had made us all relax.

"Hello there," said Dan Stein, on my doorstep, wearing a forced smile.

Erica stared at him.

My face must have been blank. The poor thing had to fill the silence.

"We had a date?" he said, "Saturday, at eight? Well this is Saturday at eight, and we have a reservation at Padua . . ."

"Oh shit!" I said.

Erica turned to look at me, her face shocked. I saw Dan's face redden.

"I'm sorry," I said. "I didn't mean it like that. Shit. What am I going to do?" I had assumed our date had gone down the drain along with my reputation, but here he was and I didn't have the heart to turn him away.

"Look, just say if you don't want . . ." He was fed up now and who could blame him?

I hesitated, torn. I had been repeatedly rude to Dan, and he had been patient and he had been kind to the children. I had no desire to go out, and not the slightest interest in a date, but he had been sweet and he didn't deserve to be stood up. Reservations at Padua are not to be sneezed at.

"What time's the reservation for?"

"Eight-thirty."

"Do I have time to put the children to bed first? It'll take me fifteen minutes to get them to sleep, then five minutes to change?

Can you ring them, tell them we'll be a few minutes late?" I turned to Erica. "Erica, could you possibly stay?"

"You're going out now?" She was disapproving. "You did not tell me."

"I'd forgotten." I nodded toward Dan, hoping she'd take pity on his face, but her eyes moved toward him and still she did not budge. "Look, Erica, I'm really sorry. I can offer you double time, it's the best I can do. The kids will be asleep."

Erica looked from him to me, and back again.

"I don't have any choice," she grumbled, "or the children will be left alone."

I opened my mouth to protest, then shut it again when I caught Dan's eye. It wasn't the time to argue. If she had to grumble that was fine.

———

Padua was a fifteen-minute walk away. I apologized about ten times for my absentmindedness and then couldn't think of anything else to say. Making small talk seemed ridiculous when what I wanted to say was what eventually burst out of me.

"Didn't your mother tell you it was a bad idea to date a murderess?"

Dan came to a halt and faced me. Of course, if I'd given it half a thought I wouldn't have put it that way.

"My mother?" he said, clearly irritated. "How old do you think I am?"

I gazed at his face. He had gray eyes and the sort of male beauty that has cheekbones and a jaw. His crew-cut hair emphasized the lines of his face. He looked a little like Adam, or rather like Adam when I first met him. I felt awfully old.

"Well?"

"I don't know," I fished for something a tad more diplomatic than I'd managed so far. "Thirty?" I suggested, adding a good half-decade to my mental estimate.

"I'm twenty-seven," he said. "What about you?"

"Thirty-five. And a half."

For a moment he said nothing.

"Wow, that's older than I thought," he said seriously. There was a moment's silence and then we both burst out laughing. But he must have known, I thought a moment later, because every detail of my life had been in the papers in the past week. Then I pushed the thought from me. I was becoming paranoid.

We laughed a lot after that. Perhaps I was just near breaking point, hovering on the rim of hysteria, but even in the best of times I think I would have found him an amusing companion. When I caught sight of myself in the mirror, a broad grin on my face, head back, I realized I hadn't laughed since before Adam died. The thought sobered me, but it was Paula's death to which we returned.

"I still think about those voices," I said as the coffee arrived. "It was a hell of a row, really vicious."

"They've split up now," he said. "The husband's moved out, and the wife and daughter are there."

"Did they know Paula Carmichael?"

Dan looked at me as though I was mad.

"Should they?" he asked. I shook my head. No reason, except that my head seemed intent on linking things together, creating a world where people talked to each other in the street, chatted over the fence, knocked on each other's doors for cups of sugar. Our world was patently not this world, it was central London, and yet I could not shake the sense that we were all connected in ways we could not fathom.

"You know," I confided, "I thought I heard voices later too, just before Paula Carmichael's fall. Did they bother to even ask you about that, or do they think I'm making it up?"

Dan shrugged. "I told D.C. Mann I was on the phone for the half hour before you got there. She didn't mention voices."

Half an hour. Much more than a manly grunt, then. I didn't dare to bring his mother into it again. A sister, perhaps, or a girlfriend. Most likely a girlfriend. I thought that probably I did not care.

"D.C. Mann came back a few days ago." Dan was running his fingers up and down the stem of his wineglass. "She asked me about the night of Adam Wills's death. I told her that you were at home when I called around."

He paused to take a sip of wine.

"And?"

"And nothing. I said that you didn't look to me like a woman who'd just committed a murder."

"Quite right."

He held my eyes.

"It's the only reason I'm here," he said, reaching out his hand briefly to touch mine, then pulling back because of something he saw in my face. "You looked kind of unhappy, and very tired, knackered actually, but you were totally calm. I don't think," he was shaking his head now, as if he was trying to convince me of my own innocence, "that someone who's just spattered someone all over their windscreen would look so at ease."

I tried to smile in grateful thanks for the support, but the bloody imagery defeated me and made me feel slightly nauseated. Let him believe what he wanted. Like Rachel Colby he had persuaded himself that I was not a murderer. For which, mentally, I thanked him. Of course I was pleased that I was not universally condemned, but frankly I was far from convinced by their logic. To Rachel I was not a murderer because I did not fit her pattern of the woman who killed her man: I had not endured years of abuse, the drip by drip erosion of my sanity. But Rachel could not know that I had felt fury. There had been days when, if Adam had walked through my door, I would have struck out at him with little thought as to what was in my hand. As for Dan, he had declared me murder-free because he couldn't conceive that someone would look calm after a crime of passion. But if you have been provoked to rage or indeed to frustrated passion, surely wiping out the source of that agitation would calm you right down.

"Besides, I could scarcely have made it back home by seven-fifteen from the Oval if I killed Adam at six forty-five," I pointed out.

"You'd have had to put your skates on," Dan said, "but I think it's doable. Anyway, I thought when he was killed it was nearer six-thirty."

"You've got inside knowledge have you?" I was feeling suddenly tired, and I know I sounded irritable.

Dan looked at me a little oddly.

"I'm just making conversation," he said.

I nodded. My head felt heavy, as though I could barely lift it. Dan had ordered a bottle of Prosecco, and my mouth tasted sour.

"I have to go home," I said. Dan raised his hand for the bill.

"You don't have to do that," I said wearily, as he got out his credit card: American Express.

"It's okay, it all goes on my mother's account," he said.

I frowned.

"Joke," he said, signed the chit with a flourish and followed me out of the restaurant. On the street outside, the cold leeched its way to my flesh. Dan took my hand, threading my arm through his. It made me feel slightly uncomfortable, but I told myself that I was just out of practice.

We reached his house before mine.

"Come in?" he asked. "See how the other half lives?"

I shook my head, disentangling my arm from his.

"Your children are asleep and your babysitter's on double time," he said. "You think she wants you back any time soon? Have a drink, that's all."

I looked at my watch. It was just before ten, and although I was exhausted, I was enjoying the freedom of an evening out.

"Just for a minute," I said.

As I stepped into the lobby I remembered that door swinging open before, Dan standing there in his coat, ready to go out. I remembered him listening to my phone call, heading out into the storm. It seemed a lifetime ago. Inside that lobby, now denuded of its antique table, we went through the door marked "A," and up the stairs to the second-floor flat. I wished that he'd been on the ground floor. It was altogether too suggestive to be following him upstairs. His home, when we entered it, was clean, ordered, uncluttered. Men, I find, fall either into the clinical or the crappy school of housekeeping and he was definitely the former. The sitting room was unremarkably furnished from IKEA, but on the walls hung framed architectural photographs, each one a work of art. Capturing stone and brick on film should of course be easy. It doesn't, after all, move. Yet the buildings in these black-and-white prints seemed to be alive.

"You're a photographer," I said, delighted, walking up close and moving from one print to another.

Dan shook his head. "I'm in personnel, I told you."

"And a traveler." I'd passed London and Chicago and reached a photo of the Potala Palace hanging next to a street scene in Jaipur.

Dan nodded. "Footloose and fancy free," he said. I realized then that we'd scarcely spoken about him in our whole evening out, but I remembered talking a lot about myself.

"No people," I commented, nodding my head at a print of Angkor Wat. "It's all bricks and mortar."

"Plenty of people," he countered, "I just don't hang them on the walls."

I followed Dan to the kitchen, just to be nosy, but my legs could barely support me I was so tired, and the kitchen was standard kitchen, so I retreated to the sofa. It was the best sort of sofa, chosen for sinkability rather than fashion. Its cushions engulfed me, and when I laid my head back, my eyes automatically closed. I heard the clatter of coffeepot and cups. I heard Dan come into the room and chuckle as he saw me, almost comatose.

"You need a head massage," he said lightly. Still half asleep, I shook my head. When I felt his fingers in my hair I sat forward abruptly, hunching over, rubbing my eyes. Dan was standing behind me, and he reached out and took me by the shoulders, pulling me back. Again I pulled forward.

"I've got to go." I stood, impelled by a premonition, sure that somehow things were going wrong.

"What?" He was indignant.

"I have to go home."

He watched me as I pulled my coat back on. "What's wrong?"

"I have to go home," I said more insistently now, embarrassed that I had let him get so close, angry for some unfathomable reason at both him and at myself.

"They can do without you for an hour." He was smiling and pleading all at once. "They're fast asleep. But I'm wide awake, and I'm not sure I can do without you."

"I'm not in the market for . . . a date," I tried to explain, reaching for my bag.

"Well, why the hell not?" He was irritated and laughing. "You're not fifteen, you're allowed out on your own."

"You're right, I'm not fifteen," I clutched at that, "I'm thirty-five, all grown up, too old for this."

He shook his head, still grinning, but he put his hands up in a gesture of defeat.

"They have names for girls like you," he murmured as I turned for the door.

Startled, I turned to look back at him, and he must have seen from my face that I was offended.

"Sorry, I'm sorry." He wasn't grinning anymore now. "I'm just, you know . . . sorry, that was a stupid thing . . . it was a bad joke . . ."

"Let's be clear," I said, looking him in the eye and speaking softly, "that was *not* coitus interruptus."

"No, of course not." The smile was back, sly now. "I have that to look forward to."

"In your dreams," I muttered and I heard him laugh behind me.

I ran down the stairs two at a time, flung open the door to the street. And there was my premonition: a siren, unremarked by my conscious mind, a siren that belonged to the police patrol car parked outside my house. As I moved toward my home, another car pulled up behind it and Finney emerged.

Chapter 22

HOW I FOUGHT OFF A KIDNAPPER
Martial arts expert Erica Schlim talks to Bill Tanning exclusively about her life as nanny to the children of murdered newsman Adam Wills, and reveals how she saved them from a shocking kidnapping attempt while their mother was out on a hot date.

Blond and bubbly Erica, 23, has revealed the dramatic goings-on in the house where the children of murdered newsman Adam Wills live with their mother, Wills's former lover, Robin Ballantyne, 35.

Just last night, Erica reveals, there was a shocking attempt to kidnap the year-old twins, Hannah and William, while Ballantyne was out on a hot date. It was only foiled when Erica, like a lioness guarding her cubs, used her judo skills to bring the kidnapper literally to his knees.

The first suspicious incident happened in the afternoon, when Erica answered the phone. "I couldn't tell if it was a man or a woman, it sounded as though whoever it was had a heavy cold," she said. "They didn't ask for Robin, just asked me to take a message. I didn't have a pen and paper to hand, so I just memorized it. They said tell Robin she's going too

far. That's all."

far. If she doesn't stop, we know where she lives. We know where the children are. Tell her this is a well-wisher."

Later, when Robin Ballantyne came in, it was only for a few minutes, and when Erica tried to tell her about the phone call, Ballantyne dismissed it and said she was going out on a date.

"I wasn't planning on babysitting," Erica told us, "but who else would have looked after the children while Robin went out with Dan, her boyfriend? She told me she was going to a restaurant with him, but later I found out she had gone back to his place. When she eventually turned up, after it was all over, she looked as though she had just got out of bed. Her hair was all over the place."

The man Erica describes as Ballantyne's boyfriend has been questioned by police, and it is believed that he has provided an alibi for Ballantyne for part of the evening of Adam Wills's death.

Erica described how, just after ten o'clock last night, a man arrived at the front door. Erica asked who he was. He pretended that he was the twins' grandfather, and that Robin had told him to wait inside for her. Once inside the house, he pushed Erica aside and walked toward the staircase that led to the children's bedroom. Erica told him to leave, but he ignored her, and she chased after him and tackled him on the landing at the top of the stairs, using her skills as a black belt judo fighter to bring him to his knees.

"I knew I had to protect the children at all costs. I used all the moves I've worked on," Erica said. "It was very satisfying to put them to use. Usually I just fight the instructor, and he yields, so he never gets hurt, but this man was soon very scared of me, and he fell down the stairs when I used the ko uchi gari on him. That's a sort of tripping throw where I use my foot to hook his out from under him. I think he hurt his arm when he fell, because he was holding his wrist when he left. He shouted that he would come back, and I was scared because I thought he might bring more people, and I could not fight them all. So I tried calling Robin's mobile, but it must have been switched off. Then I called the police, and they came very quickly. They looked for the man in the street, but he was already gone."

Ballantyne turned up just a few minutes later, still unaware how close her children had come to being abducted by a madman. "She looked stunned," said Erica, "but she didn't really thank me for what I'd done, which I find a bit hurtful, because if it wasn't for me, what would have become of her children? And I have a bruise on my leg where the man kicked me."

Erica came to London from Sweden last year to work as a nanny and to work with Britain's best judo instructors. She is the eldest of a large family and loves children, but her dream is to pursue her love of martial arts.

"The teaching here is excellent," she raves, "and when I'm fully qualified to teach judo, I'm going to give up being a nanny and do that instead."

Her judo instructor, Chaz Johns, a former national champion, describes her as "a natural." Erica's got "guts by the bucketload," he told us. "I'm not at all surprised she beat an attacker into submission."

The police confirmed that there was an incident at the Ballantyne household last night, but refused to give details, saying they were still investigating. Erica describes the would-be kidnapper as white, middle-aged, with blond hair, but very strong and tall. No one has yet been detained in connection with the incident. Robin Ballantyne could not be reached for comment.

"Robin is out a lot of the time with her social life, so I look after the children all the day and they really miss their mother," Erica told us. "They cry quite a lot. She's been difficult about money, employers often are. The house is cheap and many things are old [see pictures, right, of the children in their home, taken by Erica Schlim]. One day last week there was nothing to eat in the house, and she didn't give me any money for food. I just do the job for the children. Whatever she's like, the children deserve love and attention."

Robin Ballantyne has been suspended from work at the Corporation pending the outcome of the inquiry into her former lover's death. The attempted kidnapping is only the latest in a series of dramatic events to hit the Ballantyne household. Just two weeks ago, Paula Carmichael jumped from a window in a house opposite and died on the ground outside Miss Ballantyne's flat, where the former television producer found her body. In the past week, Ballantyne has been questioned repeatedly by police in connection with the murder of her former lover, Adam Wills. Ballantyne's car is believed to be the vehicle that killed Mr. Wills when he was crossing a street close to her home.

Chapter 23

Wᴴᴱɴ the rage at Erica's betrayal faded, it was my own guilt that remained with me. The responsibility for my children's safety resided only in me. Knowing that a threat existed, I had left them guarded only by the hired help. I had failed them.

I slept, but only to be tortured by nightmares. I dreamed that Adam and I made love, we slept in each other's arms, and then I awoke to find him lying dead and cold in a pool of blood next to me. I fled to the children's room, where I found more blood and tiny lifeless bodies, eyes staring open, rosebud mouths silenced and still. I seized their limp bodies and tried to thump life back into them, knowing I was too late, howling my despair . . . That was when I woke for real, heart pounding, terror searing through me. I switched on the light and lay on my back, staring at the ceiling, trying to shake the nightmare. But I had to get up and go to the children. They were there, of course, under their blankets, very solid, fast asleep, limbs flung wide, chests rising and falling, not a care in the world, not a pool of blood in sight. Still, I was badly shaken. I sat cross-legged on the floor in their room for a long time, leaning my back against the cool wall, just listening to them breathe. Gradually my own breathing slowed, my heartbeat returned to normal, but the fear didn't go. They were the best thing I had ever done. Now I had dreamed how it would feel to lose them, and even the presentiment was more than I could bear.

In the daylight, I reasoned with myself. The lives of my children had been precarious in my very womb. Twins are smaller, more likely to be premature, the weaker vulnerable to the needs of the stronger twin. Their birth, early but alive, was their first defiance of death, but death would dog them as it dogs us all: roads crossed in haste, planes boarded in bad weather, cigarettes smoked, chemicals inhaled or absorbed through their skin, disease, and sheer bad luck. After birth I could not, even with my constant physical presence, protect them against all that life threatened.

Erica's presence in our house was a sham. She had come back to work for us, I was now quite sure, simply to sell her story to the tabloids. She had brought a camera and she had photographed the children's tiny room, my unmade bed, our almost—but not entirely—empty food cupboards, my children while they were tired and crying. The newspaper had made a pinboard display of the lot of them. The attempted kidnapping, if such it had been, had been her opportunity. It was all so quick. I suspected that she had contacted the journalist, Bill Tanning, even before yesterday and negotiated a deal. She must have given him her story the moment she had finished giving her statement to the police, or it would not have made its way into the morning edition. She had not turned up the next morning and I had not even tried to contact her. I was too frightened of what I would do to her.

But the failings were mine. I had failed to understand her message about the threatening phone call and I had failed as a mother. I had seen it in everyone's eyes that night: Finney, my mother, D.C. Mann, the patrol officers who had turned up in answer to Erica's call. I had messed up.

"You know who it was, of course." Finney was sitting on my sofa. Against my better judgment, against every thread of logic in my head, I was pleased to see him. At first, when he turned up unannounced, I didn't know why he had come to see me or why he had greeted me with more civility than had become the norm between us. Then I saw that there was diplomacy at hand.

"He was who he said he was, Adam's father." It was obvious. Tall, white-haired rather than blond; elderly rather than middle-aged, and somewhat frail; former army, his fighting days long gone, rather overweight. But then if Erica had said that, her high kicks might have seemed a little overzealous. I thought Harold Wills could probably have been stopped with little more than a steady glare and a poke on the shoulder.

"It's Adam's funeral tomorrow," Finney said softly. "A man's allowed to go a little mad before he buries his son."

"Well he can't steal mine." My voice was thin with anger and I got to my feet and stood, looming over Finney where he sat. "And I expect you to charge him with attempted kidnapping."

"Maybe he just wanted to see them," he said, cajoling. "Try to put yourself in his shoes. He's never seen his grandchildren. His wife brings back tales of neglect and abuse. Tomorrow's his son's funeral."

"He lied his way into my home. You arrest him or I'll sue the police for harassment." My voice rose again.

Finney ran his tongue over his lips.

"Do you hear me?" I was shouting at him now.

"Of course I can hear you. Half the street can hear you."

I slumped back into the armchair, pushing my hair back from my face, irritated by its touch against my skin. Did I really want a grieving old man thrown into jail? What was happening to me? I sipped at a cup of cold coffee, but my hand was trembling. Finney was talking again and I tried to concentrate. I fixed my eyes on his.

"We've talked to Erica. She wanted to know whether you were angry with her. I said you were. Anyway, Erica didn't understand that phone call was threatening either, until she went into the *Chronicle* and sat down with Tanning, and he asked her to go through the day and tell him everything that happened. He's a worm but he's not stupid, so when he forced her to repeat exactly what had been said, or at least what she remembered, he realized the well-wisher was quite the opposite."

"You don't think Tanning was just being creative?"

"I've gone over it again with Erica and I think his interpretation was right, even if it wasn't word for word."

"I think a lot of the article was in Tanning's words," I said wearily. "Erica doesn't speak like that."

Finney nodded, then went on, "The thing is, I don't think Harold Wills made that phone call. He says he didn't, and it just doesn't make sense that he would. Adam's parents just want the children, why would they threaten you?"

"Of course he didn't make the phone call, it never occurred to me that he had," I snapped, then a thought struck me and I spoke slowly, "Unless they think threatening phone calls will convince a judge to remove the children to somewhere safer."

Finney shook his head.

"They're not up to plotting anything. The other son is here with them . . ."

"David."

"David. He's trying to hold things together, but they're both in a terrible state."

David. Adam's sweet little brother. All the talent, none of the confidence, constantly put down by his father. He'd escaped to a job that he loved and now he was recalled for death duty. I wondered how he was coping with this grief for the better-loved brother.

"You could have made the call yourself, of course." Finney was speaking quietly, and I almost missed it because my mind was on David.

"What?" I almost laughed, it was so absurd.

"You were out. You knew Erica would take a message. Threats to you make you look innocent."

I regarded him curiously, incapable of further anger.

"You don't really believe that, do you?"

His face was unreadable. He shrugged.

"Why would I kill him?" I asked dully.

"Why wouldn't you? He abandoned you with two small kids."

"So what? So I wasn't able to cope? It's a mess," I waved my hand around the sitting room. There were toys littered about, and a pile of laundry had found its way onto the coffee table. "But it wouldn't be any less of a mess with Adam here. You think he'd be tidying up?"

"You'd be less tired."

"I doubt it."

"He might at least give you financial support."

"I'm not an imbecile. I can work. We'd have got by anyway, whatever happens about Adam's will. I'm not pretending it wouldn't be great to be able to move somewhere else, but . . ." My voice trailed off.

"So you killed him because you're doing fine without him, and suddenly he's trying to elbow his way back into your lives." Finney's voice lacked all conviction, and I felt that we were playing no more than a game, a weary dutiful game.

"Make up your mind, Finney . . ." I looked across at him, and he shrugged as if to say, At least give me a comeback. "I didn't like the idea of him seeing the twins, but I was getting used to it. Anyway," I warmed to the subject, "you know what I really think? I think he wouldn't have stuck with it. We'd have seen him once a year, if that."

"That's fine with the benefit of hindsight," Finney said.

"For God's sake." I was exasperated now and I sat forward, pinning his eyes with mine, speaking fast and hard. "Tell me why I would kill the father of my children. They don't know the first thing about it now, but they will. They'll grow older, and they'll ask questions, and they'll hear what people say. Someone hated Adam enough to drive a car at him. What do you think that's going to do to his children? Well, I'm going to find out. I'm going to be dealing with this, and with my damaged children, for the rest of my life. Do you really think I'd have done that to my children? Would you do that to yours?"

Finney made a motion of surrender with his hands and hung his head. He'd puffed out his cheeks and didn't seem about to say anything.

"If you think I'm guilty, arrest me."

He raised a palm. "Don't start shouting again, I have a headache."

"If you think I'm guilty, arrest me." I came over and knelt in front of him. My eyes locked on his. I spoke as softly as I had ever spoken, but I couldn't take the intensity out of my words. "You can't because you don't have the evidence. Or you have evidence that points to someone else. I don't know which. But you know I didn't do it and I need you to say it publicly. You're just hanging me out to dry. Get me my job back. Tell Adam's parents they must stay away. For God's sake, concentrate on finding who killed Adam, so my children don't have to spend all their lives wondering whether it was their mother."

He raised his hand, pushed a strand of hair behind my ear, and my skin burned at his touch. His eyes were guarded.

"I have people to answer to," he said quietly.

I turned away from him in disgust.

"Won't anyone stand up for what they believe?" I muttered angrily. "You have a heart, you have a brain, do you need permission to use them?"

He sighed, took his head in his hands. I stayed kneeling there in front of him, not because I was begging, but because I knew if I moved away I would break the line of communication. Put me back on a chair and we'd be back at square one with weary sarcasm dripping out of his mouth and me yelling. At last he raised his head to look at me again.

"The station got a call the night Wills was killed. There's a recording. The voice was distorted. It gave your car plate number, it told us where to look. We've checked your landline and your mobile. You didn't make that call from either."

"That's not conclusive."

"Whoever drove your car wiped it clean of prints. I mean the whole thing's been polished. There's no reason for you to do that. It's your car."

"If there had only been my fingerprints, it would have proved that no one else had been in the car."

"True." He lowered his head. "Someone also dropped a tissue down on a seat."

"It could be mine."

"It's not yours. It has a few spots of blood on it, as though some-one used it to blot up a shaving wound or a nosebleed or a small cut. We have all the DNA we need, we just don't have a match. Can you think of anyone who's been in the car?"

I thought back.

"No one. And the children haven't bled in the car. I mean they're always vomiting, but . . ."

"Our scientists can tell the difference between blood and vomit."

I thought again and then there was a bolt of lightning. "I know how he did it," I said, excitement speeding my voice. "There's a piece of metal that's come loose by the door frame on the driver's side, low down by the floor. I haven't caught myself on it for ages because you only do it if you shift the seat setting, you know, if you push it back or forward."

"It would have had to cut through gloves." Finney sounded doubtful.

"Thin gloves? You've got the car, check it out," I instructed. "You have to sit in it like you're about to drive, then reach down and shift the seat."

Finney was sitting back in his chair now, looking more at ease. I realized I was clutching his knee. I removed my hand. I still didn't dare move in case I broke the spell. Because that was what it seemed like. As though I'd unlocked some magic and with it Finney's mouth.

"This stalker . . ." I said. "There is a stalker, isn't there?"

"In the two weeks before his death, Adam reported nuisance phone calls and then, just days before he died, he reported an anonymous letter."

"What did you do about it?"

Finney looked sheepish.

"We advised him to use an answering machine to screen his calls, and save the letters to show us if he got any more. Frankly, we wouldn't have done much about it. Every celebrity has their share of cranks. Most of them don't have guns."

"And some of them don't have cars," I said grimly.

We sat for a minute.

"Am I the only one with anything approaching a motive?"

Finney scrunched his face up. "There were people he'd pissed off professionally. He was an ambitious man. I don't have to tell you that."

"Richard Carmichael thought he was losing his wife, and he

thought he was losing her to Adam," I said. "How about that for motive?"

"Except for the fact that by the time Wills was killed, Paula was already dead. Motive gone."

"He blamed Adam for her death?" It was all I could come up with, but Finney shook his head. I stood up and paced around to get my circulation going again. I could tell from the expression on Finney's face that he would say no more. He too had got to his feet, and he was looking uncomfortable, annoyed with himself, as though he knew he'd said too much. He wandered over to the mantelpiece and glanced at the photographs, just as Richard Carmichael had on the morning after his wife's death. Finney picked up a framed print of myself, Jane, and Suzette. Redhead, black, and blonde, arms around each other's shoulders, strappy dresses, raising glasses of champagne. We looked like an ad for shampoo.

"Good times," he said, with that dry tone back in his voice.

"Good friends," I corrected him. "It was taken at Suzette's wedding, three years ago."

"I don't see a groom," Finney said.

"He was there somewhere. They've split up. I think he's in Australia now."

Finney replaced the photograph.

"I have to be going," he said. "I've been here too long."

Chapter 24

THE rain is falling like shards of iron, hard and fast and vicious. Above me the sky is dark. It is only ten in the morning but it might as well be dusk. My rented car is parked outside a crumbling mansion on Hill Rise, squeezed in between a minicab and a van with painted-over windows. I have grappled the double stroller out of the trunk and set it where the pavement should be but isn't. My bare head is soaked, my hair dripping onto my sodden shoulders, but the stroller has a raincover. I remove the children one by one from the shelter of the car, trying in vain to shield them from the downpour, and I strap them into the stroller with slippery fingers. By the time they are in, both they and the stroller are damp. Hannah and William are cheerful, nonetheless. I have not taken them on many outings recently, and they are prepared to be doused in water if I think it's a good idea. We maneuver our way between the cars and down the hill, then turn right and up Wood Vale, a steep incline. I am bent double, and I can see Hannah through the window in the back of the stroller, her face lifted toward the plastic of the raincover, her finger pointing, mouth burbling pleasure as raindrops splat against it. We are on our way to see David, Adam's brother. We used to be friends and I want him to help me.

For twenty-four hours I have been all but incapacitated. With Hannah and William clambering all over me, vying for my attention, I sat at home and watched the television coverage of the funeral of their father. No channel carried it live, but because of the nature of Adam's death, it had become a huge story and there were extended clips on news bulletins and lengthy reports on the state of the investigation into his death. I sat flicking from channel to channel, horribly fascinated. I was not going to make a fortune from libel suits. The lawyers must have pored over proposed scripts, cold-blooded and calculating. How much could be safely said? How much implied? The reporters, each one of them, stopped short of declaring me guilty, but there were no other suspects, no alternative paths of inquiry. Adam was killed by my car. Increasingly, it seemed to me, the only dramatic tension left in the affair was the question of when I would get my comeuppance. There was hurt outrage in the commentaries that accompanied the funeral, and I knew I was lucky that so far, aside from a single op-ed piece, no one had publicly bayed for my blood. Finney's beautiful smile was no good to me if he was too spineless to stand against the tide that was rising and threatening to engulf me.

Transfixed, I watched my friends and colleagues caricatured by the television cameras, their mourning pallor accorded a sickly hue, contours flattened, their expressions and gestures theatrical, self-conscious. Jane, her hair twisted and stabbed by two silver pins, her black cheongsam high at the neck but split to the thigh, defying death to catch her. Suzette, her dancer's body wilting under the weight of sadness, twiglike limbs in black slacks, a black sweater, her small breasts rising and falling fast, like a frightened bird, her hair loose over her shoulders and halfway down her back. I had never seen her broken like this and I thought, grudgingly, that she must really have loved him. Maeve, uncomfortable, turning her head to speak to Jane in the pew behind, then turning back, her face unhappy. A chasm lay between us. I knew that I was, in the mind of each one of them, paired with Adam in death.

I had considered going to the funeral. I would have liked to bid Adam farewell in person, but my very presence would have been news, it would have turned a funeral into a circus. So instead I was a phantom at the feast, my place set, food untouched. I bade farewell from the comfort of the sofa, my face wet with tears, the children frustrated by my distraction. I had closed the curtains against the cameras of the press, waiting for me outside.

In the front row sat Harold, Norma, and David, the wife and mother in the middle, her hands reaching out to hold the hand of her husband on one side, her son on the other. Both were seated well away from her so that she had to stretch. I willed David to move closer to his mother, to smile at her, squeeze her hand, anything to comfort her. If only he would give her the affection she craved, surely she would not need my children. My children, the other phantoms at the feast.

The inadequate priest seemed haunted by the children, his homily falling repeatedly into traps of his own making. Clearly the man had given no thought to what he would say or to how it would sound.

"Adam made such contributions to all of us," he said, his eyes blinking earnestly behind his spectacles, his voice strangely high-pitched. "He helped us understand the way the world works. He was in all ways a man of the world, a man who'd been round the block a few times and could tell us what was on the other side and make us want to go there. Adam's mother mourns him, his father mourns him." He launched into a dolorous list of those left behind. "His brother mourns him and his friends and colleagues mourn him. We who are left behind, his family and friends, mourn the man who might have been, the father to his children . . . that is, the pillar of strength to a woman, a woman that is, who might have been his wife. A filial son, like the son he never knew . . . never had, in fact . . . in his parents' declining years."

It was such a poorly worded send-off for a wordsmith that I couldn't help smiling. I saw signs of impatience on Maeve's face. If she'd been God she would have fired the man. Perhaps it was his ineptitude that stirred Norma and Harold to what came afterward. They emerged from the church but, instead of keeping on the designated path to the waiting limousines, Norma made a beeline for the press, galvanized suddenly to action. Harold chased after her, taken by surprise.

"I'd like to make a statement," she said into the nearest microphone, her voice rushed and nervous. "Nobody's brave enough to say it, but I don't care about the consequences. We all know who killed my son. My grandchildren are in danger. I beg—" But at this point Harold reached her and grabbed her arm, yanking her back.

"Don't be a bloody fool, woman," he snarled at her. He pushed her away from the press as her face crumpled, but the tapes still rolled, and they captured the curses he hissed at her.

They looked bad but I looked worse. The newspapers the next morning were united. IT'S THE WILL, STUPID, screamed one tabloid headline. The broadsheets just put it another way.

No one should be subjected to what Norma and Harold Wills have had to go through during the past week. They have lost a son and been refused access to his children. The cameras took us yesterday where we should not have gone, to the place where loss and anger meet, and it shocked us because it is an ugly place, where dignity is crushed. But push aside that shock, look with sympathy even on Harold Wills as he vents his distress on his wife, and who of us cannot say that anger is justified? Someone must pay for the loss of talent and humanity, and there must be no squeamishness about the sanctity of motherhood.

And so it was that I had to find David. I had not spoken to him since my split with Adam. The home phone number I had for him no longer worked, but a sympathetic mutual friend directed me to the Horniman Museum, where he had apparently been working for three months on a temporary project. I knew instinctively that the day after his brother's funeral he would be back at work, taking refuge. I had not telephoned to warn him of our arrival. I did not want to scare him off. As it was, I almost lost my nerve. Getting out of the house had been a nightmare, both children crying by the time I'd wrestled them through the horde outside. My escape route at the back of the house was still remarkably clear, I assumed because they were waiting for me to be arrested, and had calculated the police would have to park in front. With the virtue of hindsight I should have snuck out of the backdoor, but I hated to creep around like a criminal.

In the rain, the facade of the museum had a doleful look. The mosaic that decorates the frontage depicts a central figure, "Humanity in the House of Circumstance," bordered on either side by the gates of life and death, the latter guarded by a somber-looking figure representing resignation. We struggled, stroller and all, up the steps.

Inside, a pretty teenage girl at the reception desk regarded me with awe.

"Why didn't you bring an umbrella?" she asked me.

"Can't hold an umbrella and push a stroller at the same time," I answered, still breathless from the hill and the steps. "It's one of life's great truths."

I pulled back the raincover, drenching the children as the rain ran off the plastic in rivulets onto their heads. They blinked and looked around expectantly.

"Can you tell me where to find David Wills?" I asked, approaching the desk and flashing a smile. "We wanted to surprise him."

She stared at me, and my heart sank. There was nowhere, now, that I could go unrecognized. Even those who failed to read the newspaper every day had seen my picture on television. Surely, I thought, we looked sufficiently unthreatening. What was I going to do? Shake rain all over her? But the girl crumpled up her face in doubt.

"I'll just give him a ring then."

"Please don't," I started to say, but she was quicker than she looked, and she had already finished dialing.

"David," she dragged out the second syllable of his name, tapping her fingernails on the desk. "I've got a lady by the name of Robin Ballantyne here with her children, and she says she wants to surprise you." She turned her back to us then, and whispered into the phone. When she turned toward us and hung up, her eyes were even more anxious.

"Okay," she said grudgingly, "you'll have to leave the stroller here." She gave me directions, and I set off with one lead weight wriggling under each arm. Hannah was, at least technically, walking now, but we wouldn't get anywhere very fast.

I would have liked to linger. The children shrieked with excitement at the glass cabinets full of stuffed gorillas and emus, then stared in stunned awe at ten-foot-high tribal masks from Africa. Frederick John Horniman, nineteenth-century tea merchant and traveler, amassed such a large collection of artifacts and natural history specimens in his house that it is said his wife got thoroughly fed up.

David was waiting for us outside his office door. Shyer and slighter than Adam, with lighter coloring, he had frequently been written off (not least by his parents) as a pale imitation of his brother. His quiet scholarship had gone unnoticed and unpraised. If he felt bitter about it, he did not let it show. Now his face was worried, but as I approached I was relieved to see that his lips twitched in an involuntary smile of greeting.

"Robin, hello," he said, then peered into Hannah's face and said softly, "My God, she's the spitting image. No wonder . . ." He let his sentence trail off and turned his scrutiny to William's face.

"Hello, little man," he said softly. "Well, you're your mother's son."

"David," I blurted out, moved by his kindness. "I didn't kill Adam."

He looked at me for a moment with the same careful attention he'd given the children.

"Come in," he said.

Inside, his office could have been any academic's study, except for the presence, lying on a table in the center of the room, of an ancient Egyptian mummy in an unlidded crate, looking more like a cocoon than anything human, layers of yellowing cloth concealing the brutal interactions of time and flesh.

"I don't usually have a roommate. He's supposed to be going out on loan, but he got mislaid and ended up here." He gazed down fondly at the body. "Actually I'm getting quite used to the company. He's been here all morning, and he's heard more about my family than I care to think."

I released the children onto the floor and they scurried like insects under the table. David pointed me to the only chair, and I sat down while he perched against his desk, his bottom threatening to destabilize a leaning tower of books. He looked around for something to entertain the children with, and picked up an armful of academic magazines and put them on the floor.

"There," he said, "they can shred them for me. Save me some energy."

For a moment we watched as first William, then Hannah, got the idea, and within minutes the floor was awash with torn ethnographical treatises, footnotes scattered and bibliographies turned to confetti.

"My mother is not doing well," he said. Then, with a sigh, "Nor is my father."

"I understand all that," I said impatiently. "I'm not unsympathetic, but they have to back off. How can I make them understand that I didn't kill their son? If only I could talk to them about what happened that night. There's evidence that the police aren't releasing . . ."

"It's really not a matter of evidence, is it?" David said mildly. "You tell me you didn't kill Adam and I am prepared to believe you, but that is all it amounts to: a balance of probabilities, and those very probabilities assessed according to my subjective view of who you are . . . The longer I'm a scientist, the more I realize there is no such thing as science. There is only what we choose to believe and the accumulation of whatever evidence we require to give it some validity. I choose to believe you didn't kill Adam, and because of that I'm prepared to do what I can to help you, but my parents choose to believe the opposite and will continue to do so until they have another name and another face that they can blame."

I gazed down at the children. It would be torture for them to grow up in the world David painted, the children of a mother who might or might not be a murderer. I would not be able to expect them to defend me. If they chose to doubt me I could do nothing about it.

"How about a gesture of good faith?" I said eventually. "I won't try to convince them I didn't kill Adam, and they can visit the twins. I won't be there. They can go to my mother's house, and she will be there, and you will be there, and you will give me your word that you won't let them try anything silly."

David thought for a moment, then shook his head.

"What's the point?" he asked.

"To buy me time. To defuse them a bit."

David licked his lips.

"I don't really want to get involved," he said, carefully avoiding my eyes.

David Wills, like Frederick John Horniman, was a great traveler. David's parents had not clung to him, nor he to them. They got on with their own lives.

"I'm stuck in the middle here," he said. "I'm in a very difficult position—"

"Try my position," I snapped.

He lifted his head and his eyes met mine. He heaved a sigh.

"I'll suggest it to them," he said heavily. He returned to his perusal of the children and I watched his face. He was fascinated by them, and sad. His eyes kept returning to Hannah, so like her father.

"You must miss him," I said.

He was unable to reply. He gulped convulsively.

"He was a good brother, wasn't he?" I am not sure why I needed to say this, but I had had so little chance to talk about Adam with someone else who had loved him. It was not as though I was going to wax nostalgic with Suzette about Adam her lover.

David sighed again and covered his mouth with his hand. His head jerked and his hand went to his eyes, where tears had sprung, removing his spectacles and rubbing. He shook his head, angry at himself, and after a moment he had recovered sufficiently to speak.

"He gave me his old laptop," he said, his mouth still trembling. I frowned, not understanding the significance. Perhaps, in David's ivory tower, the gift of a laptop was the ultimate in brotherly love.

"He knew my laptop was broken and he wanted to upgrade." David cleared his throat, then went on, "And I couldn't afford a new one, so I was glad to take it. He didn't wipe the disk clean or anything, just unplugged it and handed it over."

I was beginning to see where David was headed.

"When Adam was killed I opened up some of the old files, but I can't make head or tail of it. There's so much stuff, and I don't know any of the people he refers to."

"Have you shown it to the police?"

David shook his head wearily.

"Some of it's personal," he said. "I couldn't bear to think of them reading it all in some police station somewhere. Besides, what's the point?"

"What's the point?" I echoed in exasperation. "It might tell us something about who killed him."

David snorted.

"Does it matter?" he asked. "Adam's gone. A clue here, a clue there, how is some bungling bobby going to piece together anything that approximates to the truth? We'll never understand why it happened. Any attempt to re-create the past is doomed to failure, and anything partial is flawed."

I stared at him. I had had enough of David's approach to the issue of guilt and innocence.

"Can I borrow the laptop?" I said eventually.

He nodded. Then he knelt down and started to play with the children.

Chapter 25

I plug the laptop in as soon as I reach home. I start to feel my way around. David was right. There is a huge amount of stuff here. What's more, there's no method, no order to it. In Word everything is shoved in under "My Documents": letters to the bank manager, notes to the milkman, lengthy scripts for whole television series, even what appears to be an outline for a novel. I open it, knowing he would have hated me to see it. Set in Afghanistan it is a story of derring-do, of a dashing male journalist who journeys across war-torn desert and who must decide between the importance of his story and the safety of his source, a young and stunningly beautiful Afghan woman with ebony hair and silken skin. They have a lot of sex—some of it sounds familiar.

I go to Outlook, and type in the password David has given me. The screen is filled with an inbox of old e-mails. There is one from Maeve, full of praise for a one-off documentary on the Royal family. "You struck just the right note," she writes, "no fawning, plenty of straight talking of course, but some genuine admiration. Our viewers are tired of too much cynicism, they like to switch off on an upbeat note. More of the same and your face will rarely be off the nation's television." I scowl. Perhaps I don't want to go back to documentary-making after all. Perhaps I am too jaded.

A howl. Startled, I turn to look for the children. They have both left their posts in front of the television. I rush into the kitchen.

Hannah has opened a cupboard and has pulled a heavy saucepan onto her foot. She isn't in pain, but is trying to extricate herself. I pick her up and put the pan back in the cupboard. As I walk back into the hallway, Hannah toddling behind me, I see that I have forgotten to close the gate and William is halfway up the stairs, his bottom swaying precariously, like a mountaineer on a narrow ridge. I rescue him, but the message is clear. It is time to get out of the house, something that we achieve without harassment.

————

We headed for the fair. The children were too young for the big wheel (and I was too old), but they could watch. I dragged the stroller across ridges of mud, then across the gravel that had been spread over the car park that was the site of the fair for the week. We wandered aimlessly, gazing upward at flashing lights and feats of engineering, great crashing chunks of metal thrashing around in the air purposefully, as though pounding some vital component into shape. It was a freezing damp afternoon and there were few takers. One lonely man was on the Hammer, clinging to his seat belt, his face pale, more often upside down than right way up.

The sun made a brief appearance but at four, as if by clockwork, it seemed to extinguish itself. When Hannah started to cry I realized it was getting seriously cold. I turned the stroller homeward. We passed the ticket booth for the Hammer. A small group of kids was gathered there, taking possession of a handful of tickets. I paid no attention until I saw from the corner of my eye a sudden movement, a kick, foot hard into stomach, and then heard a sob. I stopped and watched.

"Fucking wuss," one boy was saying to another. "Fucking mummy's boy."

The face of the mummy's boy contorted, and with good reason

I realized, as I recognized him. It was Kyle, Richard Carmichael's younger son, a mummy's boy whose mummy had just been buried.

The older boy—he must have been about thirteen—reached out and grabbed the collar of the Carmichael boy, who was still hugging his stomach. He began to wrestle him toward the Hammer, and the other children went along with them, so that the two were surrounded. The woman in the ticket booth watched impassively. She'd seen it all before.

"Hey," I hailed them. I felt like a fool, vulnerable and unimpressive with my strollerful of babies. "Let him go. He doesn't have to go if he doesn't want to."

The older boy turned around and the other children stood kicking their feet in the mud.

"Fuck you," he said. "It'll be good for him."

"Let him go," I said again. The Carmichael boy was trying to wriggle his way out of the older boy's grasp. Another boy in the group seemed to intercede on his behalf. Maybe he recognized me—if so, it was the only time being a suspected murderer worked to my advantage. Whatever the reason, the older boy sent Kyle packing with a last kick. He ran, stumbling toward me, and I caught him. Once in my arms he seemed reluctant to emerge, and I wasn't sure how to proceed. I knew how to deal with infants, but what did I do with this young man-boy?

"I'll take you home," I said to him, holding him by the shoulders and looking him in the face. What I saw there shocked me. He was white and trembling and the fear in his eyes hadn't departed with his tormentors, but there was recognition there too. He knew me, as I knew him.

"Are you all right?" I thought maybe something else had happened, something I hadn't witnessed, but he nodded gruffly and turned away, hands in pockets.

"Where are you going?" This bleak Common was no place for a

child in the dark. He shrugged, but he lingered there, clearly re-luctant to head off on his own.

"Come on, I'll take you home," I said again to him.

"I'm not going home," he muttered.

Was it pure altruism or sheer curiosity that prompted me to say what I said next?

"Come back with me for a while then, have something to eat. I've got hot chocolate."

He shot me a look of frank distrust.

"I'm not going to kill you," I said mildly. "I've never killed any-one in my life."

He never did say yes, just started to shamble along after me when I gave up waiting and headed off. When we reached my front door he tried to pretend he wasn't there, huddling his head down inside his collar and standing in tight to the wall, as though he didn't want his father to see him.

Once inside he paid the children no attention at all, and in fact the fresh air and the movement of the stroller had served to send both Hannah and William to sleep. Usually I would have woken them at this point—if they slept now they would be up until mid-night—but I wanted to talk to this boy and I wanted to do it in peace, so I left them tucked up. I tried not to hurry him. He fol-lowed me into the kitchen and watched while I warmed milk on the stove and stirred in chocolate powder. I scrabbled around in the cupboards, looking for something to feed him. I knew I'd got it right when I produced a packet of crisps and he made an appre-ciative grunt and practically snatched it from me. He sat there chomping crisps and I sat opposite him sipping hot chocolate, and I was afraid that his visit would pass in this noisy silence.

"Why don't you want to go home?" I asked eventually.

He sniffed and shook his head and I thought I was going to get nothing.

"Why d'you think?"

Point taken. It was obvious.

"Because your mum died," I supplied the answer.

He shrugged and pulled his mouth, which threatened to betray him, into a twisted sneer.

"Your dad's still there," I pressed on relentlessly, "you're not on your own."

This was greeted with silence. He'd finished the crisps and he rolled the packet into a greasy ball and pushed it across the table toward me, spreading crisp crumbs liberally. Something about the gesture told me that this was not how he had been brought up to behave. This was a boy who knew not to hang out at fairgrounds and knew to put rubbish in the bin. Perhaps this was what I'd heard people describe as attention-seeking behavior. Perhaps he was trying to engage me, even if only engage my irritation, by shoving trash at me.

"Doesn't your dad worry about you, doesn't he want to know where you are?"

"I'm okay."

"I can see that. I'm asking about your dad."

"He can go fuck himself."

It sounds ugly now, but when he said it, it was so full of hurt that my heart nearly broke for him. I sighed. Kyle retrieved the crisp packet and started to pick it apart, licking the salt from his fingertips.

"He'll take care of you, now your mum's gone. He's a good man."

"Take care of me?" He gave a snort. "She was too fucking busy saving the world."

"She did a lot of good," I said.

"Not for me," he came back quickly.

"She loved you."

"Yeah," he could barely speak for emotion.

I decided to change the subject.

"Your dad seems to think someone might have been with your mum that night."

"That's what he wants me to say," Kyle mumbled.

"So there wasn't anyone?"

"I don't know if there was or there wasn't. I heard the doorbell go early in the evening. I was eating in my room, it must have been about six-thirty but I don't know who it was." It was the longest thing he'd said so far, and I could hear his mid-Atlantic accent, the American drawl of his stepfather overlaid by South London prep school and the failed bravado of the fairground. "I had my head-phones on. I never know what's going on in the house when I've got my music on. I thought I heard the front door slam, and later I thought I heard the doorbell again, but I thought my mum would get it, so I wasn't interested. Then nothing. I was on the computer, listening to music. Nothing until the sirens."

Kyle's face fell, and I didn't want him to dwell on that memory.

"So your mum may have had a visitor that night?" I clarified.

Kyle shrugged.

"The doorbell rang. I guess she opened it."

"And the door slammed later—when would you say?"

"You're as bad as the police." Kyle stood up angrily, pushing his chair away from him. "I was just trying to tell them what I re-membered, but now my dad's all over me pushing me to say I saw someone, when I didn't, and the police keep asking me questions, and if I say I'm not sure whether I heard the door slam, or I'm not sure what time it was, they make out I'm lying. Can't they under-stand that I don't look at my watch every time I hear the door slam? I just don't care who comes to see Mum and Dad. It's none of my business."

He paced around angrily. He reminded me of his stepfather, the morning after Paula had died.

"I've had the same problem," I told him. "I made the mistake of saying I thought I'd heard voices just before your mum died, and they've been trying to pin me down on it ever since, but there's nothing to pin down really, it was just an impression."

Kyle came to sit down again.

"Dad's not completely out of line," he said, calmer again. "There was a man who used to call Mum up on the phone and upset her, and I know once there was a man came to visit her when Dad and I were out, because I saw him leaving the house when I was walking home. I asked her who he was, and she got angry with me for no reason. So I'm not surprised Dad's suspicious."

"Why would he keep insisting someone came that night if they didn't?"

Kyle's baleful eyes locked on mine.

"Because of the insurance," I answered my own question again. "Because it won't pay out for suicide."

"The insurance? You think my dad cares about money?" Kyle said with the level of disdain that could only be produced by the young and rich.

I stared at him. If not money, then what? I remembered what Rachel had told me, that Paula was searching, lost at sea, and that Richard knew he was losing her and was panicked by it. My mind was racing. Perhaps Kyle suspected his stepfather of killing his mother.

"Are you afraid of him?" I asked.

He looked away.

"He threw a cup of coffee at her once," he whispered, "when the man rang. Dad answered the phone and he got angry."

"That's not the same as killing someone," I told him, trying to reassure him, trying to bring him back into the present. "Besides, your stepfather has an alibi."

But Kyle was in no mood to be comforted.

"He's not stupid," he growled.

I stood and got another packet of crisps from the cupboard. I couldn't bear to see what he was doing to the empty packet. He took the pack from me and tore it open, as he had the first, as though it was the only thing he'd had to eat in days.

"Look," I said. Kyle was staring at the floor, stuffing his mouth, and the smell of sour cream and spring onion was hanging over us both like a cloud. "I mean look at me, listen to what I'm saying. Your dad is hurt because your mother killed herself. He's looking for another explanation, that's all. Right now he's all caught up in what happened, and maybe his judgment isn't as clear as it should be. He just doesn't want to think his wife killed herself."

But it was I who had misjudged the situation. Kyle's face writhed in anguish and half-masticated crisps flew from his mouth.

"She didn't kill herself," he howled in pain. "She didn't."

It was all he said before his head sank to the table and his shoulders shook, and the kitchen reverberated to the sound of his sobs. His mother couldn't have killed herself because he was her reason to live. Kyle would rather believe his stepfather had killed his mother than that she had chosen to abandon him.

Chapter 26

WILLIAM wakes up and Kyle leaves. For the rest of the evening my hands do the work of a mother while my head churns through what Kyle has told me. I am interrupted only by one phone call: Jane, reporting back, sounding weary and fed up.

"Robin, all the paperwork that had anything to do with the documentary went to Maeve when Richard Carmichael made those allegations after Paula died. I can't get near it."

"You mean it's physically in her office?"

"In a filing cabinet. Under lock and key."

"Can't you butter up her secretary?"

"I tried that. Gayle believes Maeve is the one true God, and thou shalt have no other. I even tried bribing her with tickets to a Celine Dion concert. She wouldn't budge, but I gave them to her anyway. I can't bear the woman."

"Well, thanks for trying." I tried to sound upbeat, but my head was beginning to ache from all the banging up against brick walls.

"Robin, I even waited and went in there at lunchtime when they were both out and went through her drawers, but God knows where she keeps the keys. Probably in her knickers. Short of blowing the safe sky high with dynamite, we're buggered."

"Okay. Forget the memos. Have you heard anything from Ray?"

"I took him for a drink last night. He's pissed off with you. Says can't you understand it's more than his job's worth to leak information to you. And anyway, he thinks you did it. Says Finney's under huge pressure to arrest you and he can't understand why he hasn't."

"He said all this to you? Doesn't he know you're my friend?"

"You wouldn't have thought I was your friend to hear me talk." Jane was sheepish. "I was a wee bit rude about you to get him talking. I'm surprised your ears didn't burn."

"Oh." I forced myself to sound cheerful, but it was hard work. "Well, thanks anyway."

———

It is after midnight by the time I'm off the phone with Jane. I return to Adam's computer. Late at night and on my own I feel strange sitting here, my fingers on his keyboard, as though if I rub a little a genie will appear. A computer is the imperfect imprint of its owner's mind. The things that were said or done are not here, of course, but the things thought and not pursued, directions conceived and not followed, all those are here, as well as a lot of trash. It's a bit like sorting through someone's rubbish bin, reconstructing their last meal from the food wrappers. In this case, it's a bit like finding a pizza box, but being pretty damned sure that the last meal consisted of a burger. Nothing quite adds up. What I want is a journal, a day-by-day account of his life. And death, if possible. All I can do is piece together e-mails and Word files.

I try to eliminate the dross, but I don't want to compromise evidence. I click on "History," the machine's memory of Adam's web trawls. There is a whole series of drug-related sites. I proceed in his footsteps, glancing with ghoulish fascination through the material he had sought out. I learn all about death by heroin, that a true heroin overdose is rare and slow and treatable, but that a cocktail of impure heroin and alcohol can be much more rapidly lethal. It is clearly research for some project or other, and it tells me nothing about Adam's life or death.

It dawns on me that I shouldn't have the computer at all. In the few hours I have had possession of it I could have planted anything there. Then I realize that it's too late to start worrying about evidence, and I feel free to mess around with the order of things. I create new folders and shuffle files and gradually lines begin to emerge, patterns, a sense of symmetry. Most of the information comes from e-mails, but there are Word files that tell their own story, like a curriculum vitae updated just weeks before. It started out like all the rest: date of birth, education. Then, with "Positions Held," Adam seemed to lose interest in his own career. His job description trailed off into a row of question marks and then into blank space. I assumed he had never printed this version out, but why then even create it? He must have been applying for jobs. I clicked my way back to Outlook and his e-mails suggested that he had, but not, it appeared, journalism jobs. Instead, Adam had been requesting application forms for teacher-training courses. There was more, equally baffling: e-mail conversations with a Catholic priest, a Father Joe Riberra, the same priest, if I remembered rightly, who had given Paula's funeral oration. The contents of the e-mails were not personal. Rather, Adam seemed to be requesting a theological and philosophical reading list and Riberra providing one. This was intriguing, inasmuch as the Adam I had known was dismissive of all things spiritual. But all it told me was that Adam had changed.

I did a search for e-mails to his parents and to David. There was a handful, all brief and uninformative—confirmation of a date for Sunday lunch, apologies for a birthday missed—and I suspected that most family communication was done by telephone. I searched for Paula's name, and for Suzette's. There was a spate of e-mails to Suzette about the arrangements for the *Carmichaelite*

Mission documentary. They were all brief and professional, none hinting at a torrid affair. There were several to and from Jane too, all work related. Jane had never trusted Adam and he was never comfortable in her company. Nevertheless their communications were chummy, bordering on the flirtatious, Jane's all signed with hugs and kisses. I rolled my eyes. Very Corporation.

I went to the "Deleted Items" folder in Outlook and scanned the list that came up: a lot of junk mail, offers to enlarge Adam's penis, give him free web access to pornographic sites, improve his credit rating, a proposal that he work from home, and then a message from Paula:

> My dear, he hasn't been around here. Not that I've seen anyway. I don't know what to suggest. I am incapable, now, of giving advice, because I distrust—indeed detest—my own instinct. As you see, I'm now so self-centered that I'm of no use to anyone. What can I say? Do you really think she'll thank you? The best you can probably do is take my cynicism and reject it. You have a good heart and you must follow it. The children will thank you. They will always thank you if you are not cruel to them and do not mistreat them. I cannot bear this vein of thought. I will sign off. Can we meet? Our meetings are the only thing keeping me going. Always faithfully yours, Paula.

I frowned at the screen. What was that all about then? Why delete her messages? I clicked back to the "Sent Messages" folder, and searched for the date on which Paula had sent her last message. There it was, the same day, a message from Adam to Paula. Sent on the day that Paula died.

Paula, I know we said no e-mails, but this is different. I think I've found my stalker. He eventually plucked up courage to knock on the door and introduce himself. Robin's father. The old scoundrel. Looking for his daughter. He had this address, didn't know she'd moved out. He's been staking out the house, ringing too, expecting her to pick up the phone. He wants to know where Robin is. He wants my help to contact her. My instinct, these days, is if anyone asks help from you, give it. That's what our good friend the Father says anyway, and if I have any chance of getting into heaven—and it's slight now—I need to take his advice. Still, my brain takes over and says "What if she wants nothing to do with him." I seem to remember there were rumors of scurrilous behavior. Perhaps I finally need to talk to her face to face. I'm running scared from her too. With better reason. In need of your sterling wisdom, as always, Adam."

I reread Paula's sign-off from her e-mail: "Can we meet? Our meetings are the only thing keeping me going." My eyes flicker to Adam's phrase, "I know we said no e-mails, but this is different." It sounds like a secret affair, but I have been told by Rachel Colby that one never took place.

I rub the palm of my hand over my face. I feel numb, as though I have been transported into a parallel universe and haven't quite made it back. These voices from beyond the grave are more than I can stand. Certainly they enlighten me. I know now things I did not know. I know, for instance, who Adam's stalker was. Either my father found some reason to kill Adam, or I must now eliminate the stalker as a suspect. I have further evidence too, of Paula's depression, and I have reason to believe that something had happened that made Adam rethink his life. On this level, my examination of the computer was a useful and informative exercise. But I am sitting here at two in the morning, the children's breath like a whisper from the next room, the hum of a city almost but not quite asleep from outside. A cold draft finds its way through the curtains. To hear Paula and Adam conversing is like sinking into death itself.

Chapter 27

THE next morning I went to visit Lorna and found her at the computer in her sitting room, which was bathed in sunlight. With her wrist still bandaged, she was picking out words on the keyboard at a painfully slow speed. I drew up a chair, but said nothing, aware that I would get none of her attention until she was done. Eventually she hit the "Send" button, gave a final, exasperated sigh, and turned to smile a greeting. Her red hair, always more glamorous than mine, gave her a golden halo where the sun touched her curls. The dressing on her forehead was white on white.

"Lorna," I dived right in, aware that if I hesitated I was in danger of wimping out, "I want to talk to you about our father. I think you've seen him."

Lorna's eyebrows flickered upward in surprise, and the smile fell from her lips, but she made no other response. My heart was pounding. To suggest that Lorna had defied, or even betrayed, our mother was to step into a minefield. The silence stretched between us like a wire, and I blathered on.

"I wouldn't blame you, you probably remember more than I or Tanya do about him. So if he got in contact and wanted to see you . . ."

"I never stopped seeing him," Lorna said smoothly, "at least when he was around. We've tended to lose contact when he's been in prison."

I stared at her, and she raised her eyebrows in a challenge. Since her illness began she has learnt to conserve energy even in conversation. She doesn't waste words.

"He's a con man and a thief," she told me bluntly, "just like Ma's always said. He was a doctor. He did defraud his practice. He did go on the run. He's been doing similar things ever since. He can't help himself."

My chest tightened, but I forced myself to keep on talking. I would digest this later. For the moment I must not let her stop, I must find out all I needed to know.

"You told him where to find us. Except that you gave him my old address. What's going on?"

Lorna pulled a face. She sighed, looking away from me, and for the first time there was a hint almost of apology.

"A couple of years back he decided to get in touch with you and Tanya, and I gave him your addresses almost without thinking about it. He's a very charming man. He's actually very much like you . . ." She broke off, then started again, "Then there was your pregnancy, Adam left, Tanya and Patrick were having a bad time financially, and it dawned on me that this was not the right time. Everyone had enough on their plates without Gilbert. Anyway, when I told him he wasn't to see you, we argued badly. He was hurt and angry that I thought you wouldn't want to see him. Then, a few weeks later, he was back on remand awaiting trial . . ." She looked up at me, and I shook my head slowly in disbelief, and perhaps in rebuke. "Well anyway, I got ill and he's been in prison all this time. I haven't spoken to him since our argument. I suppose he must have finished his sentence."

"Okay," I said softly. "Just one more thing and then I'll go.

Could he be violent? I mean if Adam refused to tell him where to find me, or something?"

Lorna didn't seem shocked by my question. She wiped away a tear. She gave the question a moment's consideration.

"I don't think so," she said. "When we argued, he just got hurt and petulant. He is excitable, but really . . . he's a mild man, not very physical, I can't . . ." She held the palms of her hands out toward me in supplication.

I nodded for all the world as though I understood.

———

My mother was waiting for me, her face flushed, playing hide-and-seek with Hannah and William, who were under the table.

"You were in there a good while," she commented as I entered the kitchen. She put a cup of coffee on the table next to a flapjack on a plate. I sat down, marveling that my new knowledge did not somehow show on my face. Thirty-odd years of secrecy, and still the charade could go on, if I was willing to play the game. I reached for the coffee. My mother stood watching, then pushed a pile of newspapers nearer me.

"You should read what they have to say today," she said, and I was intrigued to see that she was smiling, really smiling, for the first time in weeks. I pulled the newspapers toward me and turned to the inside pages—Adam's death no longer made the front. Still, tabloids and broadsheets alike all carried a similar story, some smaller, some larger.

In what appears to be a significant breakthrough, the police are for the first time investigating the possibility that a person other than Wills's former lover Robin Ballantyne drove her car when it ran Wills down.

Police sources say that the blood sample voluntarily supplied by Ballantyne has been tested against a bloodstain found inside her car and that there is no DNA match. It is possible, the sources say, that the bloodstain came from a cut caused by a loose strip of metal by the lever that regulates the position of the driving seat. Traces of the same unidentified blood have been found on that metal.

A police source cautioned that the discovery did not mean that another person had been driving the car on the night of the murder, only that another person had at some point been in the driving seat, but he acknowledged that this new evidence did introduce significant doubt into the case against Ballantyne.

I looked up, grinning, at my mother, only to find that she had filled a glass with something that looked suspiciously like champagne and was thrusting it toward me.

I shook my head.

"I'm not going to tempt fate," I said.

My mother shrugged, smiling.

"Well, I'm quietly confident," she said, and raised her glass to me.

I stretched my arms above my head. For the first time in weeks the air around me felt light and bright. I toasted my mother with my coffee. What pleased me most about the newspaper article was not simply the DNA evidence, but that the tone of the journalism seemed to have changed. Of course this was not the *Chronicle*.

"Look," she said happily, pushing a tabloid toward me, "there's even a little article here saying Harold Wills was once convicted of drunk driving."

I pulled a face and read through it. It was brief and of course completely irrelevant, but anything that made Adam's grieving parents look bad made me look better. It was an ugly contest. This must all, I thought, be Finney's work. If so, then he was not as spineless as I'd feared. I had hated writing him off.

I had a carefree lunch with my mother and then I tried to track down Father Joe Riberra. I called the church where Paula's funeral had taken place, where I was informed that Father Joe Riberra was not based there. They gave me the number of the office of the theological department of London University. Father Joe Riberra was, they told me, a visiting professor and he had been in the States for the past few days. They could not provide me with his number there, since he was on personal business. He was due back in a couple of days and he would return my call then if I left my number. Which I did. I e-mailed him too, because my faith in people returning calls is shaky.

I tried calling Suzette, but I couldn't reach her at home, or on her mobile, or at her office. Her assistant said that Suzette had gone on a trip, but that she couldn't say where, or when she would return. It was not clear to me whether this was incompetence or secrecy. Then I rang Rachel Colby and asked her the same thing I was going to ask Suzette: What was the last thing they filmed for the documentary before it all fell apart?

"I know where they were," she said slowly, "I mean geographically I know where they were, but I couldn't tell you who they interviewed last or anything like that."

"Geographically will do."

"They were in Penzance. Filming at a drug rehabilitation center that's funded by us, at least in part. I needed to talk to them about something just the other day, but the guy there never called me back. Still, I'll give you his name. Maybe you'll have more luck."

––––––––

Shortly after that, and just as Hannah and William emerged from their nap, I had a phone call that seemed like a gift from the gods. Tanya had a friend, a trained nursery nurse, who had just lost her job through no fault of her own. Tanya had explained the situation to her and she would be willing to babysit for the children whenever I needed her on an ad hoc basis and at an hourly rate that seemed fair. The downside was that if something better came up, she'd take it and leave me high and dry. Still, I couldn't get any higher or drier, and I liked her already for being up-front about it.

"Are you sure she's trustworthy?" I asked Tanya for the umpteenth time. And she assured me for the umpteenth time that she was.

"She's not going to photograph my children and put our pictures in the newspaper?"

"I swear to you that she will not," Tanya said. I couldn't ask for more.

I could hear Hannah upstairs, shouting to be picked up. That meant William was awake too. I couldn't face them. Every bone in my body ached with tiredness, the left side of my skull was brewing a major headache.

"Where is she?"

"Right now? She's sitting in my kitchen having a cup of coffee."

"Okay, tell her she's got a job," I said. She could take the children to the Common, I told myself, and I could telephone the drug rehabilitation center in Penzance.

"Tanya, don't hang up, I want to ask you something. Am I what you'd call excitable?"

The things Lorna had said about Gilbert were still circling in my head.

"Excitable? What the hell does that mean? If it means do you have a temper, then yes you do."

"Okay, thanks."

Tanya's friend, Carol, turned up. She was maternal and confident in a way Erica was not, and the children allowed themselves to be swept along by her warm efficiency. They were tidied up, nappies changed, dressed in cold weather clothes, all before they knew what was happening. They looked a mite surprised to be heading for the door, but they didn't complain, just looked up with curious eyes at this large woman who beamed down at them and marched them out to the strains of the "Grand Old Duke of York."

"Now get some rest," she hissed at me between verses, and saluted in farewell.

I went to bed still in my jeans. I slept, then woke as the door-bell sounded. I looked at the clock. They had been gone only twenty minutes. The children must have changed their minds about Carol. Or there had been some accident. I hurried down-stairs, almost tripping in my haste to let them in, but it was Finney.

"Oh," I said, incapable of welcome. It was raining again, pour-ing, great bombs of rain exploding against the ground. The street was empty. Where were the children?

He gave me a strange look.

"You were asleep."

"It's not illegal," I snapped. Finney always managed to wrong-foot me.

He ignored my bad temper and said he wanted to speak to me. I remembered the leaks to the papers. Finney was on my side.

"Of course." I stood aside, shut the door, and waited for him to remove his raincoat. I caught sight of myself in the hall mirror. My face was pink and puffy with sleep, my eyes huge and tired. My hair was all over the place. Well, I couldn't do anything about it now. I took Finney's raincoat and hung it over the radiator. He watched me, and I could tell he was baffled, but really I did it out of sheer habit. Whenever the children and I came home wet through, we just stripped off our wet clothes and hung them on the radiator to dry, but I was too tired to explain. Instead I went through to the sitting room. Finney knew the way, he could follow me. I sat on the edge of the sofa, curled over, my elbows on my knees, hands supporting my forehead, my body craving the sleep it had just lost. I could still feel the heavy core of it inside me.

Finney came and stood in front of me.

"Are you all right?" he said.

I twisted my head, looked up at him.

"I should thank you," I said, "for making all that stuff public."

He nodded. "My pleasure."

"I thought you were too scared to break the rules," I told him.

"It's just that I've done it once too often." He sat down at my side, leaning forward just like me.

"Facts are facts," I said, trying to marshal my head into some sort of action. "I still don't understand why you were concealing facts just because they pointed away from me. What difference does it make to the police?"

Finney rubbed his chin.

"Wills's death is very high profile," he said slowly, "which means the police service is very aware of the public perception of how it is being conducted. In this case I have a superior who has conceived a particular school of thought that says if we reveal contradictory facts it looks as though we don't know which way to turn. The public then feels insecure and starts to bay for the blood of the officer in charge—of course he doesn't put it quite like that. The public wants to see us make progress, so that is what they should see. Of course, this man would say, we'll still follow up every clue, every lead, but if we're more than sixty percent sure we've got the right person in the frame, then let's at least let the public know where we're heading."

"I'll sue his balls off," I muttered.

"He hasn't got any," Finney said, deadpan.

We turned to look at each other. I was half in tears, half laughing. Our faces were so close, and it seemed the most natural thing in the world when Finney leaned toward me and kissed me on the lips. He drew back almost at once to gauge my reaction. I smiled at him, and we kissed again as though we were devouring each other. I felt his fingers in my hair, then on my neck, my throat. We fell back against the cushions, finding each other's hands and weaving our fingers tight. My body flexed against his, heat rose from us like steam, and I thought, inasmuch as I could think at all, that never had a kiss been so much like sex.

The first time his mobile rang we both ignored it until whoever was on the line gave up. The second time even the ring tone sounded more insistent. We drew apart. He rubbed his hand over his face and cleared his throat. He glared at his phone, but when it continued to ring he grunted into it, then grunted again, in response to something.

"I'll be there," he said. He shoved the offending phone back into his trouser pocket, and we stared at each other. Then he got to his feet.

"We must do this again sometime," he said, a strained attempt at levity.

I didn't grace it with a response. I watched as he shrugged his suit into crumpled respectability. Then I stood too, and followed him into the hall, where I took his steaming raincoat from the radiator and handed it to him without a word. He put it on, then stepped toward me and we kissed again.

"I'll be back," he said.

Chapter 28

I awoke the following day to a call from Father Joe Riberra. I'd grabbed the phone in my sleep and it took me a few seconds to work out who was on the line.

"Sorry to call so early," he said when we had clarified who he was and that he was returning my call, "but I got back yesterday and my body clock is totally screwed. I think this is the opposite of how it's supposed to be. I must have slept too much on the plane."

"That's okay," I managed, pulling myself to sit upright in bed and rubbing my eyes. I looked at the clock and saw with a shock that it was eight already. Maybe if I sent the children out for a walk on the Common in a thunderstorm every day they would lie in until eight every morning.

"Plus it's urgent, right?" he said.

"It's urgent," I agreed.

"Then I'll meet you for breakfast in, say, an hour from now?"

We settled on a café that we both knew, just off the King's Road. Carol wasn't due 'til nine, so I called her mobile to redirect her to Tanya's house. Then, feeling like a total heel, I took the children and my front-door key to Patrick, because Tanya was at work. Patrick, who had just dropped their three off at school and had been looking forward to a child-free morning, looked fed up.

"I'm so sorry." My guilt provoked me to melodrama. "It's life and death."

"It always is recently," he grumbled.

In my rush I had forgotten to bring baby paraphernalia with me. No bottles, no nappies, nothing.

"They don't drink anything, they won't pee," he said grimly, and shooed me on my way.

———

Father Joe Riberra was turning heads. Out of his clerical garb he was cute in a scrubbed all-American way, and he smiled his thanks to waitstaff with huge benevolence every time they did so much as fill his water glass. He stood to shake hands with me, then wasting no time, began speaking as we sat down.

"I heard all about you from Adam," he said.

"I'm thinking of starting a fan club," I said.

He smiled, revealing even white teeth. For a moment our conversation was interrupted as we ordered breakfast, then he picked up where we had left off.

"Adam was the biggest fan of all," he said.

"Adam was a fine man in many ways," I said, "but let's not rewrite history."

Riberra nodded, then sat with his hands clasped on his lap. His scrutiny of my face was excrutiating in its detail.

"You are investigating his death," he said.

"And that of Paula Carmichael. I'm sure they're linked. You knew them both, and I believe that you counseled them both. Is there anything you can tell me?"

"You're afraid I'm going to tell you I can't pass on the secrets of the confessional," he said, apparently amused.

I nodded, sipping my coffee.

"Well, I'm not. Paula was what they call a lapsed Catholic, although how anyone could think of her as a lapsed anything I don't know. She had constructed her own belief system, a belief system that I would say ran parallel to Christianity. It had no place for Christ or God, but her concern for her fellow man and woman was, I would say, deeply religious. She thought I was misguided on the existence of God. She did not think I could commune with Him, but we did get on well and she asked my advice on matters of a spiritual or moral nature. It was Paula who introduced Adam to me. The two of them were good friends, and he was also at a point in his life where he was looking for some kind of spiritual framework. He grew up, as you know, in the Church of England, but he too would not have said he believed in a God. Neither of them felt inclined to ask me—or indeed God—to hear their confession."

The waiter delivered breakfasts to our table, and we paused to spread butter onto hot toast.

"I'm just going to carry on talking, if you don't mind," the priest said. "You eat while you listen. I'm talking to you now because of what I heard from Adam about you. I know what you mean about rewriting history, and I do respect that, but you should know that he did not take the end of your relationship lightly. I am sure you did not kill him, or I would not be talking with you now."

I nodded politely in between mouthfuls of fried egg and bacon. I knew he meant well, but I was profoundly irritated by the fact that Adam had been writing the book on my life all around town. I was also impatient. I was interested in the spiritual angst of Paula and Adam only so far as it impacted on their deaths, and I was afraid there was a way to go before Father Joe got there.

"Well, what was it that was bothering them?" It sounded dismissive, but I wanted to goad Father Joe into a response.

"I wish I could tell you," he said, his clasped hands parting in a gesture that said, That's all.

"You wish you could tell me?" I could hear the vexation in my voice.

"I have never met two such circumspect individuals," he said. "I can tell you that Paula was obsessed by what I might call sins of omission and sins of pride, and that she was overwhelmed and deeply depressed by a sense of guilt—and annoyed with herself for feeling guilt when she did not believe in a higher being who was capable of judging her. I can tell you that Adam had found in himself a sudden thirst for the meaning of life, and that he found his present state of affairs wanting in all sorts of ways. I have no doubt that the two of them had got into some sort of trouble, but in my conversations with them we talked only in the abstract and the theoretical, because as soon as I tried to probe the specifics they clammed up like a couple of schoolgirls caught smoking."

I puffed out my cheeks and exhaled slowly. Our eyes met, mine disappointed, his still curious.

"Now I have to eat," he said, "so it's your turn to talk. I want to hear about the children. Hannah and William, is that right?"

I had no desire to talk. If I was going to leave empty-handed I'd rather have done it straightaway, but my plate was clean and he still had his breakfast sitting in front of him, and common courtesy dictated that I stay and indeed that I talk. I started grudgingly, very aware that he had heard much of this from Adam. He was a good audience, however, and I soon relaxed into it. He ate steadily, pausing sometimes just to raise his eyebrows, or to grunt or chuckle. His face was expressive, and I felt as though we were having a conversation, not as though I was reciting a monologue. I wondered whether this was a technique he had perfected, something he used on his congregation. Somehow my story drew to a natural break just as he mopped his plate clear of yolk. He licked his lips, patted them with his napkin, then looked up at me.

"Adam came to see me on the afternoon of Paula's funeral," he said. "I'd already left for the airport, so I missed him."

I stared at him, and he went on speaking.

"However, he left me a package that I found on my return yesterday. He left it with instructions that it be locked in my office until I came back, and that is what happened."

He bent and picked up his briefcase from the side of his chair and drew from it a large padded brown envelope. This he placed on the table in front of me. He nodded his consent, and I reached for it and picked it up. It was unsealed. Inside were three videotapes as well as one much smaller tape about the size of a calling card that I recognized as a sixty-minute MiniDV tape. The videotapes were numbered one to three and bore the initials "CM," but were not otherwise labeled. The MiniDV tape had no marking of any sort. There was also a note. Glancing up at Father Joe Riberra, and receiving another nod, I unfolded it.

It was scrawled on headed London University paper, and I assumed it was what Adam had written in a hurry on the afternoon of the day of his death, when he realized that he could not speak to the priest face-to-face.

Dear Joe,

I need a safe place to keep this tape, and I hope you will provide it for me. Do take a look if you want to—I'm not entrapping you with pornography—but it won't mean anything to you. Nor will it put you in any danger, since no one who matters knows about this.

The thing is, I'm afraid if I keep it someone might try to take it from me or destroy it. And since I've been trying for months now to decide what to do, it would be a pity if the decision was taken out of my hands. Paula's death makes that decision urgent, and I hope that when you return we will be able to have our first proper conversation about my situation.

With deep apologies for all this 007 stuff.

Yours, Adam

I looked up and found Father Joe watching me.

"He's writing as if there's just one tape," I said, "but there are four."

"There's only one that's significant, perhaps," he offered.

"Have you watched them?" He nodded. "Including this one?" I picked up the tiny MiniDV tape.

"I borrowed a friend's camera last night," he said. "You should take it—take all of them—and watch them. It scares the crap out of me."

Chapter 29

I started at the beginning, because I didn't know where else to start. I put the videotape numbered "one" into the machine, pressed the "Play" button, and Adam's face, like his e-mailed words on the computer, rose ghostlike before me on the screen. I bit my lip. If I had descended into death to eavesdrop on their cyber conversation, today I was bringing Adam and Paula back to life.

It is immediately obvious that what I have here are the rushes, the unedited film, from *A Carmichaelite Mission,* the documentary that was never shown. There is not, at this stage in the process, any voice-over. Suzette is presumably behind the camera. Traditionally, there would be both a cameraman and a producer, but as an independent producer Suzette has chosen in many of her projects to be both, using a small but sophisticated digital camera that produces broadcast-quality footage. It is partly an economy, one less wage to pay, but largely a matter of style. She makes films that are intimate, where the viewer follows people around, eavesdrops on conversations, takes them into situations in which a large camera might be more intrusive. Her camera lives in a large brown leather shoulder bag that also contains a collection of used and unused tapes, as well as her makeup bag, her credit cards, and her palmtop computer. She had chosen to put Adam into some of the scenes with Paula, so that their conversations could be filmed. I get such pleasure from watching Adam work that I forget at first that Father Joe was scared by something. I sit back in my chair and I think how proud my children should be of their father.

There is old footage of Paula Carmichael as a child: pretty, talented, good, just as she grew up, giggling as she dances for the camera at her twelfth birthday party. Adam talks to her about her childhood. I have rarely seen him hit the wrong note, but this interview is unusual for the immediate rapport the two of them strike up. They are at ease in each other's company. There is no flirtation, rather you would believe that the two of them had been friends for years. So, when they sit down and talk about the past, Adam ends up chattering as much as she does. Partly it's a technique, to draw her out, but I've seen technique before, and it's more than that. I guess it would never have made it into the final cut, but here it is for my delight, Adam talking with real affection about his parents.

They both, Paula and Adam, had happy childhoods, and I'm glad. It helps to balance out the end. At one point Adam cracks a joke about his mother, and it touches some chord with Paula, and the two of them are practically rolling around giggling. Even I start chuckling, and then I stop short. Where is Paula's famous depression? I am expecting an earnest, dutiful Paula, struggling to be cheerful against the odds. This Paula is laughing so hard she can't speak.

I start to watch more closely and to think as I'm watching. What of Suzette, behind the camera, seeing what I'm seeing? But that's normal, I've been there, I know what it's like: three people, two of them undergoing some sort of chemical reaction in front of you. I find that when it's me behind the camera I pretty much write myself out of the equation, I see it all through a lens. Besides, if Suzette was in love with Adam, she would have seen that this thing with Paula was not sexual. Paula has not prettified herself for the camera. She looks great, she looks happy, but she looks her age.

We follow Paula to the Houses of Parliament. She gives a running commentary as the camera follows her through the corridors of power. It is funny, it is sharp.

"I could devote my life to this, you know," she says over her shoulder. "It's like a drug. You can be as bitchy as you like, and believe me when I'm in here, I'm bitchy. Even the boys are bitchy here. There's nothing that gives me a bigger high than delivering a death blow to some sad fascist on the other side of the house in a debate."

"So why don't you devote yourself to it, why bother with all the other stuff?" Adam's voice asks.

"Because it would be self-indulgent," Paula replies. "I have limited resources in terms of time and energy and I can use both to be a better person than I can be here."

"Aren't you just a little bit depressed?" I find myself muttering at her. "Not even a tiny bit?"

It is clear that she is not. It is clear, indeed, that she loves her life.

At home, Paula makes a meal for Richard and Kyle and his elder brother George. I'm not convinced she knows one end of the chopping knife from the other, but her family look pleasantly surprised when she puts roast lamb on the table for them. Richard gets out a bottle of champagne—this is clearly a special event—and carves, joking for the camera, "Now I remember why I married her." Very sweetly, at the end of the meal, Kyle gets up and goes and kisses his mother on her cheek. She looks at him with something approaching wonder, and he slopes out of the room, hands in pockets.

We follow Paula from project to project. Along the way we hear from people who work with her, from Rachel Colby, who speaks of Paula's ability to "get her hands dirty and her heart broken." We see Paula in a hostel for the homeless, at an inner city playgroup, and at a hospice, all funded to some extent by the Carmichaelites, and staffed in part by Carmichaelite volunteers. At last Paula's face shows distress, sorrow, even grief.

"I wouldn't have the motivation to do any of this if I wasn't personally involved," she tells Adam. "I know some people in the caring professions say you have to keep your distance or you won't survive. But frankly, you keep your distance, and you don't get close to what needs to be done. I tell all my volunteers to cry, howl, tear your clothes. Have sleepless nights. It's right to feel that way when things are horribly wrong."

"Don't you get depressed?" Adam asks.

"I get terribly, terribly depressed," Paula answers with a crooked smile. "There are days when life looks bleak from the moment I get up in the morning to the moment I go to bed, and everyone around me knows it. When I'm down I'm foul to be with, I've been told that enough times. Then something goes right and I'm high as a kite. I've seen kids do drugs and let me tell you, when things are going well I'm on a bigger kick than they are. I know some people would call me manic, I have great lows and great highs, but that's what propels me through life. It's the beauty of hills and valleys. I'm not going to build my house on a plain."

By now I have watched the three videotapes, and while I have been moved by what I've seen, I have not yet been scared. I dig out my 3-chip camera and put the MiniDV tape inside, then play the tape through the TV. Around about this point, absorbed as I am, I have a strong urge to pee, and a stronger urge for coffee. I am about to hit the "Pause" button when I notice something that makes me forget my bladder and my caffeine craving.

We are now at the opening ceremony for a drug rehabilitation project in Cornwall that is funded by the Carmichaelites. Rachel Colby is there to help with the media, and hanging around in the background of the picture I see a man who looks to me very much like Dan Stein. He's only there for an instant, and then he disappears. I rewind the tape, I replay it. I am ninety percent certain that the man is Dan Stein, but I tell myself that I am stressed and tired and perhaps seeing things. The man has a camera slung around his neck. Dan, the photographer who does not hang people on his walls. It doesn't mean he doesn't photograph them. I hope I am mistaken. If Dan is there, he has lied to me and to Finney, and why would he do that? This cannot be another coincidence. If it is Dan, I cannot think of an innocent explanation.

I let the tape play on then, curious to see whether he appears again, but the film makes a sudden change of place. We are in what looks like a squat, a dirty mattress against a wall that has lost most of its plaster, sheets hung across the windows as makeshift curtains. A boy, perhaps sixteen years old, is sitting on the mattress, his face blotchy. He is thin and pale, his shabby clothes hanging loose on him. It is not clear who else is in the room with him, nor who is doing the filming.

The boy looks ill. There is a sickly sheen to his skin. He unfolds a tinfoil wrap, then cooks up the drug on a spoon over the flame of a lighter. He holds a syringe in his mouth while he tightens the tourniquet around his arm and waits for the vein, but instead, his chest shudders as he begins to retch. He leans to one side, as if to vomit. The camera shot swings away from the boy and to the ground. The sound is still good.

"What's the matter?" The voice, hard, annoyed, is familiar.

"I'm going to puke," the boy groans.

"Great." Again, I hear the voice that sounds like Dan, angry and frustrated, before the screen goes blank. Presumably the boy is allowed to vomit without it being recorded for posterity. There is a limit to viewers' tolerance of the gritty, after all. When the pictures return to the screen he is sitting there again, even paler than before, if possible, beads of sweat visible on his forehead.

"Are you sure about this?" I hear Paula's voice, concerned, doubtful. "You know you don't have to do this."

"For Christ's sake, let him get on with it," the man who sounds like Dan mutters.

The boy glances toward the point from where Paula's voice has come, then at the place where the voice that may be Dan's comes from. He lifts the syringe and with a jerky impulse pushes the needle through his skin and into the vein. The camera settles for a moment on the boy's face as the drug takes effect and the tension subsides, his muscles loosening. Then, for an instant, the boy's face is suffused with panic. He convulses. Someone in the background mutters, "Shit." The camera cuts again, and this time the screen goes blank, as though they have fallen off air.

Chapter 30

THERE are days that should be cut out of our lives and pasted directly in hell. The next day was one of them. I had watched the tape over and again until late at night, then lain in bed worrying over it. When someone pounded on my front door at six the next morning, I hauled myself out of bed and went to see who it was. I realized my mistake in an instant. A camera flashed in my face and I slammed the door, but not before a man outside had hurled a rolled up newspaper inside. Shaking, I bent down to pick it up and took it into the kitchen. I removed the rubber band and unrolled it, pressing it flat on the tabletop.

It was a copy of the *Chronicle,* and when I saw the byline, Bill Tanning, I stared down at the front page with real fear. Had I ever done anything to Tanning to make him hate me, or was I just fair prey? A large black-and-white photograph took up at least half the page. At first I thought it was an ad: a picture of a man and woman kissing, his hands entangled in her hair. A headline said: SLEEPING WITH THE SUSPECT. I sat down hard on a chair and forced myself to read the story.

Detective Inspector Tom Finney, who heads the investigation into the murder of Adam Wills, is today expected to be removed from his post and suspended from duty pending a full inquiry into his passionate relationship with Robin

Ballantyne. Redhead Ballantyne, 35, was Wills's former lover, and police have repeatedly refused to rule her out as a suspect in the hit-and-run murder of the popular broadcaster. Ballantyne's car was used in the killing.

Two days ago, Detective Tom Finney passed to this newspaper alleged facts that seemed to point the investigation away from Ballantyne and toward some other, so far unnamed, killer. Journalists from our newspaper, however, were suspicious of Finney's motives. When those who are charged with upholding justice on our behalf falter in their task, then others must step into the breach. It was in this spirit that journalists from this newspaper decided to keep Finney under surveillance. Yesterday, their patience paid off and they spotted Finney, 39, engaged in passionate clinches with the supposed chief suspect.

Finney, who recently separated from his wife of five years, approached Ballantyne's house in the middle of the afternoon. Barefoot, and dressed only in jeans and a tight-fitting T-shirt, she opened the door to him and greeted him enthusiastically. He moved inside and was seen removing his coat. Ballantyne is the mother of Adam Wills's twins, Hannah and William, but there was no sign of the children.

Some time later Finney and Ballantyne were visible reclining on a sofa. They kissed repeatedly and embraced in a highly sexual way.

Contacted by this newspaper, Commander Perry of the Metropolitan Police said that if the allegations were substantiated Detective Inspector Finney would be suspended "for as long as it took." This paper has passed to Commander Perry the photographs it obtained as a result of its investigation. This newspaper has also learned that Finney was suspended for two months last year after allegations that he had acted unprofessionally in a case concerning a female suspect. Finney was cleared, but one police source told the paper Finney, "remains under a cloud to this day, and he should be watching his back, not following other parts of his anatomy."

Adam Wills's parents, contacted by this newspaper, were shocked by the news of Ballantyne's new love. "Our son is just buried," said Norma Wills, "but Robin is as hard as nails. It doesn't surprise me that the children were nowhere to be seen. She gets them out of her way whenever she can so she can have the sort of lifestyle she wants, which is very free and easy."

Robin Ballantyne and Detective Inspector Tom Finney were last night both unavailable for comment.

Chapter 31

ONLY Jane could have got through the pack of hyenas at my door. She rang me on her mobile.

"I'm coming in, be ready to open the door for me."

So I stood inside my front door and waited until I heard her voice outside.

"Out of my way, you daft buggers," I heard her shout, and they must have made way for her because the next thing she was rapping on the door and I was opening it to let her in, and pushing it closed before the rest of them fell in behind her.

I sat down on the staircase while she took her coat off and flung it over the banisters.

"You're not even dressed," she accused. "Look at you in your jammies with your head in your hands."

"It's six-thirty in the morning and I'm in shock," I informed her.

"No you're not, you wee idiot, and what were you thinking of anyway, snogging a policeman? Do you have a death wish?"

I shook my head. I didn't want to talk about it. I looked up at her and she made a face at me.

"You'll have to pull yourself together," she said, "or there's nothing I can do to help you."

I put my head back in my hands for a moment, and then I stood up, turned, and went up the stairs to get dressed.

Jane watched the *Carmichaelite Mission* tape in the sitting room while I washed the children and fed them. I didn't set her to watching the whole thing, just the last scene, with the boy. She came into the kitchen, ashen with shock, and sat down heavily without saying anything. I sat down opposite her and poured us both coffee.

"I think the man who's there when the boy shoots up is living opposite me here," I told her calmly. "I met him on the night of Paula's death. He's been trying to seduce me."

Jane screwed her face up and shook her head.

"What the fuck is going on?"

"You'll have to pull yourself together," I told her pointedly.

She puffed out her cheeks and blew, looking up at me, still shaking her head. "Have you asked Suzette about this?"

"I can't get hold of her."

"Let's try again," she said grimly.

We tried again, and then again. While I dealt with the children Jane called every number we had for Suzette, and then she tried every number anybody else had, and also rang Suzette's mother, but once it was clear Suzette wasn't there, she didn't prolong the conversation. Her mother, we knew, was frail and prone to terrible fits of anxiety. Suzette wasn't anywhere to be found. We even tried her ex-husband in Australia. God knows what time of the day it was there. Jane had to sweet-talk him, just so he didn't hang up. Anyway, he didn't know where Suzette was and he didn't much care.

"Okay," Jane said. "Suzette's gone AWOL. Time for Plan B."

Plan B, she suggested, was to confront Dan Stein. I couldn't be seen in the street or I'd be mobbed, so it had to be her. She snuck out the back way and around the block, so that in the event the hacks outside simply didn't pay any attention to a woman walking down the other side of the road and stopping outside a house that wasn't mine. I watched from the window as she rang his bell. No one came. She rang another bell, and a woman came to the door who I recognized from the top window the morning after Paula's death. Jane and the woman exchanged a few words, and a few moments later Jane was back.

"She's on the top floor," she told me, "and she hasn't seen him for the last couple of days, but that doesn't mean a thing. Do you have a home number for him?"

We tried it, but there was no answer.

"Or a work telephone?"

"He's in personnel . . ." I started to say, but realized he'd given me no company name. "No. I have nothing."

We sat in silence for a few moments, realizing we'd hit a dead end. Then we started to discuss my options, and we kept on and on for a good hour. Talk to Finney, she suggested, but I could not bear to—and besides, what if the tape was a red herring? I would look like an idiot. Like a desperate idiot.

"No," I told her, "I've got to find out what it's all about before I run to the police."

"Okay," she said.

I looked at her expectantly.

"Then don't talk to Finney," she said.

We smiled weakly at each other. My situation was dire. Hysteria was close at hand.

Talking to Maeve was similarly out of the question. Her only instinct would be to protect her backside, and anyway, I felt an obligation to Suzette. I needed to hear her side of the story. I needed to know what happened in Cornwall, who knew what and when.

"So you go to Cornwall," Jane said eventually, "and you find out what happened there."

"Okay." I nodded.

"I mean you go now."

"The children . . ." I started to say. "I'll be gone for a while, I don't know . . ."

"The children will be fine," she assured me. "Carol will get here in a minute. I'll call her and tell her to come round the back way, and then I'll call your mother and sound pathetic, and she'll help us out. We'll be fine 'til you get back."

I looked at her.

"Carol will show me what to do," she said.

I continued to stare at her.

"None of us will let any harm come to them."

I bit my lip. "That day, you know, with Erica. That call she had from the well-wisher. What if it was Dan warning me off?"

"We don't even know he's involved. We don't know anything. That video's just spooked us."

"I don't trust him. He knows the kids are here, he knows . . ." My voice trailed off. I wasn't yet prepared to voice the fears that were flooding in.

We stared at each other.

"We won't let any harm come to them," she repeated.

———

I drive fiercely at first, as though my life depends on it, south and west. I begin to find the motorway soothing, which means I am in a truly sorry state.

There was no point in splitting hairs with the *Chronicle* over the newspaper's story. I had not slept with Finney, but that wasn't really the point. I had not spoken to him before I left. I didn't know what to say. Between us I supposed that we had ruined his career, but I wasn't sure that I was required to apologize. I wanted to ask about his marriage, and I wanted to ask about the woman in the case he'd been suspended from the year before, but I was sure as hell I didn't want to know the answers. In my experience the tabloids never say it prettily, and sometimes they get it totally wrong, but, more often than not, there's a grain of truth around which they spin their pearl. We were finished before we'd begun.

I had another question. Why had Finney come to see me? Was his intention to seduce me, and if so why, or at least why then? As the tarmac sped by, my mind, now mired in paranoia, began to spin a scenario in which Finney was for some reason in league with the tabloids, plotting to ruin me. There was, as far as I could see, nothing in it for him, but whichever way you looked at it, we'd both walked headlong into trouble. I was past fury, past even being hurt.

It took me six hours to reach Penzance. I crossed the Tamar from Devon into Cornwall, thinking I must be nearly there, but the peninsula stretched for miles. On the A30 I passed fields of new age wind turbines, their propellers turning purposefully, as though they might just take off and float skyward. Around me the land swelled and dipped and the vegetation became thicker as if growing on more fertile land. As I drove southward the air that washed into the car became warmer and damper, and it seemed to carry salt on it. By the time I actually saw the sea and St. Michael's Mount, the castle rising out of the waters of the bay like the home to some imprisoned princess, the sky was already dark. The streets of granite terraces were quiet, clinging to the steep hill that sloped up from the harbor. There were pubs open, but little else, and few people around. A light drizzle added to my overwhelming impression of water and wetness: shops for surfers, bikinis and swimsuits in the windows; rainwater trickling along the gutters, down my windscreen; sea stretching away, boats bobbing in the harbor, waves beating against the promenade. Inside the car I was dry from head to toe, but I felt as though I were submerged. Eventually I found my way from the sea and up farther into the town, to Alexandra Road, a street of severe town houses, each in competition with its neighbors for the bed-and-breakfast trade.

I cruised up the street, then down, and chose an establishment with stone steps up to the door and a palm tree in the small front garden. I hoped business was bad enough that it would not turn away a potential customer on the basis that she was a suspected murderess, alleged inadequate mother, and general lowlife. Still, I approached the reception desk with some trepidation. There was a woman behind the desk, her large shoulders bent over a newspaper. She wore a flowered cardigan over a woolen dress that stretched over a substantial bosom and ballooned over a similarly substantial stomach. She wore a rectangular plastic badge on her cardigan that read "Betty."

"Do you have a room for the night?" I asked. I suddenly felt a very long way from Hannah and William. How could I spend a night so far from them? Surely it was time for me to turn around and go back home, now.

Betty was startled by my voice, and looked up, then did a double take. She looked down at the newspaper, then back up at me.

"You look just like this lass," she said.

I was caught off guard.

"Really?" I peered at the newspaper. I hadn't thought to wear a disguise, and anyway it's not as easy as it sounds. To wear sunglasses in the winter is to invite stares. I gazed at myself, upside down.

"Well, he's a fine figure of a man," she said. "Who could blame her?"

Our eyes met, and I knew instantly that she knew, but that, it seemed, was as far as Betty wanted to take it. I was, she informed me, their only guest that night, so she'd given me their best room, and I'd find it very quiet. I signed myself in as Joanna Smith.

"Very imaginative, my sweetheart," said Betty, and it was said with such generosity and such a lack of condescension that I was almost flattered.

She didn't serve food, and I ended up eating cod and chips in a café on the promenade. The proprietor, who provided newspapers, gave me a curious look too, and I lowered my head over my food and left a fat tip behind me.

Afterward, cold but no longer hungry, I returned to the B and B and made my way through the silent corridors to my room. It was decorated in pink chintz and was more quiet than I could stand. I did not want to be alone with my thoughts, and I longed for Hannah and William. I looked at my watch. They would be out of the bath, warm and soft and sweet-smelling. Here in this clear silence and the clean air and this neat and tidy room, I even felt nostalgic for the mess and muddle. I rang them on my mobile and spoke to my mother. Everything was fine, but I hung up feeling no better: I was redundant; I had left my children behind in the care of others. I had spent an entire day burning up petrol on a wild-goose chase, the deaths that haunted me as far from any solution or explanation as they had ever been. My love life was lurching from tragedy to humiliation. My career was in tatters, my dignity a farce, my very future as the mother of my children in doubt. Oh yes, and my father was a crook. It was not an evening for peaceful reflection.

I turned on Adam's computer and read halfheartedly through an e-mail or two, but Adam's cyber voice, the dead echo of his vitality, depressed me further. In the end I took a sleeping tablet and felt relief steal over me as I sank into oblivion. My last thought was of Hannah and William, of their sleeping faces.

―――

The next morning I opened the window and took a deep breath, the air like spring water. I showered, I carbo-loaded on scrambled eggs and bacon and toast, fending off the landlord's attempts at conversation. Betty had clearly shared her suspicions with her husband, and he was questioning me about where I was from and why I was in Penzance. I didn't want to talk, and he must have concluded that I was guilty. I got back in my car, and drove to the address that Jane had given me. Market Jew Street could have been a high street anywhere, complete with Boots and Woolworth's and WH Smith. Elderly women pulled shopping carts, and young mothers pushed strollers. There were few men around, and those there were had nothing to push or pull. There was no beach crowd at this time of year, just a few brave walkers, dressed professionally against the weather.

Away from the street a maze of alleys sloped up and away from the sea, and it was here, vertiginously perched just off Causewayhead, that I found a modest terraced cottage, a small hand-painted plaque next to its door confirming that it was the office of the Penzance Clear Water Rehabilitation Project. I rang the bell, but there was no response, and I realized that the windows were still dark. I turned around to leave—so much for early-morning optimism—but as I did so, a man hailed me. He was striding toward me, and I met him halfway.

"Who are you looking for?" he asked.

"You're Michael Amey," I said, recognizing him from the documentary film.

"At your service."

"Robin Ballantyne," I said, and held out my hand. He gave me an intent look, but shook my hand anyway, then led the way to the office, where he unlocked the door and pushed it open, waving me in ahead of him.

"We don't really get started until about ten," he said, brisk and businesslike, "but the day stretches into the morning at the other end. Now, tell me what I can do for you."

Amey was, I guessed, in his early fifties. He wore a tweed jacket and had a receding but distinguished hairline. He was bluff and sociable, but I imagined that he did not suffer fools gladly. He had a vaguely military air to him. I glanced at his shoes. Brown leather, well worn, but they shone. Inside the building, the original layout remained: a narrow corridor, small rooms, the thick granite walls taking up more space than any modern architect would have allowed. We sat in an office that was small but perfectly ordered, except for a mound of mail in a basket marked "In-tray."

"I've been away," Amey explained as he followed my eyes. "I'm afraid things mount up. I don't know if you know, but what we're trying to do here is keep people out of prison, even persistent offenders. We're trying to get them into detox, turn their lives around. It's a constant battle. How anyone can imagine that with a challenge like that we have time for the fine print of bureaucracy . . ." He stopped himself and took a deep breath. "But I'm sure that's not why you've come to see me."

I launched into my story, keeping my eyes glued to his. He must not think me shifty, or indeed mad. I told him about finding Paula Carmichael's body, about the death of Adam, and my conviction that the two deaths were linked. I told him that the police did not share my view, told him that I myself was a suspect in the killing of Adam. I said I believed he could help me by talking to me about Carmichael's visit during the making of the documentary. As I spoke I could see the tension rising. By the time I was finished, his jaw was set, his lips thin.

"Well, I knew a lot of that already," Amey said when I drew to a halt, "but thank you for being so candid. Tell me what you'd like to know."

"I think something happened here that put an end to the filming of the documentary," I said. "I know that there was some sort of falling out between Suzette and Paula, and that perhaps something happened that involved Adam too."

"I'm afraid I can't help you with any internal differences," he said. "If there were personality clashes between the three of them, that's nothing to do with us or our work here."

I nodded slowly, asking myself whether there was any other way to approach this.

"I understand that," I said carefully, "but I wonder how you would characterize your relations with each of those three people."

"Characterize my relations?" Amey laughed nervously, but then he caught sight of my face and the laugh disappeared. "What does it matter?"

"Well, people may have died because of it," I said quietly.

Amey raised his eyebrows, but he gave a little bow from his neck, and started to speak.

"Everything we do here is sensitive. We walk a tightrope, perhaps they didn't understand that." He paused, to give me time to digest what he'd said. "We'd talked to the production company, and we were aware in advance that the filming here would be a small part of the documentary about Paula, and about her organization, and that really we would be filmed just as an illustration of the work that organization does. Everything was fine at first. I liked Paula Carmichael, and we were all fully supportive of the documentary. In our view, and in the view of our governors, the more publicity Paula Carmichael got, the more people would be motivated to help. It's meant a lot to organizations like us, the extra funding. I can't say it's flowed, but there's been a steady trickle since Paula Carmichael came on the scene. So we were only too happy to do our bit. At first." Amey shifted in his chair, leaning forward, supporting his elbows on his knees, and pressing the tips of his fingers together. "There was a lot of filming, lots of talking, lots of interviewing. Paula was absolutely delightful, so there was absolutely no ill will, none at all. Then she wanted interviews with clients. We found a couple who were willing to talk on film, and that went well I think. Then . . ." He screwed up his face and looked away. "Much as I want to help, I'm going to ask you to keep what I tell you next confidential. You'll understand why. I'm co-operating with you, and on this I need you to cooperate with me."

"I'll try, but if this has a bearing on someone's death, then it's your responsibility as much as mine to inform the police."

He gazed at my face for a minute, the muscles at his jaw working.

"Well, I really don't think it does, so I'll take that risk. The thing is, Paula came to me and said that, in order to communicate the horror of drug abuse, she needed film of someone actually using drugs. Preferably someone young and vulnerable, she said. Well, hah!" Amey sat back in his chair. "I was stunned at the suggestion. She knows perfectly well that there have been cases where social workers have been imprisoned for allowing drug-taking on their premises. She said it didn't have to be on the premises, but any hint of our collusion, if it ever got out, would have been the end of us. I refused point blank. A scandal like that, and everything we've been working for . . . Even my volunteers don't really know what happened. They know Paula and I had a falling out—some of them may have put two and two together and got four—but this was something I tried at least to keep between Paula and myself."

Amey stopped speaking, but I knew that was not the end of the story.

"But eventually you helped her find someone," I said, trying to bluff it out of him.

"I did not," Amey protested. "I've told you, I refused point blank to have anything to do with it, and Paula dropped the subject. I never heard any more of it, but it had poisoned the atmosphere, and frankly I was glad to see them go."

I sat in silence for a moment, mulling over what he had said. I was aware that I had offended Amey, that he wished he had confided nothing, and that he was impatient for me to be gone, but I could not believe the trail ended here.

"Could you do one more thing for me?" I asked.

"Tell me first, do you believe what I've told you?" he demanded.

"I do," I said, "but I want to show you why I'm confused. Will you let me?"

He nodded, but he was still on his guard.

"Okay." I unzipped my bag, and pulled my laptop from it and set it up on the desk, moving the in-tray. I found the relevant file, then explained to Amey that I was about to show him extracts from the unedited documentary film. He nodded. I had cut the film to the minimum. First came the shot of the man I thought might be Dan Stein.

"Do you recognize him?" I asked Amey.

"Certainly," he said. His face was tense.

"Who is he?"

Amey shrugged, as if to say it wasn't important, then pulled a face that I could not read. "He's a volunteer, or he was. Name of Ned Sennet; he helps us with publicity stuff. He's an excellent photographer, so he used to get stories into the local press, and he had links with various celebrities around the place, so if you wanted someone to come and open a fund-raiser or speak after dinner, you went to Ned . . . He was always extremely helpful."

That sounded like praise, and yet Amey's tone of voice was unhappy.

"Where is he now?"

"He left a few months ago, just after the filming of the documentary. I don't know where he went. Someone was asking me how to get in contact with him just the other day . . ." Again his voice trailed off, and he seemed distracted.

"Okay, let's go back to the film," I instructed, impatient. "This follows straight on from the section filmed here in Penzance.

There's no indication on the film that we've moved to another town so I'm assuming it happened here." This time I played him the section that showed the boy shooting up. I'd included everything, from the false start, the vomit break, to the intravenous injection of the drug, the shocking spasm, and the suddenly blank screen. I kept my eyes on Amey's face throughout, and saw the blood recede and his jaw slacken with shock. He could not have faked such alarm.

"You've seen him before," I prompted.

"Where did this come from?" Amey hissed. "What is it?"

"It's the documentary that Paula made. You know who he is, don't you?"

"I don't remember his name," Amey broke off, his fists tight on his lap and his knuckles white. I gave him time to gather his thoughts. "I'm almost certain it's a boy who came here once about a year ago. Or, rather, he was dragged here by a friend. He was addicted to heroin—as I remember he'd just switched from smoking it to injecting, you know I'm sure that it's a more intense high, and it doesn't waste any—and he was in trouble with the police for housebreaking. His friend brought him here because he hoped we could get him off it. I talked to him about his options. He was an unfortunate boy. He obviously wanted to please his friend, and he wasn't happy about his life as it was. My heart went out to him, but I've seen this too often and I knew that he was not at a point where he was determined to change. I wasn't surprised when I didn't see him again—and I'm afraid," Amey's voice was solemn, "that I wasn't very surprised when a few months later I saw his picture in the newspaper, with a report of his death from a heroin overdose."

Chapter 32

I started that afternoon in the library next to Morrab Gardens, three acres of subtropical plants that on any other day I would have loved to explore. We'd gone through Michael Amey's files already. He was sure he had clipped the article: it was relevant to the work of the center, and the death had been shocking because of the youth of the boy involved. At first he refused to believe that his filing system could be anything but perfect, but he couldn't find it anywhere, and eventually, increasingly irritated and anxious, he admitted defeat. I felt stupid asking, but I asked anyway.

"Did Ned Sennet ever have access to your files?"

Amey scratched his head and sucked in his lips.

"He might have done some work in here on the computer once or twice," he said. I knew he hated having to give me an incomplete, imperfect answer. It offended his sense of control.

He was looking deeply worried as I left him. Amey thought the boy had died at around the same time as the documentary, but because he had never before connected the two events he could not be sure. Nor, he admitted, could he be one hundred percent certain that it was the same boy. What he had seen, after all, was a photograph in a newspaper, grainy, two-dimensional, and quite possibly out of date. Still, I trusted his hunch in the same way I trusted mine about Dan Stein/Ned Sennet.

When I found the boy, looking out at me from the pages of the

West Penwith Herald dated two days after Paula Carmichael's premature departure from Penzance, I knew Amey's gut instinct was right. The paper didn't say where the photograph had come from, but I guessed it had been taken by Social Services or the police. In it the teenager looked sullenly straight ahead, the collar of his sweatshirt sagging around a scrawny neck, his ears sticking out, cheeks sunken in. He was the same boy, I had no doubt of it. The report accompanying the picture was short and to the point.

> Eighteen-year-old Sean Morris died yesterday after taking a fatal overdose of heroin. Emergency services responded at three in the afternoon to an unoccupied address in Newlyn after an anonymous 999 call made from a public phone box by a woman but Morris was dead when they arrived. Sean Morris had a history of theft and drug use. He is the eighth drug fatality in the county this year, and the youngest.

I searched the newspapers for the next few days, and then for the next few weeks, and found a brief coroner's report. Morris, the coroner said, died of a sudden seizure and lung edema caused by an injection of impure heroin administered after a heavy drinking session. When he was found, the needle was still in his arm. His blood was full of alcohol. He was underweight and was still recovering from the flu. The coroner recommended a review by the relevant authorities. I could find no subsequent reference to the boy's death.

The discovery filled me with restless energy. I made copies of the two small articles I'd found, then left the library. Outside the breeze had turned into a storm. The sky was dark and rain was lashing down. I got back in the car and drove along the shore, but I couldn't stay in the car for long, despite the weather. I needed to pace, and to think. I parked opposite a bus station, then fought my way against the gale to cross a wooden bridge over the railway line and found myself on a path along the top of the beach. To my right Mount's Bay stretched toward the low rooftops, the domes and spires of Penzance. To my left lay the tiny settlement of Marazion. Out to sea the Mount itself rose medieval from the waves. The tide was out, the desert of sand stretched wet and sleek, the water beyond was like slate, the horizon a marker for a threatening sky. I breathed in deeply, filling my lungs with the good damp air. I shut my eyes for a moment, clutching my jacket closed at my neck. I abandoned myself to the wind as it battered against me and whipped my hair against my face. I hugged my new knowledge close. My instincts were vindicated. The deaths of Paula and Adam had a common root, and I had found it. I started to walk along the path. I needed to keep moving, needed to use up the adrenaline coursing through me.

In my head I can see how it happens. Suzette is concerned that her documentary is turning into fluff. So far it is all nice volunteers and helpful institutions, lots of pats on the back for Paula Carmichael, who she feels is too good to be true. Suzette wants substance, she needs an illustration of a grimmer reality.

"Paula," I see her saying, "they'll listen to you. You're the one with the clout here. I need more than this. I need something so visually shocking that our viewers really sit up and take notice and say 'God, this is so awful, I need to do something. I need to get involved.'"

And Paula wanted the documentary, of course, because it would mean so much to the cause. She had moved mountains, but she needed publicity. She'd already invested weeks of her time in the project. She might not feel comfortable about it, but Suzette was the professional. If Suzette said it was necessary, then it was necessary.

Then the picture grew cloudier. Amey says he will not be involved. My guess is that Sennet—Dan—steps in with an offer of help. I know a guy who knows a guy who knows . . . He needs some cash to do the persuading. Suzette is unhappy, but if it's the only way to get the footage . . . just don't ever tell the Corporation, Ned. Perhaps he needs cash for the drug too . . . Suzette doesn't want to know where the heroin comes from. Probably she doesn't even want to be present when they film the boy. Perhaps Sennet does the whole thing on his own. He knows the boy is just a baby, knows the boy's been drinking, that he's sick, knows he needs the cash and is desperate for the drug. Suzette at least thinks she's buying a pro, some hardened addict. If she had been there, if she had seen him, then surely she would put a stop to what happens next— but then why didn't Paula put a stop to it? And what did Adam know of what took place? Four people, bonded together by guilt. Two of them dead, one missing.

Deep in my thoughts, I lose all sense of time. There is no one else on the beach, no one in sight. The sky is getting darker, but the wind is losing none of its power, and I am beginning to be more aware of the cold and the wet, the beach and the railway tracks. Then, out of nowhere, comes a voice from behind me.

"Small world."

I start, turn, knowing already who I will find.

Dan Stein—Ned Sennet—is walking just behind me.

For an instant I try to formulate words—I will challenge him, demand the truth—but he is in no mood to talk. He takes advantage of my hesitation by walking straight toward me so that I have no alternative but to step backward, off the path.

He smiles at me, licks the rain off his lips. He is wearing jogging pants and a black waterproof jacket, its hood over his crew-cut head. Until now I have seen him in the chinos and button-down collars that make every man look the same size. Now, for the first time, I realize that he is large and athletic. We are both wet through.

"Funny running into you here," he says, shouting over the storm. He is still coming toward me, and when I step backward once more I feel the low chicken-wire fence behind me. For a moment I lose my footing, and the chicken wire gives way. Behind me is a steep embankment, and below that the railway line.

"Are you sure you don't want to go out with me?" he yells, still grinning. I realize that on top of the noise of the storm there is now another sound, an approaching train. Dan leans over me, making me bend even farther back to avoid the touch of his body, puckering his lips, laughing when I turn my face away. As the train approaches, I raise my knee into his groin, but he jumps backward before it makes contact and my sudden movement makes me lose my balance. I am slipping. The train roars toward us, and I see the driver's face, frozen in alarm as he catches sight of us. I fall forward, pulling myself away from the embankment. Then the train is gone.

"I know what happened to the boy," I yell at Dan through the rain, fury overwhelming fear.

He turns his face away for an instant, then turns back to me.

"The boy was a mistake, forget about him," he yells back. "Remember what happened to Paula." He comes closer again and this time I stand my ground. He leans in close and still I don't move. My jaw is set. I don't even want to run, I want to fight.

"You'll never find me," he says, his mouth so close to my ear that he doesn't have to shout, "but I can always find you."

I feel his tongue on my ear and slap him hard across the face. He laughs, steps away from me.

"Why are you here?" I shout.

"Remember Paula," he mouths at me. He blows me a kiss and, grinning, turns and walks away. I start to walk after him, and when he starts to jog, I break into a run too. We are heading toward the

Mount but the rain is getting heavier, the sky is black, and Dan pulls away from me into the downpour. Then, all at once, as the path divides, I have lost sight of him. I bend over, hands on knees, panting. My legs are shaking, and my heart is pounding, and I am soaked to the skin.

Up in the town, away from the shore, I found a coffee shop open. I was the only customer, and the tables were all set with white lace tablecloths. The waitress, a young woman with blond streaks in her hair and a tight pink T-shirt that rode up over her stomach, looked at me in horror as I dripped through the door.

"Did you get caught in the rain?" she asked, full of sympathy.

I nodded. I'd got caught and nearly killed in the rain, but I wasn't ready to share that.

"Isn't it awful. I'll get you a towel," she said, and I stood and waited, not daring to plant my soaking self on one of her white chairs. I dug my mobile phone out of my pocket, but then realized it had run out of power.

When the waitress got back I dried myself as best I could and thanked her profusely. Then I asked for a coffee and the use of her telephone.

I rang my home number and Carol answered. She reported that the children were fine, although by the time she had arrived the day before Jane had put Hannah's nappy on back to front and had the contents of the old nappy smeared down her skirt. Between them Jane, Carol, and my mother seem to have a schedule worked out. Carol will do the daytime shift while my mother is at work. My mother will do the night shift and stay until Carol returns in the morning. Jane has been demoted to logistical support in the form of grocery shopping. "She needs to feel useful," Carol confided. The children are cheerful without me, and when I speak to them briefly, they do not break down in floods of tears. Before I hang up I remind Carol that she must not open the door to strangers.

Relieved and reinvigorated by the knowledge that all was well at home, I rang Amey to tell him that he was right, that the boy on the video was the boy he remembered from the newspaper, but he had already taken that for granted.

"You need to come over here now," he told me, his voice tight. "There's someone you need to talk to."

Amey was waiting for me in his office, and with him was a young woman, slim and attractive, her dark hair gathered in a ponytail on top of her head, her ears and fingers heavy with silver jewelry. She was seated at Amey's desk, and she looked apprehensive. Amey was standing, stone-faced.

"Becky is my assistant here," he said, his voice clipped. I nodded at her, and she dipped her head at me, but Amey was not in a mood for social niceties. "I asked her days ago whether she'd seen Ned, and she said no. Now she tells me she's been talking to him on a daily . . ."

"Mike, you told me someone was looking for him, and you asked if I'd seen him," Becky interrupted, defiant. "I told you I hadn't seen him because I *hadn't* seen him. I'd just talked to him on the phone. I didn't know where he was."

"Why on earth didn't you give me his phone number?"

"I don't know, I just didn't think . . . It was only today, when you said a boy died, that I realized it was important. I thought you were just mad at him for walking out on us."

At which Amey's face turned purple. He was appalled at her idiocy, but I wasn't convinced by her story. He was about to harangue her, but I gestured at him that I wanted to speak, and he shut up, shaking his head in frustration.

"Becky, Ned told you not to give anyone his phone number, didn't he?"

Becky fixed me with a speculative eye. She didn't reply.

"Were the two of you seeing each other?" I asked her.

She nodded minutely, a single jerk of the head.

"And he told you he wanted to continue his relationship with you?"

Another nod of assent.

"But he didn't want everyone calling him, he just wanted you."

"He felt put upon here." Becky glared at Amey. "They'd been asking too much of him because he was so good at things. He wanted to break off contact with them, but not with me."

"So when Mike told you someone wanted to get in touch with Ned, you lied."

"I told Mike I didn't know where he was," Becky said, "which was true, but I passed the message on to Ned. I told him exactly what Mike said to me, that a journalist from the *West Penwith Herald* was trying to track him down to ask him some questions about some boy. Ned said he didn't want anything to do with any journalist, so I wasn't to let on how to contact him."

I turned to Amey.

"That's who wanted to contact him?" I demanded. "A journalist from the *West Penwith Herald*?"

"Neil Bovin. I thought nothing of it," Amey said defensively.

"Did he say why he wanted to speak to Ned?"

Amey sighed. He looked a good ten years older than he had that morning.

"All right. Look, when I told him Ned didn't work for us anymore he wanted to know whether there had been any problem with him. I asked what sort of problem, and he asked whether Ned had dealt drugs. Well, there had never been the slightest suggestion of anything like that, so I'm afraid I gave him short shrift. I did try ringing the producer woman, Milner, because I thought she might have a contact number for him. I think I may even have told her what the journalist had said about Ned, I'd found the allegation so disturbing, but she didn't know where he was either, and I decided there was nothing more I could be expected to do."

Amey was red in the face, as though he felt he should have done more to trace Ned Sennet, or as though he should have admitted that he'd been warned about Ned, but it would have made no difference to the substance of what had happened. Sean Morris was already dead.

"The journalist rang me too," Becky said quietly. "I told him I didn't know where Ned was, but he didn't ask me about the dealing, or I'd have said something."

"For Christ's sake," Amey exclaimed, "is there anyone else we should know about?"

"The woman from the TV crew," Becky said, "the blond one, she rang me too, looking for Ned. I told her I didn't know where he was."

"But you passed the message on," I prompted her.

"I told Ned," she agreed. "He said he'd deal with it."

———

Amey drove me to a pub in Newlyn, where the journalist from the *West Penwith Herald* had agreed to meet us. I was still wet from the rain. My feet were particularly uncomfortable, soggy in my boots. I could feel angry vibrations coming from Amey.

"Is this how you always work?" he snapped, eventually, unable to contain himself any longer, his knuckles white on the steering wheel.

"I don't know what you mean." We stopped at a traffic light, and he turned a glare on me.

"I mean you journalists. Is that how you work, getting boys to kill themselves in front of you? Playing with people's lives? Like children let loose with a camera, meddling in things you don't understand?"

"Of course not. Something went wrong."

I stared out of the window.

"Went wrong?" He was angrier than ever. "Sean was a good kid with a foul life. People like Sean take heroin because it's a painkiller. There's nothing evil about it, they just want a break from the misery. The dealers boost their profits by cutting the stuff with drain cleaner or cement dust or baby powder. That's the poison these kids end up injecting into their veins. The government washes its hands by criminalizing everyone including the kids like Sean. And then some arrogant do-gooder comes along and says please inject more, so I can have a nice picture. And you tell me something went wrong? In my book that's as good as murder."

I stared silently out at the angry sea. If only they had come forward. If only they had come clean about what had happened. But Sean was dead. Their careers would have been in tatters. I wanted to find a way of defending them, but there was none.

"You're right," I said at last.

———————

In the bar, Neil Bovin was waiting for us and nursing a beer. It was still early evening, and he had the place to himself. As soon as he saw us he drained his glass, stubbed out his cigarette, and stood up.

We introduced ourselves, shaking hands. Bovin looked like a surfer. He had shoulder-length blond hair, hazel eyes, and a tan, and he looked vaguely contemptuous of Amey's obvious anxiety.

Still, a journalist is a journalist. He knew the smell of a story, and he knew how to dig.

I would have been fairly circumspect about what I said, but Amey just blurted it all out. I sat and listened to his account of what we knew, or what he thought we knew. Any sense of loyalty I'd had toward Suzette or Paula had dissipated in a cloud of disgust at what they'd done.

"So what we need to know from you," Amey rounded off, "is how you knew about Ned Sennet."

Bovin pursed his lips and gave me a little smile.

"There's someone you need to meet," he said, "but I need an agreement from you, Robin, that I get to write this first. I mean, without what I'm about to show you, you don't have a story."

I stared at him.

"I'm not interested in writing this for anyone. That's not the point."

He raised his eyebrows.

"I thought you were a journalist," he said, standing up, "but that's okay by me. You do the police, I'll do the papers. This is one for the nationals. Let's go."

————

Bovin led us to the outskirts of the small town, to a road of small, terraced cement-clad houses.

The three of us walked up to the front door of one of these—the only house with a garden that had been left to grow wild. With fertile soil and all the sun and rain that it could need, the tiny space had turned into a jungle. The windows were boarded up, the bell hung out of the wall, the wire bare. From inside came the sound of a radio chat show. Bovin rapped on the door. Then he yelled.

"Kenny, it's Neil."

The radio fell silent and a moment later the door opened. A boy with an acne-covered face and bare feet stood there.

"C'min," he muttered.

Amey whispered in my ear, "It's the boy, the friend."

We filed past him, and found ourselves in a room that contained only a TV and an armchair, both in a condition that suggested they had been salvaged from a dump. There was a smell of cigarettes and male feet and chips.

There was nowhere for us all to sit, so we stood in a semicircle, and Kenny came and stood with us, completing the circle, uncowed by his visitors, reaching into his pockets for a packet of cigarettes and a box of matches.

"This is about Sean—" Neil told him.

Kenny cut him short. "I know."

"I want you to tell them what you told me," Neil said.

Kenny lit up slowly, taking the opportunity to give Amey a good look up and down. It was a thorough inspection—face, clothing, general demeanor.

"Hello again," he said.

Amey nodded.

"Sean was my friend from school," Kenny said, and when he started to talk he had a voice that was easy to listen to, low and measured, taking the same slow pleasure in his vowels that I heard when Betty spoke. "He was always in trouble, he'd been in and out of detention, then he came to live with me when he got out. His dad didn't want anything to do with him. The moment he got out he started to drink, and he did whatever drugs he could get his hands on. When he began to inject I took him to see you," he nodded at Amey, "but he wouldn't listen to me. He got sick too. I took him to the doctor, and he said it was a virus, something like glandular fever, but Sean said it was boring being at home in bed. I had some money from a job, so one night we went to the pub.

He was going on about how much he wanted a hit, and I told him to keep his voice down, but this guy came over and started talking to us. I didn't trust him, but he's telling Sean how he works at this drug center, and how he can get hold of anything Sean wants. His name was Ned. Sean was over the bloody moon. The two of them got to whispering and I knew they were making arrangements to meet up, but I wanted nothing of it. Next day, Sean goes out, won't tell me where he's going. He comes back high and sicker than ever. Next day he goes out again, only this time he never comes back."

"Why didn't you tell the police?" I wanted to know.

"Don't want anything to do with them," he replied, with the same simple directness that had characterized his whole account.

"He tried to contact me," Bovin said. "He rang the paper and asked who to speak to about a drug death. They put him through to me, but I was busy on something else, and anyway I thought he was just a druggy with a sob story. When I did agree to meet him, I thought there might be some truth in what he was saying, so I began to try and check it out. I rang you," he indicated Amey, "because this Ned guy had said he worked at a drug rehabilitation center. And obviously you did know who he was. When you told me to get lost I tried talking to Becky, but she just clammed up."

We were all quiet for a moment.

"Well, Ned found me," Kenny said into the silence. "Last night. He brought me money." He fished in his jeans pocket and pulled out five twenty-pound notes. "Told me he hadn't seen Sean since the night we went to the pub. Sorry to hear he's dead, oh and here's some cash. And he'll drop by again soon, and if I'm lucky he'll bring me some more cash. But he's heard I've talked to a journalist, and I'm not to do that anymore because they might misinterpret it. And look what happened to Sean when he got involved with journalists."

"He threatened you?"

"Not in so many words, but he kept saying what a pity it was when boys got involved with the media and died of overdoses and the police just weren't interested."

"So this guy threatens you, and you take his money?" That was Bovin, getting the facts straight for his story.

"I'm brighter than Sean was," Kenny said. "I thanked him."

Chapter 33

IT was past nine by the time I returned to Betty's B and B. She greeted me like an old friend, but something in my face must have told her that I was not in the mood to chat. My only thought was that I must speak to Finney. My embarrassment at the thought of talking to him, after what had happened between us, was now outweighed by urgency. In my room I emptied the contents of my pocketbook onto the bed, swearing when I realized that I had not brought my mobile phone charger with me.

There was no phone in the room, so I ran down the stairs in search of a pay phone. I found it in the lounge, then sought out Betty who sold me a telephone card. She did not comment on my trembling hand as I handed her a banknote, except to ask whether I had eaten. I shook my head. I had not eaten and I was terribly hungry, but I was also nauseous with anxiety. I felt light-headed and shaky, and not entirely in control. Still, food was low on my list of priorities.

I returned to the lounge and started dialing. I would speak to Finney, but first I must try one last time to find Suzette. I worked my way through all the numbers that Jane and I had found for her—including her increasingly irate ex in Australia—all without luck. Then I rang Maeve at home. She was in the middle of a dinner party and didn't want to speak. No, she knew nothing about the whereabouts of Suzette, hadn't seen her for weeks. Why, I could hear her thinking, was I bothering her with this? I tried ringing Jane, but her phone was busy. I got through to Terry. He was pleasantly surprised to hear from me. No, he hadn't seen Suzette.

"Is everything all right?" he asked. "You sound distressed."

I took a deep breath. This was not the time to break down.

"I'm fine, Terry."

"May I take you for dinner soon? I feel I need to apologize for my behavior . . . I've had Jane reading me the riot act, and of course she's quite right. I'm afraid I handled the situation badly."

"Of course we'll have dinner," I told him, and found myself feeling better despite everything as I hung up.

I rang Suzette's mother last of all. I had not wanted to worry her, but by now I had no choice. Her voice was distant, and I was not sure how much of what I said to her she was capable of grasping. As far as I could gather she did not know where exactly Suzette was, but she was not worried.

"Suzette rings me every week on the telephone," she told me. "I'm sure she would tell me if there was something wrong."

I asked when Suzette had rung last, and although her mother couldn't name a day it was clear that it could have been as much as a week ago, perhaps more, but she clearly hadn't done the math.

"May I take a message and get her to call you?" she asked.

I closed my eyes.

"Would you?" I asked. I left my name and the hotel number, but I feared it was hopeless.

I hung up and turned away from the telephone. Betty had placed a bowl of steaming soup and a bread roll on the table. Betty herself was sitting in a reclining armchair, her feet up, the TV remote control in her hand. She was watching the news, but the sound was muted.

I smiled at her gratefully and began to spoon the soup greedily into my mouth. It was mushroom, from one of the better class of cans. The bread was fresh and warm, and the butter melted into it. I didn't speak for several minutes, just concentrated on getting nourishment into my blood.

"Thank you," I said to Betty eventually, mopping my mouth with a napkin. "I needed that."

"That's what I thought." She nodded her satisfaction.

I turned back to the telephone and hesitated, but Betty made no move to leave. I rang my home number, but the phone was busy, and I hung up. I had a strange compulsion to explain to Betty.

"I wanted to check the children are all right," I told her, "but I can't get through."

"Little mites, you must miss them."

I nodded, hesitated. The question burst out of me. "You know I'm the woman in the newspaper, don't you?"

"Of course I do, my darling." Her voice was soothing. The term of endearment was no such thing, just habit, but at least it suggested that friendship was a possibility.

"And you don't mind?"

"I don't believe everything I read in the newspapers, my love. Besides," she waved her arm around the empty lounge, "business is business, and my husband did inform the officer from the local constabulary that you were here."

I nodded.

"Shouldn't you be ringing your policeman friend now?" she inquired.

"Yes," I told her, "I should."

I was about to dial Finney's mobile, when the phone rang. I started with surprise, then took up the receiver.

"Robin?"

"Suze, where have you been? I thought you were dead."

"Don't say that!" Her voice was high, verging on hysteria.

"Robin, he's stolen my car, I'm stuck here all alone in the middle of nowhere—"

"Suze," I interrupted her, "where are you?"

"I've rented this place on the road to Mousehole," she wailed, as if it were the most obvious thing in the world. "I'm only a couple of miles from you, but I can't drive anywhere because I haven't got a car, and he's going to come back and—"

"Suze," I took a deep breath, "who's going to come back?"

"He's called Ned." Suzette's voice became falsetto. "He's a lunatic."

For a moment I didn't reply. Sean Morris's death returned to me with a force that took me by surprise.

"Were you there when the boy died?" I demanded.

"What?" For a moment I had shocked Suzette back to baffled normality. There was, after all, no way she could know that I knew. Her voice was a full octave lower.

"Were you there when he died? Amey knows he died. Did you see what you'd done?"

I heard Suzette whimper, and then she broke down. She was talking, but I couldn't make head or tail of it: She was speaking into the phone, then away from it, her voice a sobbing, shrieking mess. Eventually the words got clearer, and I understood that she was denying my allegation, and that she was angry.

"How can you think I would do that?" Her voice was low, intense, accusatory. "You are my friend, you should believe in me. Did I ever accuse you of killing Adam? Did I?"

I was silent, and she carried on speaking, fast and furious.

"Even when everyone else thought you did it, I didn't. Did I even ask you? Did I show any doubt?"

I thought back to our meeting in the Corporation canteen after Adam's death. No, Suzette had not doubted me. Everyone else had wanted something from me, either a denial or an explanation, even Jane.

Suzette was still speaking.

"You think you're better than me, that you have some moral high ground? You think I'm some sort of sleaze, capable of murder, and you're not?"

"Suzette, where are you?" I broke in. She was right. I owed her more than this.

"Why do you care?" She was fanning the flames of her own anger.

"We should talk," I said. "You're right. I want to talk to you."

She didn't exactly warm to me, but she calmed down enough to give me an address. When I hung up I checked the directions with Betty and she drew me a map. I was to head for the esplanade, drive toward Newlyn. In Newlyn I was not to head inland, but instead keep to the coast and go from Fore Street to Cliff Road. Somewhere along that road Suzette had said I would see a painted sign to the house. Finney would have to wait.

Chapter 34

SOMEHOW, in the dark, I found her. It was a tiny place, a one-story converted barn, set back all on its own, about fifty yards in-land from the coastal road. I stepped out of the car onto earth and took a deep breath of night air. The rain had stopped but the wind was still up, and it made me shiver. Above me I could see the stars, around me the hills, behind and below me the sea. Nowhere could I see a car. I banged on the door, which was a two-piece affair that had once belonged on a stable, and Suzette let me in and hugged me. The entrance hall was lit by a glass lamp overhead, and it cast a ghostly pallor over her face. Suzette's eyes were red-rimmed and her hands were shaking. Even in good lighting she would have looked a wreck.

"Christ, I needed to see a friendly face," she said to me, and she teetered on the edge of tears again, biting her lip and shaking her head. She headed through a door into a kitchen beyond. It was a cozy room. A pine dresser was filled with willow pattern plates and a red cloth covered a dining table that could have seated six. There was an open fireplace with logs of wood stacked next to it.

I perched on a wooden stool, but Suzette was too hyper to sit down. She couldn't keep still.

"Why are you here?" I asked her.

"I felt so awful about the boy," she said, sitting down for a moment, then getting up again to pace some more. "I came back to try and put things right. I wanted to find his family, I wanted to help them out."

"He didn't have any, or none that wanted to know him."

"I know that now," she wailed. "And then I saw Ned in town yesterday, he was following me and I got scared, so I came back here, and I haven't been out since. Then, when I got your message from my mother, I thought I'd drive into Penzance and see you. So I go outside and the car's vanished. I've looked everywhere, it's just gone. Bloody Sennet and his stupid bloody pranks . . . Robbie, I'm so scared. I have to get out of here tonight, can you take me? You know what happened to Paula, I'm not going to hang around and wait for him to push me off a cliff."

There was a bag packed on the floor by the door. I could feel her fear and for a moment I shared the impulse to flee.

"You have to tell me what happened first."

"I don't want to hang around here. Aren't you scared of him?" She was incredulous. "If you know about the boy, you're on his list too."

I gave it a moment's consideration, but no more. I did not know why I was not scared, but I wasn't. If Ned had wanted to kill me, he could have done it on the beach.

"Tell me what happened," I repeated.

She shook her head in exasperation, but she was desperate to get out of there and I was the one with the car.

"I didn't know." She took a shuddering breath. "You have to believe me. I didn't know what Sennet was doing. He was always messing around, but he was funny, you know, always on the right side of jokey. He stopped before you got fed up with him. And you got the idea that he knew what he was doing. He wanted to make films professionally, and I was supportive. I gave him advice and he showed me some of his work. It was great. Anyway, one day he just said he wanted to borrow my camera and I'd like the results, so I let him. I know it was stupid but I let him. I didn't realize, but he took Paula with him too. Apparently he told her that it was something I'd asked him to film. Then they came back to the hotel that night looking like ghosts, and I asked them what happened, and he tried to shut her up, but Paula told me this boy had died. I just couldn't believe it. I mean, I just couldn't believe either of them would be so stupid—or that someone could die that fast. Paula got sick. I mean really sick. She was throwing up in the bathroom. So it was just me and Ned, and I said to him, 'Come on, we've got to tell the police,' and that was when he said it." Suzette seemed momentarily unable to get her breath, and I went to the sink and ran her a glass of water. She gulped, then continued talking. "He said he'd kill me if I went to the police," she said. "And I laughed, because I thought it was a sick joke, but there was something in his eyes that . . . I just knew it wasn't a joke."

She stopped speaking and drank again. She stared into my face, as though she was looking there for validation.

"I knew it was wrong not to tell anyone. I felt sick at myself, but I knew he would kill me."

"So what did you do?"

She shrugged, as if I should have guessed.

"Nothing. We left. We agreed that the documentary had to be ditched."

"And Ned?"

"He killed Paula. She was getting so depressed over what happened that he thought she would just blurt it out. Then he killed Adam, because Paula had told Adam what happened to the boy, and after Paula died, Adam told Ned he was going to the police."

I gazed at her. It all made sense for the first time, the knot of horror at the center of things, and then the unraveling. Telling the story seemed to have comforted her, and she had stopped shaking. I gazed at her. Her face had shrunk in on itself so that she was all cheekbone and eye socket, her skin so translucent I could see the capillaries underneath. Her hair shone white and brittle as straw in this strange light. She looked tiny and vulnerable, her birdlike limbs twisted around themselves, all elbows and knees, her shoulders contorted to hug herself tight.

"How did you know about the boy?" she asked.

"Adam," I said. "He left me a message."

She frowned, and seemed about to speak, but I cut her off. "Why don't we get going?"

She nodded slowly and got to her feet.

"Are you all set?" I asked.

She rubbed her hand over her face.

"I'll just lock up."

I picked up her bag and took it out to the car. With the house lights switched off it was pitch dark, and I was scrabbling around trying to get the trunk open when a moment later she followed me outside. I glanced up. All I could see was a dim outline against the whitewashed walls of the cottage. She'd got dressed up warm, and I wished I had too.

I opened the trunk, then turned to her. What she'd told me was playing over and over again in my head, but something kept catching like a scratch on a record.

"What happened to the film?" I asked her.

"Ned destroyed it," she said. "I saw him do it. Paula was screaming at him to get rid of it, and neither of them wanted any evidence. He threw it into the fire. I saw it burn."

For a heartbeat all I heard was the wind in the trees.

Over her voice came the sound of a car approaching on the coast road. I turned to look and saw lights drawing near below us.

"Come on," Suzette said urgently, "that must be Ned."

She stepped toward the car and I bent over to pick up her bag, my mind rewinding, replaying. Suzette's story, Suzette's face, her voice. What is fear and what is a breakdown of reason? Her story is beautiful in its simplicity. Its logic and symmetry attract me. It is aesthetically pleasing, well produced. What she said is true: She never doubted that I had not killed Adam, never questioned me. She was my one true friend.

I hear the sound of spray curling and leaping as the wave rises to the shore. I hear the car engine purr, coming closer. Suzette shifts from one foot to the other, uneasily. My eyes are getting accustomed to the darkness. As I straighten and turn to throw the bag into the trunk, the shape of the house emerges from the black sky and the clear outline of a garage built on the coastal side defines itself. Somewhere a gull calls. If I don't believe her, the time to confront her is now, before she steps into my car, before I drive through the night with her at my side. Perhaps Suzette had good reason to believe me innocent of Adam's murder: not faith in my good character but some more sinister knowledge. I realize that the sound of the car is receding. It has not turned off Cliff Road toward the house. Its taillights are vanishing into the distance. I hear a footfall. I glance around to tell Suzette that the car is nothing to do with us, to tell her that if we are going anywhere, we are going to the police. I see the birdlike arm is raised, and in its claw a hatchet of polished metal reflects the moon. The moon falls, dealing a blow on my skull that fells me to the unflinching granite, and my fading mind struggles to comprehend how the moon can fall again and again and again.

Chapter 35

I lie on the operating table, my skull bared, hair hacked and shaved, and there is blood and skin, some neatly cut, some torn, and a team of surgeons breathing into masks, leaning anxiously over me, tying knots, sewing stitches in holes where blood still leaks hours after surgery began and should not. When they started operating they played a jazz CD. It relaxes them, makes their muscles less tense. Now they operate in silence. I can feel nothing and I will sleep after this for days. They are afraid that I will never wake up—they are afraid that if I wake, I will not be me. Outside the operating theater, in the corridor that doubles as a waiting room, D.C. Mann watches Finney pace, cursing his own stupidity.

Finney, not long before, is sitting at home, suspended. He's in a space too big and too unfamiliar since his wife left him eighteen months ago to go and live with her boss. He is drinking beer and working his way through Paula Carmichael's voluminous diaries, the diaries that have been abandoned along with the investigation into Paula's death. He reads about me there, about my life, or at least what Paula has observed, and what she has heard from Adam. He knows more about me, now, than I do about him.

Then Finney realizes what should have been realized weeks ago. There is a missing diary. The dates do not add up. He leaves his house and goes to find Carmichael. They talk, they argue, and eventually Carmichael produces what he has been hiding since his

wife's death: the missing diary, and in it an account of the death of
Sean Morris. The one volume Paula has kept apart from all the
others, under lock and key in the safe; the volume Carmichael goes
to after his wife's death, after he has made allegations about the
documentary. When he reads what is there, he decides to shut up.
The subject of the documentary is safer left untouched. Full and
unexpurgated, in the diary Paula beats her breast with the guilt and
the awfulness of it.

Paula is there, with Ned Sennet who has provided the heroin for
Sean Morris to do his bit on film. It is Ned too, who has found the
abandoned shed as an appropriately grotty setting for the filming.
Paula is there with Suzette, who has the camera. After Sean Morris vomits, the boy briefly seems to lose interest in the drug. Ned
starts haranguing him. They had an arrangement, he reminds the
boy. Suzette snaps at Sean. Things are getting out of hand and she
is panicking. Paula tries to pour oil on troubled water. She tells
Ned and Suzette to shut up. She goes and talks to the boy.

"If you don't want to do this, don't," I told him. "Don't listen to them. You can just go home." The boy looked at Ned,
and I could see he wanted to, of course he wanted to, vomiting or not. It was only afterwards I realized there was money
involved too. What was I thinking? Just walk away, I said, but
that was for me, covering my back, pretending I'd given him
a choice. This boy, hardly older than Kyle, had no family to
go home to, not a penny in his pocket, and his body was
screaming at him for heroin. I've been over it in my head a
million times to find some excuse for myself, and there is no
escaping it. Murder? Manslaughter? I was at best criminally
naive. And still there is more. I was speaking to him the way
I speak to Kyle if there's something I want him to do but he's
reluctant. I've learned the more I push Kyle, the less likely he

is to do it. So I tell him, it's okay, you don't have to. I pretend I don't care. And then Kyle shrugs and does whatever it is. I tell myself that what I said made no difference, Sean wanted to do it. So why do I spend every minute of every day sick at myself?

Sean injects the drug, and Paula watches as he dies, and records and replays the scene in her mind for the months of her life that remain. With every replay her conscience condemns her. Yet Paula remains silent. She listens, blankly, to Suzette's logic. If Paula reveals what has happened, all that she has worked for will be destroyed, the good work will stop, the volunteers will return to cynicism. The boy was a drug addict, Suzette says, he would have died anyway. They were unfortunate bystanders, in the wrong place at the wrong time, that is all. Paula, stunned by what has happened, knows something Suzette does not. Paula is already covering up the theft of Carmichaelite funds. One scandal might be weathered, but two will bring the whole thing tumbling down around her ears. If she makes a public mea culpa for her involvement in the boy's death, the press will take the Carmichaelite organization to pieces. The theft of funds will be discovered, and then the cover-up. The organization will not survive. Paula hears what Suzette says, stays silent for a day, then for a week, and Ned, like a vulture, knows his prey. "You've stayed silent," he says to her, "that's enough to condemn you. Now I want money." So, from simple silence she progresses to the payoff. It starts at five hundred pounds a month and goes up to a thousand. Paula has already forked out thousands to cover up the theft. Now the drain on their finances is enough to make even Richard Carmichael take notice that something is wrong.

Here then, among the papers Richard Carmichael has hidden, is the true suicide note.

I have tried to go on knowing that I am flawed, and recognizing that we are all flawed. I've even tried to convince myself that this makes me a better and more tolerant person. But Ned has moved in a few doors down, like the devil himself, and he comes by and knocks on the door once in a while, when he thinks no one else is in, and I put cash in his hand. I am incapable now even of believing words like "better," "more tolerant." I of all people. I of ALL people. I OF ALL PEOPLE. I am a shoddy thing. I have sold my soul. I can no longer contemplate my own reflection. Tonight he came here. I told him there would be no more. I refused to give him anything and he became angry. For a full hour, with Kyle in the other room, Ned berated me. If I cut off the payments, he'll expose me. I was shaking. I was crying, but I will not be spineless again. I stuck to my vow. I will not pay you, I told him. I would rather die. He left, and I realized that in fact now I have no option but to die. He will expose me. My children will hate me. I have no choice.

Finney knows what he has found. He scratches his head, scribbles notes on a pad, frowning. The phone rings, and it is a call from D.C. Mann. Is he okay? Of course, he snaps, he's fine. She is used to him snapping and talks over him. She thinks he might be interested to know that the Penzance police rang earlier to say, just for your information, that Ballantyne is there, staying at a B and B. Finney grunts, hangs up, scratches his head again. He wonders where Sennet is, and who he is, and whether the police have ever questioned Suzette Milner in connection with anything at all. He shakes his head and consults his map. He does not like the thought of me alone at the end of the earth.

It is Finney who finds me, not long after the attack they think. Early enough, they hope, to save me. He drives southwest through the night, disturbs Betty from her bed, pesters her for directions until she rolls her eyes and decides to accompany him because he's so dense, and heaves her flowery nightgown into the passenger seat. Without Betty he would have driven past the track that led to Suzette's cottage, foot hard down on the accelerator until he reached Land's End. They find an abandoned cottage, my abandoned car, a garage, doors left wide open, my body all but lifeless, bloodied, beaten around the head, dragged to the sea, and left for dead at the water's edge, my feet already floating, lifted by the tide.

D.C. Mann arrives hours later, dispatched by an embarrassed superior. Chief suspect beaten nearly to death, and by whom? Another suspect, until now unsuspected. The humbled and humiliated suspect-lover, Finney, is quietly reinstated, but D.C. Mann is sent to save the day. She can speak to the press. She looks a treat on camera, and she at least will not break down if the former chief suspect dies, as is half expected. The same cannot be said of Finney.

Betty has been a good listener. She is able to tell D.C. Mann who I've spoken to and what I've said. D.C. Mann is quite capable of putting two and two together. She murmurs these pieces of information to Finney in the waiting room, but he is not interested, so Mann leaves the hospital and goes to find Amey. Amey is not sleeping, has not slept since I knocked on his door the day before. He knows he must tell the truth—even if his project dies, and with it the people he tries to save. He tells Mann what she needs to know, he leads her to Bovin and to Kenny. She contacts her superiors in London, who contact Maeve, whose heart almost stops. The police search my house and take away the tapes. Copies are made.

Suzette is running. She is falling apart. She was never cut out for this. Ever since Sean Morris's death she has barely been holding herself together. When Paula died she thought she would expire from fear. When she killed Adam, she thought she would disintegrate. Now, with her murderous attack on me, there is no more of herself to keep together. Everywhere she tries to run, people look at her. They can see on her face what she has done. Everywhere she runs, she sees Ned. He never did steal her car, she hid it in the garage herself, but she is truly frightened of him because she believes he killed Paula. She abandons her car. She heads for a train station and stands for an age in front of the departure board. There is nowhere she can go and not be found. She catches a train, and then another, until she arrives at Heathrow. She stands and stares at another departure board. She is shaking and crying, and everyone is staring.

Ned Sennet hears what has happened on the radio news while he is driving. His mouth forms a silent "Oh," and then an admonitory, "Suzette." He drives on to Plymouth, parks his hired car, retrieves his luggage, and walks away. He will keep on the move, and he will invent another new identity. He hasn't killed anyone, and he has little in the way of a conscience, but he knows that people will come looking for him now.

My mother clasps my children to her breast and sobs, relieved only that she does not have to find words to tell them what has happened. They are so young. They will forget me. She stays in London, huddled tight with my sisters and my children until the surgery is over and word comes that I am at least still breathing. Then, in the middle of the night, Tanya piles them all into her car and drives them southwest, to join the party in the waiting room. Lorna sits in her chair staring out of the window. She has been told. She is with me. I can feel her.

Chapter 36

MONTHS have passed, months of recuperation first in the hospital and then at home, months of letting go of my children so that others can look after them while I am bedbound. My mother is still busy at work, so she has organized a corps of helpers. Even Lorna has been drafted in to sit with me.

"This is a change," I said to her the first time she appeared in my sickroom.

"As if I've got nothing better to do," she said good-naturedly.

She stroked my shaved head for a moment, then settled down in the armchair next to my bed. We talked a little, laughed a little, and after a while we both closed our eyes for a rest.

Father Joe Riberra came to visit, all eaten up with guilt.

"I should have just gone to the police," he berated himself, "but Adam had entrusted me with those tapes, and it seemed like it would be some kind of a betrayal just to run to the police. I don't know what I was thinking of."

Lorna was there at the time. She told him I had only myself to blame.

"You're only human," she said in her beautiful voice, "we all do the best we can."

Riberra looked properly at Lorna then, and I could see that he noticed for the first time the halo of golden red ringlets and the luminous porcelain skin. They have spoken since on the telephone, and I suspect they may have met, but that's another story.

David, Adam's brother, brought the children more academic journals to tear up and showed them how to make paper airplanes. My mother had a talk with Norma and Harold Wills too. Several talks, I suspect. Then one day they arrived at my bedside, contrite. After an awkward minute or so of groveling apologies, Harold elbowed his wife in her ribs, and she embarked on a little speech.

"I'll understand entirely if you say no," Norma said, "but we would love to be able to help with the children. I mean we'd love to see them, but we'd love to help you out too. We've been thinking about it, and we'll understand absolutely if you don't want to see us, although perhaps we could just come and collect them sometimes and deliver them back, and you really wouldn't have to see us at all . . ."

My mother and I both gazed at Norma in amazement. She was practically on her knees in this orgy of self-flagellation. I looked to my mother for help, but she was leaving this one up to me.

"Perhaps one day you can come around and spend some time with all of us, so the twins see us all together and know we're all . . ." I nearly choked and had to try again, "know we're all . . . a family." I got it out at last, and they were bowled over, thanking me as they retreated out of the door, afraid to stay longer in case I changed my mind. Behind their backs, my mother rolled her eyes.

Jane came one day and took Hannah and William to the playground and returned with them as victorious as if she had scaled Everest. She came back a week later with Quentin in tow and did it again. When she brought them back the second time she came in to see me and confided that she and Quentin were thinking of having a baby because Hannah and William were so sweet. Which they were. Both on their feet, hurtling around, bottoms wiggling with the sheer joy of mobility.

"Actually we're doing more than think about it," Jane said, and roared with laughter.

"Very wise," I told her weakly.

Three times the front doorbell has rung, and that has been followed by a low conversation downstairs involving a male voice. Each time, shortly afterward Carol has come up to my room with a bunch of lilies. The first time this happened I thought they were from Finney and seized the card, only to drop it with alarm when I saw that it bore the words "With best wishes for your rapid recovery, Gilbert." I have not encouraged him, and nor have I told Carol to turn my father away. I accept his flowers. I notice he has never come to the house when my mother is around and realize that one day when he comes to call it will be me who opens the door to him. I will cross that bridge when I come to it.

Next week I'm going back to work. My head has healed and my hair has grown back, but it's still short, and a great white streak has appeared. I've dyed the streak blond, because I'm not ready to go gray. My first outing has been to buy a new wardrobe for my new life. When I look in the mirror I think I look strong. Ready for anything. There is no spare flesh on me, and when I look into my eyes I see little in the way of frivolity there. I'll have to work on that.

The editorial pages did a 180-degree turn in the space of twenty-four hours when it became clear that I was not a murderess, and the Corporation got a beating for not giving me their full support. As the story emerged, with the details of the death of Sean Morris, Maeve clung to me for dear life. If she could show herself to be on the side of the wronged party, that is me, her career would survive. I let her cling and exploited it ruthlessly. She agreed I could return to work on full pay, first two days, rising slowly to three, four, perhaps five days a week if and when I felt able, and I had carte blanche to make pretty much whatever documentary films I wanted.

"Perhaps you could do a series on miscarriages of justice," said Maeve helpfully, her eye on the ratings.

"Ballantyne's World," I suggested drily, and she muttered something under her breath and changed the subject.

Now, a week before I return to work, I am moving home, out of my little nest and into Adam's flat. The Carmichaels—those who are left of them—have already sold up and moved to a house in the country. Richard has dropped by a few times over the last few months, and so has Kyle, but always separately. Richard has brought books and magazines and Kyle has brought me chocolates. I had one long talk with Richard. He is not a happy man, but he has become more settled, more tranquil, for the sake of Kyle. He is sad that his wife's reputation has been so battered, but he is still proud of her. Kyle is having a tough time with his mother's suicide. For a while there was talk of him moving back to live with his real father, but Richard seemed glad when he decided in the end that he preferred to stay where he was. Richard wants him to move to a more supportive school and to get him specialist help. George has been in trouble at school for drunkenness, but he is a kind older brother to Kyle.

With Dan gone too, the street is empty of my ghosts, but I've been having nightmares about that night, about the whispers in the wind and Paula's fall. I have a private theory, that if I heard a voice that night just before she fell, it was the voice of Paula herself shouting into the storm, declaring her guilt to the world. She needed to do it, and she did it standing on the balcony before she threw herself off. It was, I like to think, her last confession. A confession not to God, but to humanity.

I can't go on having nightmares. I know I need to go. I need to leave the security of my hibernation and reclaim my place in the world. Adam's flat will be a new start. Carol will come with us. She's agreed to live in for the next year, to help me with the children while I find my feet. Jane thinks it weird that I should go and live in Adam's home, and of course it has occurred to me that one way or another he will still be there, but I trust he will be a friendly ghost, and we should all probably get to know him. Adam was far from perfect, but he was, after all, Hannah and William's father.

———————

The moving men, all of them Australian, are just about done. My life is in boxes. The children are at Norma and Harold's for the day. My only worry about them being with Adam's parents is that they always come home on such a sugar high that it's impossible to get them to bed, but in the scale of things, a sugar high does not rank as a problem. I'm standing in the hallway trying not to get in the way of the movers. The front door is wide open and D.C. Mann appears there, except that now she's a sergeant.

There is nothing strange about her visit. She has come here often over the past few months. There was a time when they didn't think I would be able to testify at Suzette's trial, and Mann was charged with monitoring my mental health—she and a battery of psychiatrists. She also filled me in on the life and times of D.C.I. Finney. She told me one day how his wife walked out on him, to go and live with her boss in Manchester. Another day she told me about the case that got Finney in trouble a year ago. It had indeed involved another woman, and one Finney had been fond of, but this one had been seventy years old, a woman who had been beaten up in her own home by her nephew. "It wasn't," Mann said carefully, determined that I should understand, "at all a romantic thing. He just liked her and bent the rules to make sure she was okay." Now, whenever she gets the chance, she tells me little stories, and the point is always the same: Finney is a good man and he is a lonely man. All this I knew. I like to hear the stories, but in all this time Finney has never been to see me.

Mann comes in without knocking, and squeezes against the wall while two of my Australians stride by, boxes of books on their shoulders, biceps bursting. She flashes a grin at one of them, then looks over the scene of devastation. With my furniture gone the house looks grubby.

"Do you have time for a walk?" she asks me.

I know this means there is news. I tell my men I'm taking a break, and go out into the early summer sun. I fall into step beside her.

"Sennet's been detained in Wales," she tells me, "and he's talking."

"You mean he's made a deal. Let me guess—he won't be charged with supplying the drugs that killed Sean Morris?"

"It would have been almost impossible to make it stick. He claims Morris brought his own drugs, and he says he didn't pay Morris for shooting up on film—and since Morris dropped dead before any money could change hands, that's technically true. We've got Paula's account of what happened, but she's dead."

"And the cash gone from her account for the blackmail," I said. "Surely that's proof of something?"

"Could have been charitable donations. Anyway, the point is Stein, Sennet, whatever you want to call him, is giving us what we need to nail Suzette's motive for killing Adam. He's going to describe how Morris died. He heard Suzette swear Paula and Adam to secrecy in the hotel bar that night. He heard the row over what should happen to the film. Adam promised to stay silent about Morris's death, but only if he got the tape. He promised to destroy it." Mann trailed off and sighed. She loved her story, how it grew and made more sense with every fact she uncovered, but she hated this bit. "Why did Adam want the tape at all? That's the bit I don't get," she said. "Why say you'll stay silent but preserve the evidence? It doesn't make sense."

It did to me. No real journalist can bear to destroy the historical record. You can bury it, you can hide it for a thousand years, but destroy it and you'll be hit by a thunderbolt. Besides, maybe Adam knew that even if he was prepared to stay silent about Morris's death in the short term, in the long term he might change his mind. Adam was a pragmatist. Never burn your bridges. I guessed the only reason he'd agreed to stay silent at all was out of loyalty to Paula, and perhaps to Suzette too. By all accounts Suzette and Adam had indeed been having a relationship, as Suzette had told me, but their friends and colleagues agreed they had not been seen together after the documentary had been abandoned.

Mann went on talking, as if reciting by heart the facts of the case. "Then on the day of Paula's funeral Suzette overheard you telling Finney that Adam was coming to see you. Suzette knew Adam was going through hell after Paula killed herself. She had watched him walk out of Paula's funeral. She must have known what was going through his head. Maybe they even talked about it. She must have thought he was about to bare his soul to you. She drove over to your house in her own car. She was wearing her hair up, covered in a knitted hat, with a scarf over half her face, a basic disguise, nothing fancy. She probably told herself she was going to confront him, or just scare him. In fact she would probably have killed him in her own car. Then she got lucky. She saw yours and recognized it. She parked her own in the next street, tried the door of yours, it opened. You'd even left the keys in the ignition. Well, we won't go over just how stupid that was."

"Thank you."

"We've got a witness now, who saw Suzette stop by your car. She got in. She was wearing gloves, but when she adjusted the seat to reach the steering wheel she cut her hand on that bit of metal on the floor. She mopped up the blood with a paper hanky, then for some reason she got careless. Perhaps she saw Adam walking along the street, getting ready to cross the road in front of her. She dropped the tissue. We've got her. She must have thought she could throw us off the scent by trying to frame you."

"She was right," I pointed out, but Mann wouldn't be led down that road. She returned to her story.

"She thought she was getting away with it, and then Michael Amey rings her, trying to track down Ned Sennet after Bovin called him. Amey is all heated up, and he tells her of Bovin's allegations that Sennet had dealt drugs. Suzette panics. She's totally paranoid by now. She returns to Cornwall to try to find out what is going on. Well, the rest you know only too well."

I sighed. I wanted to go home, to build my new home around me. I'd been through this a million times. Suzette's trial had been hanging over me ever since my mother told me she had been picked up trying to board a plane to New York the day after she attacked me and left me for dead. It was clear to me that Suzette was effectively out of control by the time she killed Adam. It was a risky, opportunistic murder, panicked and last-minute and ill thought-out. Then, when she attacked me, she hadn't even stopped to make sure I was dead.

"I'm glad you got Dan," I said, "but I hate to think of him walking away from this."

Mann and I had walked by this time all the way up and all the way down the street. She nodded at the estate agent's sign outside the front door.

"Did you get a good price?" she asked.

"Not bad," I said. But I'd taken the first offer I'd got. I hadn't the heart for a hard sell, and when the surveyor came around I came clean and told him the roof leaked. Still, once I'd paid off the mortgage, the rest was profit. With the legacy of Adam's flat I could see light at the end of the financial tunnel.

I was back at my house, and Mann said she'd come in for a cup of coffee to get a better look at the Australians, but as we were about to walk inside another car pulled up, and her face broke into a broad grin.

"Hello, sir," she hailed him.

Finney wound down the window and gave her a lopsided smile. I could have sworn he blushed.

Mann pulled a face at me.

"I'll be off then," she said.

Finney and I watched her go. He looked over at me, but he didn't get out and my heart twisted. I walked over to the car.

"You're going," he said.

"Not far."

He nodded. Then he reached behind him and picked a bunch of red roses off the backseat. He handed them through the window to me.

"For the new house," he said.

"You haven't been to see me. All this time."

He shook his head, apparently incapable of speaking. He stared straight ahead. I looked back at the house, but it was no time to invite anyone in. I walked around the car, opened the passenger door, and sat down beside him, roses on my lap. I could feel the thorns on my thighs.

He turned toward me. He reached out and touched my short hair.

"You're blond."

"In parts," I said. "I heard they have more fun."

We smiled at each other then, shy at first, then just sheer happy. He stretched his hand, palm upward, toward me, and I put my hand in his. His fingers tightened around mine. I leaned back against the headrest. I was sitting in a police car, double-parked in the middle of a south London street, and I was home.

"I can't mess things up again," he said. "I'm off the case, but the defense could still make something of it. So could the press."

"You're here today."

"I wanted to wish you well. With work and . . ." His voice trailed off. "Well, just with everything."

We sat in silence. The sun was setting over the rooftops, but the dusk was warm and slow. The Australians lugged the last box into their truck and slammed the doors. They waved at me and shouted that they'd see me tomorrow morning, then they beeped their horn in farewell and my belongings bumped off down the street. We sat in silence for a while longer.

Suzette's trial would not go away. Even after it was over, it would stay with me forever, like Adam's death and Paula's before that. Hard, dark moments in my life—but I would not let my life, or Hannah's, or William's, be lived in gloom.

"When the trial's over," I said, "you could give me a couple of weeks. Then you could call me, and we could have dinner. If you wanted to. Or we could take the kids somewhere."

He breathed in deeply.

"Dinner sounds good," he said.

I nodded.

"To me too."

"I would need your new number," he said.

So I wrote it for him in his notebook, the number I had called and called on the night of Adam's death, and Finney took it and put it in his jacket pocket.

"I won't lose it," he said.

"Don't," I told him. I leaned over and kissed him lightly on his cheek, then opened the door and got out. He sat immobile for several seconds, looking out at me and smiling. Then he raised his hand in farewell, and he drove away.

More
Catherine Sampson!

Please turn this page
for a preview of

Out of Mind

available in hardcover.

Chapter 1

WHEN I awoke the twins were playing quietly in the patch of sunlight at the foot of my bed. I pretended to be asleep and through half-closed eyes watched them squatting, bottoms stuck out, in their pajamas. Hannah and William are three years old. Hannah has the willpower of a Sherman tank and William the devastating cunning of a stealth bomber. They were sorting through my jewelry box, draping strings of beads around their necks. William had a bangle dangling from one ear, and Hannah had devised for herself a crown. Once in a while, Hannah would thwack William, and he would obediently hand over whatever treasure she coveted, then steal it back when she wasn't looking. They were so busy that they had forgotten even to demand food and drink.

Their father, Adam, was murdered nearly two years ago and anyway was never really a father to them. Perhaps, I thought wistfully as I watched them play, this was what parenting would be like as they grew older. They would require only the occasional meal or dose of moral guidance, and I could recline on the sofa and admire them as they quietly bathed and dressed themselves and bent their heads dutifully over their homework.

Half an hour later, when Finney arrived, Hannah was sitting stark naked on the stairs and screaming, and William was clinging to my leg, trying to pull me toward his train set. Finney took in the scene in one sweep of the eyes, settling on.Hannah to give her a look he would usually reserve for the drunk and disorderly.

"We're going to be late," he growled.

Long weekend drives in the country with my children in the backseat are not Finney's idea of fun, but I had asked him to come along because I needed the eyes of a detective chief inspector. And he agreed because he has fallen in love with me, even if he has not fallen in love with my children. We were heading south on the A23 toward Reigate, to a manor house on the edge of London, a place known among my fellow journalists as the War School. Here in rural England, journalists learn from former elite forces soldiers how to duck and dive in deadly games of hide-and-seek. Or how to stanch the bleeding of a fallen colleague whose stomach has been blown open or eye dislodged. His screams are amateur dramatics and the torn flesh is bread soaked in animal blood, none of which makes it any less a matter of life and death.

Because of the number of journalists who have died in the past decade in war zones, news organizations now realize they must try to protect their employees, at least with knowledge and sometimes with arms, too.

"You know this is a wild goose chase," Finney shouted over the children's yelling. I was driving, and he was in the passenger seat, stoically ignoring Hannah, who was stretching out her legs to kick the back of his seat. "If there was anything to find, Coburn would have found it six months ago when she disappeared."

Finney can be pretty scathing about the incompetence of his colleagues, even about DCI Coburn, who headed the investigation into Melanie's disappearance. But the police force is his family, not mine, and I didn't want to get into a fight.

"I promised Melanie's parents. I can't not go."

Corporation camerawoman Melanie Jacobs had disappeared on January 10, a Friday six months earlier, from the War School, which is officially called HazPrep. The Corporation employs thousands of people. It is like a very little country, or a big school. You have a few colleagues who are blood brothers, lots of people you know to say hi to, and legions you know by reputation only. I worked just once with Melanie, but I was impressed by her seriousness and attention to detail. Since then I have heard colleagues speak with approval, and sometimes with disbelief, about her bravery in war zones. Shortly after she covered a particularly bloody civil war, I saw her in the canteen and went over to say hello.

Melanie was tall and agile and strong. She let her dark hair grow long and straight, and when she was working she generally tied it back behind her head. That was when you could see that her left ear bore not one but a row of six gold studs. She nodded in greeting but she did not smile. I looked into her eyes and saw that something had changed.

"It must have been hard," I said. I don't know why I said it. It's not the sort of thing journalists normally say to each other.

"It's a job," she muttered, shrugging.

I don't know if she intended it in the way that it hit me, but I walked away bathed in guilt. I had the same job as her. I'd started out as a television producer, but I'd learned how to operate a camera, and sometimes I filmed my own material. We were both journalists. But I'd said no to war zones with scarcely a second thought because I am the single mother of two small children. Melanie had no children to hold her back, and she had taken the decision to risk her own life day after day to record human atrocity. It seemed to me that this was the purest form of journalism, to put the factual record above one's own survival. I did not know Melanie well enough to ask her motivation. I could not believe that she sought glory—camera operators do not, in general, achieve glory however good their work. But could such a dangerous decision be entirely selfless?

On another occasion I bumped into Melanie with her parents at King's Cross. So when she went missing a few weeks later, I telephoned them to see if there was anything I could do to help. Melanie's mother, Beatrice, worried sick but polite nevertheless, thanked me for my concern and asked simply that I keep in touch, which I did. Beatrice and Melanie's father, Elliot, lived in Durham, and Elliot's health had deteriorated rapidly after his daughter's disappearance. Beatrice did not like to leave him for more than a few hours, but the lengthy train journey to London was more than he could stand. She was the sort of person who by instinct would have dug around to find out what had happened to her daughter, but her circumstances made her feel impotent and cut off. She was frustrated at the lack of news and upset that the police investigation seemed to be running out of steam.

"DCI Coburn tells me there's no evidence that she's dead. He says it's possible she's had a nervous breakdown, and that she just upped and went, but I find that hard to believe of Melanie."

Desperately apologetic, she'd asked me whether I would mind keeping my ears open within the Corporation for any word at all on what might have happened to Melanie.

"Who have you spoken to inside the Corporation?" I asked Beatrice. "There must be someone who's the contact point for the police."

"There is a man called Ivor Collins," Beatrice said, "who has been very kind. He came up on the train to see us, and he brought us Melanie's things. He talked with us for a long time, but he seemed to be completely mystified, too. He said he would let us know anything he found out, but . . ." Her voice trailed off unhappily.

"He hasn't contacted you?" I was incredulous.

"Oh yes, he has, he's rung us every week. He's been very kind. But he hasn't had any news for us. Maybe he feels until there's something definite, he can't tell us. But that's not what I want. . . . Melanie had friends, she had colleagues, they must be talking about her disappearance, people must have theories, there must be rumors. I want—" Her voice cracked, and she fell silent. I could hear her trying to control herself, breathing hard and slow into the telephone.

She wanted what I would want. She wanted every tiny speck of information, she wanted to know she had left no stone unturned. She wanted to know she had done everything she could for her daughter.

I knew the name Ivor Collins. Usually you glimpse him in the distance, like a star in the night sky. Occasionally, if there is a morale issue, Collins visits the rank and file to dispense encouraging words, pat backs, and nose around to see where—or with whom—the trouble lies. When I had spoken to Beatrice, I looked Ivor Collins up in the directory and found that he was HCP(R, H), which stood for Head of Corporate Policy, parens Resources comma Human, close parens.

The next day, I made an appointment to see him and found his comfortably appointed office in the far reaches of the management empire. He greeted me with a warm handshake and invited me to sit in an armchair opposite his. He had startling blue eyes and snowy white hair cut very short. His body was narrow, and his long face seemed even longer because of its unusual thinness. He looked like an exclamation mark.

"You wanted to talk to me about Melanie Jacobs," he said, cocking his long head to one side.

"Her parents are frustrated by the lack of news," I told him, "and they asked me to keep my ears open."

He nodded thoughtfully. "And what have you learned?"

"You're the first person I've asked."

"Well . . ." He heaved a sigh and spoke in a voice that was so low, it was almost not there. Whether this indicated a desire for ultimate deniability or simply a throat infection, I could not tell.

"I find it hard to speak to Beatrice and Elliot every Monday, as I do, when I can't tell them any more than they've read in the papers. All of us here have been helping the police in whatever ways we can, but there has been little to say to them. Melanie was supremely brave, extremely talented, and we valued her highly. We have no idea why she disappeared."

I left Collins's office ten minutes later, empty-handed. As I trod the lengths of corridor back to my office, I felt increasingly dissatisfied. Collins had not dismissed me, he had not tried to stop me asking questions, but he had met each of my inquiries with a sad shake of the head and an apology that there was nothing new he could tell me, his blue eyes filled with concern that looked genuine.

Surely, I thought, it was impossible that Collins had no more information now than the day Melanie vanished. I simply could not believe it. And as I thought it over, the whole thing began to ring alarm bells in my head. When Adam Wills had been killed, I had become chief suspect, and the Corporation had failed to stand behind me. Was the Corporation now abandoning Melanie to her fate as it had abandoned me? I had been a suspect in a murder investigation. It was perhaps understandable that my employer should want to pretend I had nothing to do with them. But there was no such stain on Melanie's reputation.

The next day, Beatrice rang me and asked whether I would mind terribly going to HazPrep and checking one last time whether there was something, anything, that the police might have missed. I agreed immediately. If Collins was not going to stand up for Melanie, then I would have to. I found myself fired by an angry zeal that, had I been honest with myself, I would have realized had more to do with what had happened to me nearly two years earlier than with what had or had not happened to Melanie.

Now, as hedgerow gave way to high brick wall topped with razor-sharp wire, I recognized the War School from the TV coverage of Melanie's disappearance. HazPrep had not allowed journalists inside to film in their grounds at the time, nor had it allowed its staff to give interviews, with the exception of the director, Andrew Bentley. So there had been lots of pictures of this exterior wall and the blue metal gate. I called Bentley from my mobile, as he'd instructed, and the gate slid open.

We parked by the manor house, a sprawling stone building surrounded with topiary at the top of a small hill. Bentley was waiting. I had expected combat fatigues, but he wore a dark blue business suit and what looked to my amateur eyes like a regimental tie. All I knew of his history was that he had been an officer in the Special Boat Service. His short dark hair receded to show a large circle of glossy bald head, his shoulders pushed the suit to its limits, and his unbuttoned jacket revealed a chest that sat above his waist like a V. I could see my face in his shoes.

"Hello?" Bentley greeted Finney with an interrogative and shook his hand.

"This is Tom Finney," I said, and left it at that.

"Good God, you've got a carful." Bentley peered into the backseat.

"It's the weekend . . . ," I started, but he waved away my excuses.

"Plenty of space for them to run around. I've got kids myself."

I was pleased to find someone who didn't blanch at the sight of children, but by the time I'd managed to dislodge William and Hannah from the car, Bentley and Finney had turned and were already heading toward the house. It was an English summer's day, the early sun now overcast with clouds that threatened rain, and Finney was wearing a leather jacket and jeans. Unlike Bentley, who made a suit look like a uniform, Finney was incapable of making even a suit look like a suit. I hadn't introduced Finney as a police officer, but it seemed to me, as they strode off together, that the two men had recognized in each other the formal manner of men who work in hierarchical institutions and the bearing of those who expect a certain measure of respect. They were deep in conversation.

I gathered up the children and hurried after them. Inside the house, we followed Bentley along a ground-floor corridor, and he stopped outside a door, the top half of which was glass.

"This is one of our seminar rooms," he said quietly. "It's being used, but you're welcome to take a look. A lot of what we teach is risk assessment and self-awareness. We need to tell camera operators like Melanie that their camera looks like a rocket-propelled grenade launcher. They may think they look innocent enough, but they don't. And a camera operator needs minimum four seconds of film, which is a long time to stick your neck out with bullets flying "

I stepped up and looked through the glass. A dozen men were in there, sitting on metal chairs chosen for function rather than comfort, arranged in a circle, each with a notebook at his elbow. Two of them were passing notes to each other. A third looked close to sleep. I recognized only one of them, a man called Max Amsel. Max is one of the Corporation's war correspondents. Short and stout, he is German Austrian by birth and was once told by a Corporation executive that he would never make a broadcaster because his accent was too strong. Now he speaks a smooth standard English. Only if you listen very closely can you hear the slightest of clipped edges.

An instructor stood at the front of the class, holding up a flak jacket and describing its many fine properties. Props were stacked on shelves around the edges of the room—first-aid kits, helmets, a pair of boots, and what I assumed were models of grenades, land mines, and mortar shells. Two old-fashioned blackboards stood at the front of the room, and a large flat-screen TV was mounted on the wall. On the blackboard were diagrams of explosions, of the trajectory of shrapnel, with stick figures crouching, ducking, running. On the second, there was writing in white chalk:

"Be the Grey Man."

"Shut the Fuck Up or Die," was scrawled in pink chalk beneath it. Someone had wiped over the words in a halfhearted attempt to erase them, but they were still clearly legible.

Bentley followed my eyes. "In a group hostage situation it's generally good policy to keep your head down," he murmured in my ear. "I think the commentary was added by one of our clients. Some of them think they're real jokers."

I moved aside to let Finney take a look through the glass, and then we moved on. We climbed the staircase to the room Melanie had occupied.

The single bed was covered in a grass green counterpane. There was a small chest of drawers beside it, olive green curtains hung at the window, the carpet was moss green, the walls beige. It was a room in camouflage. This must be what happens when you leave interior decoration up to a bunch of former soldiers. A narrow wardrobe was empty of anything but hangers. Through another door, a shower room was hung with pristine towels. The room had long ago been wiped clean of any vestige of Melanie.

"The police sealed it off." Bentley was standing in the doorway, as though crossing the threshold might make hims disappear as Melanie had. "They turned it upside down, but as far as I know they didn't find anything unusual, and there was no sign of forced entry. In the end someone from the Corporation came and packed up her things."

"Who was that?"

Bentley shrugged. "I don't remember the name. We shook hands. She was late thirties, perhaps early forties, light brown hair. I can check with my secretary if it's important."

"If you could. Did you spend any time with Melanie?"

Bentley shook his head. "I had meetings in London the first two days she was here. The course runs like clockwork. My instructors don't need me breathing down their necks."

We followed Bentley outside again and along a dirt path from the dining room toward the woods. A light rain was falling, and the children galloped around us, shrieking with delight as they got wet and the soggy earth began to cling to their sandals.

"Am I right in remembering it had snowed?" Finney asked. "Did Melanie leave tracks?"

"The snow hadn't settled on the path around the house itself—there was too much foot traffic. After that . . . well, we don't know which direction she took, of course. The guard at the gate did not see her. There was snow and ice on this path down to the wood, but no one even noticed Melanie was gone until midday on January eleventh. When she didn't turn up at class, the instructor assumed she was sick and had stayed in her room. So the alarm wasn't raised until the afternoon. By which time we'd had a dozen men and women tramping up and down here. I think the sun even shone. So all we had left was sludge. Look."

Bentley came to a halt and pointed up ahead. "We call this the booby trap trail, we want our clients to learn how to use their eyes and their brains. Here, look, the path forks and one route has been blocked off with a log. You should ask yourself, Who did that? Why did they do that? Is someone you can't see forcing you to choose this path through the woods? There's a hut over there, it would provide excellent shelter. Someone's piled firewood in the doorway—you'd have to clear it away before you could get in—"

"And it would blow up in your face," Finney said, finishing the sentence for him. Bentley nodded.

Bentley's analysis of what we saw around us was delivered with clinical calm. I felt a chill creep into my bones. The beech trees in these woods had been here for a century or more, their thick foliage keeping out what little daylight there was. Even the rain fell more thinly here.

"And here's our execution ground," Bentley said, his voice still bare of inflection. He stood in a clearing in the trees. A perfectly circular patch of ground had been concreted over and a high brick wall constructed along one section of the perimeter with rough windows built into it. It looked like a theater set.

"Not that an execution ground has to look like anything in particular, but when we're doing this exercise we want our clients to be able to identify this as a defined area, a killing zone, in which their efforts to save themselves take place."

William hurtled past me and ran out into the center of the concreted area, then stopped and shouted something unintelligible toward me. We all stared at him. I had to stop myself from bodily seizing him up and carrying him out of this godforsaken place.

"William wants a ball, Mummy," Hannah told me.

I told her that I didn't have a ball with me, and she ran to William to pass on the message. He started to scream and stamp his feet.

"What happened that day?" Finney asked Bentley. "Did Melanie say the right thing, did she talk herself out of it, or would she have been executed?"

Bentley puffed out his cheeks, and I thought he seemed uncomfortable with Finney's question. When he spoke he had to raise his voice so that he we could hear him over William's tantrum.

"We don't deal in right or wrong answers here. We preach first psychological preparation and avoidance, and if that fails we teach problem-solving techniques. No one pretended to execute Melanie that day, if that's what you're asking. We're not here to terrorize people. There's no need to. Our clients are not stupid. They know what they are getting themselves into. As I understand it, Melanie had extricated herself from some tight situations."

William had fallen silent and was gazing at the ground as the drizzle became heavier, the raindrops fatter. They fell and burst against the concrete stage like ten thousand tiny explosions. Bentley glanced at his watch.

"My men will be using this area for a training exercise in a few minutes. Let's go and get some lunch."

The dining room was almost empty, just a few tables occupied by people who looked like staff getting an early lunch. We took a table by the window and sat down. Bentley pointed out the adjoining bar, where Melanie had last been seen. She had been on the course for three days and was due to leave on the fourth. The bar had a separate exit into the grounds. It was through this exit that Melanie had left the bar at ten p.m.

"Why go outside at all?" I asked. "Wouldn't it have been quicker to go through the dining room?"

"It would have been quicker. Also it was dark outside, and cold. But there is another entrance by the bedroom wing, and people do take the overland route. Usually to have a cigarette or make a phone call. The entire building is a no-smoking zone, including the bar. And mobile phone reception is bad inside the building and marginally better outside. I seem to remember someone said they thought she was speaking spoking into her mobile just before she left."

"Her mobile . . ." Finney was thinking aloud. "I don't think it's been found, am I right?"

"Right," I agreed. My knowledge of the newspaper reporting on Melanie's disappearance was second to none. "The police checked her phone records, and there was an electronic signal logging off from the local transmitter shortly after ten that night."

"Which means either that the battery ran out or that someone switched the phone off," Finney said, "but either way the phone was somewhere in this area at that point."

"The transmitter's footprint covers a much greater area than just HazPrep, of course," Bentley said quickly. "And we shouldn't forget that she might have switched it off herself as she left the area, so she couldn't be tracked."

"She hasn't used it since," I pointed out.

"Anyone who's technologically literate would know not to use their mobile if they wanted to disappear," Bentley responded. "From what I've seen of these guys, camera operators are using sat phones and video-phones, and GPS units, and digital editing. If she's out there, Melanie Jacobs knows what she's doing."

As he spoke, I felt a warm, wet sensation spread over my lap. Hannah, more asleep than awake, had done the inevitable. I could feel the urine trickle down my legs and see it splashing into a little puddle on the floor.

"Here—" I dumped William on Finney's lap and grabbed a handful of paper napkins from the table. "I'm sorry, we're going to need someone with a mop over here."

Andrew Bentley looked blankly at the pool, then waved a waitress over with some urgency. Hannah and I retreated to the ladies' to mop up in privacy, but she was embarrassed and would not stop howling. I picked her up and cuddled her and looked at the two of us in the mirror. You wouldn't have thought we were related. Hannah had her dead father's dark good looks. Huge tears were running from swollen eyes down her plump freckled cheeks, and her mouth was wobbling. In the mirror I was pale in comparison, my red blond hair cut in a short, messy bob. My eyes were huge with tiredness, and I was thin from running around chasing after the children and trying to work and having too little time to eat.

When I returned to the table, I found William also melting down. He had slid off Finney's lap and was standing there screaming for me, arms stiff by his side, cheeks red, face awash with tears. Andrew Bentley was trying to jolly him along, but his initial child-friendliness was clearly being stretched to the limit, as indeed was mine.

I gave William a hug—which outraged Hannah even more—and grabbed a plate from the table.

"I'm going to take them outside. The lawn's not mined or anything, is it?"

Andrew Bentley looked taken aback, said, "No, no, no," and made a "very sorry to lose you" face that reached only as far as his lips.

It was not a dignified retreat, Hannah and William competing for ugliest child and clinging to my urine-soaked skirt. Me balancing the plate of chips in one hand, clasping their two little hands in the other. The lawn was still wet from the rain, but I found a bench that was almost dry under the canopy of a large beech tree. Gradually the children's sobs subsided sufficiently for chips to be eaten.

I contemplated the parkland that dropped away from me into the valley. I could hear a muffled explosion from the woods below, and then the rattle of automatic gunfire. I knew that I was not in danger, but that didn't stop my heart rate increasing. My senses were more alive to threats than they had been. Ever since Adam was murdered and I was attacked by his killer, I had not been able to regain my sense of safety. The moment I relaxed, my brain played tricks on me. I would go to sleep, then awaken well before dawn, my ears straining for the sound of movement, my eyes raking the darkness for intruders. I no longer trusted security or those who offered it to me.

I knew I'd been giving Finney a hard time. Neither of us have what you would call a traditional family background. My family is almost completely female—it's a long story, and not one that inspires confidence in the reliability of men. Finney has nothing by way of family, male or female. Yet it was Finney who seemed to be thinking about permanence and togetherness, Finney who seemed to be offering me security, whereas I felt safer on my own. If I stayed separate, emotionally as well as practically, then I would never have to relearn independence when he left. That, at least, was my logic. But I knew that Finney could sense me keeping him at arm's length. Perhaps Finney's very lack of family also frightened me. It is one thing to be one of many relationships in someone's life, but it is quite another to be everything to that person. I looked back at the house and saw Finney talking with Bentley. He glanced toward me. I raised my hand in greeting, and he smiled briefly before turning back toward the conversation.

People began to emerge from the woods, the group from the seminar room with their instructors. As they came nearer, I could see that there were men in full military kit walking slightly apart from the group, talking quietly among themselves. One had what appeared to be an automatic rifle slung over his shoulder. Another carried a mesh bag that seemed to be full of grenades. Soldiers and journalists, male to a man, they walked past us, their minds elsewhere. Only one of the group gave me a second look as he passed, then he turned to walk across the lawn toward me.

"Hi, Max." I stood and greeted him.

"Robin"—his eyes went to the children—"this is an eccentric choice for a family outing."

"It's Saturday, I brought them along for the ride. How's it going?"

"A laugh a minute."

"Any tips?"

"Grenade shrapnel travels up to forty yards in an inverted cone. Hit the ground with your feet pointing toward the grenade, legs crossed, hands on your head."

"I'll remember that."

Max smiled slightly and nodded.

"Melanie Jacobs' parents wanted me to ask a few questions on their behalf," I told him. "They still have no idea why she would have gone missing."

Max had turned slightly away from me and was gazing out over the valley. "I don't know if it's relevant . . . I've been away, so I haven't followed the news . . . but has it been suggested that Melanie had met one of the instructors before she came here?"

I shook my head, intrigued. "I don't think so."

Behind Max, I could see Finney and Bentley approaching, deep in conversation. I caught Finney's eye, and he must have got the message that I didn't want to be interrupted just then, because he stopped dead in his tracks and Bentley had no choice but to stop, too. Finney was doing most of the listening, nodding, interjecting the questions that kept Bentley talking.

"I don't know whether it's important," Max said carefully. "In the entrance hall there are pictures of all the staff, with their names written underneath. When I arrived here yesterday there was no one at reception, so I spent some time kicking my heels there. One of the staff members is called Mike Darling. This took me by surprise, because I have seen a photograph of Darling with Melanie."

I understood why Max seemed unhappy. He was not a journalist given to speculation. He would hate to be the one to give birth to a rumor.

Bentley started walking toward us again. Max watched him approach.

"Ask him," he said, and set off after his colleagues, nodding to Bentley as he passed. I stared after him. Max Amsel didn't make mistakes.

"Mike Darling was one of Melanie's instructors that day, wasn't he?" I asked Bentley as he reached me. Both men looked at me in surprise.

Bentley frowned. "I would have to check."

"I'd have thought," I said pleasantly, "you'd know every detail of that day off by heart by now."

"Why are you interested in Darling?" The words came like bullets.

"Darling and Melanie had met before," I said. "Darling did tell you, didn't he?"

Bentley stared. I could see the headlines unfurling behind his eyes.

"My wife is waiting for me. I'll take you to your car now." The mask of charm was dislodged, the depth of his disquiet revealed, but he forced the words out nevertheless: "It's been a pleasure." He turned to walk away.

"I'd like to talk to Mike Darling," I said.

Bentley swung back round, his face tense. "No."

"No?" I was startled by the abruptness of the reply.

"I'm afraid that won't be possible," he said. "Mike's no longer with us."